© Stacy Sodolak

A NOTE ABOUT THE AUTHOR

DOMINIC SMITH is the author of the *New York Times* bestseller *The Last Painting of Sara de Vos*, as well as three other novels: *Bright and Distant Shores*, *The Beautiful Miscellaneous*, and *The Mercury Visions of Louis Daguerre*. His writing has appeared widely, in such publications as *The New York Times*, *The Atlantic*, *Texas Monthly*, and *The Australian*. He has received literature grants from the National Endowment for the Arts and the Australia Council for the Arts. Smith grew up in Sydney, Australia, and now lives in Seattle, Washington. He teaches in the Warren Wilson College MFA Program for Writers.

ALSO BY DOMINIC SMITH

THE
ELECTRIC
HOTEL

THE
ELECTRIC
HOTEL

DOMINIC SMITH

PICADOR

FARRAR, STRAUS AND GIROUX

NEW YORK

Picador
120 Broadway, New York 10271

Printed in the United States of America
Published in 2019 by Sarah Crichton Books /
Farrar, Straus and Giroux
First Picador paperback edition, 2020

Owing to limitations of space, illustration credits can be found on pages 333–336.

The Library of Congress has cataloged the Sarah Crichton Books hardcover edition as follows:
Names: Smith, Dominic, 1971– author.
Title: The electric hotel / Dominic Smith.
Description: First edition. | New York : Sarah Crichton Books ; Farrar, Straus and Giroux, 2019.
Identifiers: LCCN 2018045335 | ISBN 9780374146856 (hardcover)
Subjects: LCSH: Cinematographers—Fiction. | Film historians—Fiction.
Classification: LCC PS3619.M5815 E44 2019 | DDC 813/.6—dc23
LC record available at https://lccn.loc.gov/2018045335

Picador Paperback ISBN: 978-1-250-61967-9

Designed by Jonathan D. Lippincott

1 3 5 7 9 10 8 6 4 2

For James Magnuson, who taught us how to love the work

The cinema is an invention without a future.
—attributed to Louis Lumière

Author's Note

According to the Library of Congress, more than 75 percent of all silent films have been lost. Much of that is due to the unstable medium itself—celluloid nitrate is both highly flammable and prone to decay. Every now and again, a film thought to be lost forever shows up somewhere in the world, in an archive drawer or as a foreign print sitting in a far-flung attic or basement.

The Electric Hotel is the name of a silent "trick film" made by the early Spanish director Segundo de Chomón and released as *El hotel eléctrico* in 1908. Thought to be lost for many years, the film was rediscovered and now resides in the Filmoteca Española film archive. I've borrowed the germ of the film, and the title, for my own dramatic purposes.

THE
ELECTRIC
HOTEL

1

The Knickerbocker

Each morning, for more than thirty years, Claude Ballard returned to the hotel lobby with two cameras strapped across his chest and a tote bag full of foraged mushrooms and herbs. His long walking circuit took in Little Armenia, where he photographed rug sellers smoking cigarettes in the dawning light or, more recently, the homeless college dropouts and beatniks along Sunset Boulevard, *striplings*, the doorman called them, the ambassadors of Hollywood ruin. This morning—a crisp sunny day in December of 1962—he'd also foraged up into the hills and canyons and now sat in his usual chair, leaning over a coffee table with a pair of nail scissors, trimming the stems of oyster mushrooms and the lacy fronds of wild fennel. He wore a threadbare glen plaid suit with Swiss mountaineering boots, a crumpled white handkerchief flaming like a moth orchid from his breast pocket.

His appointment was late so he began to delicately insert the trimmed plants into envelopes, the hotel manager's English setter, Elsie, nuzzled and sleeping at his feet. Claude could remember a lineage of hotel setters and bloodhounds, purebreds that slept in the lobby and rode the elevators when they were bored or hungry. Speck, the first mascot, was a forager in his own right, moving between the eleven floors where residents and guests left out their breakfast dishes. D. W. Griffith, who'd made the first American epic, used to coax Speck into his room with bacon and eggs. When he died of a stroke under the lobby chandelier in 1948, all but forgotten, the dog kept vigil outside his room every morning for a month.

Claude watched Elsie breathe and twitch at his feet, transported into a dream chase, he imagined, by the smell of damp underbrush and ragweed that clung to his trousers and boots. He looked out through the glass doors for a sign of his visitor, but only the doorman, Sid, was standing there in his gold-trimmed cap and epaulets. From this vantage point, he appeared to Claude like a war-weary admiral standing alone on a dock, staring out to sea, hands clasped behind his back. He still dressed as if he opened doors for Bob Hope and Jack Benny.

But the truth was the Knickerbocker Hotel's best days were far behind it. If the lobby had once resembled an elegant Spanish Colonial outpost, with its stenciled, hand-painted ceilings and Moorish tapestries, it now resembled a Madrid funeral home on hard times. Frayed cordovan carpets, dusty ferns in copper pots, velvet gondola couches marooned in pools of fifteen-watt lamplight. Celebrities once sat in easy chairs smoking cigars or reading *Variety*, but now an unemployed screenwriter was taking his pet iguana for a morning stroll and Susan Berg, an actress of the silent era, stood in her robe whispering a monologue to an empty chaise longue.

Over the rim of Claude's bifocals, Susan appeared as a winking silhouette, a corona of daylight streaming in behind her from the street. Her words were mostly lost, her face turned away, her voice soft and worn. She delivered this speech a few mornings a week, always in the same alcove, where insurance clerks or secretaries on their way to the Guaranty Office Building might glimpse her through the front windows. These were the last lines she'd ever spoken on camera, dialogue intended not to be heard but to be printed on intertitle cards. Claude sometimes caught a single phrase or word from the murmured speech, and the line *Why single me out for revenge?* had stayed with him. She'd told him that it was from a 1922 Western called *Comanche Bride*, but Claude couldn't recall it. By the time of its release, his directing days were over and the medium was dead to him.

•

There were other refugees of the silent era still living at the hotel—a one-time makeup artist who cut hair in her room, a master carpenter who did odd jobs around the neighborhood, a widowed British actor who'd barricaded himself in his two-room suite during the Cuban missile crisis back in October. Claude kept an eye out for them, offered to pick up prescriptions or newspapers on his walks, brought takeout up from the lobby when one of them was under the weather, but although they were friendly they never talked about the old days. And they never mentioned Susan Berg's lobby monologues or the silent era memorabilia Claude had stashed away in his small suite.

When Claude thought about the hotel's heyday, he remembered the house band, the Hungarian Symphonette, playing out on the Lido patio while celebrities danced or, later, Houdini's widow holding a séance on the rooftop to commune with the escape artist, or the time that Elvis recorded "Love Me Tender" in room 1016. He'd witnessed and photographed the passing of a golden, burnished epoch. A passenger sitting at the window on a train at dusk, it seemed to him now. In 1954, Claude had met Marilyn Monroe in the elevator after she'd eloped with Joe DiMaggio, a canvas bag of mushrooms hung over Claude's shoulder, and she'd been kind enough to ask him about his foraging expeditions. Somewhere in his suite, he had an undeveloped negative of the actress holding up a black elfin saddle mushroom as if it were a dead mouse. Later, in the lobby, she blew him a kiss and called him the mushroom hunter from the elevator, oblivious to the fact that he was a film pioneer.

When the newspapers reported Marilyn Monroe's suicide in her Brentwood home back in August, he'd thought about her in the elevator, imagined her forever rising between floors toward the sundeck. He remembered her holding a towel and a transistor radio, smelling of rose-hip shampoo and cigarettes, girlish and shy behind her oversized sunglasses. That was how history showed up at the Knickerbocker, fleetingly and behind smoked glass. The hotel was once a place to be seen and now it was a place to hide or disappear, sometimes forever.

For the most part, the suicides on the eleventh floor were gruesomely quiet affairs—barbiturate overdoses or the lancing of arteries in a bathtub. But in

November, a costume designer had left the world noisily and it rattled Claude in a way he couldn't explain. He'd been out on the sidewalk talking to Sid, returning from one of his walks, perhaps holding up an exemplary sprig of chervil into the sunlight, when he looked up and saw Irene Lentz—he would learn her name later—sitting on the ledge of a bathroom window on the top floor. She sat there calmly for a moment, kicking her bare feet back and forth, testing the air as if it were a swimming pool, and then she edged off the sill. She shot down toward the concrete awning, flailing and screaming, and Claude felt his hands rise involuntarily above his head as she fell. She landed right behind the neon Hollywood sign with a sound that left nothing to the imagination.

1962 had already featured a man going into space orbit and the Russians pointing nuclear missiles at Florida, but it was somehow the sight of Irene Lentz's covered body being lowered by medics on a gurney with ropes that shook something loose in him. For months, he'd been reading but not responding to the earnest, flattering letters of a film graduate student, and it was the afternoon of the suicide when he finally wrote back to suggest a meeting. It was time to tell the story of how he'd ended up on this desolate shoreline, time to wave back at the spinning world.

In one of his letters, Martin Embry had referred to Claude's first silent feature, *The Electric Hotel*, as a lost masterpiece, and now Claude found it difficult to square that phrasing with the fact that his correspondent was fifteen minutes late. Did one keep an eighty-five-year-old master waiting? As if summoned by this thought, Sid opened one of the glass doors for a shaggy blond man in his twenties, wearing a tan suede coat and a bolo tie. The doorman pointed in Claude's direction and then fell in behind the visitor. Claude busied himself with his mushrooms and fennel fronds because it was bad manners to be late but it was worse manners to notice.

Claude looked up and smiled when he heard the sound of boot heels on the terra-cotta tiles. He sometimes photographed this kind of apparition out on Hollywood Boulevard, among the music and creative types, the urban cowboy with the unruly sideburns and big belt buckle who's just moved out of his parent's basement in Van Nuys. To Claude's mind he didn't look anything like a Ph.D. student in film history. The doorman gestured to Claude, and the man in western wear grinned and nodded.

—Mr. Claude Ballard, in the flesh, said Sid. Cinematic genius, forager of edible plants, and permanent resident of this fine establishment since 1929.

—You're making me feel like I'm part of a museum exhibition, said Claude.

—I'm Martin Embry. It is an enormous and distinct pleasure.

He extended his hand to Claude and they shook. Sid picked up a newspaper and returned to his post at the front doors.

—Please, have a seat, Claude said.

Martin sat in the armchair opposite and leaned down to rub Elsie's rump. The dog quivered but continued to sleep.

—She is dreaming of chasing a rabbit, Claude said, which I am inclined to think always ends with a meal. Before she got so old I used to take her out foraging.

—I grew up with dogs. I miss them out here.

—You are not from here?

—Texas. I moved out here for graduate school.

A silence settled between them as they both watched the sleeping dog.

—I must apologize for not replying to your letters sooner, Claude said. You see, I have been out of the correspondence business for many years.

—I understand completely.

—Very kind. Would you mind terribly if I took some footage of you?

—Are you making a film?

—I like to document what happens to me each day. Call it an old habit.

Claude lifted the 16 mm Bell & Howell from around his chest and filmed several seconds of Martin blinking and smiling into the lens. Then he took out a small spiral notebook from his jacket and jotted down the date, time, and subject.

—I wondered if I might take you out for breakfast. I'd love to ask you about your career.

—There's a diner around the corner, Claude said. I have trained them to make omelets the way I like them.

Claude rested the camera against his rib cage and attached the lens cap. He gathered his envelopes of herbs and mushrooms, stood up, stepped over Elsie, and continued to the corner of the lobby, where Susan Berg was looping through a second murmured run at the monologue. Claude heard Martin's boot heels behind him as he delicately touched the arm of Susan's robe.

—Wonderful, wonderful work this morning, Susan. I see something new every time. Now, I'm headed out for breakfast at the diner and I wondered if you would like me to see if they have any bones for your soup broth?

Her papery, girlish face lived inside a halo of silver-white hair. She blinked and swallowed, her eyes a startling blue that put Claude in mind of tropical fish darting behind aquarium glass.

—I'd like that very much, thank you, Claude.

Claude handed her a small sprig of lilac verbena and she brought it to her nose.

—Go on up to your room and I'll stop by after breakfast.

Susan nodded and the scene dropped away from her face and hands as she headed for the elevators.

They walked into the high chrome of the Los Angeles morning and headed for Claude's usual diner on Hollywood Boulevard. Claude took a few images with the still camera as they walked along—their own reflections in the chrome whorl of a hubcap, a sparrow standing up to a pigeon over a bread crust in the gutter, a cat sleeping on a sunny stoop. A few of the indigent men on the boulevard waved to Claude, and one of them, a dropout named Billy, a tall kid in overalls and an army surplus jacket, asked for his photo to be taken. Claude obliged and told his subject to look off into the distance instead of at the camera. *Pretend you are staring back at Iowa*, Claude said, snapping the image.

The diner straddled a corner, a wedge of checkerboard linoleum and two rows of booths forming a wide V along the big windows. A middle-aged waitress named Gail showed them to Claude's favorite booth, in the apex of the V, where he could see the street as well as the rest of the diners. She handed them menus and he handed her a paper envelope of herbs and mushrooms for the kitchen. Claude cleaned his black-rimmed bifocals with a paper napkin—framing a distorted Martin briefly inside one smudged lens—before unstrapping his cameras and placing them on the leather bench. He watched Martin scanning the laminated menu.

—I am biased, but I recommend the omelet they call the Frenchman.

—Did they name it after you?

Claude smiled, gave a modest, Gallic shrug.

—It's possible I gave them the idea of adding fresh herbs and mushrooms with grated Gruyère. They pay me a little for my foraged herbs and they give me a regular's discount.

Gail arrived back at the table and they both ordered omelets and coffee. When the coffee arrived, Claude took a meditative sip and lingered his eyes on the street. A few bright-scarved secretaries were coming out of the studio and record label offices for a cigarette break, walking a little dazedly into the sunshine. Claude picked up the still camera, took some shots of the women smoking at the curbstone, wrote the details in his notebook.

—Strangers have always interested me, Claude said. The way they illuminate their own sorrows or joys when you least expect it. It might be half a second of staring into space, then it vanishes. In English, we say *perfect strangers*, which is very apt, I think.

He looked over at Martin, who was sipping his coffee.

—Nobody remembers my work anymore. How do you know it?

—I'm writing my dissertation on innovation in American silent film before 1914.

—And there is someone in existence who would read such a thing?

—Other film scholars mostly. Listen, my classmates aren't going to believe I'm having breakfast with Claude Ballard.

Claude waved a hand dismissively.

—How did you come to these studies?

—My grandparents raised me and they owned a movie theater out in the Hill Country, west of San Antonio. I was a certified projectionist by the time I was ten. You could say the silents are in my blood.

—I didn't become a projectionist and cameraman until I was nearly twenty.

—I'm guessing cinema hadn't been invented when you were ten.

—That's correct. My first job with a camera was in a hospital in Paris where they were studying hysteria. Then I took a job as a concession agent for the Lumière brothers. I was the first agent to show projected images in America and Australia. The brothers sent projectionists all over the world . . . India, Cuba, Brazil, China, Russia . . . sometimes the locals treated us like gods, sometimes like heretics . . .

Before too long their omelets arrived and they ate for a few minutes without talking.

—This is by far the best omelet I've ever eaten, Martin said.

—The secret is creating a little egg pouch around the cheese and herbs. And lots of butter. And the outside of the omelet should never be browned. Like most Frenchmen, I have opinions about food . . .

Martin took a bite and wiped his mouth with his napkin.

—They still teach you in film schools, you know.

A consideration of a smile played on Claude's lower lip.

—And what do they teach?

—That you practically invented the close-up.

—Heavens no, that was not me.

—That you were the first one to use a professional stuntman and to shoot at night.

—More or less this is true.

—I assume that was before the first war?

—Yes, before we all drowned in our own excesses.

Claude looked out at the street across the rim of his coffee cup.

—And what do they teach you in film school about the end of my career? The dénouement?

—That you never worked again after *The Electric Hotel*. That you went to film in Europe during the first war and had some kind of nervous breakdown . . .

—No, no, there was nothing nervous about it. It was quite decisive. And after the war, I came back to America and supported myself for decades as a wedding photographer. For the most part, no one ever knew who the Frenchman was behind the viewfinder.

Martin used the edge of his fork to slice into the perfectly rolled omelet. Claude had never understood the American aversion to keeping a knife in hand during a meal.

—Your studio was in New Jersey? Where you made the first feature?

—Perched right above the Hudson, near the town of Fort Lee. A big production stage under a glass roof, like a greenhouse, right up on the Palisades. We used to haul in actors from Manhattan on the ferries and we could shoot melodramas and westerns out on the cliff tops. Did you know the term *cliffhanger* comes from those early films shot on the Palisades?

Martin chewed, nodded.

—I'd heard that. Or read about it.

—Sabine Montrose or Lillian Gish at the edge of a cliff with a bandit bearing down on her. Then cut, *finis*, come back next week to pay a quarter to find out whether Sabine lives or dies.

—What ever happened to her?

—Who?

—Sabine Montrose. She never acted again after you made *The Electric Hotel* together.

Claude felt his mind slacken and go blank, as if someone had lowered an awning over his thoughts. He rested his hands flat on the tabletop, studied the whites of his knuckles, the sunspots that resembled tiny brown planets.

—Well, let's see . . . Ah, I remember: she ate my entrails like a feral dog and then she vanished into thin air.

Claude dabbed at his mouth with a napkin, aware of Martin staring at him.

—Forgive me, it's been many years since I've spoken of her. She wronged me, it's true, but you might also say that I killed her off.

—What do you mean?

—That will take some explaining.

Claude flagged down Gail for some more coffee and asked if the kitchen had any extra bones they could spare for Susan Berg's soup broth. Gail topped up their cups and said she'd check.

—Susan Berg is the woman back at the hotel?

Claude nodded.

—I am afraid that if she stops making her treacherous soups and coming down to the lobby to perform her monologue she will simply float away. She was a famous actress once but her voice didn't make the transition to sound. She whispers a lot because I think she's always been ashamed of her creaking voice. A director once said that her voice sounded like a burglar creeping down an old wooden staircase, and she never recovered. Poor Susan . . .

Martin finished his omelet and retired his fork.

—The silent era must seem like an eternity ago. Are there directors you still follow? Hitchcock? Didn't he start out with some silent features? I seem to remember he made a silent in Austria called *The Mountain Eagle* that was supposed to be set in Kentucky.

—I must make a confession.

—Please.

—I haven't seen a film since 1920.

Martin blinked and blew some air between his lips. It reminded Claude of Chip Spalding, the Australian stuntman from the New Jersey studio, a man who walked through his days blowing air between his lips and looking astonished. What had ever happened to Chip? Were there unanswered letters from him somewhere in Claude's suite?

—How is that possible?

—I don't own a television and I don't go to the movies.

—So you've never seen a movie with sound?

Claude gave another Gallic shrug, this time with his whole body, and Martin laughed.

—What's so funny?

—I would call that the biggest shrug in the history of shrugging. It was almost existential in its scope and delivery.

Claude smiled, moved his plate to the side.

—I have kept some prints and photographs and equipment from the old days in my hotel suite. Would you like to see them?

Martin drummed his fingers on the edge of the table, trying to contain a grin.

—Oh God, that would be incredible. Thank you so much.

Gail arrived with the bill and a brown paper bag of bones. Martin left some money on the table and they headed out into the street.

Back at the hotel, Claude gave one of the bones to Elsie in the lobby and took the rest up to the ninth floor. Susan Berg appeared in the darkened doorway of 905, her hair now in curlers. She took the bag, kissed Claude on the cheek, and retreated into a cluttered interior hung with bedclothes. In the clanking cage elevator, Claude told Martin that he could remember Susan dancing a tango with Buster Keaton out on the Lido deck.

—It happened a lifetime ago. They sailed across the terra-cotta tile like a couple of Spanish galleons, Claude said, while we all just watched in awe.

They stopped in front of 1013 and Claude moved his cameras to one side to dig for his keys in a coat pocket. When he opened the door, he saw Martin flinch and hold the back of his sleeve up to his nose.

—Is something the matter?

—You don't smell it?

—What?

—Vinegar syndrome, Martin said gently, in the old celluloid.

Claude said nothing, but he felt his jaw tighten as he switched on the lights in the living room and kitchenette. The décor hadn't changed much since the 1930s—gold-and-green-flecked carpet, a tropically themed couch, art deco lampshades, a nest of walnut end tables covered in newspapers. Over the years, Claude had done his best to categorize the reels and press clippings and photographs. He'd organized the canisters into suitcases and metal trunks, arranged the issues of *The Moving Picture World* in chronological order and stacked them against one wall. The vintage projectors were in a state of disrepair, he admitted, and it was possible that he'd been using an early cinema camera as a plant stand for twenty years.

—How often do you handle the old reels?

—They haven't been touched in decades.

Martin hummed nervously. Claude folded his arms, bit his lower lip.

—Do you smoke?

—Not anymore.

—Gas or electric stove?

—The gas stove doesn't work anymore. I have an electric hotplate.

—Good. Please don't ever light a match in here. The nitrates—

Martin crossed to the suitcases and reached into one to pick up a metal canister.

—May I?

Claude nodded. When Martin removed the canister lid, he pointed at the tiny silver shards of nitrate that were flaking along one edge of the reel.

THE ELECTRIC HOTEL

—See how it's already flaking and buckling in places?
Claude said nothing.
—I have a grad school friend who can duplicate and restore some of these.
—No, no, I cannot let you take them out of here.
—For some of the reels, it's probably too late. They're lost forever. But some of them can be salvaged in a lab.
Claude walked over to the window to escape the suffocating air of accusation. The sky above Hollywood was paling away into bands of washed-out blue and tin white. He couldn't name the emotion that was cutting through him but he felt his throat thicken with it.
—I don't think this was a good idea. I'm sorry, Claude said. I am suddenly very tired.
Martin carefully replaced the canister into the battered-looking suitcase and wiped his hands down his jeans.
—Perhaps just think about it. I'll come back next week to see if you'd like to have breakfast again. I have lots of questions I'd like to ask you. I'll leave a message with the front desk.
Martin headed for the door and Claude waited at the window until he heard the latch.

That night, and for a week after, Claude smelled nothing but vinegar in his hotel suite—in his bedclothes, in the icebox, on the backs of his hands. The phrase *vinegar syndrome* kept coming back to him with the euphemistic menace of nineteenth-century plagues—*consumption, scarlet fever, typhus* . . . Did vinegar syndrome affect humans, or just degrade the emulsion along a stretch of celluloid?

He found himself emptying his closet, laying his plaid and mustard-colored suits and dress shirts across his bed. Along the white shirt collars he noticed a jaundiced seam of yellow and it made him think of photographic paper on the verge of exposure. He opened all the windows in the suite, but the noise of the street annoyed him during the day and kept him awake at night. He lay in bed, staring up at the ceiling, picturing a chemical fog drifting from room to room, the way his breakfast bananas were spotting in the bromide atmosphere. He saw himself shambling down Hollywood Boulevard in his yellowed shirt collars every morning, Gail wincing at his briny smell when she took his order at the diner. A terrifying thought gripped him: I have been pickling myself for thirty years.

After Martin left a message at the front desk, Claude sat in the lobby in a dry-cleaned suit and a new white dress shirt, a single canister in his hands. Tiny starbursts and cankers of rust surrounded a flaking, foxed label that read *The Early Reels*. Handing it to Martin, he said that these were the images that launched his career. *Will you see what can be saved?* Martin carried the canister to the diner and kept touching it with one hand all during breakfast. He asked Claude to take him back to the beginning. Claude stared out through the big windows along Hollywood Boulevard, conjuring Paris of the 1890s.

   —When I dream of that old life I see it like a strip of burning celluloid. It smokes and curls in the air, but it's impossible to hold between my fingers.

2

The Silver Quickening

When Claude remembered seeing those first Lumière reels in the basement of a Paris hotel in the winter of 1895, he closed his eyes and smelled the warming nitrates of the celluloid. He recalled the smell of damp wool as the photographic society members brushed snow from their coats, the high sweet chemistry of gelatin on his hands from the hospital darkroom. It struck him that the olfactory world was right there, burned into his memories, while the first glimmer of motion somehow evaded him. Was it a baby eating breakfast or a factory worker astride a bicycle? Was it a street scene or the sight of a woman and four boys plunging into the ocean?

He'd moved to Paris a year earlier, following his older sister as she began treatments for tuberculosis. He'd found a job not far from the consumption institute, working as a photographic apprentice for Albert Londe at La Salpêtrière asylum and hospital. The wards were full of women—hysterics, epileptics, lunatics, the destitute—and his task was to fix images of their behavior. A team of neurologists wanted to uncover patterns and characterize the phases of hysteria and epilepsy or the mounting nervous tics of a compulsive. In the early evenings, when the workday was over, he walked to the consumption ward and sat with Odette and read to her from their father's botanical letters, about his escapades collecting mushrooms and wild herbs in the woods. As her illness worsened, it was a comfort to picture their father out with the farm dogs and his leather satchel, pulling on his pipe, tramping through the same square mile of northeastern France he'd known all his life.

Claude thought of his widowed father, a fierce patriot, as the Lumière brothers told the gathered members that the invention began with their own father's grudge against the American inventor Thomas Edison. Auguste Lumière did most of the talking, the older brother and commercial manager of the family factory in Lyon that produced fifteen million photographic plates a year. They stood on a makeshift stage in front of a canvas screen, their invention draped under a cloth down in the aisle between the seats.

—You see, friends, Auguste said, some years ago our father went to an exhibition where he saw Edison's crude peepshow device . . .

—The Kinetoscope, added Louis Lumière.

They were both in their thirties, bow-tied in elegant black frockcoats, looking more like wealthy aldermen, it seemed to Claude, than prodigious inventors. He moved his tattered stovepipe hat from his lap to beneath his seat, then he took out a pencil and a leather-bound notebook, the one he used to document his thoughts and photographs at the hospital. He'd been sent to the meeting by Albert Londe to see if there was anything to this new development. Claude wrote down *invention = patriotic grudge*.

—Edison's arcade novelty, Auguste continued, demands that the viewer drop a coin into the slot of a big wooden cabinet and watch through a view-finder while a tiny motor churns the pictures in front of an electric light bulb. But who wants to hunch over a cabinet all by themselves? Our father heard that Edison wanted to start manufacturing and selling these kineto-scopes in France and he couldn't abide it . . . so he comes to my brother and me with a sample of a kinetoscope reel and a proposition. *Free the light*, he says to us, *and you will make Edison's invention look like a child's trinket and make yourselves rich in the process.*

Claude wrote *I believe you are already rich* in his notebook, then he looked up at the younger brother launching onto the balls of his feet, suddenly brimming and boyish.

—Indeed, we asked ourselves, Louis said, why keep the images cooped up inside a wooden cabinet? What if there was a way to project the views

onto a wall? The technical problem, *alors*, was the movement of the celluloid strip. How to thread at just the right speed, that was the question, and
I am happy to report that we solved it as precisely as astronomers using
mathematics to locate a new star or planet . . .

Louis put his hands into his pockets and looked down at the floor, as if
he'd caught himself prattling to dinner guests.

—My brother is being far too modest and *cosmique*, said Auguste. During one of his bouts of insomnia, he has suffered nervous complaints and
headaches his whole life, you see; regardless, one night he stumbled downstairs and took apart our mother's sewing machine and began to copy the
mechanism that pulls the hem of a garment under the grip of the churning needle. She was not very happy, I can assure you, but the claw mechanism Louis designed was our great huzzah! In a way, gentlemen, you could
say that we learned how to stitch light together . . . heavens, now I am the
one being *cosmique* . . .

An older society member in the front row, an optician from the Latin
Quarter with a monocle, folded his arms and bellowed up at the stage.

—Perhaps, esteemed brothers, now that you've stitched so many words
together, we can see the damn thing work?

Auguste smiled weakly and bent into a continental bow. He gestured
for Louis to take his place down in the aisle with the covered contraption.

—The public exhibition will be after Christmas, said Auguste, so we'd
appreciate your discretion until then. Behold, gentlemen, the *cinématographe*: a working camera, projector, and printer. A photographic trinity, if
you will. *Amusez-vous bien!*

Claude expected Louis to remove the cloth with a stage magician's flourish, but the younger brother delicately lifted each corner and revealed the
machine by degrees. Claude cleaned his spectacles with a silk cloth and
put them back on. He was sitting on the end of a row, and as the gaslight
sconces were dimmed he leaned into the aisle to study the device. It resembled a wooden sawhorse with a ten-inch box camera mounted on one
end and a metallic lamphouse on the other. There was a hand-powered
crank on one side of the camera and a narrow strip of silver-black film
coiled onto a spool above. Louis Lumière opened a hatch on the lamphouse
and lit the limelight, then he began to steadily turn the hand crank, the
air sharpening with quicklime and emulsion. Claude would remember his

eyes smarting and a swallow, a moment of suspension before everything changed.

A space opened out behind the stage, a catacomb of dappling motion and light. Dozens of workers came silently bustling through the wall of the hotel basement, surging between the enormous metal doors of a factory at the end of a day, a man astride a wobbling bicycle, women in hats and sturdy shoes with aprons and baskets, a brown dog circling and tail-wagging in the foreground. They were all suspended in midair, slightly jittered and staccato in their motions, accelerating toward evening, as if under the unwinding tension of a spring, toward dinners and children, toward taverns and lovers. Claude felt their humanity in his chest, the headlong plunge toward home, even as he thought of a million drops of mercury teeming on the surface of a daguerreotype, a chemical rain that somehow atomized and animated these figures to life.

When a horse-drawn carriage barreled out of the factory's darkened, gaping mouth, the optician in the front row gave a start, threw up his hands, and dropped his monocle as the horse veered toward him. Another member, a funeral photographer not much older than Claude, stood up and began to ghost toward the screen, a sleepwalker roused by otherworldly music. He drifted down the aisle, right by Louis Lumière, and suddenly his monstrous shadow crossed into the projector's arc and was pinned against the wall, blotting out the factory scene to a volley of French insults and expletives. The first matinee heckle, Claude would think in years to come. The forty-six-second reel came to an end and Louis began to thread another, looping the strip of shining celluloid between a series of spools.

Later, Claude would forget the exact sequence of the views. A prankster with a garden hose; a congress of photographers arriving by boat in Lyon with their equipment; a baby being held up to the rim of an enormous glass bowl filled with goldfish, a grinning, white-frocked monster wobbling above her watery domain. There was a reel, perhaps the final one, consisting of a woman and four boys, probably her boisterous, wiry sons, running out along a wooden plank in their bathing suits and jumping into the gunmetal sea. Each of the ten reels was less than a minute long, just long enough to peer into the crevice of a human life, but they would all run together in his mind, a confluence that came bursting over him like shards of recovered memory. And although the order of the images remained hazy, he would never forget the revelation that fell through him as he sat in the half light, the sound and smell of Louis hand-cranking the shimmerings of existence in front of the limelight.

O-mouthed, transfixed, Claude watched the screen, but he also felt some part of him pulling away to his childhood in Alsace, to the autumn his mother died of smallpox while he lay in bed with his own fever. The fever had distorted his vision and he could remember lying up under the eaves of the attic as the shapes of the room fell out of focus. For a month, while his mother slipped away in the room next door, the edges of objects began to slowly quake and fringe. When the village doctor finally sent him to an ophthalmologist, a bearded man who spoke gravely of the fever warping his corneas, Claude emerged with a wire-frame prescription wrapped behind his ears and it was suddenly as if he'd swum to the surface of a very deep lake. The world rushed back in as the coppered edge of an October leaf, the crinoline hem of his teacher's skirt, the yellow-white flange of a chanterelle mushroom on his father's foraging table. And with each new Lumière reel, that was the sensation he had now, of being startled from a haze. He was a diver emerging from the murky, myopic depths into a bell jar of crystalline edges and forms.

The fever and his mother's death turned him into a devout watcher the year he turned eleven, the bespectacled, motherless boy at school who was always flitting his eyes between a sketch pad and the horizon, who fell in behind his father and the dogs as they collected and foraged some order back into the callous universe. Seeing the woman jump into the ocean in one of the reels, he thought of his mother's habit of alpine swimming, the way she grimaced before the icy plunge but always emerged shivering and roaring with joy, and then he imagined her all these years later on a strip of celluloid, swimming, laughing, waving, forty-five seconds of her tenure on the planet. Nothing would ever be the same in the photographic world, Claude understood as he watched. Magic lanterns had been used for centuries to project mechanical slides, but they were glimpses through a keyhole, a shifting geometric pattern or resolving image. In each Lumière view, every inch of the screen was alive, and it was the background of fluttering leaves, or rippling waves, or drifting clouds that captivated the eye as much as the foregrounded subject. You burrowed into the screen, dug it out with your gaze. In the span of ten minutes, in a hotel basement, the still image and the projected slide had become the slow-witted cousins to this shimmering colossus.

At the end of the screening, while the members of the photographic society continued to sit in awed silence, the brothers turned up the gaslight sconces and discussed their plans for the invention from the stage. They wanted to hire a small army of concession agents to proselytize the cinématographe into the far corners of the world, a grand tour of sorts, to beat Edison at his own game of colonizing human appetites and curiosities.

—The Lumière concession agents, Auguste said, will project views of Paris and London and Rome for the locals, but they will also make filmstrips of their new surroundings as they travel. They will sell the cinématographes and filmstrips to showmen and photography buffs alike. Imagine, if you will, a tribe of Esquimaux or the bushmen of the Australian desert or the philosophers of Buenos Aires seeing their own lives glowing back at them.

—Now, said Louis, we would be happy to take your questions.

Not a single member of the photographic society raised a hand. In a sense, they'd been leveled by what they'd witnessed. To ask how the sprockets fed the loop inside the box camera, or whether electricity could be used to fuel the lamphouse, or where the cinématographe could be purchased, was to quibble with wonder. To ask about the mechanics was to grind the air with so much noise. After a long enough silence, the members began to reclaim their coats and hats, the first cigars were lit, and Claude heard one of the veteran members say *I don't know what that was, but it has weakened my heart considerably.* Claude stayed in his seat, cleaned his glasses again as if it might polish his thinking, and stood in the aisle. As he came toward the Lumière brothers he realized there were tears on his cheeks, and he paused to dab them away with his sleeve.

—Were you moved by the views, young man?
Auguste asked it with a note of fatherly concern in his voice.

—More than I can say, Claude said.

Louis, who'd begun to roll up the canvas screen, looked over at Claude.

—I must learn how to make my own views.

There was a slight stammer in Claude's voice.

—What is your name? asked Auguste.

—Claude Ballard, sir.

—Do you have any experience with photography? Louis asked.

The brothers studied Claude at the lip of the stage, his wrinkled stovepipe hat in his hands.

—I work as a photographic apprentice at La Salpêtrière, under Albert Londe.

Auguste gave an affirming nod and reached into his coat pocket. On the back of a business card, he wrote down the name of an optical store on the Left Bank. Then he wrote *Noon on March 1, 1896* and handed the card to Claude.

—Ask for Yves at the optical shop. He will make you a licensed cinématographe.

—And the date?

—If you come back here at that time, we will be hiring our first concession agents. Make some views for us to watch and we would be happy to consider you.

—What should I photograph?

—Surprise us, Louis said. That is the only requirement.

Claude noticed Auguste Lumière studying his scuffed shoes and the frayed felt of his hat brim. He felt himself flush in the sconce light and looked down at the floor. He put the card into a deep pocket of his shapeless coat, forced his eyes back up at the brothers, thanked them for their demonstration, and rushed for the stairwell. Auguste called after him.

—And tell Albert Londe that he might grace us with his presence sometime, instead of just sending his apprentice. Tell him that we just showed you the goddamn moon and stars!

Claude took the stairs two at a time, rushing out into the glittering cold Parisian daylight. His glasses fogged in the open air, and for a moment the street came at him as if through a sheet of ice, everything muted, the pedestrians living as dashes and daubs of color. He stepped under a tobacconist's awning to let his glasses defog. As he stared through his freshly cleared lenses, he found himself already auditioning passersby for reels—the shopgirls bundling along, arm in arm, their breath smoking in the chill as they gossiped, the butcher hauling a marbled side of beef over his shoulder behind a glass storefront, the ravaged old flâneur idling along with a spaniel and a cane and a wilting flower in his lapel.

Claude entered the fray of the street again, wending his way back toward the hospital. In the photographic plate of a clothier's window he saw his own image fixed, saw himself the way the Lumières or a Parisian passerby might—a tall provincial kid in a stovepipe hat too tight in the brim, a slouching sack coat and wrinkled black wool trousers, a bespectacled, unblinking expression that was earnest, if he was being kind, and hangdog if he was being honest. For a year, he'd wanted to believe his wiry build and high-bridged nose might distract Parisians from his mawkish clothes and big-knuckled hands shoved into his trouser pockets, but he understood now that he looked like he'd borrowed a fat uncle's funereal suit. He peered into the store window at a rack of tailored nankeen jackets, a walnut table of neckties, a wall of brogues the color of brandy and oxblood. He combed through the voluminous pockets of his coat, counted out his money, including part of next month's rent, and stepped through the clothier's doorway. His prodigious future, he felt sure, involved a Nile-blue necktie.

When Claude returned to the hospital in a mushroom-colored jacket with a blue silk necktie and caramel-colored shoes, the doctors and nurses of the neurology wing took notice. As he walked down the long white corridor, one nurse called him Casanova, another called him a duke of the provinces, and a physiologist, a bespectacled, dapper dresser in his own right, said, *Welcome aboard!*

Albert Londe's secretary said he was in meetings, so Claude decided to finish developing some plates in the darkroom. This narrow space was his sanctuary. Eyeglasses folded, moving by feel, rinsing and hanging exposures under an amber bulb. It always seemed to him in here that he was graceful and unencumbered, that there was someone with perfect eyesight moving inside him. Only once the prints were dry did he put his glasses back on and study the distorted postures of hysterics, the knuckled spines and bowed arms. He placed the better images into a dossier for Albert Londe to present to a panel of neurologists.

Today, while a woman's buckled torso dissolved into view from a chemical bath, he felt a thickening line of dread in his throat. He saw himself in the darkroom for the next year while Albert Londe enlisted him to put the cinématographe to gainful medical use. He believed in science, in the photographic study of human movement and disease, but the idea of only making filmstrips of the hobbled and the stricken and projecting them for amphitheaters full of medical students was unthinkable. The Lumières had worked out how to reduce life to an emulsion and smear it onto a narrow strip of celluloid. To limit their invention to hospitals and lunatic asylums was to miss its point entirely. It was to stage an opera inside a train station.

When Claude emerged from the darkroom, Albert Londe stood waiting for his dispatch from the monthly meeting of the photographic society. Bearded with his dark hair cropped close to his ears, his coat buttoned almost to the knot of his necktie, a clipboard in his hands, he carried an air of scientific heft and certitude. On the neurology ward, they called him the Walrus. Claude was still wearing an apron from the darkroom, but something about his appearance clearly bothered his employer, perhaps the blue necktie flashing above the small island of bromide on his white apron. He searched for something in Claude's countenance.

—Have they done it? he asked. How does it compare to Marey's photographic gun? I doubt they have bettered twelve consecutive frames per second in a single sequence. Am I right?

Claude hesitated, didn't know where to begin. Londe had developed a camera with nine lenses that could render human movement to a tenth of a second. But compared to the cinématographe, it was a painting on a cave wall.

—Well, Ballard? What did you see?

For a moment, Claude wanted to tell him that he'd seen his own future etched into the basement wall of the hotel. He could also imagine telling Londe how the invention parsed the images into a continuous, seamless stream, that the study of the human figure would never be the same. But when he finally spoke it was to protect what he'd witnessed and felt, to keep it as his own.

—Sadly, sir, I don't believe this will be of interest to your work. In one image, we see Auguste Lumière and his wife feeding their infant daughter a meal. Breakfast, I believe it was, out in the countryside.

Albert Londe broke into a smile, then a chuckle, shaking his head slightly. He touched a brass button on his coat.

—*Vraiment*, babies eating a bucolic breakfast? That is what all the fuss is about? I have long said that the brothers Lumière aren't committed to scientific photography. They are commercialists, factory owners, business-men . . .

He turned his attention to his clipboard, paged through a handwrit-ten schedule.

—Now, Claude, can you set up the studio for tomorrow morning's studies? We have a delegation of physicians arriving from Vienna.

Claude nodded and watched Albert Londe disappear down the corridor.

It wasn't until he sat with Odette that evening in the consumption hospital that Claude grasped the magnitude of his lie. Within days, or weeks, Albert Londe would hear about the Lumière exhibition from other members of the photographic fraternity and wonder why his apprentice had down-played its impact. He might hear of Claude coming forward, tears on his cheeks, to ask where to obtain a working cinématographe. He felt sure he had sabotaged his own chances at La Salpêtrière, jeopardized the wages that helped pay for Odette's treatments.

He watched his sister as she slept beneath the blue windowpane, night de-scending over the rooftops of the thirteenth arrondissement. Snow flurries whirred above her head, a spinning halo that brought him back to the reels in the basement, to the beautifully calibrated mirage. Her eyes fluttered and she woke coughing, her chest shaking. In the last month she'd become feverish and weak and luminously pale, her long blond hair turning flaxen. The attending physician had been a disciple of the doctor who'd invented the stethoscope, had traveled the world studying pulmonary consumption, insisted visitors cover their mouths and noses with cloth masks, kept the windows cracked to allow ventilation, but it was clear he'd run aground with Odette's case. The disease was winning.

Claude poured her a glass of water from a jug beside the bed and propped her up with pillows. She took a sip of water, licked her lips, smiled through a sigh.

—Have you joined the circus, *mon petit frère?*

—I bought some new clothes.

—Father always said you'd become a dandy in Paris. Next it will be absinthe . . . and poems about the sadness of the moon.

On the nightstand lay a bible full of pressed wildflowers, a gift from their dead mother, open to the Book of Psalms. Claude glanced down at a vellum page and read the words *Let me know how transient I am.*

—I saw something today, he said.

—A madwoman pulling her hair out?

Claude shot out a laugh, felt his breath hot against the face mask.

—The Walrus sent me to another meeting of the photographic society.

—Did someone bring back photographs of the North Pole again?

She coughed again, dabbed at her mouth.

—I'd rather see almost anything . . . than all that ice and whiteness, she said.

—The Lumière brothers from Lyon did a demonstration of something they call the cinématographe. I've never seen anything like it.

—Tell me.

—The machine projects images onto the wall. Only they're not photographs, exactly, but something else entirely. You see people moving and going about their normal lives, as if you are watching them from a window. Everything is silver and quiet. They walk along, smile, ride bicycles . . . it's as if you're watching your own dreams or memories up there. Everything is moving before you, over you, all of it quickening along . . . and you could touch it, it's so real. There was a woman and her sons running out along a wooden plank and jumping into the ocean. I thought of Mama . . .

He watched her staring out the window into the falling dark.

—This woman thrashed about in the waves like a happy dog in a mountain lake, Claude said.

She blinked slowly and smiled, her voice coming from far away.

—And what will they do with this silver quickening?

—The brothers are hiring concession agents to demonstrate the device all over the world.

—Will you join them? she asked plainly. After I'm gone?

Claude watched Odette's eyes come back from the window and settle on him. Until now, they'd carried the possibility of her death in the gaps and silences that gathered around their words, in the lingering gazes they cast out the window onto the rooftops. Now she'd said it aloud and he couldn't look at her. He had promised his father that he would take care of her, assured him that Paris doctors were a league above the country hacks in the north. And yet he surely must have admitted defeat the second he'd taken the business card and imagined showing his reels to the Lumières. As long as Odette was alive, there was no chance he would leave Paris. But if she died, he was suddenly and terrifyingly free. He looked down at his hands, then at the impossible vanity of his toffee-colored shoes. He felt a tear well up and wiped it away with the back of his hand.

—Dear brother, I'm not afraid of it. I never have been. Who knows? Maybe death is its own silver quickening. You hate La Salpêtrière . . . photographing all those poor derelict women for men in white coats. You should work for the brothers from Lyon . . . travel the world. Do you know that I have always wanted to go to Brazil?

—If I wanted to apply, I'd have to purchase a cinématographe and make some views of my own.

—Views?

—The moving photographs.

She closed her eyes for a long time, then startled awake.

—I'm tired again. It's like quicksand, always pulling me back down.

—You must rest. I will sit here with you while you sleep.

He watched as she closed her eyes, tried to imagine what rippled through her thoughts and fitful dreams.

Within a week, the optical supply store had made Claude's cinématographe and he'd parted with a month's wages. The box camera, without the projection stand, was small enough to fit inside a carrycase, and he brought it with him wherever he went. He captured lovers in doorways, a juggler in the Tuileries Garden, a woman selling bread and hothouse roses from the basket of her bicycle. It reminded him of foraging with a satchel and a pair of hand shears, of excavating a copse of trees or a riverbank with his eyes. For a year, he'd pinned Parisians behind his eyeglasses, imagined their lives, and now he arranged them behind the brass-mounted lens. He liked the way the box camera felt in his hand or on a tripod, the mechanical click and certainty of its gears. But none of his initial views were novel. Like the Lumière reels, they were all filmed outside in daylight, and they captured strangers either going about their business or performing a feat for the camera. The camera glanced about but it didn't reveal.

The Lumières, he felt sure, had underestimated their own invention and he wanted to show them what was possible. Louis Lumière had told him to surprise them, after all. The camera could be placed low to the ground in the street so that an omnibus appeared to be careening toward it. Or it could look down from a height, widening out the landscape and miniaturizing horses and people. And what if it could film indoors, with the right lighting coming from outside the frame? During his second weekend with the device, he filmed a view from a tethered hot-air balloon, the Seine like a slate-gray ribbon. And he captured the otherworldly stares of the monstrous sea creatures at the Trocadéro aquarium, the dreadnought grace of a shark that loomed and then vanished into the underwater shadows.

At first, he'd bristled at the idea of putting the cinématographe to scientific use, but then he found himself re-creating one of Marey's famous experiments that depicted a falling cat righting itself in midair. One night he flooded Albert Londe's photographic studio with medical arc lamps and paid a nurse to drop one of the cats that perennially slept in the courtyard from a height of six feet onto a mattress on the floor. He filmed a dozen descents and sure-footed landings. And when Londe asked him to photograph an old hysteric after she'd undergone hydrotherapy, he positioned the cinématographe next to the regular plate camera. Under the direction of a neurology nurse, the woman removed her gown and walked back and forth along a Persian rug. Claude made the still images for Londe before repeating the exercise for the Lumières.

When he told Odette of his mounting collection of views she added her own images to the list: a basket of writhing fish at the market, a Sunday picnic where a child flies a kite above the trees and then lets it blow free into the upper drafts. He wanted to capture the images dredged from his dying sister's consumptive dreams, but it was the end of winter. There were no kites in the air, no fish in the open-air markets. Her lips had turned blue-white and she frequently called out from the undertow of her fevered sleep. She called out their mother's name, the names of long-deceased family pets, questions about Paris street names and train schedules. One time, she startled awake, whispered to Claude that the rabbit was out of its hutch, and promptly fell back asleep. While she slept, he held her hand and sang one of their mother's Austrian folk songs, something about a nightingale winging its way through a valley.

Then one wintry night Claude arrived from a day of filming around the city to find a somber doctor posted outside Odette's room. He gave a downcast nod that Claude felt in his bones and gestured to the open doorway with a face mask in one hand. Claude told the doctor to fetch the priest, that his father would want that. He set his camera and tripod down, strapped the mask in place, and stepped across the threshold with his equipment to see his sister in her final delirium. Her blankets were thrown back and she lay under a thin cotton sheet. A cloth was pressed to her forehead, and the window had been flung wide so that the cold air flowed over her. She had been sick for years, a slow winnowing, but nothing prepared Claude for her tubercular end, the soughing breath and the ragged sound of a thousand drownings from within.

For a long moment, he stood motionless six feet from her bed, paralyzed by this desolate, violent act of nature. He rested his equipment on the floor and came closer, felt the chill air on his hands and forehead and neck. He found himself removing his coat to cover Odette, even as her chest barreled up and she writhed with the fever. The coat dropped to the floor, but she kept grabbing at her chest with her flushed hands to remove a terrible weight that was pressing down on her. *La table*, she murmured, *lis le*. He turned to see that on the nightstand, resting on the bible full of pressed wildflowers, was a folded note with his name on it and another for their father. He opened his letter to find a few sentences written in trembling cursive: *Beloved brother, take me with you when you travel the world. In your heart and memories, but also in that little box of dusk you carry around. The first human death captured on film—that is something the Lyonnais brothers and their audiences could never ignore. Remind them how transient we all are. Always yours, Odette.*

•

Claude wanted to bellow out the open window, wanted to lie down on the narrow bed beside Odette and hold her until the shaking subsided. But he knew she wanted to offer up this gift, to be granulized into a medium she would never see. Here is my own transience, she might think in her final moments, captured forever. He wiped the tears away, kissed her on the forehead through his face mask, and placed the cinématographe onto the tripod.

When Claude arrived in the hotel basement at noon on March 1, 1896, he found a secretary from the Lumière factory sitting at a small table taking down names, and a few dozen clerks, shopkeepers, and photographers lined up in a hallway, cinématographes clutched to their chests or resting in their laps. Until that moment, it hadn't occurred to him that this was an audition, not a private screening for the brothers. Suddenly nervous, he gave his name and stood by himself with his own equipment. He had developed ten reels, each forty-five seconds long, and he found himself looping through them in his mind while he waited.

Eventually, the secretary called his name and he followed her into the big darkened room where the brothers sat under a canopy of cigar smoke. He shook hands with each man and Auguste complimented Claude's clothes and shoes. The concession agents, Claude suddenly understood, were ambassadors for the Lumière name. Louis gestured to the wooden stand where he could mount his cinématographe. The lamphouse had been attached to electrical wires, and Claude wondered if this was a concession to Edison. The Frenchmen would take moving images but they would concede direct current to the American tycoon.

Claude began with his filmstrips of Paris—the rose seller, the lovers in doorways, a fog-draped view from Notre Dame. Louis stared up at the screen, expressionless, and Auguste shifted in his seat. Then Claude showed them the view from the tethered balloon, and Louis said that he never knew how many fishing boats were in the Seine. It was clear they'd already seen the novelties of boulevards and sight lines from previous applicants. Even the barreling omnibus failed to get the response Claude wanted. Auguste just nodded and said it was an interesting trick of perspective.

—This next view is an adaptation of Marey's *The Falling Cat.*

Louis thinned his lips, brushed some lint from his trousers.

—We all know the proverb that a cat always lands on its feet, Claude said. Well, here is living proof that our grandmothers were right.

Against a black background, a white cat drops from a height of six feet, its back briefly toward the floor. There's a flashing, midair scramble, a twisting motion as the cat rights itself—the feet kicking and cantering, the tail swinging out like a boom. It lands on all fours, ears back, after a plummet of less than a second.

—Within point-two-five meters it has already moved its legs to the downward position, Claude said.

He liked that it sounded precise and definitive, as if he'd watched and filmed a hundred cats falling from a height.

—Might we view that one again? Perhaps more slowly, said Louis.

Claude cranked the footage again, this time at half speed. Louis tapped his bottom lip as the cat flipped in midair, now slowed to the calculus of the human eye.

—Very nice, said Auguste, what's next?

Claude told them that the next view was part of Londe's scientific study and they both leaned in, eager to glimpse a rival's work.

—At the hospital, we have a research laboratory for physiological experiments. I help photograph some of the studies so that we can better understand animal mechanics, for example. We also photograph certain autopsies. This shows the distorted gait of a hysteric . . .

A naked, silver-haired woman hobbles away from the camera under a skylight, elbows jutting, legs bowed, hips cocked. Her hair is tightly cropped, revealing the whiteness of her scalp and neck as she moves. The spine is knuckled and distended and her black leather shoes with pulled-up socks somehow exaggerate her off-kilter walk.

—Londe says that women diagnosed with hysteria have a gait that refuses to be coordinated, that every step is excessive and exaggerated.

The woman bird-toes down the length of a narrow Persian rug, toward a pale velvet curtain.

—I suppose that crazed walk is part of her inner rebellion . . .

It was Louis who said it, a little sarcastically, but his face was completely transfixed in the ricochet of projected light.

The woman rights herself for a turn, her face in profile, and the filmstrip dissolves to black.

—The hysteric's family, Claude said, insisted we keep her face concealed in our studies.

Claude loaded the final strip, the scintillation he knew would force them to either offer him the job or show him the door. He took his time, adjusted the lamphouse, felt the blood beating in his chest. He swallowed, pretended to tinker with the cinématographe, pushed some air up behind his lips.

—Gentlemen, may I present the first human death captured on moving celluloid.

A hospital room gauzy with winter light. Under an open window, a young woman languishes on a metal cot, draped in nothing but a sheet, staring up at the ceiling. A priest by the bed with a bible and rosary beads, his lips soundlessly murmuring. Ten seconds of midwinter pall and quietude. Then a finch on the snowy windowsill, a hapless spectator. The patient raises a hand from below the sheet and holds it up to the priest. He takes it, their fingers draped in beads of threaded glass. Then the woman's chest barrels up through a coughing fit, her face incredulous. The bed shakes, the bird flies away, and the camera continues to crank. Right before it goes to black she reaches toward the corner, toward the camera, her hand clenching an invisible rope.

Claude felt the chill through the open window of the hospital room as he watched. He felt his hot breath against the cloth mask, heard the terrible pneumatic sound of Odette's final breath and the enormous calm that followed. In the darkened room, when the reel was over, he wiped his face with a handkerchief and tried to collect himself. There was a long, smoky pause before the brothers brought themselves back to the room and their cigars. Louis got up and slowly opened the curtains, flooding the space with daylight. Auguste—managerial and efficient—thanked Claude for his time and attention to detail. A letter would be sent with the results. They asked him to ensure he gave his current address to their secretary at the desk outside. Claude quietly packed up his equipment. He shook hands with the brothers and wrote his address in the secretary's journal.

•

Then he was out in the Paris streets, the streets slick with runoff from the abattoirs and the tanneries, striations of offal and blood in the gutters. It was all too much to look at, so he removed his spectacles and panned the middle distances, the dead spot where faces floated in a fog. An enormous sorrow suddenly bruised up to the surface, lodged in the back of his throat. He huddled under a shop awning, glasses in hand, and shuddered into his grief.

When the letter came the next morning—hand-delivered and on Lumière stationery—he was heading out the door, on his way to the hospital. He kept it unopened in his breast pocket until he got inside the darkroom and read it under the amber bulb. *It is our privilege to inform you that you have been chosen as an official concessionaire and operator for the Fraternité des Cinématographe. Over the next year or so, you will be assigned to a tour in America and Australia.* He read the letter several times before putting it back in his pocket. All the women in his life had vanished, burned off like alcohol-blue flames, beset by fevers and pox. He felt ashamed for still being alive, for a year in Paris without a single friend to console him. But then he heard himself whispering in the darkness and he realized that he was praying, not to God, but to Odette. He heard himself say *I promise to keep you forever spooling and therefore still alive.*

A Magnificent Outburst

The cinématographe made its New York debut four months later, on June 29, 1896, in a Union Square vaudeville theater. Years later, Claude would tell interviewers that this was not only the birth of cinema in America, but the night he fell in love with the French stage actress Sabine Montrose, who would later maul him like a tiger, and the night Hal Bender, a teenager whose family ran a struggling amusement parlor in Brooklyn, saw himself delivered like a penitent onto the nitrate shoals of cinematic projection. This is how we came together, Claude would say, the genesis of our troubled moviemaking family.

And it happened in two adjacent theaters divided by a common redbrick wall. On one side, in a cavernous auditorium that rose behind gothic archways and festooned columns, Sabine Montrose stood onstage as Hamlet on her fortieth birthday, determined to prove to the world—and Sarah Bernhardt—that she could channel a young, grief-addled Danish prince. On the other side, in what resembled an enormous vaudeville drawing room, with burnished nickel railings and allegorical figures on the drop curtain, Claude stood cranking the cinématographe, projecting onto a large silk screen the ten reels he'd perfected back in Paris. Hal Bender, future producer and impresario, sat in the front row of the balcony, dumbstruck in the hemisphere of silver-blue light.

•

Sabine's Hamlet was channeled from her days as a young runaway on the Paris streets. Her face pale, her blue-black hair pinned back, she played the prince as an impetuous street waif, a playful mimic one second and a brooding melancholic the next. There was a choked-up quality to her soliloquys, the suggestion of a mind ravaged by thought. She had just delivered the lines *O God! God! How weary, stale, flat, and unprofitable, seem to me all the uses of this world!* in the second scene of the first act when an uproar rose, seemingly from deep inside the lengthwise wall of the auditorium. It was not a scream, per se, but a collective gasp, a horde of the bewildered, of people loosed from their senses. It came to her, from somewhere inside the frail, transparent envelope of Hamlet's character, that all three hundred theatergoers, women in pearls, bow-tied men with monocles and opera glasses, had snapped their heads to the north, a herd or pilgrimage startled by some otherworldly calamity nearby. Was it a fire? A patron plunging from a high balcony into the orchestra pit below?

The disruption opened out like a wound. She felt it as a knife blade running across a skein of delicate thoughts and emotions. Then she felt herself blanch and stammer under the floodlights. In all her years onstage, whether as Phaedra or Floria Tosca or Cleopatra, she had never flubbed a line, and she prided herself on seducing her audiences. She did not come to them; they came to her. She had sung arias and floated monologues through blackouts and coughing fits and mezzanine heart attacks, but this kind of interruption was unprecedented. Fleetingly, while she stumbled through *Frailty, thy name is woman*, she allowed herself to look at Pavel Rachenko, her acting coach and spiritual advisor sitting in the front row. Pavel had been instructing her in the latest approaches to naturalism, sat through her performances with a splayed notebook, pencil in hand, wearing an embroidered waistcoat hung with two gold fob watches, one set to local time and the other to Greenwich mean time. Without ever saying so, he seemed to imply that the prime meridian was a yardstick against which the world's falsehoods and relativities could be measured, an anchor in the sands of illusion, but now he was gaping with the rest of them in the direction of the moaning.

•

On the vaudeville side of the wall, the audience was recovering from an omnibus bearing down on them from a spectral height. It seemed to descend from the Hellenic ceiling, tumbling out of a constellation of Greek gods and their consorts. Hal Bender, whose novelty parlor was full of Edison gramophones and kinetoscopes, had watched the entire thing through cupped hands, through his own improvised viewfinder. He couldn't get his mind around the dappling scene loosed from the winding intestines of the projector, couldn't fathom that the Lumière brothers and this tall, bespectacled Frenchman had worked out how to unfurl time itself onto a silk screen. For the next reel, he sat on his hands and let everything wash over him. The catlike concession agent tended the machine for a moment and began turning the hand crank again. The machine threw its silver palings of light, then it widened out until Hal was sitting at the bottom of a big blue river.

Swimmers running out of the ocean at dusk. A blonde girl trots up the sand, her face upturned, making a show of her chill, her freckled shoulders raised, her hands clenched. She grins at the camera, shivering and exhilarated, then takes off running. The waves ripple and spume as she runs along the beach . . .

Hal could feel the salt air cooling against her skin and smell the briny damp under the pier at Far Rockaway where his dead father used to take him to fish and play dice on summer afternoons. When he closed his eyes for a moment there was a second life burning behind his eyelids. The French had made all this conjuring look easy, like spreading a piece of toast with butter. He folded his arms and braced himself in the darkness for the next view. While he waited, he let his mind tick over with numbers. The audience for a peepshow was typically a workingman with time to spare and a few coins in his pocket. You kept the machines humming twelve hours a day, but it was a grain of sand compared to this beachhead—hundreds of people for ten reels, a thirty-minute show at twenty-five cents a ticket. He swallowed and wiped his hands down his trouser legs, a sinner who'd stumbled his way into the church of perpetual motion. The Lumière brothers, he was certain, had delivered him from the novelty parlor's long slump.

Down in the aisle, the auditorium at his back, Claude had the sensation that he was hand-cranking Paris and Normandy into existence, that the bustling pedestrians and the lazing seasiders came into being only through the braiding of silver emulsion with limelight. He couldn't bring himself to spool Odette's death, not yet, not here, but he hovered the view from Notre Dame, the gothic spires and mansard rooflines piercing the morning fog, and the beachgoers reading novels in plashes of sunshine or strolling along the shoreline and the cat falling and the naked old hysteric crab-walking down a strip of Persian rug. Each time a new audience saw the omnibus careening toward them, the camera low to the ground, he felt their booming voices in his rib cage.

Sabine suffered three of these outbursts before the intermission. From her side of the wall, she had no way of knowing that each round of hollering came from a new audience for the exhibition, that the vaudeville theater was cycling patrons every thirty minutes. Instead, she imagined the same colossal crowd unhinged at regular intervals. After the second scene in the third act of Hamlet, *When churchyards yawn, and hell itself breathes out*, she had fifteen minutes to gather her senses in her dressing room with Pavel. She removed the sword from her scabbard and laid it across the makeup table, between the bouquets of flowers and the birthday cards from colleagues and fans. She loosened her doublet and lit a cigarette. With her free hand, she dusted some white powder under her eyes and across the bridge of her nose.

—Every time I look toward the back of the house I see people drifting out, Pavel, as if this were some flea circus with peanut shells and sawdust on the floor.

—This will pass. Remember to stay natural.

Through a scrim of smoke, she fixed a cauterizing stare at him in the mirror.

—Will you go next door and see what in good Christ is happening? And tell the stage manager to stand with the prompt book at the trapdoor.

—I've never seen you forget a line.

She blew smoke above their heads, waved it away.

—Every time they look at the wall I feel my mind go blank. Now, let me think for a few minutes before they send me back into that coliseum . . .

She watched him compare the time between his twin fob watches before walking out into the hallway. She looked at her gaunt face in the mirror, the way her neck papered above the laced and ribboned collar. Forty was a practical joke, a celestial prank engineered for her mortification.

Back onstage, Sabine favored the apron near the open trapdoor for the rest of the performance. Her fellow actors, Ophelia, Guildenstern, the king and queen and all the rest, had to trail after her downstage, their blocking sabotaged as she stayed within earshot of the prompter. The stage manager, a balding man in rolled shirtsleeves and suspenders, had positioned an enormous boulder made of mastic, papier-mâché, and wire in front of the open trapdoor, to conceal it from the audience, and now he stood with the annotated script, a disembodied head blinking from the floorboards, his baldness glinting under the stage lights. And because the trapdoor led down into the orchestra pit, the transition music, the trumpets and snares and violins, shot up from the crawlspace below the stage as the actors settled into the opening lines of each scene.

By the first scene of act 5, Sabine still hadn't taken a prompt. Then the final outburst erupted from inside the wall—a woman's muffled shriek, followed by a communal groan. It was during Ophelia's burial scene, as Hamlet stood with Horatio in a copse of artificial trees and watched the queen scatter flowers into the grave. Sabine said to Horatio, *What, the fair Ophelia?* just as the audience shifted in their seats, scowled at the wall of noise, whispered to one another with annoyance. During the queen's speech and Laertes's lament for his dead sister, Sabine looked out into the house, saw a flurry of white gloves and watch chains and glinting pearls. The front row had thinned out beyond the lip of the orchestra pit, and it occurred to her that Pavel had never returned from his errand next door. He'd deserted her for whatever was causing so many people to cry out. She stood for a long time in the cardboard trees, their silk leaves rustling in the cross-breeze of a fan in the wings. She stared out into the twilight of the house, waiting for an impulse or a line to galvanize her into action, but she was suddenly sinking and receding, saw herself underground, standing alone under the high ceiling of a limestone cave.

Just as she heard a page of the promptbook peel up under the stage manager's thumb, she burst from the copse toward the grave by the boulder.

—What is he whose grief bears such an emphasis? whose phrase of sorrow conjures the wand'ring stars, and makes them stand like wonder-wounded hearers? This is I, Hamlet the Dane.

She heard her voice hollow out the space in front of her, heard it coiling inside the brass bells of the orchestra horns. Not a scream, but a voice pierced and unraveled by grief. The world on the other side of the proscenium went silent and still, the pale, dotted faces turning back to her from the mezzanine and the balcony and she felt their rapt attention in her spine, in the hairs on her neck.

The script and rehearsals called for a skirmish between Laertes and Hamlet, demanded that grief-stricken Hamlet should follow Laertes into the burial pit, but the staging had been uprooted and nothing was in its proper place. Laertes was wringing his hands down on the apron, sweating in the sodium aura of a floodlight, too far from the silk-draped body of his sister over by the boulder. Sabine rushed up to the prompt's trapdoor, the stage manager a vigilant, blinking prairie dog, and put her boot heel on his bald head and gave it a nudge. When he ducked below for cover, she jumped in after him, down into the cavity under the stage to signify her descent into madness and Ophelia's burial pit. She couldn't stand at full height, so she crouched, arms outstretched, and barreled, yelling *Hold off thy hand!* in the direction of the orchestra pit. As she moved through a rummage of broken theater seats and discarded props, she heard the actor's boot heels scraping along the floorboards after her, following her movements and voice as if she'd been whisked from a shelf of ice into a swift river below.

She emerged between the woodwinds and the brass section, at the left, tuxedoed elbow of the stunned French horn player. There was a jolt of exhilaration as she drew her sword and climbed over the railing toward her real nemesis, not the brother of her lover and son of the king's chief councilor, but the bored, dopey Upper East Siders and Iowans and Long Islanders masquerading as her audience.

Lines were dropped, whole actions erased, because here was Hamlet ranting in the aisles, his androgynous voice rubbed hoarse, his sword extended into the space above the raked seats, *I loved Ophelia!* Sabine

wailed. *Forty thousand brothers could not, with all their quantity of love,
make up my sum. What wilt thou do for her?* And from the back acres of
the stage came the king's well-trained, scoffing voice, *O, he is mad,
Laertes,* and the proof was in the walled-back eyes of the theatergoers in
the middle rows, who sat under the electricity of Hamlet's sword and
words. After the queen made her entreaty from the stage, *This is mere
madness,* Hamlet fell down in the aisle, prostrate under the tiny cone of
illumination on J117, and finished his outpouring. *Let Hercules himself do
what he may, the cat will mew, and dog will have his day.* And it was Horatio who finally moved from the circle of the other actors onstage to
come down into the house and retrieve the wrecked Dane. They hobbled back toward the orchestra pit and the stage, Sabine's arm around
Horatio's neck, the silence unwinding into murmured appreciation and
then cascading into applause. From the apron of the stage, she looked
down to see Pavel standing in the back of the house, clapping and
cheering *bravo* with the rest of them.

Act 5 unfolded as written and rehearsed. When Sabine uttered Hamlet's
last words, *the rest is silence,* as she lay dying in Horatio's arms, she closed
her eyes and felt herself slacken into a void of exhaustion. Motionless, her
breathing a tiny purr in the back of her throat, she heard Horatio and
Fortinbras and the ambassador finish out the scene, their voices scudding
through the darkness all around her. She had died thousands of times onstage and fallen asleep only once, after a fellow actor forgot to drag her
corpse from the stage and she'd lain there poisoned and murdered for an
entire act. But she realized she'd drifted off as slain Hamlet when the mechanical curtain winch ground to life and the audience erupted into applause. Horatio, who'd been side-mouthing comments to her all through
the evening's disruptions, nudged her with his shoe and whispered, *Wake
the hell up, the whole place is on its feet.*

During the final curtain call, after Sabine gestured magnanimously down
into the orchestra pit and toward her director in the front row, she flung an
arm out toward the redbrick wall, at the unnamed saboteur of her play,
and the theatergoers laughed en masse and directed their clapping at the
vaudeville side of the divide. The curtain came down and Sabine moved
toward her dressing room without speaking or making eye contact with

the ensemble. Pavel waited in a lounge chair with his notebook and fob watches.

—I thought you'd abandoned me, she said.

—I stayed a little while to see what all the fuss was about.

—And?

—The Lumière brothers have sent a concession agent to show the Americans their new invention.

—Don't they sell chemicals in Lyon or someplace?

—Photographic plates, actually. They're calling it the cinématographe . . .

She pulled off her buckskin boots, rubbed the soles of her stockinged feet.

—I hurt my goddamn ankle on that stunt below the stage . . . And what does it do, this invention, burn a hole into the brainbox of any idiot who sees it?

—It turns life into moving pictures.

She winced into the mirror.

—Theater turns life into moving pictures, into flesh-and-blood persons moving on a stage in front of a breathing audience. Imagine it. And, what, all that screaming was for this magic lantern show? You should talk to the booking manager. It was horrific, an outrage.

Pavel nodded, crossed his legs.

—As a student of naturalism, I thought you would want to see this. So I took the liberty of inviting the projectionist to come to the hotel suite later tonight for a private exhibition.

—I'd rather have my legs removed.

—He said that he and the Lumière brothers were enormous fans of your work and it would be a great honor. *A patriotic privilege*, I believe is the phrase he used. Besides, I have an idea you might like.

—Tell me.

—After you see the show.

—Very well, but I must take a nap first. I'm a wreck.

Pavel stood and gave her a nod.

—I will tell him to come a little after midnight.

Sabine heard Pavel close the door behind him and she turned her attention back to her swollen feet.

Hal Bender emerged from the vaudeville theater in a trance and a funk. He'd paid to sit through six or seven screenings, he couldn't remember which, and was now walking along Broadway in the general direction of the Brooklyn Bridge. Everything seemed crude, slow, and hard-edged compared to that silver-skinned river of light. He intended to walk all the way back to Fulton Street, that much was clear to him, slouching along with his hands in his pockets, the night folded out in the middle. Flossy Bender was always at him for wearing his shoes down at the heel, duck-footed she called him, a trait he got from his dead father, Chester Bender. But now Hal appreciated his splayed-foot inheritance because all he wanted to do was think and walk slow, to amble along on his crooked heels.

From the bridge, he watched the East River blink red and blue with navigation lights. Somewhere down there were the remains of Chester's ketch, a bloated, waterlogged affair that was taken out on weekends and on summer weeknights. Eel fishing with the Germans from Staten Island, clamming with giant metal tongs, all three brothers dragging down the stern. Shortly before his father was shot for his gambling debts, the boat had been set on fire by a disgruntled creditor and sent to the bottom of the river. In Hal's mind, Chester Bender was down there with his sunken sailboat, standing in the mud and murk with the eels, whistling bubbles up to the surface.

Chester had always been an inveterate whistler, and Hal missed that puckering as much as anything else. When he made it back to the Brooklyn side of the bridge, he took a detour down Columbia Heights and formulated his father's brassy signature tune with his mouth as he passed the site where they'd found his body. Dr. Shepard's Turkish Baths for Malaise was the spot where Chester, who'd trained as a daguerreotypist and spent too much time with mercury vapors, took his nervous complaints for a medicinal soak. He'd come down off the front stoop, Hal remembered, hair slicked, cheeks flushed, replenished and light, puckering into the sunlight, daydreaming about one of his moneymaking schemes, perhaps, the portrait-studio-cum-barbershop, the floating bandstand, while he smoked and melodized down the street. He returned to the apartment above the novelty parlor with a new amplitude in his joints and limbs and mind, floated through the apartment smelling of camphor or birch leaves—*venik*, he said it was called—the younger boys hanging off him, slipping their hands into his trouser pockets for coins or mints, pausing his whistle to kiss his wife on the lips on the way down the hallway to dinner, and then he'd come to Hal, his eldest, and they'd shake hands like two diplomats signing a treaty. *What's the word, Harold Bender,* he'd ask, *all good among your chiefdoms?*

And Hal would tell him of his exploits out at the Coney Island handball courts, back before he'd left school to take over the novelty parlor. Smelling of hot oil and minerals, Chester would listen and marvel and chuckle in all the right places. Slapping old tennis balls against the dilapidated wooden jetties with his friends turned into competitive matches against the Italians and the Irish. For the year before Chester's death, Hal was the reigning champion in single-wall handball, trouncing the older, shirtless boys with stubble and massive wingspans. Chester sometimes trekked out there to cheer him on and take bets from the sidelines with a coffee can. But those stories about his summer afternoon triumphs and the coffee cans full of his winnings already felt like another lifetime. Two years ago, in the wake of his father's murder, he'd left his childhood behind.

And he'd been running the novelty parlor as if it were a small shipping empire ever since, determined to turn a profit as a way of getting even with a stone-hearted universe. He tallied receipts, plotted revenue curves on graphing paper, mailed viewing surveys to his neighbors, negotiated better terms with creditors. If they entered a Sunday afternoon slump, when the post-church crowd were flushed from their porches and doorways after a pot-roast lunch, he walked out onto Flatbush or Fulton in his derby hat and necktie to drum up a fresh round of peepers, rocking on his heels like a clapboard evangelist, *a nickel to change your day, see real life like never before with Edison's latest marvel.* He greeted customers and prospects by name and knew how to read strangers in the street from a distance of fifty feet. If he saw a lonely punter shambling toward him, eyes averted, hands in pockets, he stopped barking like a sideshow carnie and simply held out the sandwich board sign he'd painted by hand: *A happy man has no use for fun. For everyone else, there's Edison's kinetoscope!*

•

While Hal tended the front of the house and the daily ledger, his mother supervised the novelty parlor itself. She kept out the rabble-rousers, walked the aisles between phonographs and kinetoscopes with a ready quip or admonishment. Because Flossy Bender had lost her husband to drink and vice, she conducted the business with an even, virtuous hand. Management reserved the right to deny entry or turn off a peepshow midstream if some lunatic from Red Hook or Young Dublin started yelling down into the peephole. On moral grounds, she didn't exhibit boxing matches or female contortionists. She preferred scenes that were wholesome or patriotic, or suggested purification—brass band parades, a family flying a kite from a hillside, surfers on the Atlantic, a tenement rat-catcher plying his trade.

Ticket sales were down, though, and the slump hung over the Benders all that summer. Hal called it their kinetoscopic revenue gap and drew charts that demonstrated the effect of showing a single boxing match at a nickel a round. Flossy said she had no appetite for blood sport and complained that he was already becoming an authority on everything under the sun, just like his buried old man. She sometimes speculated that Chester Bender had been shot with his mouth open, mid-opinion, holding forth at the Turkish bathhouse like a country parson.

By the time Hal reached the parlor, he was sweating and also appalled at the thought of turning on the kinetoscopes and phonographs in the morning. At the end of a row of phonographs, their stethoscope earphones neatly folded across the top, Flossy had posted a sign that read *Dancing in the Aisles Strictly Prohibited*. At the other end, in an alcove devoted to kinetoscopes, a daguerreotype portrait of a young Thomas Edison hung above the franchise certificate on the wall, a look of distracted genius and scarlet fever in his eyes. Occasionally, Hal heard his mother offer up a kind of commercial prayer to the patron saint of nickel entertainments—*Let it rain on Saturday so people are driven indoors to distraction and can't be bothered schlepping out to Coney Island.*

As he looked around the dimly lit space now, he realized the peepshow was officially dead, the parlor a museum. A slug of lead dropped into his stomach when he tried to guess how many months they could remain in business. Even if he could convince his mother to buy a peepshow reel like one of the infamous Leonard-Cushing fight, confined to the viewfinder it was merely a fitful breath before drowning. He knew his mother's moods and dispositions like his own, the way she'd give her sons Hood's Sarsaparilla to fortify their blood, make them scrub twice a week with an ammonia-soaked sponge as a safeguard against disease and destitution. Rationing would ensue and roast beef would become a thing of the past because here it was, the other bullet in the revolver. The French brothers and their invention had finished what Chester's killer had begun—the complete annihilation of the Bender clan. But *what if,* Hal wondered aloud, he could get his hands on a cinématographe?

When he got into the apartment above the parlor, there was a plate of food on the kitchen table covered with a saucepan lid. Beside it was a note in Flossy's signature deadpan: *Trust the animal spectacle didn't ruin your appetite.* Did she know what he'd witnessed? Then he remembered that he'd told her and his younger brothers that he was meeting an old classmate to go see the menagerie in Central Park. He took off his shoes and ate his dinner in the silence of the kitchen, in the light of a sewing lamp. Up on the wall was a daguerreotype of his father—bearded, blithe, looking out from the puzzle of the afterlife. Hal looked up at his father's silvered double and said, *You should have seen the crowd.*

When Sabine woke from her nap, just after midnight, it was to the smell of oranges and lilies. Even with her silk blindfold in place, she could tell the penthouse was choking with flowers and baskets of fruit from well-wishers. She lifted the blindfold, looked at the clock, blinked up at the ceiling. That night's performance of Hamlet and her birthday, now technically elapsed, came back to her slowly. As a number, 40 seemed unsightly and implausible. She'd thought it might look stately and dignified when she imagined it presiding over her life, but now she saw that the 4 was a wiry man with his arm in a sling, and that the 0 was her own astonished mouth. She sat up in the lamplight and read three of the letters that had been brought in with the assorted packages, fruit baskets, and flowers.

Dear Sabine Montrose,
    *I am collecting the autographs of luminaries in various fields and you
will confer a personal favor by enclosing me yours in duplicate, on the ac-
companying cards, which I shall ever appreciate with feelings of gratitude.*
    Yours,
    Muriel Kingsley
    20 High Street, Boston

Miss:
    *I have written a play (enclosed) and can't get it performed anywhere.
What do you suppose is the cause of my failure? The role of the Countess
was written with your visage in mind.*
    Respectfully,
    Simon Portney

Sabine Montrose,
    *Permit a humble admirer of your genius to express the following lines
on the occasion of your Fortieth Birthday.*

    Sabine, the years are going
    And your hair is silvery growing;
    Age is the flower of Youth
    Full-blown
    Yielding pain from anguish sown.
    Hurry on through mists of tears
    Toward the spot your laughter clears
    Find amid the young a hiding from that Foe, who day or dark,
    Ever seeks a shining.

    H. C. Cooper

She heard her maid's insistent knuckles rapping on the door, called out *Je
dors!*, but Helena Favre came in anyway. She stepped briskly across the room
and handed Sabine a warm facecloth. She was in her fifties and childless, a
pragmatist from Burgundy who sent postcards to her invalid mother from
every town and country they visited. Sabine set the letters aside, took the
cloth, and pressed it to her face.

—Pavel says the projectionist is expected any minute.

Sabine put on her robe and went out into the hotel suite's living room—another little province of tropical flowers and fruit and plush furniture. Her feet still hurt and the floral intensity of the room made her light-headed. Pavel had changed out of his embroidered waistcoat and now sat in a kaftan and deerskin moccasins, a steaming cup of tea in one hand and Madame Blavatsky's *The Secret Doctrine* open beside him on the velvet sofa. Although Pavel was a Russian émigré who'd spent most of his life in London and Paris, he could, in certain clothes and aspects, put Sabine in mind of a bearded hermit flushed onto the streets of St. Petersburg or Istanbul.

But that relentless flint-gray regard had not been honed in solitude but during dinnertime debate and philosophical argument. It was the cold unwavering scrutiny of a man who seldom apologized and had never been in love. And his inability to lie was another trait that never failed to surprise her. In response to a simple question like *How was my performance tonight?* Pavel's answer was uncompromising, flat-toned, a little distracted, as if he'd just asked someone to hand him a bowl of almonds—*You were pinched in the throat and overblown in your gestures. Forget the Comédie-Française, with its wooden mechanics and ostrich-feather hats. We are aiming at something truthful beyond all that.* Then he would look about the room, or return to his book, not noticing the utter devastation roiling through Sabine's chest and face.

Helena busied herself organizing the twenty-six trunks that had come across the Atlantic on the steamer, each one labeled in French—*chapeaux, robes, bijoux*. Pavel drew his legs under his kaftan, sipped his tea.

—Did the little sleep replenish you?

Sabine's English wasn't perfect either, but she wished he could retain the word *nap*. In the middle of his eloquent monologues she often came upon a blunder, a little rodent in his garden of criticism.

—I slept wonderfully. When is the Frenchman who killed my Hamlet arriving?

—Any minute.

Pavel looked around the room, blew across the rim of his cup, studied the arabesque of the carpet and the drapes.

—How terrible was it tonight? Sabine asked.

Pavel leaned his head to one side, squinted as if listening to difficult, exotic music.

—I invent nothing. You are the one slaying the demons out there in front of humanity every night. Who am I to ever judge what you do?

—It hasn't stopped you in the past.

—I study people's minds and hearts, the little stories of daily life. I'm no expert.

—Get on with it. And please take account of the insanity that came from the vaudeville house next door.

—Disruptions can be wrecking balls, or they can be mental mosquitoes. But we are concerned with the smoke of human emotion wafting up from those boards without a single lie. That is the criteria.

He examined the fingernails on one hand while Sabine looked out the windows toward Fifth Avenue. Her fortieth birthday had vanished and it occurred to her that one day she would be an old woman living alone in Brittany, scalding and nagging herself in a cottage by the sea. She saw it as plainly as her own hands, the long white days of solitude.

—And on this front, how did I fare?

—Until the magnificent outburst of you jumping into Ophelia's burial pit, it was a series of formulas and chess moves by a beautiful expert.

She folded her arms, felt her earlobes flush.

—Has a woman ever consented to sleep with you? It's impossible to imagine a seduction with you in the starring role.

Pavel smiled into his teacup.

—As it happens, I'm not much interested in that variety of flesh. Carnality zaps a man's vital energies. Oh, but your graveyard scene, when you climbed over the railing of the orchestra pit, you should have seen the look on the faces of Gramercy Park matrons! It made me want to bring back Aristotle from the dead. It made me want to write sonnets. So honest and exhilarating, your own anger and grief tearing at your throat. It was Hamlet beating at the walls of his own paralysis. I have the chicken skin just thinking of it.

—Goose bumps.

—All languages are bastards. I let my speech fornicate with whatever happens by. How did you *feel* out there?

She ran a hand along the plush of her chair, closed her eyes, steadied her voice. For a moment, she could feel Shakespeare's iambs throbbing in her throat like five lingering heartbeats.

—Full of rage and anguish. As if my life had ended.

—The secret, said Pavel, was forgetting.

She opened her eyes, looked at him.

—Your riddles have always bored me.

—You forgot to enunciate and project. You forgot that hundreds of people had paid to see you pretending to be a grief-stricken prince. You forgot that you are famous, entitled, spoiled, divorced, and middle-aged. You also forgot that you're a woman. It was a marvelous thing to behold.

Helena announced that the projectionist was waiting out in the hallway. Sabine told her to let him in, and through the open doorway she glimpsed her disruptor and saboteur, top hat in hand, standing out there with a room service cart loaded with equipment. Helena showed him in and he wheeled in a tripod, a metal carrycase, an electric lamphouse, a big wooden box with a fixed lens, and a hand crank. He was tall, skinny, bespectacled. He moved lightly and precisely on his feet. Hands by his side, he nodded into a deferential bow.

—Claude Ballard, at your service, madame.

—And what service is that? Ruining my tragedy?

Claude looked down at his hat, then at his shoes.

—My apologies. Monsieur Rachenko told me what happened. I can speak with the booking agent and perhaps secure a different time slot. I wasn't quite expecting the uproar.

—Five of them, if I'm not mistaken, said Sabine. *Cinq tumultes!*

—Thank you for coming, said Pavel, getting up from the couch.

The two men shook hands and exchanged pleasantries in French. Sabine listened and made a perimeter check around Claude Ballard's accent and upbringing. He said he was from a small town outside of Belfort, that his mother was Austrian and his father was French. He had a handsome, patrician face behind those wire-rimmed eyeglasses, blue eyes that were bright and quick. In the debit column was a pair of frayed shoelaces on his brandy-colored brogues and hands that were far too big for his wrists. She wondered why God had placed a potato farmer's hands onto the body of a figure skater. She enjoyed watching him as he made furtive glances at Pavel's kaftan and the suety yard of leg above his moccasins.

—Alsace, it seems to me, is not quite German and not fully French, said Sabine. Perhaps you should all form your own country up there and leave the rest of us alone.

—I am happy to report that Belfort has never been annexed by the Germans.

—That's something, I suppose.

—And I've lived in Paris since the age of eighteen. I moved to the city to become a man of science.

—And what science is that? Pavel asked.

—Motion of the human figure, sir. I worked as a hospital photographer at La Salpêtrière before joining the Lumière brothers. I'll be taking my exhibition to Australia next, if you can believe it. Lumière concession agents are going out to the ends of the earth. Russia, Egypt, Mexico, Japan . . .

—I played Camille and Tosca in Australia some years back, before all the trouble with the unions and the radicals, said Sabine. Wonderful people . . . though none of them spoke even a smidgeon of French . . . We had to give them booklets in translation and keep the house lights up so they could follow along.

—Isn't there some kind of economic trouble down there in the colonies? asked Pavel. A depression, a drought?

—That might be, said Claude. But I'm told that Sydney already has two Edison kinetoscope parlors that sell more tickets than all of London.

—So you're also being sent there to slay the competition, said Pavel.

—I suppose so.

While Pavel and Claude talked, Sabine found herself remembering her Sydney lover, Adrien Loir, nephew to Louis Pasteur. He'd been sent to solve the country's rabbit plague and holed up with his test tubes and microscopes on an island in Sydney Harbour, in a little cottage where Sabine spent her nights after her theater performances. Even the words *chicken cholera* could sound appealing when they left Adrien Loir's sensual mouth. That epic mustache camouflaged the fullest lips and the most beautiful teeth she'd ever seen on a man. Sabine interrupted Pavel's monologue about the importance of a workingman seeing his own life and emotions on the stage.

—Now that you've come all this way, Monsieur Ballard, perhaps you'll show us?

—Of course. May I borrow a bedsheet as a makeshift screen?

•

Sabine disliked the inconsistency of hotel bed linens, so she always traveled with her own. She asked Helena to dig through one of the trunks. Claude took the white sheet, unfolded it, and hung it between two picture frames on the wall. Sabine thought she noticed him leaning in slightly, as if to smell the cotton. Helena liked to roll up sprigs of dried lavender in the steamer trunks so that Sabine's bedding and clothes smelled like the fields of Provence. Claude set up his cart in the middle of the room, behind the divan where Sabine and Pavel now sat. He illuminated the lamphouse and a chemical whiff sharpened the air. He opened the front of the wooden box, cabling the light through an aperture.

—This is one of the most popular Lumière views, with scenes from Paris.

In a few moments they were watching schoolchildren setting toy boats afloat on a pond and picnickers reading novels in the sun. Helena came and stood beside the divan, cooing with homesick delight. The sky was pewter, the shadows inky and amorphous. The quality of the shimmering light reminded Sabine of waking as a child, of coming back dreamily to a world hemorrhaging daylight. In her attic bedroom she had learned the art of sleeping away an afternoon and waking at dusk, a habit that infuriated her father. When the sun got low enough, the twilight spangled shapes from the garden up against her ceiling—linden branches and slantwise fence palings shifting with each passing second. She recognized the same suspension on the bedsheet—the teeming world shining and magnified by some trick of light. She thought: Twilight makes everything fathomless.

—What else do you have? asked Pavel.

—I have some scenes from the Lumière factory and Auguste having breakfast with his wife and baby.

—Even with the dazzling presentation, there's a limit to what can be made interesting, said Pavel. You and the Lumières need to be thinking about the real power of this invention.

—I would agree with you, said Claude. How about a falling cat?

—Oh, I must see that! said Helena, clapping.

Pavel and Sabine indulged the maid and let Claude thread the plummeting feline into the wooden box. They watched it three times, once at slow

speed, while Claude gave an impromptu lecture on the mechanics of the cinématographe, about how it doubled as a camera and a projector. He
opened up the front of the box and showed them the rotating disk that
parsed and shuttered the outbound images. When he threaded and projected the omnibus reel, only Helena gave a start.

—That was what made all those people scream through the wall?
asked Sabine.

—You have to remember it was in the dark on a big screen, said Claude.

Sabine yawned, feeling a little bored, looked at the clock and realized
she was two hours into her forty-first year and no one had sung to her or
raised a toast. She asked Helena to have some champagne on ice sent up.

When the champagne arrived, they sang *Bon anniversaire*, insisted that the
whole year Sabine *be gentle and light*, which was an impossibility, she told
them. Then they toasted various portions of her life and career. There was the
final escape from the Burgundy countryside, her birth into the theater,
the ex-husband who tried to steal her away from the stage on a Mediterranean
island. Sabine braided her memories in French and English. Gently drunk,
Claude told stories about foraging for mushrooms and truffles in the northern woods, about how his father had filled every book and bible in their
house with pressed flowers. Sabine watched him over her champagne flute.
He was twenty, perhaps, and not yet fully formed. Earnest, a touch morose,
something devout in his gaze, either faith or conviction. She'd always had a
leaning toward young men of science, she realized, because she wanted to
free them from that pious, burdened look in their eyes.

Claude told them about his arrival in Paris, about the hospital where he
photographed the deranged and the hobbled in the name of physiology.
Pavel's accent took a Slavic turn when he drank champagne, and Sabine
listened to his metaphors coarsen. *The mind is a bear*, he said, *and cannot be
tamed by documenting an old woman's hysterical gait with photographs. No, the
mind winters and sleeps in the insane, but emerges from the cave famished and ready
for spring . . .* He raised a glass to the bear minds of the world. Sabine over-
heard Helena, who was unpacking trunks on the periphery of the room,
murmur to herself, *Surprise, the Russian charlatan is drunk again.* The maid
had been with her for twenty years, since Sabine's first successes in the theater, and she regarded Pavel as a stray mutt that Sabine had let in off the
street. Only the mongrel had been given the place of honor by the hearth.

Sabine took in the room while the conversation moved on without her. Steamer trunks and flowers and bottles of Brut Réserve—these were the props of her carefully managed life.

An hour later, Helena had gone to bed and Pavel slept fitfully on the divan. At one point, a big baritone snore startled him briefly awake and Sabine said, *Now that is a magnificent outburst!* Claude looked at her blankly and she came to sit in the wingback chair beside him.

—Are you married, Monsieur Ballard?

—No, madame.

—Maybe you'll find a wife in Australia. You'd be a dapper fellow if you lost that undertaker's hat and most of your Rhiny accent. How many people in your hometown?

—A few hundred, farmers and vintners mostly.

—Just as I feared. No one judges a hayseed like another bumpkin. I mashed the Burgundy grapes before I could walk, toes the color of mulberries.

Claude nodded, swallowed, drank up.

—You have lovely blue eyes, she said.

Claude shrugged, looked away.

—They remind me of the church domes on Santorini.

—Madame, you are very kind. But I should let you retire. You must be exhausted.

—Nonsense, I'll be up all night. Until the night clerk comes with my newspaper critics at four. Let's see if they crucify my performance tonight. Do stay. Do you have something else you could show me? Something I've never seen before.

Claude looked into his champagne flute.

—I hear that Edison wants to film two trains colliding. That would be something to behold.

He took a long sip, drained his glass, blinked back something she couldn't quite read. Then she felt it all around her. Only regret or grief doused a room like that.

—What is it?

—I took a view of my sister dying of consumption in the Paris hospital where I worked. I showed it to the Lumière brothers when they interviewed me. It's probably why they gave me the job . . .

Sabine watched him in profile, his face turned to the wall.

—She comes to me in my dreams, singing and baking bread in the sunny kitchen. My mother died when I was young and she cooked for my father and me.

She touched his arm gently. With his face turned away, his jaw faintly trembling, she stole a glance at the metal carrycase that held all those tiny lives. The dying sister is coiled inside there, she thought, her actual final breath. She'd seen two dead bodies in her lifetime. A peasant fieldworker who'd dropped dead one harvest season—wrapped in a blanket and stiff as firewood—and then her mother in a casket, her cheeks rouged and gaunt, a courtesan made up for eternity. A death captured on film was somehow comforting to her—the dark angel brought down to the same plane as flickering toy sailboats and kites in the wind.

—I lost my mother also. She ended her own life. It's part of what drew me to the theater, the ache of it.

Claude grazed his bottom lip with his teeth.

—I am sorry for that.

—Perhaps you were honoring your sister's memory.

—I told myself I was holding Odette close to my chest. But, the truth is, I fear I have offended God and decency. I have not shown it to anyone since my interview with the Lumières. I'm thinking of destroying it . . .

Sabine watched him. He was new to the world, a tightly wound spring waiting to uncoil. He might burn up in Australia, might end up marrying the first pug who lifted her leg. She wanted, somehow, to save him from all that. But in return she also wanted a demonstration of affection and loyalty, the thing she inevitably asked of new lovers and friends.

—Will you show me her death, Claude? We can watch her passing from this world together.

She put her hand on his and left it there.

They watched the reel in the silver hush of the lamplight. Afterward, the lamphouse smelled like snuffed quicklime and it reminded Sabine of a burning fuse, of the disappointment that always followed a fireworks display. Partway into the viewing—right when the bird flew from the windowsill—she had decided to sleep with Claude Ballard. As he cranked and jittered his sister's death back to life, he gave out a fluttery sigh and she sensed the weight he carried. He was trapped and transfixed by everything around him—the grit of a city street, faces at dusk, a bird on a fence paling—and she wanted to offer up a tonic, a way to quell his need to end-lessly observe and catalogue. She also wanted to forget herself for a few hours, to lie in that peaceful blue room that always waited, in her mind, at the top of a darkened stairwell.

After he'd extinguished his machine, she took him by the hand and led him to the bedroom while Pavel continued to snore on the divan. She closed the door behind them and lit a lantern by the bedside. Someone had delivered a pineapple wrapped in cellophane as a birthday gift and they both stared at it for a moment as if it were a tribal effigy. The smell of flowers and ripen-ing fruit was overpowering.

From Claude's perspective, this was not a seduction by the standards of the novels or sonnets he'd read in his Paris garret, or by the measure of the one fumbling escapade he'd had with a nurse at the hospital. That had taken place in a medicine closet and the memory was soaked through with iodine. This was another thing entirely. She stood in front of a bed the size of a swimming pool, floating in a sea of kerosene-light, and slowly untied her robe so that it fell around her ankles. It was an offering, the unveiling of a bronzed explorer in a municipal park. Oceans had been conquered, new continents discovered, and here was the tribute—her long dark hair falling down across her big, puckered breasts and onto her pale stomach.

To ease the tension, Claude made a joke, in French, about which time zone of the bed she would like to occupy and this got him a shushing finger to her lips. Mainly, he didn't know what to do with his hands. He settled on putting them behind his back, but then he felt them fidgeting nervously.

—Would you like me to help you out of your clothes, Monsieur Ballard?

He shook his head. She watched him kneel down to untie his shoe-laces with the precision of a surgeon removing sutures. He stood, removed his coat and trousers, unbuttoned his shirt, and folded everything neatly onto an armchair. He stood in his black, darned socks and his flannel draw-ers and eyeglasses.

—Come over to the bed.

When he got there she took his big knuckles and kissed them one by one, then the palms and the slender wrists. She lifted her face to his.

—*Êtes-vous prêt?* she whispered. You will leave your spectacles on?

He nodded but couldn't speak. No one had ever looked at him like that.

What followed was a meticulous blocking out of his sensual performance. She peeled back the fragrant bedclothes and took him by the hand, as if helping him aboard a yacht. Flattening her stomach against the mattress, she said, *Kiss my neck, then my shoulders and down to the small of my back.* Claude complied, moving his lips down her body. There were two dimples in the small of her back—two inverted commas spanning an invisible quote—and he lingered there, drunk on the smell of her, on the headiness of jasmine and musk. She said, *Now kiss the arches of my feet.*

In his anatomical speculations Claude had never considered feet to be implicated in lovemaking, but here he was grazing his lips against her silvery pale instep while she murmured into her pillow. When she turned over he retraced his steps, working back toward her head, getting a whispered *bon* or *oui* as he passed the russet, malty inlet of her groin, kissing each rib on his ascent.

He thought this tender choreography might continue for some time, but then she told him to tie her wrists to the bedframe with a silk blindfold. When he hesitated, she asked him again, then she accused him of being an Alsatian milksop in a tone that was softened by a whisper. *Don't make me do it myself,* she said. He took the blindfold and cinched both her hands to the wooden headboard. She smiled up at him from the pillow. *Merde,* she said, *you still have your chaussettes and drawers on.* He removed his undergarments and tossed them theatrically over the cellophane-wrapped pineapple by the bed. They both laughed and he fell into a grinning kiss.

The actual lovemaking was a series of cryptic clues and concealed pleasures. A sensual treasure hunt. She asked for something, then changed her mind. He made adjustments and calibrations, awaited further instruction.

For most of the proceedings he felt his own desire as if it were tethered to a wire, a bright red balloon floating in his peripheral vision, but eventually he burst through. It was toward the end, as their breathing quickened. Her stage directions had stalled out into silence. He looked to his right and noticed the scene in the smoky lens of the mirror above the bureau, saw his own body move with the steady rhythm of a bellows blowing air at the base of a fire. It brought back the early experiments at the photographic society in Paris, the wiring of a bird's feet to a camera-gun, the mounting tension and uplift before a surge of exasperated flight. His own face looking back in the mirror—open-mouthed, flushed, euphoric—was a wild, strange thing to him. A beguiled stranger he'd never met, held in place by an infinite loop. Then his eyes locked on Sabine's in the mirror and he could see that she was pleased with her staging, with her hair fanning across the pillow, with the way her ankles locked about his calves so that her long white feet formed a perfect V. And it was the act of looking back at the filmstrip juddering above the bureau that sent her into a final boisterous delirium. She bit his shoulder, then whispered into the mirror— *nous voilà*, catching her breath, *here we are.*

When it was over she lit candles and brushed out her hair at the edge of the bed. He curled behind her, kissing her hips and rubbing the small of her back. When she lay back in the lavendered sheets, they talked until she grew sleepy. About the trapdoor of the past, about the loss of a mother at an early age.

—I spent my adolescence seeking attention and adoration, performing skits and plays for anyone who would watch, she said.

—I missed the singing, after she died. My father has a farmer's curiosity for the world, but the truth is he prefers fish and fungus to people. My mother liked to cook for people and hear their stories. I remember her always throwing open the windows in the summertime . . .

She closed her eyes and he suddenly felt self-conscious, as if he were prattling.

—How would you like to be filmed tomorrow?

—Pardon?

—Mr. Rachenko asked me if I would make a view of you tomorrow. Something that would capture the world's attention and lift the veil of mystery on the real Sabine Montrose.

—Did he now? Well, let me sleep on it. Perhaps the answer will come to me in my dreams.

•

Within minutes she had fallen asleep with her blindfold on. Claude lay awake for hours, staring into the whorl of darkness just below the ceiling, his eyeglasses folded by the bed, his life a baffling and beautiful mystery. If there was an anchor point, some place to go back to and say here was the beginning of his ruin, it was here, in that hotel room, a hazy twilight floating between him and the molded ceiling. He felt weightless, invisible, out of time. Something enormous had been roused in him and he thought Sabine Montrose was the cause of it.

∞

When Claude woke, it was to sunlight streaming in through the windows along Fifth Avenue. Sabine lay on her back, her hair draped across the pillows, the silk blindfold across her eyes, a stack of newspapers across her chest. Somehow she'd been up and reading the theater reviews without him noticing. He lifted the sheet and took in her nakedness—she was pale-breasted and leggy, her hips as curved as the bouts of a viola. Her hands were folded across her stomach, fingers laced. Claude breathed in the underworld of the bedclothes, hoping to catch something of the actual event. He wanted it to smell earthy and coital, a little olfactory proof of his exploits, but it smelled sedate and freshly laundered. Looking around the room, he tallied the moments from the night before and reached for his eyeglasses.

The Russian appeared in the doorway in his embroidered waistcoat drinking a small tumbler of grape juice, a fob watch dangling between his fingers. He refused to look directly over at the bed, but stared off at the brightening windows.

—All right, my sleepyheads, everything is prepared. Is the light optimal at present, Monsieur Ballard, for the making of a view? We are almost upon eleven o'clock. I want Sabine to look very natural, you understand.

Sabine removed her blindfold and propped her head onto one hand, causing the newspapers to fall off the side of the bed. She flinched at the light from the windows and held out one hand to block it. Claude could see the rise of her breasts against the hem of the bedsheet.

—The solar conditions look promising, said Claude.

—Pavey, what are you talking about? asked Sabine.

—All you need is your robe. Congratulations on your reviews, by the way. The critics love to build you shrines out of newspaper. Now hurry along! I'll meet you out in the hallway.

A few minutes later, Pavel was leading them up a darkened stairwell at the far end of the penthouse floor. Sabine was in her robe, hair unbrushed, an afghan wrapped around her shoulders. Claude carried his equipment, the cinématographe in one hand, a tripod over one shoulder. When they reached the top of the stairs, Pavel held open a metal door and they came out onto the hotel's rooftop. An expanse of flagstone opened out toward a conservatory at one end, a tiny chapel of iron and glass winking in the sunshine. Behind it, the city teemed with water towers and smokestacks and custodian perches. Seeing the city from this vantage point, Claude realized that New York kept her crown jewels, her terraced rooftop gardens and statuary, right next to her broom closets, her generators, her winches and coal shovels. The Paris skyline—the mansard roofs and gargoyled nooks and spires, the zinced dormers—was much more sedate.

As they walked toward the conservatory, they saw a profusion of plants blooming and greening behind the windowpanes and transparent turrets.
—What is it? asked Sabine, tightening the afghan about her shoulders. Pavel sipped his grape juice, pleased with himself.
—Don't you love it? A glasshouse modeled on the Crystal Palace in London. The hotel wanted an all-weather tearoom up here but they couldn't get the permits. The doorman told me that a botanist from Columbia University has adopted it.
—Are we to make the view up here? asked Claude.
—In there, said Pavel, gesturing to the open conservatory doors.

Stepping inside, Claude had the sensation of entering a cloister of glass and humid gasses, the cerulean blue of the sky and the woody, green smells somehow magnified. He could smell peat and pollen and something damp and lingering, a fungal afternote. There were bromeliads, ferns, and palms pushing against the walls, orchids hanging and cantilevering from the high ledges, outcroppings of passionflowers and hibiscuses. A tiny bog garden lay encircled by Venus flytraps. It was very warm inside and he could see rivulets of condensation running down the glass ceiling. A room that had its own air and weather, tiny zephyrs whistling above their heads between open glass panels. In the center of the conservatory, an enormous cast-iron and porcelain bathtub had been placed under a canopy of maidenhair and staghorn ferns. Pavel stood in front of the tub, very pleased with himself, as if he'd made all this by hand during the night.

—It took six porters and an unspeakable gratuity to get this tub up here, Pavel said. They are on their way up with buckets of hot water.

—I don't understand, said Sabine.

—There is nothing more natural or compelling than a beautiful woman bathing. And what better way to capitalize on your debut in a moving picture. As Monsieur Ballard travels the world, he will also be publicizing your theatrical appearances . . . We will capture you with all due modesty, of course.

When Pavel had suggested a promotional reel of Sabine Montrose backstage at the Union Square vaudeville house, Claude had pictured Sabine walking through Manhattan dressed as the prince of Denmark, a troupe of grocers and shopgirls in her wake. He imagined the camera perched high, looking down at her from above. But now he saw this cinematic coup plainly: a famous French actress bathing in a rooftop glasshouse. It was beautiful and theatrical and natural, and he couldn't reconcile the conceit with this Russian who carried two fob watches and leisured in a kaftan. He thought of the letter he would write to the Lumière brothers describing the new addition: *I have made a view of one of the world's great talents, a household theatrical name. Attendance at screenings is up 60%.*

They both watched Sabine standing at the porcelain lip, staring down into the tub as if it were a mineshaft or a well. Along the ledge was a crystal bowl of bath salts and another of lavender soap flakes.

—Sabine Montrose stripped bare, down to flesh and blood, she said. Seen like never before . . .

She heard herself speak and for a second couldn't discern her own tone, wasn't sure if she was pondering or mocking the idea. Then she saw the old woman in Brittany, the stranger wandering toward her from the future, alone and probably bereft, and the ten thousand nights of looking at herself disintegrate in the makeup mirror of theater dressing rooms. *Find amid the*

young a hiding from that Foe, who day or dark, ever seeks a shining . . . a snippet
from a fan letter's birthday poem, read the night before, came to the surface
of her mind and she couldn't understand why she'd memorized it. She wasn't
terrified of getting old or losing her looks, but she was vengeful about it,
wanted nothing more than to drive a small dagger into the spleen of old age.

—If I do it, she said to Claude, we must split the ticket sales for my
appearance in the view.
—Madame, I am not authorized to pay film subjects.
—Given the proceedings of last night, *madame* seems quite formal,
don't you think?
Claude blushed under the glassed-in sky.
—Based on those extravagant newspaper reviews, I think thirty
percent is the right number, said Sabine. That's roughly a three-way split
between each brother and me.
She liked the look of the number *30*—it began with a woman's ample
buttocks.
—I will have to write to the Lumières and ask them how to proceed.
—Very well, in the meantime, Claude, when you take the view, you
must shroud me in orchids and ferns and soap bubbles. I am not making
some backroom parlor image.

They heard a door banging from the other end of the rooftop and turned to
see a small army of porters carrying buckets of steaming water over their
shoulders. *Places, everybody*, said Pavel, probably a phrase that came from the
theater but one that Claude would use from now on, whenever he was directing a view. Long before there was *action!* there were *places*. Claude attached the cinématographe to the tripod, a blank film already loaded and
waiting inside the darkness of the chamber. He positioned the camera so
that he could take in the backdrop of the city behind the tub. The porters
emptied their steaming water and were sent dutifully from the rooftop.
Sabine removed her robe and stepped into the tub. She began to soap up
the water while Claude arranged ferns and flowers in the foreground. When
he looked through the viewfinder he immediately saw a Greek myth of revenge or lust, a bare-breasted Electra bathing above her conquered citadel.

4

The Fiery Splash

Claude never did write to the Lumières about splitting ticket sales with Sabine Montrose. Instead, he bundled along the footage of her bathing on a Midtown rooftop on the steamer to Sydney, Australia. Onboard, below-decks, and in the kind of barrooms and taverns where only men gathered, it outperformed his other reels. He liked to show it after the careening omnibus and the falling cat but before Odette's hospital room death, a view now in the regular lineup. Each time he showed it, when he heard the men cheering and groaning with pleasure, he felt his one night with Sabine roaring through him, his blood pounding in his ears.

He didn't include the bathtub scene at the Lyceum Theatre on Pitt Street, where he exhibited reels for an audience that included women and children. On the weekends, each performance pulled a crowd of hundreds and they hollered up at the careening omnibus just like their New York counterparts. That sound stayed with him when he came out of the theater, cinématographe and tripod in hand, and walked past the two Edison kinetoscope parlors, both of them small storefronts of half a dozen machines, with viewfinders and twenty-second loops at a shilling a turn. His pockets full of money, he hurried down Pitt Street to the Strand Arcade and passed under the tinted glass roof. The Strand was a commercial conservatory in its own right, a retail cathedral of ironwork and marble columns and carved balustrades, the upper galleries full of hatters and haberdashers and tailors, illuminated below the gas-jet and electric chandeliers that hung from the roof trusses. He had an arrangement with a jeweler on the upper floor to store his ticket sales in the shop safe until the banks opened on Monday morning, but as he climbed the cedar stairs, he thought about the paneled transparent roof, about how a film stage could be built under a ceiling of glass.

After he'd deposited his takings, he continued down to Circular Quay to take in the gunflint blue of the harbor, to make views among the ferries and tourists. As a city, Sydney was a paradox. Her Paris-inspired town hall held a concert venue with the world's largest pipe organ, behind an ornate facade carved with lions, and her elite lived in sandstone mansions along the shoreline, and the streets were full of crinoline and top hats and morning suits, but there was also the edge of something darker, a vestige of her convict past. Down at the Rocks, among the gambling houses and weatherboard pubs, there were larrikin gangs known to prey upon outsiders. They wore black bell-bottomed pants and no waistcoats, swaggered along in collarless shirts and neckerchiefs. Claude had been told on several occasions at his hotel to never go walking alone at night, that foreign dandies like him could end up robbed and with their throats slit.

On the Sunday afternoon when he met Chip Spalding, the next and final member of his moviemaking family, Claude wondered whether this fifteen-year-old runaway was a surfside cousin to the hoodlums who preyed on tourists down in The Rocks. He was all sinew and lank muscle, fearless and pigeon-chested, a teenage daredevil in a loincloth. Claude had taken the tramline out to Fletcher's Glen behind Tamarama Beach and walked down to take in the amusements at the Royal Aquarium and Pleasure Grounds. There was a promenade concert, a sea pond stocked with stingrays and sharks, a seal and penguin enclose, a switchback railway that undulated above the sand. A troupe of acrobats twirled from a tethered balloon. Not to be outdone by the aquariums at Manly and Coogee, the proprietors employed a small team of gymnasts and daredevils, and Chip Spalding was one of them. He hand-fed the sharks and set himself on fire before plunging into the Pacific from a tightrope suspended cliff to cliff.

Hearing of the fiery stunt, Claude had arranged with the foreman of the pleasure grounds to take his equipment up into the tethered balloon and film it from above.

Chip Spalding, wearing nothing but his loincloth, lathered up with a gel he made from sheep's-wool fat and doused himself with kerosene. He was oblivious to Claude hand-cranking the cinématographe from the balloon. Eyes straight out, breath tucked in his gut, he balanced out toward the midpoint of the inlet, some thirty feet above the roiling surf, a wooden pole lit at both ends. The crowd watched from the sand as he slid the burning pole toward his body and made contact. A ruffle of blue-yellow flame kindled up his torso, then curled gently out to his limbs. A few women shrieked from under their wide-brim sunhats down on the sand, while he stood there very still, holding his breath now so that he wouldn't scorch his throat. Arms outstretched before an arrow-like plunge into the surf below.

All the way down he heard the sputter of the flames and the awed silence of the onlookers. Then the moment of impact came like a blow to the head, shooting the air from his lungs and bruising his knuckles and fingertips. Everything went dark and cold. He'd once been thrown by his father through a small-town pub window, and that was a holiday compared to this particular descent. Each time he heard himself scream underwater he thought he might black out. When he came up for air, the crowd always chanted his nickname from the beach—*Blazer! Blazer! Blazer!*—and he wished his mother out west could hear that clapping and cheering. He swam to the shore and ran from the surf, fists in the air like a prizefighter, a wild grin on his face. He died and got reborn every single day.

In return for this spectacle and for feeding the wobbegong and tiger sharks, Chip earned a few pounds a week plus room and board and an illegal little hut in the scrubby crown land that abutted the pleasure grounds. He didn't like the bunkroom where the acrobats bedded down because the troupe included some godless gamblers and womanizers who rarely bathed. He washed himself every morning from a spigot he'd drilled into the sandstone wall behind the hut. A pure spring catacombing through the sandstone headland, flowing out into a tiny stream and gulley. It was a source of strength that fortified his stunts, this water, and he liked to picture it flowing in reverse, out to the drought-stricken hinterland, the patch of stony ground his bastard father raised sheep on.

After bathing, he performed his calisthenics, climbed his tree ropes to stay limber, and read his vellum-paged bible, a birthday present from his mother. Although he'd run away to escape his father and the stricken sheep farm, he kept up the habits of his mother's household. She was English and cut from finer cloth. He ate his tea when she did (five sharp), polished his boots on Sunday afternoons, read scriptures every day, and tried to continue his studies in reading and writing. He kept a list of words he heard among the wealthy holidaymakers as they strolled about the pleasure grounds— *gallant, incognito, audacious*—and looked them up in his travel-sized dictionary. He knew himself to be an audacious person and it pleased him to be in their orbit of fancy words. Sometimes he put the collected words into the letters he wrote to his mother. Every day he renewed the commitment to improve his body and mind. If he had vices, it was possible they included "cleaning his rifle" a little too often, swearing, and a taste for practical jokes. He once put a stingray he'd found washed up on the beach inside a gypsy acrobat's dressing room because the man had beaten his wife.

When Claude descended from the balloon and hiked up the glen that Sunday afternoon, Chip was inspecting his body for new burns and scrapes from the tightrope fall. His freckled arms, legs, and chest were hairless and there were crescents and discs from old burns, patches of marbled skin, dark runs on the backs of his forearms and shins. A childhood spent lighting bonfires and falling off barbed-wire fences, barns, and horses had been written into his body. A map of boyhood rebellion. He washed the ash and grease out of his hair and eyebrows, rubbed down his legs and arms with a soapy washcloth. The wool fat compound never really washed off; it just crusted over and had to be scraped off with a twig. He liked to smear the scrapings on the bark of the trees, each one like a notch on a leather belt.

He saw the French projectionist walking up through the scrub— bespectacled eyes on the ground, hands butterflying behind his back, a beachside scholar running his mind. This bloke was different from the foreigners in the bunkhouse; his hands were big plates of bone china and he smelled of lemons. A few nights ago, Monsieur Ballard had been invited by

the pleasure grounds to put on his light show in one of the canvas sideshow tents. Chip had sat on the ground because all the chairs were full,
and he'd been close enough to smell the Frenchman's aroma, to watch his
hand turn the crank. Because Paris and New York were as unfathomable to
Chip Spalding as distant planets, he got a lump in his throat when he saw
the shaky little pictures of northern cities, especially the one with the tall,
big-bosomed actress bathing herself like an empress above the city.

Chip could hardly talk when the nude scene was over and his cheeks were
searing in the dark as he walked barefoot back through the glen, his crotch
throbbing and burning. He had to lean up against a silky oak to relieve
himself of that particular burden and then go inside the hut to read scriptures by candlelight and apologize to God for besmirching his own sanc-
tity. He'd made a commitment to clean his rifle only once a month and now
he'd fallen short. Plus she was old enough to be his mother. Deep down,
though, he knew he'd do it again if he ever saw that woman sudsing herself
in a bathtub under the noonday sun, her hair pulled to the nape of her neck.

Claude stopped ten feet short.
　—I hope I'm not intruding.
　The Frenchman, it seemed to Chip, was made of manners and tweed.
Chip was naked except for an old bath towel around his waist, still taking
inventory of his scars and welts. He looked up, shrugged. The foreigner's
shoulders were bent forward, an invisible weight around his neck.
　—Doesn't matter to me.
　Claude came closer and briefly had the sensation of approaching a wild
animal in a clearing.
　—As soon as I develop the film I'll show you your work. It was quite
wonderful, especially from a height.
　—I never seen it, obviously, but they tell me the fiery splash makes certain ladies faint. The fat ones mostly, on account of the heat and sun. They
stand out there like sausages bursting from their casings.
　Claude laughed and looked across the glen toward the beach. Then he
asked the question that had been troubling him for hours: *Why do you do it?*

Chip made a show of studying his scars. When people asked him why, he
shrugged and pretended he'd never thought about it. How could he explain

that to live inside the slicked skin of a new stunt—a fall, a burn, a backward somersault off a cliff—was to lance your own fate like a wasp to a corkboard? The knot of fear began as a swollen fist around his heart and then it opened out, right before the leap, his limbs electrified and unbreakable. Each time he felt washed clean, *exalted* in the vellum words of his mother's old bible. Did you hear that ruckus on the beach, he wanted to ask the Frenchman, the way they worship me like some blue-headed Hindu god? Matronly women sometimes brought him flowers; young girls with organdy bows in their hair offered him ice cream cones or money, their fathers nudging them forward. Back home, on the hectares of dust and cane grass that passed for a sheep station, he was invisible at the bottom of a big brood of twelve kids. The runt of the hardscrabble Catholic clan. The older siblings had all left, fled to the coasts, and unless his father was on a bender and marking him for a hiding, he was free to go skiving off school and live out among the scrub and ghost gums, tethering ropes between the trees and setting fires down in the stony riverbed. On the night he'd run away, he burned down the clanking old windmill just to make sure they'd all notice he was gone. The rusting blades shanking through the night had always given him nightmares anyway.

Chip grinned and said, *Who the hell knows why I do it?* as he backed into his lean-to. Claude stood in the doorway, peering into the darkness. There was a small cot, a hurricane lantern, a desk made from a packing crate with a bible on top. And then there was what appeared to be a tiny shrine, a ledge brimming with flowers and foreign postcards, sea glass and cockles. A leather-clad seaweed album lay on a chair, open to an emerald-haired specimen.

—They tell me you're from out in the country? Claude asked.

—Out west.

—What is it like?

Chip picked through a small pile of neatly folded clothes and put on a pair of trousers under his towel.

—Hot and dry. The flies get bad in the summer. Bush flies the size of currawongs.

—Currawongs?

Chip let the silence and confusion gather, buttoned his pants. He wasn't put on the earth to explain Australia's flora and fauna to every foreigner who happened upon its shores. He shrugged, inspected one hairless, spackled arm, slung it through a singlet.

—It's a bird. A fucking savage. Excuse the French.

—But it's not French.

They both laughed. Then Claude understood that he was not going to be invited in, so he collected his thoughts in the darkening glen.

—As an agent for the Lumière brothers, I wish to retain an assistant, someone who might help make moving pictures. I have come to see if you might consider it. It would mean traveling around Australia and then back to America, possibly to Europe. You would also be in some of the films, with your daredevil work.

Chip looked him dead in the eyes.

—America's far. What's it pay?

—Handsomely.

—How handsomely?

—As prettily as Sabine Montrose bathing in the reel the other night.

Claude saw the boy blush as he tried to smooth out the wrinkles of a cotton shirt.

—What about me job here?

—If we can agree on a price, I will speak with the owners and see if they will let you leave. You might be gone a year or more. I am also willing to pay them. A finder's fee, let's call it.

—Nope, they didn't find me. I found them. Rode a neighbor's gelding for three weeks and slept in chook houses.

As he buttoned up his shirt, Chip tried to think of a number that would shock the Frenchman.

—Five pounds a week, plus meals, including afternoon tea all the seven days. Each stunt is extra, depending on its peculiar hazards.

—That seems fair.

—That means I could have asked for more.

Claude shrugged amiably.

—Who'll feed the sharks when I'm gone?

—Perhaps one of the Hungarian acrobats.

—I reckon the tiger sharks might get a taste for gypsy blood.

He ran a bone-handled comb through his hair, something he'd bought with his own money. Fire and falling fed and clothed him and now they were going to bear him across oceans. He wished his husk of an old man could know that he'd become a shining colossus.

—Consider us under contract if the owners agree to let me quit.

He liked the official way that sounded. Claude moved off the doorframe and extended his hand to the boy. When they shook, Claude felt the callused skin on Chip's palm and fingertips. It made him embarrassed of his own big fleshy hand at the end of his tweed sleeve.

5

The Bender Bijoux

Everyone agreed that Hal Bender had brought something beautiful to the corner of Flatbush Avenue and Fulton Street, even if they didn't know what to call it. Something between a glorified storefront, a vaudeville theater, and a novelty parlor. The facade was stucco and rusticated imitation stone, but the flourishes—sculpted garlands and goddesses—were molded plaster, painted to a high gloss. From a distance, it looked like a curbside basilica, something hand-chiseled by neighborhood sinners and aspirants, but inside there were eight rows of red-plush opera chairs and the velvet drapes were tied back with golden, tasseled ropes. There was a Kimball pump organ, a mounted screen of white silk, and a stage where vaudeville acts could perform between reels.

The renovation, financed by Chester Bender's pawnbroker and loan shark connections, had taken the old parlor down to the studs, engulfed the adjacent delicatessen, knocked down walls, run electricity to a constellation of incandescent light bulbs. Flossy's kinetoscopes and phonographs were relegated to a single row in an alcove of the lobby, and Thomas Edison's portrait now hung in a storage closet. The American inventor had released the projecting Vitascope to compete with the Lumières, but Hal had declared his allegiance to the French brothers by purchasing the Cinématographe

Model B, which projected views all during construction from one curtained-off end of the parlor. It had arrived in a wooden crate, packed in straw, accompanied by a French clerk who'd personally overseen its passage across the Atlantic. He'd presented Hal with an instruction manual, a certificate of authenticity, and a handwritten note from the brothers themselves, all in French. The first time Hal turned the projector on to run a test loop, he let himself tear up when the warming nitrates smarted his eyes. More than anything, he wished his father could have seen that cloud of granulated light.

Hal had written to invite Claude Ballard to exhibit his work at the grand opening of the Bender Bijoux, scheduled for December of 1900. By now, Claude's footage had become legendary for its risqué subject matter and its ability to draw a paying crowd. He'd also designed and built a magazine for the cinématographe that housed ten reels spliced together, expanding a film's duration from forty-five seconds to seven and a half minutes. In his letter, Hal described his epiphany in the Union Square vaudeville theater, wrote about the girl running along the beach and smelling the salt on her skin. *It's as if you projected something directly behind my eyelids, Monsieur Ballard, and for that I will always be in your debt.* Then he offered Claude Ballard $500 to come opening weekend and stay for a month, to project the seven-minute reel that featured a burning boy and a naked famous actress, the reel they called *The Haymaker* and *that everyone talks about but which the Lumières say has never existed.* The letter had to be forwarded three times before it reached Claude, who was still filming and exhibiting in Australia. When he wrote back to accept the offer, Claude noted, *Please understand that I am now an independent moving picture agent with no association with the Lumière brothers. I will also need board and room for my assistant.*

When Sabine read about Claude Ballard's exhibition at a newly remodeled theater in Brooklyn, the day before its grand opening, she was surprised by the sense of betrayal that cut through her. She was back in New York after a hiatus in Paris, rehearsing for another run of *Hamlet* in the spring, sharing her usual penthouse hotel suite with Pavel and Helena. The half-page advertisement that Hal Bender had taken out in *The New York Times* did not mention her by name, but it promised *a famous personage seen like never before.*

During Claude's long absence, he'd sent her a series of lovelorn letters—*the memory of our twin faces in the lens of the hotel mirror still intoxicates me*—along with her end of ticket sales. In return, she'd mailed him friendly travel reflections written on hotel stationery and postcards of foreign monuments. She didn't pick up the amorous tempo of his letters, but neither did she rebuff him (she remembered scenting at least one envelope with bergamot). But sometime during the past year, it occurred to her that the letters and bathtub royalties had dwindled and then stopped altogether. And why hadn't he written to tell her of his return to America?

The idea that Claude Ballard's affections for her had waned left a ragged edge to her thoughts. Young men were usually simple in their affections and in their understanding of love and art. They wanted to be understood, to transmit themselves out into the void like a telegram, and she'd always found this to be an infuriating mediocrity. Most of the time she wanted to rescue them from it, to provide an education in ambiguity and nuance, but occasionally she also wanted to warm her hands by the bonfires of their devotion. No matter how true, modern, or sophisticated doubt seemed, it still ran thin and pale next to the exhilaration of belief. Even Hamlet had grown weary of doubt and indecision.

She told Helena and Pavel that she'd like to spend Saturday evening—on her day off from rehearsals—going out to Brooklyn to see the theater grand opening and that they were to accompany her. They both looked at her as if she'd announced a trip to Outer Mongolia. *In Brooklyn?* Helena asked. Somewhat dramatically, Sabine said, *Yes, and I will travel in disguise.*

And so the next day, courtesy of a Broadway theater's wardrobe department, she dressed as a ragged gypsy immigrant—a headscarf, a frayed workaday blouse, a bodice with a Bohemian print, a pair of scuffed boots buckled to the mid-calf. She had always adored the transformative power of costumes and disguises, had found her way to the theater through her grandmother's cherrywood wardrobe. Wrapped in another woman's clothes, she felt invisible and reckless. They hired a driver for the day and set off in a hansom toward Brooklyn, the three of them squeezed onto the covered bench seat.

Along Flatbush Avenue, there was little danger of Sabine Montrose being recognized, even without her elaborate disguise. In this stretch of Brooklyn, people were more likely to go see an acrobat, a magician, or a little blackface comedy at the local vaudeville house than cross the river for *Hamlet* or *Othello*. A few might have glimpsed her face on a Manhattan theater poster, but she was invisible to the rest. By the next day, though, every husband, bachelor, and grocery clerk would know about her. At construction sites and in lunchrooms, the *rooftop nude* would become shorthand for everything that was new and titillating in the world.

It was mild for December, and a big crowd had turned out for the five o'clock show. As the hansom pulled up in front of the theater, Sabine was surprised to see that those waiting were all men—local businessmen and clerks and storekeepers in derby hats and dun-colored coats, jostling and smoking in the twilight, eager to kill off an hour. A line began in front of the nickel-and-chrome ticket booth and stretched around onto Fulton Street. The marquee read:

THE BENDER BIJOUX
A VAUDEVILLE THEATER FEATURING THE
LUMIÈRE CINÉMATOGRAPHE!
MIXED COMPANY SHOWS EVERY HOUR &
GENTLEMEN ONLY EXHIBITIONS AFTER 5

Pavel confirmed with both of his fob watches that the local time was ten minutes before five. From her window, Sabine took in the overblown facade, the tessellations of blue tile under the awning, the image of Saturn wielding an imitation stone sickle above the street. After a moment, she sent Pavel into the throng to find Claude Ballard because, at the very least, she wanted an explanation for his silence. And if, in fact, he was preparing to show her unlicensed breasts, glimpsed among fernery and orchids in a rooftop conservatory, to the paying male public, then she was certainly going to seek retribution. Pavel stepped down from the carriage in his waistcoat and wool cloak, parting the crowd with his Baltic gravitas and heft.

•

Hal Bender was at the ticket booth because he didn't trust his mother or two younger brothers to handle this volume of cash. He'd have to make a drop payment to Alroy Healy, his largest creditor, before the night was out. Above and beyond the principal and interest, Alroy was in for a percentage of the door take. When Hal saw the burly, cloaked man bustling toward him, he lifted his eyes to take in the hansom cab and saw the woman in a headscarf peering directly at him. The man arrived at the front of the line, his accent lavishly foreign.

—I am Pavel Rachenko, sent by the noted thespian Sabine Montrose. She would like to speak with Claude Ballard, the French projectionist. Is he within?

A few delivery clerks in line snickered at the Russian dandy, but Hal kept a straight face.

—Is she *here?* Hal asked.

Pavel glanced back toward the hansom, faintly keeping up the pretense of Sabine's disguise. When Hal looked over, he caught Sabine's dark eyes flinting above the rim of her shawl, and a flash of her waving naked from the bathtub hit him square in the chest. Three days earlier, Claude Ballard and his assistant had arrived and projected the *Haymaker* reel while Hal and his brothers stood in the empty theater. Angus, Hal's twelve-year-old brother who played piano and turned pages for the church organist, sat at the Kimball pump organ, ready to accompany whatever scenes might hover onto the screen. But as soon as Sabine Montrose came into view, singing and soaping herself up in all that glassy light, Angus went slack-jawed and the organ sputtered into a reedy, pneumatic stupor. Thinking of it now, Hal had to swallow before speaking again.

—Please wait here and I will go find him. We're about to start a new show any minute.

Hal took off at a trot through the lobby, past Flossy's glass-fronted cake emporium, where she'd been selling baked goods and cider and kettle corn at a scandalous markup all day, and into the theater. The auditorium was still being cleaned because, apparently, Brooklynites were content to throw peanut shells, ticket stubs, and cake doilies onto the floorboards. They'd shown half a dozen screenings, interspersed with comedy sketches and vaudeville acts, since ten in the morning. Now that the evening was upon them, Hal had convinced Flossy to take the night off, to go put her feet up before the reels were switched over for the men-only performances. He'd kept the *Haymaker* reel from her and she was probably doing some needle-point under the sewing lamp in the upstairs apartment, oblivious, while every manner of scandal was about to play out below—a buxom nude, a bloody fight, a burning boy, a consumptive's final breath. Not ten feet be-low his mother's scuffed carpet slippers, while she stitched the edges of a millpond, life's appetites and sorrows would spangle and warp against a bolt of silk.

Claude and Chip were up on the projector stand that resembled a gun tur-ret, bent over the cinématographe, its hatch open, making small calibra-tions with a screwdriver. The Model B looped Edison-format reels, no longer doubling as a camera, and they'd been discovering the projector's quirks ever since their arrival. Hal, a little breathless, gestured out toward the lobby and the street.

—The actress, Sabine Montrose, is outside and asking to speak with you, Claude.

Claude straightened slowly behind the projector, removed a small cloth from his breast pocket, and cleaned his eyeglasses. After three years of film-ing and exhibiting in Australia, capturing everything from the Melbourne Cup to Aborigines at Ayers Rock to deep-sea divers emerging from the Coral Sea, Claude's face and hands had weathered and bronzed. His lips were chapped and there were creases in his neck and forehead and sun streaks in his thick brown hair. When he put his glasses back on and blinked, letting the news settle over him, Hal thought that there was something dazed and windblown in his bearing, as if he'd been walking through a blizzard or dust storm for a very long time. Claude nodded, scratched the side of his face, looked at Chip, and launched a big existential shrug.

By the time he'd buttoned his blazer and stepped down off the gun-turret projector stand, Sabine Montrose was already parting the crowd of ticket-holders in the lobby, Pavel in her wake. The men stepped aside to let in this beautiful, wayward gypsy, perhaps a fortune-teller brought in special for the evening's vaudeville performance, and now her Baltic valet in his embroidered waistcoat and wool cloak made sense, because the pair clearly came from distant lands where people spoke inscrutable languages, wore outlandish clothes, and ate strange foods, and where oracles wore headscarves and lived in forests. Claude saw her walk under the houselights and squint in the direction of the stage. When she completed the visual line to see him standing in front of the projector turret, he realized he was shaking and that his hands were over his head, waving like a signalman lost at sea, a man with a semaphore in a fog. In three years he'd been involved with a few women, secretaries and governesses awed by his display of exotic views, but he'd also kept vigil to Sabine in his letters and daydreams and now the sight of her, drawing nearer, made his blood jump.

Chip Spalding, crouching beside the projector, whispered up at Claude, *Is that who I think it is?* but then retreated for the stage on the pretext of some errand. In his mind, the rooftop scene had transformed Sabine Montrose into a solar eclipse. He'd go blind or turn into an imbecile if he stared at her for any length of time. Hal found himself standing between Sabine and Claude, anchored in place by their silence.

　　—Would you consider being our guest of honor tomorrow, Miss Montrose? Hal asked. We're about to start the first of two men-only shows right now, but tomorrow I can set up a private viewing area during the mixed-company screenings, for you and your associates.

Hal wondered about the word *associates*. Hadn't his father's associates put him in the ground? Sabine smiled and folded her arms, relishing the skittish look on Claude's face. His nose and ears looked sunburnt, she thought, even in December, then she remembered the inverted summers in the antipodes. They were upside down over there, a nation of January sunbathers. From his sheepishness, she understood that her nudity had traveled far and wide, had unspooled in distant clubs and backrooms, mesmerizing factory owners and delivery boys and coal miners, the same ragtag crowd that was now waiting to enter the theater. She knew in that instant that her end of the profits was much larger than he'd sent her.

　　—Thank you, she said to Hal, but I'm not a guest here. Since I am owed a commission for every screening of my rooftop scene, I believe we are all business partners.

—Thirty percent for each rooftop scintillation, said Pavel, arriving at the projector stand.

Claude cleared his throat.

—It is very nice to see you again, madame. However, the rooftop scene is now spliced with many other images into a single, seven-minute reel. So, you see, everything is run together now and there is no separate accounting.

Sabine shrugged, thinned her lips.

—Again, said Hal, this will be a men-only exhibition, Miss Montrose. My apologies.

Sabine turned to look at the young proprietor for the first time and put her hands on her hips.

—If I am not entitled to see my own breasts in a starring role then the world will never make sense to me again.

Hal flushed under the houselights, put his hands into his pockets.

—There are other actualities in the reel, he said. Things that might unsettle you . . .

Sabine loosened the knot on her headscarf and pushed some strands of hair behind her ears.

—Unless there is brain surgery or cannibalism, I am not the least bit queasy. Now, I believe those gentlemen out there have paid to see *a famous personage like never before*. Were those the words in the newspaper advertisement?

Hal said nothing but he stared out into the lobby, where Angus, dressed in his organist's tails and bow tie, was holding back the rabble behind a velvet rope.

—All right, Angus, Hal called out, let's start seating them. Miss Montrose and Mr. Rachenko, if you will follow me.

Sabine gave Claude a curt nod and fell in behind Hal. There was no private viewing area, per se, but Hal cordoned off the space right in front of the projector turret—a bower for the famous actress, tucked right beneath the limelight. Against his mother's protests, he brought down the wing-backed lounge chair from the upstairs apartment for her to sit in. It had been his father's chair, a basecamp for evening declarations and whiskeyed rants. The maid, he was told, had decided to stay in the hansom cab and the Russian could make do with a wooden chair from the kitchen.

•

Once the men were seated, the houselights went down and a few vaudeville acts took to the stage, one after the other. A rope trickster, a pair of
wrestling midgets, a contortionist, a juggler, a terrifyingly dull mime, a
comic in green socks who did impressions. Angus pumped out marches and
circus themes from the organ, accompanied pratfalls and the juggling of
knives. An usher in a red cummerbund brought Sabine an endless supply
of cider and teacakes on a silver tray. It was half an hour before the projector
started up, and Sabine thought she was going to faint from the migraine of
tedium settling behind her eyes.

The Haymaker began with a clown on roller skates, wearing a baggy suit
jacket and a top hat. He smoked a cigar, spun around, coattails flapping,
dropped his hat. When he bent over to pick it up, a white handprint
appeared on the seat of his pants and the circle of men watching in some
Melbourne municipal park, wearing straw boaters in November, laughed
and cheered. Their distant Brooklyn cousins did the same now and Sabine
wished she'd stayed back in her hotel suite. Then came the falling cat,
which she'd already seen, so she closed her eyes to make it all vanish. She
listened to Claude Ballard hand-cranking the machine up on the turret
behind her. He did it with a steady, pneumatic clip that made her think of
trains clacking through the countryside, of yachts coming about and spin-
nakers being raised on the open ocean. She wanted to escape her life, to sail
away with somebody whose love for her was a terrible demon.

A second before she opened her eyes she heard the sound of 150 men sighing.
There came an erotic murmur and a single *Oh Christ, here it is* from up the
back. When she looked up at the screen she saw herself in the glass conservatory as a resplendent, middle-aged stranger. Who was *she*? She'd been
carrying this allure like a ball of wax in her pocket since the age of thirteen,
since the first time she'd run away to Paris, carried it as a burden and a gift,
but seeing it captured on the first day of her fifth decade, on the morning
after her fortieth birthday, she understood that it was a form of electricity, a
pulse of magnetism. Edison had learned how to send a filament of lightning
across the tiny cosmos of an incandescent bulb, but he'd merely channeled a
universal spark, a source of energy that flowed everywhere, between lovers
and strangers, and she saw it now in the gaze of this woman at the height of

her sensual powers. For a hundredth of a second, she thought she would live for a thousand years and die at the height of her bloom. She smiled and leaned back into her armchair as the men whispered and quietly refuted what they were seeing in the shared darkness. Over on the Kimball pump organ, Angus played a melodic minor scale with an Eastern edge.

An overhang of maidenhair ferns and orchid tendrils, the camera low, her breasts glimpsed from the side, above the rim of the porcelain tub. She seems to be singing a serenade to the city, to the welter of smokestacks and water towers and box-hedged terraces that skew and buckle behind the walls of glass. A singing Amazon in a cube of light and air. She leans back and stares up into the lush canopy as if it were the night sky, luxuriating in a sea of soap bubbles, and then she sits up, grinning, one slicked arm along the side of the tub. The cameraman has said something funny or clever and she laughs before waving and blowing a soapy kiss in our direction . . .

The men cheered and blew kisses back at her, called her a French darlin' and things she knew to be more vulgar but which she didn't understand. They might have lingered, or asked to see it again, if it weren't for the pigeon-chested boy in the loincloth walking out over the sea on a tightrope. The audience floated above him, a slight sway and jostle in their field of vision as he carried a pole lit at both ends. At the midpoint, he stood very still and let the flames kindle along his arms until he resembled a burning post. Then he dropped the pole and reached his arms slowly above his head. When he fell into a knifelike plunge, a contrail of smoke and fire shot out behind him until he hit the water.

In the cheering dark, Sabine turned to the projector stand and clapped for Chip Spalding, who pretended not to notice, and then she turned her attention to Claude, who was peering up at the screen. From her vantage point, he was braiding a silver rope of light from one spinning hand. She blew him a kiss—just like the one from the rooftop conservatory—and for a few seconds the next filmstrip jittered into slow motion as Claude's hand slackened. Pavel leaned in beside her and said, *He's managed to trap real life, right down to the follicle,* and Sabine knew it to be true.

Right as the dying sister appeared in the hospital room, Sabine decided she needed some fresh air. It was a mistake to follow the rousing of a man's appetites with a reminder of his own mortality, she thought, moving into the aisle. She left Pavel staring up at the screen in a wordless, meditative funk, a single tear on his cheek, and as she passed the projector stand, she caught the bruised, abandoned look on Claude's face. When she got to the doorway that led into the foyer, a workingman who'd been forced to stand at the back recognized her. She'd loosened the headscarf by now and some of her dark hair spilled down around her face. The man tilted his head slowly and doffed his billycock hat as she walked by. A second later, she heard him say from behind, *Holy hell, it's her, it's the bathtub nude!* He said it loud enough to bring dozens of other men scrambling from their seats.

Flossy Bender happened to be standing at the foot of the stairs that led to the apartment. She'd come down to see what the rabble-rousers were watching and to count the day's earnings in the back office. Even if Hal had taken over the day-to-day, she still had a key to the metal strongbox, wore it on a chain dangling from her pinafore. She'd counted over two hundred dollars, including cake and pastry receipts, most of it in nickels and dimes. For that kind of money, she was willing to turn a blind eye and pretend that a woman's anatomy could edify a bachelor and keep a married man from straying. Edison had filmed an eighteen-second kiss, after all, so the slipstream was moving along with or without her. When she saw the beautiful gypsy coming toward her, a red-faced man in pursuit, she ushered the woman upstairs and out of sight.

By the time the horde of curious men arrived in the lobby all they could see was Flossy Bender standing there in her housedress and carpet slippers. The workingman was still holding his billycock hat in his hands, apparently rendered delusional by all that kinked time and light. He pointed wanly up the stairs, toward the apartment and his celestial vision, and they all laughed.

The disruption had emptied half the theater so Claude stopped the projector. It occurred to him as he watched Hal walking out toward the lobby that Sabine Montrose had finally gotten even for the night he'd sabotaged her performance of Hamlet.

Hal came toward his mother on the stairs, braced for a moral scolding.
    —You're just like Chester, for better or worse, Flossy said.

There was a tone of resignation in her voice and he guessed that she'd seen the reel.

—We made more today than we ever did with six months of kinetoscopes.

—I know, she said, I counted the take.

She held up the key to the lockbox between two fingers.

—And there's still one more showing, Hal said.

—I'm making some dinner upstairs and there's plenty for everybody. Invite the foreigners if you like. We'll celebrate.

It occurred to Hal that his mother had no idea who Sabine Montrose was.

—I need to deliver Healy's percentage after the next show.

—He can wait, she said.

She put her hands into the pockets of her pinafore and looked down at his feet.

—What is it? he asked.

—If you'd come to me I would have told you. But they lent you that money as if you were the head of this household.

—Told me what?

—I always thought Alroy Healy was the one behind it. Your father owed him more than I ever knew.

Hal watched his mother's eyes come up from the floor slowly, by degrees, but they never made it to his face. She looked out toward Flatbush Avenue where the crowd milled and gossiped and rekindled certain scenes from *The Haymaker* for the incoming ticketholders. She kissed him on the cheek and turned to climb the stairs, still without acknowledging the desolation raking through him. He watched her go up, her hand along the railing, and it fell through him like a hammer that he'd made them all beholden to his father's murderer.

All through dinner, after the final show, Hal kept looking up at the daguerreotype of his father. It hung directly above Sabine Montrose, the guest of honor at the head of the table. She sat between his two younger brothers, Angus and Michael, who were brimming with her attentions and blushing from her playful taunts. She taught them how to hold their knives while they ate, how to fold their napkins into a swan, how to say *my cat is very sleepy* in French. Flossy served them all roast beef and mashed potatoes and custard for dessert. She wore her good silver earrings and poured sherry from the crystal decanter. Already, there was talk of expanded hours, of the reels they would make together, the burning feats and rousing spectacles. Pavel, sitting between Sabine and Claude, was already brokering a new deal for the actress's appearances. Hal looked up at his father's portrait, a ghost grinning through mercury vapors, and thought about how he would have approved of all this commotion, how there'd be a kick in his step and a whistle in his mouth if he'd lived to see the opening. Claude Ballard raised his sherry glass for a toast and they all looked at him as he smiled at Sabine. *Here's to everything that waits for us inside the viewfinder,* he said.

6

The Lost Film

Every Thursday morning, for four months, Claude waited in the lobby with his cameras, a canvas bag of foraged plants, and a new canister of footage. After breakfast at the diner, Martin took the reel to be restored—some of it too mottled and damaged to repair—and returned some weeks later with a duplicate. The originals and a master copy were placed in an archive drawer at the University of Southern California. In April, Claude showed up in the hotel lobby empty-handed.

—There are no more films? Martin asked.

—I don't know that I'm ready for the next batch.

They walked to the diner, where Claude avoided the topic of his films and instead asked Martin about his upbringing, about how he came to the vanished silent era.

—I was raised in the projection booth, Martin said.

—How so?

—After my parents died, when I was ten, I went to live with my grandparents, who ran an old movie house west of San Antonio. Every Sunday they showed a double silent feature for the matinee, my grandfather on the Wurlitzer organ, my grandmother in the lobby, and me up in the projection booth.

Martin cut into his omelet and took a bite. He chewed, considered, looked out onto Hollywood Boulevard.

—At one point, I was the youngest licensed projectionist in the state of Texas. I used to wear a little cap like a train conductor.

—Extraordinary, said Claude.

He wiped his mouth with the corner of his napkin and took a sip of coffee. His two cameras were on the table beside his plate and he gave each lens cap a quarter turn.

—And what happened to your grandparents' cinema?

—Sold off when they passed. Now it's a bowling alley.

—Tragic.

—I agree. But my trade came in handy. I paid my way through college as a projectionist at the local drive-in.

—But you never wanted to make films yourself?

—Not really. I just wanted to watch them in my dorm room on a little 16 mm projector. I used to drive my roommates nuts. They'd come home from a party and all the lights would be out and I'd be projecting Chaplin or Jean Renoir up on the bedroom wall.

Claude could see this very clearly, Martin as a college freshman reclined on his bed, looking up at a marbled wall of images. He smiled thinking of it, then he thought of himself in Paris at nineteen, saw the tiny garret apartment where he projected his first test reels on the cinématographe in the days after his sister's death. The impossibility of that time and that myopic kid from Alsace never ceased to amaze him.

—You were born in the wrong decade, Claude said, maybe the wrong century.

—During my senior year, I had a film professor who told me to go to grad school and become a film historian. So here I am.

Claude watched Martin cut into the slice of orange garnish on the side of his plate. The American custom of putting fruit onto a savory plate of food had never made sense to Claude.

—Why would they still teach ancient relics like me in film school?

Martin nodded, poured some cream into his coffee, and took a sip.

—You were the generation that made all the big breakthroughs— crosscutting, the montage, the close-up, the feature-length drama. Half the time, Hitchcock is just copying something D. W. Griffith did fifty years ago.

Claude dismissed this flattery of the silent directors with a wave of his napkin.

—We also took thirty years to work out how to synchronize sound with pictures. But I blame our slow progress, like many things, on Edison's stranglehold on anything with motion, light, or sound. He couldn't beat the French on a level playing field, so he bought up every patent he could and dragged us all through the courts.

—After he formed the Trust?

Claude saw that his own fists were now clenched in his lap. He felt a surge of blood pressure in his fingertips.

—Christ, if it wasn't for Edison's Trust, Hollywood might never have happened. He drove filmmakers out here by the dozens. The weather was better for year-round moviemaking, but they were also on the run from Edison's lawsuits.

—But your studio stayed in New Jersey?

—We fled to Europe to film the first war after what Edison did to *The Electric Hotel*.

—What do you mean?

Claude folded his napkin lengthwise and looked at the boulevard dimming under a bank of rain clouds.

—Come, I'll show you.

It was suddenly raining outside and they watched as Angelenos on their coffee breaks dashed along with newspapers and jackets spread over their heads. Under the awning of the diner, Claude removed an umbrella from his canvas foraging bag and opened it. Martin stepped in close beside him and they walked along the boulevard back toward the hotel. They passed the art deco facade of the Pantages Theatre, a movie palace from the 1920s whose ticket lobby resembled a mausoleum trimmed in black marble and gold. Every time they walked to the diner, Claude shuffled past it without ever looking over.

In the hotel suite, Claude took off his jacket, turned on the table lamps, and began digging through the rummage of papers and canisters. Every now and then a patch of wall or floor space would open up, the pale, nubby velvet of the wallpaper, or the gold-and-green geometry of the carpet. Eventually he went into the bedroom, and a short while later Martin followed. Claude was on all fours, pulling a battered metal trunk from under his bed. When he opened the lid, it gave out a damp, briny smell. Inside were more than a dozen rusting canisters, the labels flaking and foxed with age. There was also a sheath of letters, press clippings, publicity stills, and a bound copy of the photoplay for *The Electric Hotel.*

—After Sabine betrayed me, I took everything I could from the studio and put it in a storage locker down in Edgewater.

Claude began to carefully lift each canister out of the trunk and place it on the floor.

—With some luck, there should be an intact print of *The Electric Hotel* in these reels.

Martin kneeled beside the trunk, his breath thickening.

—Christ, we all thought it was lost. In the film history books, they call it your lost masterpiece.

—Hogwash. It's never been lost. It's just that no one has ever asked to see it.

Martin opened one of the canisters and held a frame up to the light so that they were both staring into the ghostly image of a zeppelin above a river. Martin set the reel down gently and took up a black-and-white publicity photograph from the trunk. It was captioned *The Cast and Crew Relaxing on Lester Summers's Yacht.* Sabine Montrose flanked by men in white dinner jackets, her hair pulled up, her gaze directed at something beyond the camera. Martin pointed to a young Claude at her side, his hair slicked back, his big-knuckled hands banished to his trouser pockets.

Claude handed Martin a letter inside a creped, yellowed envelope.

—You can consider this Edison's wrecking ball.

Martin removed the letter from the envelope and began to read it. It was from a Manhattan law firm. At the bottom, it was signed *Thomas A. Edison,* the left side of the *T* thrown up and over the other letters like a bullwhip uncoiling through the air.

7

Across the River

It was the age of invention. The vacuum cleaner, air-conditioning, the radar. Edison had been riding the wave for decades, filing patents, assembling the future in his laboratories. He lit the filaments inside their incandescent glass bulbs and cut the grooves onto phonograph wax cylinders. But he'd come to motion pictures half-heartedly and late, trailing the French in projecting images into the collective darkness instead of through a viewfinder. By the time he caught up, he was determined to dominate by zealously filing and defending his own patents. He sent private detectives to rival film shoots to see if his camera or film copyrights were being infringed upon. It became standard practice, among early directors, to keep the cameras covered in case Edison's men came around.

The inventor's motion picture empire hinged, in part, on looping mechanisms and perforated film stock. Each Edison frame was four perforations long, the strip one-and-three-eighths of an inch across. Like a railway track, every filmstrip had a gauge, and competing widths were part of the cinematic battle. On a single day in 1886, tens of thousands of railway workers had pulled the spikes from the west rail of all the broad-gauge lines in the South, moved them three inches, and spiked them back into place. Practically overnight, America became a single-gauge railway nation—

four feet, nine inches—and Edison wanted a similar coup in the world of celluloid.

For the first five years of the Bender Bijoux's operation, Hal watched Edison put a stranglehold on the competition. The Lumières had already lost the war on format—their projector now ran celluloid with Edison-style perforations instead of the single-perforation format they'd invented—and by 1905, the Lumières closed their American operations and withdrew from the motion picture business altogether. Meanwhile, Edison was releasing dozens of reels a week to titillate the viewing public. He'd begun this campaign with the first kiss of the medium, back in 1896, an eighteen-second smooch in *The Widow Jones*, but now it continued with the electrocution of an Asian elephant at Coney Island after the animal killed a zookeeper, and the collision of two locomotives on a stretch of rented railway track. Edison might have showed up late to the motion picture party, but now he was swaggering through a crowded house like vaudeville's hooligan younger brother.

Hal ordered as much spectacle as he could, Edison's included, but it was impossible to source enough celluloid to show at the Brooklyn theater. They ran twenty screenings a day, seven days a week, and if the projectionist overcranked the reels they could squeeze in one extra viewing per night. The audiences cycled through the titles within a week and then they wanted something different.

So Hal began to think about expansion. He knew there was more money to be made upriver, by making his own films, and he'd managed to make a handful of reels with Sabine, Claude, and Chip. But it was nearly impossible to assemble them all in the same place for a shoot, and besides, he was always at the Bijoux, nights and weekends, making sure the seats were full and his mother remembered to turn off the cast-iron kettles at the concession stand before she went to bed.

Late at night, alone in the office, Hal tallied their ticket sales and filed the bank statements with their accumulating savings. He also read economics, studying vertical integration, the way a shoe factory might also own a cattle ranch, a tannery, and a storefront. Edison was trying to annihilate the competition by controlling the means of production—the camera, the film, the method of projection and distribution. Hal pictured his own moviemaking studio, a factory that made and released images like so many widgets. But until he got out from under the debt he carried with Alroy Healy, the man suspected of killing Chester Bender, there was no possibility of expansion. Healy was in for 20 percent of ticket sales until the principal was paid back, so that, in Hal's mind, a fifth of every projected reel was tainted with his father's blood.

Unable to face him for years, Hal sent his debt repayments to Alroy via a messenger every Monday morning, once the weekend box office had been tallied. But one morning in the summer of 1905, Hal decided to go settle his accounts with Healy, to look him in the eyes and see what floated there.

Healy owned a number of businesses on disreputable blocks of Fulton Street and Myrtle Avenue, including a saloon, a flophouse, a mattress store, three pawnshops, and two underground poolrooms. His unofficial headquarters was behind the bar inside the Brazen Head, the watering hole he'd inherited from his father. Hal suspected he liked to maintain the pretense of being a barkeep so that he could poison his boozing enemies, keep an eye on the street, and reach for a revolver he was rumored to keep behind a bag of onions. Ordering a drink in Alroy's saloon got you a small plate of sliced onions with some crumbling cheese alongside.

When Hal walked into the Brazen Head just after ten in the morning, the place was mostly empty. Alroy stood hunched over the back counter, filleting a twenty-pound bluefish, its silver scales iridescent in the gaslight of the saloon. The barroom was dug belowground, a root cellar smelling of beer and sawdust. Alroy looked up at Hal, wiped his bloody hands down his white apron.

Fuck me dainty, look who's graced us with his presence, Alroy said to his bookkeeper, an elderly man named John Burns who had a blunt, expressionless face and a beer between two palsied hands. It was said that the old bookkeeper kept not only a meticulous ledger of outstanding debts but a running list of a borrower's relatives and relations, a family tree, in case the loans went south. Hal's father had been a regular here and he'd once developed a daguerreotype portrait of Alroy as a way to pay off a poolroom loss. It now hung behind the bar—Alroy staring out audaciously beside a mantel, arms folded in houndstooth, a wall of mounted deer heads and hunting rifles in the background. He was short, ginger-bearded, going bald, slouching into middle age with an ale drinker's paunch and drooping eyelids.

Is it from the Hudson? Hal asked, taking a stool at the bar and gesturing to the enormous fish. He knew you had to start with small talk when it came to these men. Brooklyn was full of criminals who liked to talk about baseball and the weather before they shot you in broad daylight or robbed you blind.

—She's a beauty, don't you think? Hauled her up off Red Hook, down by the navy yards. And to what do we owe this pleasure?

He brought the knife down on the silver tail and squared it off. Hal thought about the noxious smell of the water down in Red Hook, the way it hung over Brooklyn when the wind blew wrong.

—I'm just stopping by. To work out what I owe.

Alroy turned to the bookkeeper.

—If memory serves, Chester's boy is already up to date. Didn't that goose drop the funds yesterday? Regular as prune juice, that shaper.

—No, I mean all of it, said Hal.

Alroy set the knife down on the steel countertop and wiped his hands again.

—Leaving for China, are you? Flossy won't like that.

—I'm branching out and want to get things squared away.

Alroy smiled, nodded.

—Branching out? What, like a tree?

Hal felt his pulse thickening behind his ears.

—I'm prepared to pay out the rest of the loan plus interest. All of it up front, but then we're settled.

Alroy washed his hands methodically with soap in the bar sink and walked toward Hal, his fingertips dripping and raised like a scrubbed surgeon's.

—Sounds big, like something your investors might like. What is it? Another theater where you're going to show some bird's flickering old tits and a couple of drunks in a street brawl?

It occurred to Hal that even as his biggest creditor, Alroy had never stepped foot inside the Bender Bijoux, that everything he knew of the operation was based on hearsay, that it was no different in his mind from a flophouse or a pawnshop, just another way to filch coins from a working-man's pockets.

—I'm going to start shooting my own films across the river. A couple a week. Over in New Jersey.

—That so? Remind me, what's your brother's name, the one who used to turn pages for the organ-grinder in church?

—Angus.

—So Angus and your mother will run the parlor down the road?

—I'll still keep an eye on the place.

Alroy nodded, puckered.

—Sounds like a fucking disaster. Your mother'll be showing picnics and nuns on bicycles again in no time.

Alroy turned his back on Hal and spoke to the bookkeeper.

—Suppose, John, we were to let Hal Bender here walk away into the clear sunshine, what would that hypothetical number look like?

Old John took a sip of his beer and consulted a ledger that resembled a hymnal. Debtors called it the House Bible or the Fulton Street Book of the Dead, the brain trust of the Healy empire that always sat at the bar, smelling of ale and onions, guarded by the proprietor and put in the safe at night. John flipped shakily through some pages.

—We would have to factor in increased ticket sales over time, since we're in for a take.

—We're already showing reels twenty times a day and attendance is dropping. That's why I need to make new product, Hal said.

—Assume full houses for the term of the loan, one year remaining, plus the interest, said Alroy.

John Burns wobbled a few numbers down on the back of an envelope and completed some long multiplication. He took another sip of his beer and handed the envelope to Alroy, who inspected the total, nodded in approval, then slid it across the bar to Hal. Underlined three times in pencil was the number: $3,565.22.

—You'll have it by the end of the month, said Hal.

There was a moment of squinting hesitation, as if a better deal might have been brokered, before Alroy looked at John, who looked into his beer. Acquiescence came in the form of the bookkeeper's meditative sip, then a slow blink. Alroy turned and extended his hand over the bar to Hal.

—I'll give you one thing, Hal Bender, you manage money a hell of a lot better than your old man ever did.

When he put Alroy's wet hand in his, Hal felt voltage in his scalp. It was a question prickling through his skin: had he just shaken the iodine-smelling hand of his father's murderer? He wanted to test the waters with Alroy, to open up his own ledger page for a future repayment.

—My mother would agree with you. He owed a lot of people money when he died.

Alroy dried his hands and began moving some glassware onto a shelf, his eyes averted.

—It was unfortunate, that whole business. Some men should never leave the house.

—My youngest brother, Michael, barely remembers him. You knew him pretty well?

Hal saw the bookkeeper look up from his beer at the other end of the bar. Alroy still with his eyes down.

—He used to come in here sometimes, or one of the poolrooms or pawnshops. Quick with a joke or a story, old Chester, but always with some calamity chasing him down like a rabid fucking dog.

For years, Hal had read people out in the street as he tried to lure them into the parlor. He prided himself on knowing the difference between shyness and worry, between distraction and cunning. What he saw now was a man trying very hard to look occupied with glassware. Hal looked back at the bookkeeper and said, *Who knows? Maybe someday they'll find out who killed him.* He got off his stool and walked toward the front door. From behind him, he heard Alroy's steady voice saying *I wouldn't hold your breath*, and he felt the force of it between his shoulder blades.

Between May and October each year, they filmed scenes and scenarios along the Hudson. Cliffside rescues of a distressed Sabine, or Chip Spalding, doubled as an actor, leaping from the prow of a sinking ketch. There were lynchings, barroom brawls between Mexicans and Indians, kidnapped wives taken to remote cabins, vengeful grand finales in stockades and stone quarries.

Their first narratives were disjointed and unedited; they exposed a single reel for each sequence, filmed until they had five sections, each under two minutes, then Claude spliced them all together. A new set of reels drew paying customers at the Bender Bijoux for a week, but then the audience tapered off and the films had to be swapped out. In the early days, Claude made positives of the longer reels so that Hal could sell the copies in Pittsburgh and Boston and Chicago, to operators who weren't competing for the same actors and audiences.

This ad hoc arrangement continued until 1908. Since Claude, Chip, and Sabine were all foreigners, Hal had to ensure that they left the country twice a year to avoid complications with immigration. Sabine wintered back in Paris most years, while Chip and Claude made three-day trips to Montreal or Toronto to appease the officials. Meanwhile, Hal saw that moviegoers were losing their appetite for slapstick and spectacle. They wanted stories of intricate peril and promise, not just pratfalls and pranks. He also saw that his makeshift production company was wearing itself ragged. Every summer was a dash for scenarios and locations. In the papers, Edison was offering fifteen dollars per story treatment and receiving thousands of submissions a week. Americans, especially the workaday crowd, were film crazed. Anyone with a dime in his pockets could wade onto those nitrate shoals. The boom wouldn't last forever, though, so Hal began to explore his options for boosting production by building a permanent studio across the Hudson.

They had filmed many times in Fort Lee, New Jersey, a small town with hotels, saloons, and livery stables that catered to summer tourists. Rambo's Hotel rented out its upstairs as dressing rooms and the actors were allowed to eat out back, at wooden picnic tables under the apple trees. Magistrates and Comanche braves and cigar girls sat eating corned beef and cabbage, drinking mugs of ale and smoking cigarettes between scenes. Surrounded by woods and fields and the dramatic Palisades vistas over the Hudson, Fort Lee was a moviemaking idyll. You could film a dry goods merchant coming out of a hotel or bank on Main Street, move a few minutes away, and capture a bloody Indian standing over a wounded soldier on a cliff top. The Wild West could be improvised on rocky bluffs and down in sunless ravines. Chip, who'd grown up wrangling and droving, stabled a few trick horses on Main Street and had easy access to them throughout a summer of daylong shoots.

One Sunday in the summer of 1908, Hal invited Sabine, Chip, and Claude to go scouting for a permanent moviemaking home. They rode the ferry across the Hudson to Edgewater, where a real-estate agent met them with a touring motorcar. They took in Fort Lee, Coytesville, and Shadyville in a single day. Offhandedly, the agent mentioned that he'd recently taken another group out on a similar tour. They were going to build a film studio on a dead-end street in Coytesville. *Some nickelodeon men sick of paying Edison hand over fist*, said the man.

That summer, Edison was in the midst of forming the Motion Picture Patents Company, a group of ten producers and distributors who wanted to control how films looped and projected, which celluloid was used (Eastman Kodak with Edison-style perforations), even how a movie theater could obtain their reels (sales replaced by rentals). But a small band of independent operators were braced to defy Edison's cinematic land grab and Hal Bender wanted to be among them.

The agent took them out to a twenty-acre ruin on the edge of the Palisades, overlooking the Hudson. It was upriver from the Palisades Amusement Park, a crowded summer destination that featured a midway freak show, high divers, and dirigible rides over the river. No one had lived on the property for twenty years.

There was a big, dilapidated clapboard house that needed to be demolished but the old stone stables were still in working order. There were cabins where day actors could bunk down, fields and woods and exposed cliff faces for filming. Hal saw the blueprint of the future etched into the terrain and outbuildings. They would rent out horses to the other production studios, build a film lab where they could import uncut French celluloid, make their own perforations, develop their own negatives, and bypass the Edison system entirely.

·

And in the rusting hothouse of iron and glass, Claude saw the hotel's rooftop conservatory where he'd first captured Sabine bathing, or the trussed, transparent ceiling of the Strand Arcade back in Sydney, and he imagined a new prototype for a production stage. By filming under glass he could keep out the elements while minimizing shadow and reducing lighting costs. He watched Sabine standing at the edge of the cliffs, imagined her moving through pools of glassy sunlight.

Hal asked Sabine if she would consider spending her summers at the studio. She stood with a parasol shielding her from the sun, looking across the river at the Manhattan skyline. She turned from the shining blue slate of the river to look at him squarely. Claude and Chip stood on either side of Hal, their faces shadowed under hat brims, and the real-estate agent stood in the background, holding his straw boater, awaiting a verdict.

It was midday, Sabine realized, and she'd been lured out to the cliffs in the best possible weather and light for a noonday seduction.

—On two conditions. First, my name must appear prominently at the beginning of each filmstrip. Second, I will need my own little cottage, not too far from the cliffs and the river. Is it possible? Nothing lavish, perhaps made from local stone, and you must promise to situate the actors' bunkhouses as far away as possible.

By Hal's reckoning, that was three conditions, but he was just relieved she didn't need more convincing. He'd prepared a speech in case she wavered, an account of his own cinematic baptism in the Union Square theater, of his vision of a vertically integrated factory of images.

—I think the cottage should have a front porch, don't you, Hal said, so you can sit out here in the evenings?

This made her smile under her parasol. Hal turned to Claude and Chip.

—And you, gentlemen?

—It's got everything I need, said Chip. Stables, open fields, cliffs to jump from . . . I'll build a living space above the stables, if that's all right. The smell of horses has always been a comfort to me.

Claude, who now wore a camera lens on a lanyard wherever he went, held Sabine's refracted image inside a cubic inch of glass. She looked away, folded her arms. When they were out filming in a ravine or on a cliff top, she was often tender and warm, but then there were days of aloofness he felt as a chill in his bones. He turned the peephole back toward the old house in a wide sweeping shot that made him dizzy. He lowered the lens, steadied himself.

—When they demolish the house, Hal, have them burn it down instead of using a wrecking ball. I'd like to film the blaze and use it for a future film.

Hal Bender ran the studio like the benevolent owner of a piano factory or a glassworks. He devised schemes to increase efficiency and cut costs, but he never took his eye off the beauty of the end product. The indoor scenes were shot in the glasshouse, its roof constructed like a cantilevered bridge to minimize the shadowy interference of columns and trusses. There was a raised steel walkway, where the camera could be positioned on a trolley that glided on ball bearings.

The downpour of daylight through the glass, coupled with side lighting, tended to flatten actors against the set and wash out their faces. So Claude and Hal devised a system of mounting bedsheets over wooden frames to soften the glare. They built boxes of white gravel and placed them in front of the actors, rounding out their features. Remembering his father's oval-shaped daguerreotype frames, Hal told Claude to use coffee cans around the camera lens to shade the corners of the film. It made certain scenes appear hooded and nostalgic, as if they floated through the haze of memory.

Hal also streamlined the messy business of casting. He hired local Fort Lee residents as extras, and if he had to import actors from across the river, he dispensed roles only to performers with their own makeup and costumes, and with access to a telephone. The calls were made at five in the morning, to Manhattan rooming houses and hotel lobbies, and the actors had better be standing by. First call to the studio was at seven sharp. Actors trundled up the hill from the ferry terminal or took the trolley up the cobblestone road cut into the Palisades. They carried suitcases of costumes, props, wigs, little tubs of greasepaint.

•

Along the Palisades, Chip corralled horses and kept a small menagerie of exotic animals, including a wallaby, an Alaskan bear, and a Siberian tiger. All three had been retired from the Bronx Zoo. He knew nothing about wild animals outside the occasional brumby he'd broken at the childhood farm, so they hired an animal trainer from the nearby amusement park and soon they were renting out the animals to other shoots—trainer included— for fifty dollars a day. Chip also built a permanent stage along the edge of the Palisades, a mounted scaffold with mattresses that was perfect for filming cliffhangers.

Hal managed not only the studio's budget and production schedule but the difficult personalities of his two principal moviemakers, Sabine and Claude. Although he was still single at twenty-eight, and didn't have much experience in the realm of love, he instinctively understood Claude's obsession with Sabine. Even into her early fifties, she was a shining enigma, a drop of quicksilver rolling across a tabletop.

One night at a party to celebrate the end of a shoot, Hal watched Claude study Sabine from across a crowded room. Claude leaned against a wall, blinking behind his eyeglasses, while she stood under a chandelier surrounded by a group of admirers. She wore a red silk dress threaded with glass beads and cabochons, her dark hair pulled up into a French twist, her neckline decidedly low and Parisian. Her girlish laughter broke through the wall of people, little guffaws of self-deprecation and delight. At one point, she touched a dashing young man's tuxedo sleeve when he told the story of his grandmother walking her infirm spaniel down a busy Manhattan sidewalk, and Hal saw Claude wince and walk out into the night.

A week later, at a different gathering, Sabine appeared in the darkened corners of the same room, dressed in a man's waistcoat and breeches, looking severe and brooding as she stood talking quietly with Pavel. She turned several admirers away, telling them that she had important business to discuss with her acting mentor. Hal stood nearby and watched as she beckoned Claude over from the sidelines. Claude arrived with a glass of wine in hand, flushed in the cheeks, the viewfinder around his neck. She asked him if her death scene that day had been convincing and Claude said he'd have to look at the negatives once they were developed. Hal looked over in time to see Sabine's face harden.

—*Merde*, you do not know what you saw with your own eyes? she asked.

Then she turned her back to Claude and continued her conversation with Pavel. Hal heard her say that dying a thousand times onstage was a dress rehearsal for the real thing, that playing Phaedra had given her dreams of swimming in a pool of blue poison. Claude stood there blushing behind her back, one big hand in his pocket.

Loving a woman like that, Hal thought, was chasing smoke. He was sure that love could buoy a man, but it could also drag him down, and it was clear that Claude Ballard was sinking into the mires and backwaters of unrequited love. He wore his longing like a hangover—it left him tender and dazed and easily riled—and if he went under, the entire studio would suffer, since future productions hinged on harmony between Claude and Sabine, between the camera and its primary subject. So Hal perfected the role of confidant, peacemaker, and diplomat, consoling Sabine and Claude as the tiffs and slights became ever more explosive.

One source of disquiet was Lavinia Merryweather, a woman from Hoboken whom Claude had courted sporadically for years. Lavinia was a romantic contingency plan, an understudy to Sabine, and Claude freely admitted that she was his attempt to remedy his doomed infatuation with the actress. But they routinely broke things off and Claude liked to talk about their spats on location or sitting out on the patio at night with a bottle of burgundy. He had a Gallic talent for meditative suffering and epic sighs. Meanwhile, Sabine dispensed mean-spirited advice, told him to throw Lavinia from a bridge into the Hudson with house bricks in her coat pockets.

Claude would laugh, then fume. A drunken fight would break out, in English then French, two streams of invective and profanity that ran together and threatened Hal's production schedule. Hal would give Chip Spalding a nod and Chip would take the sulking Frenchman out for a walk to cool off, as if he were bridling an unbroken horse. Eventually Chip would sober him up and deliver him to his own bed. Chip would report back to Hal, who would go smooth things over with Sabine. The next day they would all be back out filming, oblivious to the spat, Claude angling the camera to filch another strand of sunlight from Sabine's hair or dress. During lunch in the canteen, Hal would sit between them, monitoring their beer or wine consumption, ready to broker a peace agreement if one of them spoke out of turn.

The Idea

Loving Sabine Montrose was a migraine. Claude never knew when a bout of longing might seize him, leaving his eyeballs tender, his mouth dry, climbing for days through a mental fog. He might be watching the daily rushes and stop a frame of her face, or standing on set as she walked by in a vapor cloud of bergamot, or leafing through the pages of a screenplay, and then the big maw would open up and swallow him whole. For years, he'd tried to banish this ache in another hemisphere, had taken regular doses of Lavinia Merryweather as a tonic against this kind of debilitating want, but it was no use. He felt sickened in his heart and throat, weakened and appalled by his own need.

Constrained to the viewfinder, Sabine was all nuance and feeling, but she moved through the real world as an infuriating paradox. She was cruel and aloof, then loving and kind, all in the same hour. He was forever trying to recapture that spark of recognition in the hotel suite overcome by flowers and gifts, when the grinding of his sister's death through the cinématographe pushed something to the surface between them. Sabine had dragged him ashore in that colossal bed with its lavendered sheets, directing his lovemaking so he could better himself in the coital arts.

When it was over she'd lit candles and brushed out her violet-dark hair at the edge of the bed while he curled behind her, kissing the milky flesh above her hipbones. They talked about their childhoods, and then she suddenly got sleepy and bored, turned her back to him while he lay awake for hours touching the tips of her hair. In the morning, as they negotiated the terms of the filming, it felt as if she'd folded up her affections like a breakfast newspaper. That was the exact moment, he thought, when this terrible plague began.

It continued throughout that day and every day after—a kind of platonic malaise. A cheek kiss here, a straightened collar there, but not the boundless thing itself. The unstinting, shining world had been splayed before him, its broadsheets laid flat, and now it lay quartered on the nightstand. For twelve years he'd been marooned within the fabric of that single night and he felt sure it had ruined him for anything sedate or wholesome. When he made love to Lavinia there were no candles or wrists tied in silk; she came to bed in the dark, dressed in a petticoat, smelling of her supper.

For all these years he'd not only wanted to make love to Sabine again—to fall back into that trance—but to contain her in life the way he could in the viewfinder. On camera, she allowed herself to be pressed into the nitrate emulsion like an exotic, venomous spider in amber, but loving Sabine on a Tuesday afternoon in New Jersey was a vial of ether in your trouser pocket, an act of staring into vapors. She shifted, fidgeted, grew distracted, begrudged your affections, dissolved before your eyes. Claude imagined that he might cure this romantic disease if he killed Sabine off in a film with the morose precision of a Russian novel, with such veracity that his mind would finally be his own again. He pictured a frayed knot, finally untied, or an enormous boulder dropping into the river far below. His own great unburdening.

In Paris, Claude had sometimes attended the midnight plays at the Théâtre Chaptal, a run-down gothic chapel in Montmartre that had been taken over by a theater company. The director and playwright specialized in naturalistic displays of violence, in harrowing tales of cruelty and insanity, so that he found himself sitting in the dark of the converted sanctuary that now resembled an operating room or asylum. The theater was famous for its fake-blood recipe—a mixture of carmine and glycerin—and used it lavishly in every show: as the jilted husband performed brain surgery on his wife's lover, as two hags plied an ice pick to blind a beautiful young inmate, as the barber opened out a customer's throat with a straight razor. There were also, Claude remembered, subtler effects—Schubert playing from a gramophone in one corner, a white housecat that prowled among the audience's legs, a grim-faced actor who sat among the ticketholders until he walked on-stage to commit murder.

Claude didn't want to make a film that was quite so gruesome, but he wondered if he might bring some of the Chaptal's bewitched atmosphere to a dark melodrama. As an antidote to his longing, he daydreamed about all the ways Sabine's character might die on-screen—chasing a hallucination down a staircase or being murdered in her sleep or burning up with tubercular fevers.

Then one night he was driving the studio's Oldsmobile back from Manhattan after seeing a concert with Lavinia. He'd taken her to see a touring orchestra and she leaned back in the passenger seat, smoking a cigarette, calling it a *shabby little performance*, and wasn't the venerable old European maestro *an absolute fraud*, and Claude hummed to mask his annoyance. The performance had been rousing and majestic, a bursting, symphonic love poem. He decided to take a detour through some New Jersey backwoods while she talked—they'd been scouting for a stone quarry as a film location—and in a forgotten pocket of farmland he came upon a painted sign that made him slow and turn around: *The Gladehill Hotel—Newly Electrified, Traveling Businessmen Welcome.*

He drove partway down the long gravel driveway until a bluestone mansion came into view through the trees, every room lit up as if for surgery. There was a wide canvas awning overhanging a driving circle but not a single automobile in sight. Claude stared up at the blaze of lights, waited for a shadow or silhouette to appear behind a window, trying to imagine how traveling salesmen would ever find such a place. He got out of the Oldsmobile, took a few crunching steps along the gravel, when someone appeared behind a high window. It was a child's silhouette, no more than a flicker, and then the light in that room was snuffed. Lavinia was suddenly behind him, blowing smoke into the night sky and saying *No, sir, I am not staying here, not even for a single night. It's the most desolate thing I've ever seen in my life.*

On the drive back to the studio, Lavinia fell asleep and Claude began to devise film plots, the headlights picking through the trees and brush and his own imaginings. He thought about the house in D. W. Griffith's *The Lonely Villa*, about the way Billy Bitzer, the cameraman, had framed the view from below, so that you were staring up at the austere villa hunkered on the brow of the hill. As the attackers planned their assault—the camera like a fourth accomplice—the house sat as a sanctuary, like an ornate mahogany figurine poised to fall from a table. But what if the house or villa or hotel were the source of the menace itself?

When they climbed the stairs to Claude's room in the main studio house, Lavinia took off her shoes and lay on the bed while Claude sat at the portable typewriter he kept by the window. He went through several sheets of paper, whittling and sharpening the idea until it had all the elements he wanted. Sometime in the small hours, he typed a synopsis onto a single index card:

THE ELECTRIC HOTEL

A hotelier dies suddenly, leaving his consumptive wife to run their country hotel and raise their two young children. Situated on a rambling estate, the gothic hotel falls into disrepair and the widow decides to modernize to attract paying customers. She electrifies the hotel and advertises, which draws a fresh wave of guests— mostly traveling businessmen and salesmen. Many of the guests are never seen again.

Claude didn't yet know exactly what the widow did to these men, but he was sure a writer could flesh that out. He switched off the lamp and got in bed beside a gently snoring Lavinia. While he waited for sleep, he lay there pondering all the horrifying cinematic deaths he might bestow on Sabine Montrose.

The next piece of the narrative puzzle fell into place on Halloween 1909. Hal Bender threw a party for his employees, the off-season crew from the amusement park, and any Fort Lee residents who wanted to make the wagon ride out to the studio acres. Especially for the occasion, Hal obtained a film from Fox Entertainments—William Selig's sixteen-minute *Dr. Jekyll and Mr. Hyde*—which had come out the previous year and terrified audiences. Hal wanted to stay ahead of the competition, to branch out into thrillers and crime dramas, so he regularly obtained competitor films so he and Claude could study them. Claude had not yet told Hal about his feature film idea; he would pitch the idea once all the key details were in place and Sabine had agreed to do it. For the Halloween screening of *Jekyll and Hyde*, Hal asked Claude to come up with a frightening way to show Selig's film.

But it was Chip who came up with the idea of the cliffside viewing. They would project the film above the river, on a framed screen that hung below a dirigible on loan from the amusement park. Chip had befriended the young aeronaut who flew the Strobel airship, a seventeen-year-old named Jimmy Thorpe. The Palisades Amusement Park billed him as the world's youngest aeronaut and sent him on publicity flights across the river. During the summer, he circled Grant's Tomb and floated above Broadway, delighting Midtown pedestrians, but tonight he would just sit in the sixty-foot airship while reels were projected on the screen below, the gondola tethered with steel cables to the cliff face. Chip, who loved a good prank, had instructed Jimmy on a harmless stunt to be performed at a climactic moment of the film.

Claude had invited Sabine to see the film and he arrived at her cottage in the guise of an escaped murderer—leg chains and a work gang uniform spattered with stage blood made from the Chaptal recipe. Claude couldn't remember ever seeing Sabine frightened and hoped the sight of the blood and the filmstrip floating through the night would be enough to unsettle her. He remembered a carpenter severing his finger on set one day and her regarding it with cold scrutiny, asking the man whether he could still move it and touching the fingertip with a grease pencil. And in the audience of a movie house she never flinched, no matter what violence passed across the screen. A pugilist dabbing his facial wounds or a herd animal being brought down by a bounding predator—it was merely so much orchestrated motion and light.

•

Pavel answered the door in a tunic and moccasins, a treatise on homeopathy under one arm. He looked at the blood splattered across Claude's work-gang uniform and folded his arms.

—You look festive.

—Is this your Halloween costume? Claude asked.

—Just my everyday. A suit contorts a man, constricts his thinking. I prefer to swim loose.

Claude stood in the doorway while Pavel went to fetch Sabine. He wondered, not for the first time, where Pavel slept when he stayed over at the studio. A dozen suitcases and trunks were lined up along the floor, some of them open and half-packed. Sabine, Pavel, and Helena were due to return to Paris for the winter recess in early December and would come back in the spring for a new filming season.

Sabine emerged from the back of the cottage as an oracle—a hunchbacked crone with a walking staff and nettles in her hair. She carried a silver goblet of mulled wine in one hand. Pavel walked her to the door and she stepped out onto the flagstone porch. When the door closed behind her, she took a sip of wine from her silver goblet and looked down toward the cliffs. The night smelled of damp leaves and wood smoke. The crew had built a big bonfire at the other end of the cliffs, far from the outdoor theater, and they could hear it faintly crackling in the cold air.

—*Vous êtes macabre*, Claude said.

—*Et vous.*

—You don't look a day over three hundred.

—I've always wanted to be an oracle, an old hag from Delphi. Tonight I intend to dispense ambiguous alarms about people's futures.

—And what is my ambiguous alarm?

—Yours is not so ambiguous.

She tightened a tattered shawl around her shoulders.

—You have been cursed to love the wrong woman.

She stepped down from the porch, goblet in hand, her hair spilling against her shoulders. Claude could see that she had streaked her hair with talcum powder to whiten it. He watched her as she moved down the path, that old feeling mangling through his chest and thoughts. Did she mean *she* was the wrong woman to love or Lavinia? His ankle chains jangled as he stepped off the porch and followed a few feet behind. He was determined not to provoke her, so he sidled up beside her and extended his elbow.

—Chip mixed up the stunt blood for me. I'm an escaped murderer.

—Did you finally bludgeon that glorified barmaid from Hoboken in her sleep?

She pronounced Hoboken as *O-bock-aine*. He swallowed, refused to be baited.

—She's actually visiting her mother in Connecticut. I look like this because I murdered a man in cold blood for his pocket watch.

Sabine liked this answer and took his arm. Even in the envelope of a brisk fall night, she still smelled like Provence, like lemons and sun-bleached limestone.

—I've got a surprise for you. A spectacle, he said.

—Are there any left to be had?

—A few. I'm working on a new idea for a film I'd like you to star in. It will be an hour long.

—Who would sit in darkness for an hour?

They came along the pathway and onto the grassy flats adjacent to the Palisades. The airship—secured perpendicular to the cliff—swayed a little in the pockets of turbulence above the Hudson. It hovered thirty feet or so from the edge, a framed canvas screen below. Except for the undercarriage and the faint silhouette of the aeronaut and his anonymous passenger, wearing a top hat, it looked as if the filmstrip were projecting directly into a rent of darkening sky above the river.

Claude had instructed Chip to run a starter reel he'd spliced of Sabine in various roles, a montage of her as pioneer wife, kidnapped countess, empress in a long flowing robe. She stopped when she saw these enormous projected images, then continued walking slowly. An organ had been set up at the edge of the cliffs, played by Hal's brother Angus, and it fog-horned through the riverine night, into the canyon of falling dark between the studio and Manhattan.

—Bordel de merde! I look gargantuan and impossibly old up there. My mouth is the size of a cave. And, what, we are playing a funeral march to accompany my mortification?

Claude felt a bite of anger but said nothing. He would kill her off in his film so convincingly that everyone in America would assume she'd really perished, that she'd finally snubbed them all for the vanity of her own private afterlife. And it would be his masterpiece, his rallying cry to Edison, Selig, and D. W. Griffith.

He led her down into the gathering crowd, Fort Lee residents and their children dressed as witches and monsters and lions. A few of them recognized Sabine and they gave her a round of applause. She blew them a kiss and waved. The animal trainer had brought out the bear and the tiger into separate enclosures just for the occasion. A few young wolves and warlocks stood throwing pieces of jerky and bread out toward the animals.

Down at the cliffs, Chip manned the projector dressed as a racehorse jockey, his pet wallaby leashed and lying on its haunches at his feet. Earlier, Claude had set up a private viewing area on the stunt stage, the mattress and scaffolding that lay suspended six feet below the edge. They climbed down the wooden ladder—Claude slowly, one chained foot at a time, Sabine with her goblet and staff still in hand—and settled against a makeshift divan of pillows and sheepskin. A bottle of champagne stood propped inside a bucket of ice, two flutes nearby.

Claude knew that he had staged a seduction scene, but he wasn't sure if it was strictly a seduction of Sabine or whether he was trying to seduce himself, that part of his mind that could conjure the dark narrative coil of a melodrama. He imagined the widow, heard her fitful breathing as she looked out a frosted window of the hotel. He imagined an overgrown yew maze in the foreground and knew that she liked to stare into it from above, trying to fathom its design. But he couldn't make out her expression in the windowpane—it was a blank sheet of glass.

Sabine settled back against the plush cushions, nursing her goblet of spiced wine. When she was done with her drink, she let Claude pour her some champagne and they watched the last of her montage in silence, a dozen disguises and characters. Claude looked off at the opalescent city against the other shoreline, the Hudson breathing and lapping far below, and felt momentarily suspended in time, floating high above the intricate workings of his own life. He thought: Something new is going to happen.

—Does my insurance cover this particular location? Sabine asked.

She sipped her champagne. Claude smiled but said nothing. The film opened with the raising of a curtain on a title card:

> *In each of us, two natures are at war.*
> *But in our own hands lies the power to choose—what we want*
> *most to be, we are.*

The organ music above their heads became a fugue.

—Have you read the book? I think the quote is Stevenson, Claude whispered.

Sabine shook her head and brought her finger to her lips to shush him.

A woman stands by an open French window in the drawing room of a London town-house. Agnes, daughter of Sir Danvers, is waiting for her fiancé, Dr. Henry Jekyll. The father sits playing chess with his lawyer nearby. Their conversation, spanning half a dozen title cards, details Jekyll's recent erratic behavior, then the story of a strange man brutally assaulting a woman out in the street.

A few moments later, the camera cuts to the young doctor arriving at the open window. But he stops a few feet short, seized by an idea.

—I am possessed of a fiend, wearing at times another shape, vile, monstrous, hideous beyond belief. I must break things off with Agnes. To save her poor soul.

He backs away from the window and quickens across the square. But both Agnes and Danvers see him leave.

—An important case, no doubt.

—There he goes now, through the trees. Look, Papa. The moon is coming up . . . it is beautiful.

The screen blanches with moonlight. A few moments later, the fiancé appears again, this time bent and haggard, stopping to drink from the fountain in the square.

He wipes his mouth with the back of a sleeve and looks up at the window, at the camera, at Danvers and Agnes at the window.

The cliffside audience—monsters and ghouls at the precipice—murmured as they watched him lope toward the open window.

—Leave the room, Agnes. Do as I bid you, child.

The doctor, now transformed into Mr. Hyde, walks closer, something erratic in his hands and shoulders and breathing. He cranes up into the halo of a gaslight. Claude could see the whites of his eyes, the grinding set of his jaws. It was the same actor playing Jekyll, but his face and body had been completely altered.

—Call Agnes back, I say. I saw her face through the window, and I like it.

—My daughter's name! Why, what's that to you?

Hyde reaches through the window, places his gnarled hands against the aristocrat's throat, and forces him to the ground. Claude looked over at Sabine, her flute of champagne halfway to her mouth, her face unblinking. He watched her swallow, hoping she was terrified.

Just as Hyde strangled the life out of Danvers, a series of piercing notes erupted from the organ and Jimmy Thorpe, the aeronaut, lit a lantern in the gondola of the airship and threw his anonymous passenger over the side. The figure dangled from a long rope, his neck wrenched and limp inside a noose. His top hat fell, end over end, curling down toward the Hudson far below. Women and children and goblins screamed from the edge of New Jersey until they saw, in the slumping of the figure, in his misshapen trouser legs stuffed with cotton and rags, that this was a Halloween hoax. Jimmy had executed the stunt exactly as Chip had instructed, following Angus's organ cue. Claude watched Sabine's face wash with relief, a single adrenal tear in one of her eyes, then she smacked his bloodied shoulder, called him an imbecile, and folded her arms.

There was a long pause on the cliff top, then a volley of energetic cheering and applause to clear out the lingering terror. The aeronaut waved to the crowd and turned off his lantern, but left the lynched dummy dangling below.

A few minutes later, during a scene with Hyde in a lodging house, Claude finally understood how Sabine as the widow had to appear in the film. *Hyde*

*has just come in from the street and sits at a table with a candle burning before him.
He looks up at his own distorted shadow on the wall.*

*—I thought someone followed me in from the street, but it is merely this—this
that I love. My own self is my sanctuary.*

Hyde's face changes. His eyes soften, his mouth becomes supple and imploring.

Claude thought: *This that I love* is a thing he carries through the glinting
rooms and days of the living, his own secret self-infatuation. Claude suddenly saw the widow's face at the window of the hotel as she looked down
into the puzzle of the yew maze. Her reflection, he realized, was not bleak
and pallid, but radiant, her face burning and somehow purified by the tubercular fevers. He remembered seeing that look in his own sister before
her death—her face smooth and pale as soapstone, her eyes green and flinty
and shining, her lips full and blood-red. Had she been seducing death in her
final days, or was she courting that other eternal self at the windowpane?
Her dark and eternal *this that I love.*

The men who checked into the electric hotel—he saw it now—fell under
her spell, because a kind of hypnotism was at work. Lights went out when
she entered a room, suitcases unpacked themselves, and each night one of
these stupefied guests climbed the stairs to her attic bedroom. And she was
somehow sustained by these seductions, drawing down sustenance like so
much DC current. Eventually, when the traveling salesmen and merchants
didn't check out of the hotel, the townspeople would descend on the property, convinced that the widow was a witch, a whore, a murderess, or all
three. They wanted to burn her alive. But the truth was, Claude realized,
she'd been burning alive for some time, in love with her own apparition in
the windowpane.

Selig's film was winding down, Hyde disappearing behind the facade of
Jekyll after the monster takes a dose of the poisonous tonic. The devil, the
rogue traveler, retreated again into the shadows. A curtain came down at the
end of the reel and they heard the audience above begin to disperse, some of
them walking down toward the bonfire.

Claude looked over at Sabine, who was now wrapped in a blanket.

—Did you like it?

She nodded.

—But it made me very cold.

She leaned toward him and he wrapped the sheepskin around her shoulders. They looked out from their perch at the airship. Jimmy Thorpe released the steel cables and began to motor back toward the aerodrome where he stored the Strobel. His lantern picked through the fog above the river. Up above, they heard Chip call, *A very nice exhibition, Jimmy! Top-notch!* The aeronaut shrugged, the words lost in the night air, and waved as he drifted by.

Claude watched the airship buoy through the darkness for a moment.

—When we advertise this film, we will use the airship to display your image high above the streets of Manhattan. We might even use it in the film itself.

—Ah, I see, like a floating advertisement for baking soda or hemorrhoid cream. Put your arm around me, *je gèle.*

Claude complied.

—Did it frighten you, the film?

Sabine blew into her hands.

—Give me your knee. I need to have something warm between my hands.

He cocked his left knee and angled it toward her. She placed her hands on his kneecap, fingers laced.

—What is the idea for the picture?

—There is a widow overcome by consumption . . .

—It sounds morbid already. I will need more champagne.

—You have to promise not to interrupt. *Vous promettez?*

She nodded, held out her flute. Claude poured the last of the champagne into her glass and settled back against the cushions.

—The widow runs a hotel out in the country and lives there with her two children. To modernize and attract paying guests, she electrifies the hotel. But she continues to die. Only she gets more beautiful the closer she gets to death. Every day, as she is dying, she stands at the window staring down into a yew maze.

—What is a yew? A sheep? *Un mouton?*

—You promised. A kind of tree. Traveling salesmen and merchants check in to the hotel, but they fall under her spell and never leave. Eventually, they're found stupefied and shuffling endlessly through the garden maze. Or some of them are found dead in their rooms.

—What happens to the children?

—They wander through the hotel and the grounds, as if lost.

—Did she kill the husband? Poison him?

—No, I don't think so.

A silence.

—What else?

He continued to improvise the script while they both stared north, up into the dark gaping mouth of the Hudson Valley. He knew exactly which aspects to emphasize to draw her in—the widow's mounting beauty, her seductive powers, the silk dresses she wears to the dinner table, a ghost who's drifted in from a glittering spectral ballroom. He told her everything in elaborate detail except for the film's ending. He didn't know exactly how her terrible death would unfold, but he wanted to keep it from her as long as possible. When he was done he waited, braced himself for her cynicism.

—I am too old to have small children. No one would believe that.

—It will be part of your supernatural powers. We would begin filming in the spring.

—Could she be foreign, French, like me?

—Perhaps.

—What are you calling it?

—*The Electric Hotel.* We would release it next Halloween.

She thought for a moment, looking off into the distance. He felt the hand pressure on his knee tighten.

—You should set the picture as if it were taking place right here above the river. We're always pretending New Jersey is somewhere else.

—Agreed.

She peered into the space in front of her, letting it all take shape.

—Yes, your film needs a beautiful monster, a shockingly pale woman in a black silk gown.

—I was thinking white.

—No, no, black will bring out the lavender powder on her cheeks.

—I'm so pleased you like the idea.

He put his hand on top of hers, the one gripping his knee. She left her hand there for a moment, then removed it and looked into her empty champagne glass.

—I don't know why you've loved me like this all these years. It's pure but also monstrous.

Claude stared down at the river. Hal Bender's dead father had a boat lying at the bottom of the Hudson, and Claude imagined it there in an underwater cemetery, a riverscape of mud and sunken scows and bloated keg barrels. Life is nothing but flotsam, he thought, floating all around us while we slowly drown.

—The poison that Dr. Jekyll carries in his pocket . . . This is loving you. I take a sip and there you are again, ready to put a knife through my shoulder blades.

She lifted her hands in front of her, opened her fingers wide.

—Look, there is no knife in my hands. There never has been . . .

—I'm going to ask Hal to spend fifty thousand dollars on this film. It will be unlike anything else that's ever been made. Will you do it?

Sabine, still with nettles in her hair, examined her champagne flute and gave it a sudden toss. They heard a tiny, far-off shattering of glass against the cliff face. She smiled faintly but didn't look at him.

—We used to smash our glasses before opening night at the Théâtre Libre. It's a gesture of good luck for a new beginning. It signals the death of the past. Of course I will do it.

Claude tossed his own glass off the cliff and they listened for the far-off shattering.

9

The Feature

"THE ELECTRIC HOTEL"
A DARK MELODRAMA
PHOTOPLAY

<u>Principals:</u>
The Widow, Rosalind Bernaud--Madame Sabine Montrose
The Besotted Hotel Guest--Lester Summers
Director--Claude Ballard
Producer--Hal Bender
Master of Stunts--Chip Spalding

ACT I

1. EXTERIOR HOTEL (NIGHT)
The camera is stationary as the fade comes in. The Palisades
in moonlight, the dark river below. A gothic hotel, hunkered
and foreboding, looms above a ruined garden. A single light
shines from a circular attic window: a portal into another
world.

.

In the foreground, something prowls: a menacing silhouette. The beast slinks up the stairs and onto the porch, lying across the entranceway. In the pall, we see its piercing eyes. A tiger. Blink, then it's gone.

2. TITLE CARD: *THE ELECTRIC HOTEL, starring MADAME SABINE MONTROSE*

3. TITLE CARD: *A consumptive widow and her two children are forced to fend for themselves in their country hotel . . . But Rosalind, the widow, possesses a dark secret . . .*

DISSOLVE TO:

4. CROSS-SECTION OF HOTEL--ATTIC (NIGHT)
The rooms in profile, as if the facade has been sliced away. In the attic, the WIDOW is dressing for the evening, standing in front of a full-length mirror in a long black décolleté gown. Her hair is long and dark, framing a pale and sensual face. The attic appears to be her makeshift bedroom: a large four-poster bed stands behind her. Suddenly stricken, she coughs into a white handkerchief, one hand at her throat.

5. INSERT CLOSE VIEW: A tiny island of blood on the hand-kerchief.

6. CROSS-SECTION OF HOTEL--CHILDREN'S BEDROOM
The attic dims and a bedroom lamp comes up a floor below. The widow's CHILDREN stand before a dollhouse. The BOY wears a tattered dressing gown, a wooden sword tucked into his cinched belt. The GIRL is wearing her nightgown and placing a cloth doll inside one of the miniature rooms.

The bedroom is disheveled--breakfast dishes, piles of clothes, two small unmade beds.

•

But as we peer into the dollhouse, we see figures and furniture
moving under their own volition. The children watch this
miniature life intently.

7. CROSS-SECTION OF HOTEL--DESCENDING
The widow in her long dress, descending the stairs. Each room
is briefly lit up as she zigzags through the stairwell, down
three levels. She passes hotel rooms with numbers on the doors.
There are mounted deer and bear heads looking out, antique
clocks and paintings. In one painting, we see the dead husband looking back from death, his cheeks ablaze.

She arrives at the front door, drapes a cloak around her
shoulders, and steps out into the night with the lantern. The
tiger rises on its haunches, tame as a spaniel, and they walk
down the front stairs together.

8. EXTERIOR, THE PALISADES (NIGHT)
The camera floats in midair. The widow and the tiger saunter
toward the edge of the cliffs, high above the darkening
river below. A gaslit Manhattan glimmers from the other
shore. Her hair is loose and her face is peaceful as she
watches the view in the moonlight. The tiger blinks into the
wind. For a second, it looks as if she might jump . . .

9. EXTERIOR FACADE OF HOTEL, CHILDREN'S BEDROOM WINDOW (NIGHT)
The boy and the girl are pressed to the windowpane, looking
out into the night at their mother.

10. EXTERIOR, THE PALISADES (NIGHT)
A dirigible floats into view, descending from the upper drafts.
It hovers above the cliffs for a moment before a rope ladder
is lowered. In her gown, the widow carefully climbs up, one
foot and hand at a time. The tiger watches, roars once, then
sits, sphinxlike, as the airship rises into the night sky . . .

In the early months of 1910, Hal Bender pitched the opening sequence
of *The Electric Hotel* to potential investors, claiming it would become the

most captivating and expensive stretch of celluloid in the history of moving pictures. He handed around the first two pages of the photoplay and told them that he wasn't just competing with Edison, Fox, and Biograph anymore, but with the medium itself, with the limits of emulsified light.

He met with bankers, factory owners, stockbrokers, real-estate speculators. He prepared charts that mapped out return on investment and a wall poster featuring a solid blue profit line soaring into an upward bend. He sometimes brought along a Manhattan ophthalmologist who attested to the fact that, contrary to popular belief, a motion picture running more than twenty minutes would not damage the moviegoer's retinas.

These were men who made their money investing in apartment buildings and foreign currencies, who stored deeds of trust in bank vaults, so he was surprised by how little they cared for the economics of filmmaking. High risk seemed to be part of the equation; in their minds, investing in a film was equivalent to gambling on the weather, on the movement of clouds. In return for a smattering of projected profits, they were willing to sink a few thousand apiece into an hour-long feature, shot mostly at night, with risqué themes, so long as it featured Sabine Montrose under exclusive contract. Hal showed them the rooftop bathtub scene as a teaser, presented it matter-of-factly and then watched their faces flush in the half light. Magnified against a white wall, floating on a current of cigar and pipe smoke, she bathed and sang in her glasshouse bower, Manhattan marbled and glinting through the walls behind her. Then, as a clincher, Hal passed around a full-page ad he intended to run in *The Moving Picture World*.

A SELLING CYCLONE

Every State Right Buyer in the Business Is Eager to Secure

The Marvel and Miracle of Photoplays

MADAME SABINE

MONTROSE

in the Emotional Masterpiece

"THE ELECTRIC HOTEL"

A Multi-Reel Dark Melodrama
A Glorious Record of Genius

Montrose is under an ironclad contract not to pose for others in motion pictures. This photoplay is unique and exclusive.	*ANY AND ALL INFRINGEMENTS OF COPYRIGHT WILL BE MERCILESSLY PROSECUTED*	These are the only motion pictures of Montrose in *The Electric Hotel*.

★ ★ ★ ★ ★

Sabine Montrose in "The Electric Hotel" is better than U.S. Government Bonds. Prospective purchasers must hurry, for much is sold and all remaining territory is in negotiation. What a very Goddess of the Theater is Montrose! Empress-queen of the Stage Play and the Photoplay, her picture "The Electric Hotel" will break all records for popularity with State Right Investors. We are flooded with enquiries. Deluged with checks. Telegrams rain in upon us. Buyers throng our offices. Selling surely—Selling fast—Selling enthusiastically—It's a selling riot!

Bender & Ballard Productions, Fort Lee, New Jersey

Be it known to all and forgotten by no one that these pictures are copyrighted and that all infringements will be relentlessly prosecuted to the full extent of the law. There is but one Montrose "Electric Hotel" in the world of photoplays. Our attorneys are House, Grossman & Vorhaus, New York, and Albert Mayer, Paris and London.

•

With the lights back on, and while the potential investors passed around the
broadsheet advertisement, Hal walked among them, looking into their
faces. It was not all that different from enticing a peeper into a show at the
novelty parlor in Brooklyn during his teens. He leaned back on his heels and
pushed his voice up from his stomach, a trick his father had taught him
to convey confidence.

—Be a part of moviemaking history, gentlemen, while making a handsome return. This is not something Edison can offer you—a seat at the
table. His new trust prevents any of you from entering into the motion picture business. And if you happen to own a movie house in Toledo or Schenectady, he will rent you a film, but you could never be part of making your
own. But timing is everything and we're almost fully funded . . .

This got a steady round of head-nodding in the clubhouse or private
dining room where he delivered his pitch. Each time, when he packed up
the projector and charts and went out into the street he patted a handful of
signed checks in his breast pocket.

What Hal didn't tell the investors was that the first few pages of the photoplay were the only ones written, that Lester Summers had not yet signed
on to the film, and that he intended to violate the Edison Motion Picture
Trust by illegally importing uncut French celluloid and perforating it in the
studio's New Jersey laboratory.

SCENARIO WRITERS!
If your scenarios do not sell find out why. The author of "Tech-
nique of the Photoplay," Winthrop Major, will give your manuscript personal criticism and revision for a fee of only $2.

The first scriptwriter they hired—fired after only a week—was a former
vaudeville critic who advertised in the celluloid trades. Winthrop Major
arrived at the studio wearing a beaver-felt hat and driving moccasins,
stepping down from his motorcar with a meerschaum pipe clenched between gapped teeth. Claude showed him to one of the actors' bunkhouses,
where he insisted that, as per the addendum to his retainer agreement,

private accommodations were to be provided. He was put up in a top-floor bedroom in the main house, where his pacing, adenoidal muttering, and midnight tapping on his typewriter wore Hal's nerves ragged. At breakfast one morning, as Winthrop repacked his pipe, Hal asked him how the photoplay was coming along and whether a scene could be worked in that featured the widow playing with her pet tiger.

—To show she has some special connection with the world of beasts, Hal said.

—Remember, as per my advertisement, two dollars per simple question, Mr. Bender. And I believe that's a five-dollar question.

He smiled into his breakfast plate, chuffed.

—I'm not kidding, said Hal.

Winthrop looked up, struck a match, lit his pipe. There was a slight shunting noise in the back of his throat as he drew air through the burning plug. His words came out on the first ribbons of smoke.

—The photoplay is a blueprint and a scale model. It requires an architect's eye to achieve its intentions. I do not believe for one second that a consumptive widow would be playing fetch with a Bengal tiger. In fact, I recommend cutting the preposterous animal altogether.

Claude sat marmalade-ing a piece of toast at the other end of the table.

—But audiences like dangerous animals in films. They have played quite well in previous reels, said Claude.

—Be that as it may, gentlemen, I cannot allow the logical construct to be disrupted by false effects.

Winthrop was fired by the end of the day. Even the horn on his motorcar had a pompous, adenoidal quality as he honked angrily driving out of the studio gates.

The second writer was a failed novelist who specialized in South Sea adventures. He lasted two weeks, but was let go after writing a long sequence that had the widow taking the airship to New Zealand, where she married a Maori chief and was honored as a goddess by the local savages. He spent three days on this muddle before showing the pages to Hal and Claude.

The third writer was a retired newspaper editor, the fourth a copywriter, the fifth a poet and amateur photographer named Nash Sully. Finally, they had found someone who thought in images and who needed the money badly enough that he was willing to take Hal and Claude's unending prescriptive notes. Nash Sully brought their ideas back to them as polished visual gems, little motifs and suggestive lines of intertitle dialogue, lovely asides about the experiences of the camera, as if it were the probing eye of a sentient being instead of a crystal-ground lens. *Camera pulls back into oblivion* or *Camera ghosts after the distraught widow.* His final sequence—a mob descending on the hotel with burning torches, a dirigible going up in flames— was unlike anything ever filmed. Hal and Claude agreed to remove those final two pages from Sabine's copy of the photoplay.

10

The Actress Prepares

Miss, I lik you so Please send me yur auto graf plus $10. I am 20 years old. I cant rite good. Bil says I can. I don't beleive Bil Wilson. I wuz sik last winter. I hav got a Baby. Her name is Sabine Montrose Kane cauz I like your picturs. bil reads to me and I know about your life. Send me money and rite soon. Address Miss Abbie Kane mother of Sabine Montrose Kane, Union Missouri. Grandma saw you in St. Louis and was filled with wunder.

To "Sabine Montrose"
Dear Madame,
I trust I am not taking too much liberty in asking you to kindly name your favorite flower and why? My object in soliciting this favor is that I may write an article on the favorite flowers of prominent people. I have received answers from several noteworthy personages in politics and the arts.
Sincerely,
Beatrice Windermere

Vixen,
A man's appetites can be exploited for the devil's work, or the Lord's. Seeing your feminine form in a bathtub on a rooftop galvanized my wrath

*some years back. Now I see you whoring in other moving pictures as a
Comanche bride or woodsman's lover. You turn the Holy Scriptures into
ridicule. To think I once stood applauding for you during your Hamlet
curtain call.*

 A Once Great Admirer

Sabine made the mistake of opening some of the correspondence she'd bundled across the Atlantic. Two weeks before shooting was scheduled to begin,
she rode alone in a motorcar from the Hoboken docks to the studio, certain
that the world was a hateful place. She'd spent the off-season performing
in a naturalistic adaptation of the Zola novel *Thérèse Raquin* at the Odéon in
Paris. Eight weeks of playing the lead—a nervous, feckless, adulterous
woman who felt smothered by life's demands—had left Sabine raked through
with boredom and disappointment. Unhappiness loomed everywhere. Her
days could be plundered by the bitterness of spoiled fruit or someone un-
pleasant entering a room, and she could never pinpoint how the initial dis-
pleasure, the bitter apple or the poseur, quickly attached itself to some
greater existential sadness. Unhelpfully, Pavel told her she was experienc-
ing *toska*, the Russian word for a spiritual malaise.

As she traveled along the road outside Fort Lee she suspected that *Thérèse
Raquin* was responsible for her *toska*. She looked out her motorcar window,
beyond the mud in the ditches, and noticed half a dozen filthy dun-brown
cows ogling eternity from behind a split rail fence. She blinked back a tear,
closed her eyes, and felt her thoughts turn apocalyptic. The newspapers were
reporting that the planet was going to arc into the poisonous, gassy tail of
Halley's Comet later in the spring. Of course, she thought, now we will all
choke in our beds. Opening her eyes again, she studied the upholstery of the
motorcar to avoid the bovine misery out in the fields, but then she noticed
the seat leather was cracked and brittle.

She looked at the grease-stained envelope from Union, Missouri, where
Sabine Montrose Kane had been named by an illiterate mother hoping for
$10. It all seemed impossible, these dispatches from life's ragged edges. Her
only consolation was being alone inside this noxious mood. After they'd
arrived at the docks, she'd banished Pavel and Helena into a second motorcar with the suitcases and trunks.

•

The winter had been a particularly lonely time for her. Pavel and André Antoine, the director of the Odéon, were determined to take naturalism to its highest calling. Together, they coached her toward a style of acting that was unadorned and naked—small, contained gestures, no formalized speeches or exits, so that she sometimes felt like she wandered on and off the stage like a daydreaming child. They also sent her out to observe and study the archetypes of Paris, because Zola had insisted his novel, and therefore the play, was a study in temperament, not character. Zola drew his characters from ancient Greece, from Galen's humors and types—the crippled aunt was choleric, Thérèse melancholic, her lover sanguine, and the duped husband phlegmatic. They were fated to their actions based on some dominance of bile, phlegm, or blood.

To prepare for her role, Sabine was sent out into the Paris streets in disguise, often at night, to locate the city's melancholics. Her main character study was a barmaid at a Montmartre tavern, middle-aged and slumped in the shoulders, a sallow-faced woman of small exasperations, who polished the glasses with something that approached fanaticism. Every smudge or thumbprint was a personal affront to the barmaid and Sabine sometimes saw the woman's eyes narrow when a paying customer took up a glass of Bordeaux or beer. She chatted and complained about life's adversities, about the struggling shopgirl daughter and the flatulent husband who worked for the postal service, but all the while she stood transfixed by a developing whorl of thumb grease pressing into her polished glass. For a perfectionist melancholic, Sabine knew this was a miniature death of the soul.

Back at the theater, Antoine and Pavel were thrilled with her progress. She stopped acting with studied gestures and let her emotions surge through her. Her face and head and voice were left battered by the blunt force of Thérèse's personality. Antoine was famous for his naturalistic staging and effects—the chickens pecking onstage, the crowd scenes with vagrants off the street, the drunken fights fueled by real absinthe—and he saw his actors as an extension of life's chaotic, naked rhythms. He asked Sabine to stop washing her hair so that she could sense her own body's wild inclinations. By the end of her eight-week run, some of her matted hair had to be cut from the crown of her head.

•

Pavel, meanwhile, had developed his own fully fledged system that brought together smatterings of Stanislavski and Darwin and blended them with homeopathy, theosophy, anthropology, and yogic breathing exercises. He called his new approach the Emotive-Pneumatic Practice, inspired by the Hellenic idea that it was pneuma—a kind of spiritual breath—that coursed through human arteries instead of blood. By the spring of 1910, he'd delivered lectures on his *occult science of the imagination and emotional intellect* at academies of dramatic art in Paris, London, and St. Petersburg.

Publicly, he touted Sabine Montrose as his most famous protégé, but privately he suspected she only half believed in his methods. It was not uncommon for her to banish him to another hotel room or railcar when she grew tired of his pedagogy. En route to his temporary exile, he would tell her, *Either we swim in the underground river or it drowns us.*

At the entrance to the studio property, a uniformed security guard greeted the two motorcars and checked their names off a list. It was the studio's new protection against Edison's private detectives who went out looking for patent and copyright infringements. They drove down toward the main building and the cottage. It annoyed Sabine that Claude hadn't bothered to meet the steamer, despite the fact that she'd telegraphed her itinerary. He'd sent a curt reply—*Chaos and much excitement here. Please come directly. Bon voyage!* Now she saw what he meant about chaos. The entire lot was in upheaval.

Workmen stood on scaffolding to paint the facade of a three-story gothic hotel—a single imitation wall fronted with windows and shutters, but hollowed out in the back, supported by diagonal beams. There were platforms and suspended walkways behind certain windows, presumably where an actor might stand to be glimpsed by the camera.

In front of the facade, a ruined garden and a maze were being painstakingly assembled from unsheathed trees and shrubs. A moss-ravaged fountain taking shape from mastic and wire, its creator standing by with a trowel. As her motorcar drove toward the stone cottage, Sabine noticed a series of cross-sectioned rooms under the glasshouse of the filming stage, the empty living spaces stacked like so many boxes. Then, down by the cliffs, she saw Chip

Spalding and Jimmy Thorpe practicing some kind of aerial maneuver from the tethered dirigible, the Australian suspended from the gondola in a harness. He was going to plunge to his death—she was certain of it.

Her mood brightened, briefly, when she discovered her favorite flowers and chocolates inside the cottage: white lilies and cherries covered in bittersweet chocolate. This was another new dimension to her moods—the fleeting euphoria of her favorite tastes and smells. She let a chocolate-covered cherry melt on her tongue and took a deep breath. The vase of lilies contained the aromatic cloud of her childhood, a dozen feral summers performing for her younger brother and sister in the barn and running through the flowerbeds. Her mother didn't like flowers in the house, found the browning anthers of a dying lily on a mantel intolerably morbid, so she let them bloom in the beds every year to the heady edge of rotting before they went to seed. That florid, operatic smell was somehow a comfort to Sabine; it evoked her mother as a woman of strong opinions instead of the sad woman in the sealed room at the end of the hallway.

In the kitchen, there was another bundle of letters and a copy of the revised photoplay waiting for her on the table. She didn't have the stomach for more letters from strangers, so she picked up the photoplay and began to turn pages. Claude had mailed the script to her in Paris, where both she and Pavel critiqued it for errors of naturalistic judgment before sending it back. She'd also begun some research of her own on consumption, writing away to several sanitariums before receiving a promising reply.

Six months ago she'd sat listening to Claude under a sheepskin rug as he described his idea for a feature film about a tubercular widow. She was going to play a beautiful monster, a seductress with an otherworldly allure. She sometimes felt like a coil of wire, a medium for the unraveling ideas of men, for storytellers and visionaries. Zola, Pavel, Chekhov, Shakespeare, Antoine, dead and some living, they all needed a filament inside their glass bulbs, something to electrify an inkling they had about human nature and convert it to a shock of recognition.

She studied the roles, saw the world through the vapored lens of Ophelia or Thérèse, but she also knew her own emotional landscape as if it were fixed and painted plainly on a wall—the shame that had scoured her insides since the age of twelve, when she sensed her family lived apart from the world after her mother's suicide, or the later thrill of commanding a room's full attention, of being seen again, the freedom and terror that came with being adored and coveted by men. All these motifs were available to her at any time; it was like lying in bed at the top of a great, darkened house and sensing every room below, omniscient and clairvoyant as she plumbed the concealed spaces in her mind. If she set her mind to it, she could empathize with a cup of tea cooling on a nightstand in a bedroom far below, feel into its tiny universe of despair as its erstwhile drinker dozed off. Where had this emotional gift and burden come from?

Pavel came into the kitchen and stood with the photoplay over by the window, tsking and sighing as he flipped pages. Helena was outside with the motorcars, overseeing the unloading of the luggage. Sabine took a glass down from the cupboard and drank some water from the tap. It tasted like silt. She poured it out and set the glass on the sink. She wondered what the Montmartre barmaid was doing right at this moment. When the trunks had been arranged for unpacking, Helena, who ran the mess hall during the filming season, came into Sabine's kitchen and said she was going to walk over to the communal kitchen.

—Apparently, they hired a summer camp cook from the Catskills during the off-season. I will need to examine his credentials.

—As a test of culinary skill, have him make me an omelet. Oh, and would you tell Messieurs Ballard and Bender that I won't be receiving any visitors today. But I would like to discuss the photoplay here at ten o'clock tomorrow morning.

Helena nodded as she headed out the door.

Pavel continued to stand in her kitchen with the photoplay.

—You read it first, then bring it back to me before bed, said Sabine. See if they made our changes.

—I thought I would stay here during our preparations.

Sabine sat in a chair to take off her shoes.

—Dear God, look at these feet! No, no, I must be alone, Pavey. Go bed down in the main house or one of the actors' bunkhouses.

Pavel stared at her over the edge of the photoplay. She knew better than to look into that Baltic wall of inscrutable knowing.

—You grow tired of people and lash out. It's a fault.

—Agreed. Now take your suitcase with you.

In the morning, they assembled at the cottage to discuss the photoplay. Sabine had read it in the early hours, after Pavel had dog-eared and bordered the pages with his Cyrillic-looking criticism—*kill the grand entrance, no speechifying, pray the actor doesn't opt for a death-flop here.* Claude and Hal arrived looking harried, having spent half the night supervising set construction. Sabine kissed each man on both cheeks, her face barely touching theirs. Pavel didn't shake hands with either of them but he gave them a deferential Eastern bow before sitting on the divan in his waistcoat with a sprig of rosemary in one hand. This was a new affectation—ruminating with a sprig of fresh herb or a wildflower between two fingers, twirling it back and forth, sometimes pausing to savor its fragrance. Sabine had made some Japanese tea and served it from a glazed-blue porcelain teapot on a lacquered tray, pouring out four tiny ceramic bowls. The tea set had been a gift from a Tokyo lover years ago, a young theater booking agent with samurai blood.

Once everyone had a bowl of tea in the sitting room, Sabine said:

—Has Mr. Summers arrived? I'm anxious to meet the man I will seduce into ruin.

Claude looked at her.

—Harold Spruce is the character's name, said Claude.

—He's expected any minute now. His family owns some sugar plantations in the Caribbean and he's been sailing through the Bahamas on his yacht. Not a bad sideline for an actor, said Hal.

Claude delicately rested his tea bowl on his knee.

—Did you have a chance to read the revised script, Sabine?

She noticed that his hands were shaking slightly.

—We did, said Pavel.

—And? asked Hal.

Sabine shifted in her chair.

—All things considered, it's a very nice melodrama. The role feels demanding and complex. Are there pages still missing? The ending seems incomplete.

—Nash Sully is still working on the ending, but we're all set to start shooting on May first, said Claude.

Pavel leaned forward to set his tea down on the low table, took out the annotated photoplay from under the cashmere shawl draped around his shoulders.

—We have itemized some additional modifications. But first, I'm curious how you will film all these nocturnal scenes?

—Medical carbon arc lamps. They use them to treat skin conditions. We've bought dozens of them, said Claude.

Pavel continued flipping through his notes.

—I do hope I won't have to wear dark glasses between scenes, said Sabine.

—We have a way of filtering out some of the glare, said Claude.

Pavel repositioned the photoplay in his lap.

—We crossed out the exeunts and entrances on the grand staircase, the elocutional speeches—is this how you say it?—the muttering she is making all the time into the windowpane. Wherever possible, we want Sabine to be natural. We watch her like a little fly on the wall . . .

Pavel placed the photoplay facedown on the table.

—Now, we are still not understanding the airship.

—It's for stunt work and aerial shots, said Hal.

Pavel turned another page, pressed the rosemary sprig to his nose.

—And, tell me, what business does a tubercular widow have riding in a zeppelin as if it were a Packard? We asked this question on the last version and never received a reply.

Claude turned to Sabine instead of Pavel.

—She has one foot in the afterlife, floats through her days . . .

Sabine, her face turned to the windows, said nothing.

—And she also floats above the river, Pavel said. Well, obviously, Sabine's feet won't leave the ground, so you will need to double her for those scenes.

—Naturally, said Claude.

There was a long silence. They all watched Pavel flip pages.

—Then there is the question of additional preparation.

—What kind of preparation? asked Hal.

Sabine let her gaze drift into the hazy blue air above the Hudson. Claude studied her faraway expression, a look that suggested the talk had turned to horse racing or the stock market. Her eyes suddenly narrowed and came back to the room as she removed a torn and tattered newspaper advertisement from her pocket and handed it to Claude. He read it several times before passing it to Hal.

WANTED: A GOOD HOME FOR
SOON-TO-BE ORPHANS

Two children, boy and girl. Mother an addled, consumptive widow; father tragically deceased. Contact Salvation Army Headquarters in Albany, New York, for adoption particulars.

—I found this advertisement in one of the American newspapers and it broke my heart. I kept wondering why a neighbor or family member hadn't taken in the children, both under the age of twelve. Why did they have to resort to advertising in the newspaper? So I took the liberty of corresponding with the Salvation Army and then the sanitarium superintendent. The husband was a railway tycoon and left behind a large estate. Dorothy, the widow, is still alive. And she has agreed to a visit.

Claude sipped his tea, tried to steady his voice.

—A visit?

—I want to meet a real consumptive widow and her children. She is in a sanitarium upstate.

—To prepare properly for the role, Pavel added.

A new mood took hold of the room. Any delays could plunder the budget. Claude crossed his legs, tapped the rim of his tea bowl. He felt a headache coming on, two thumbs pressing behind his eyes. Hal abruptly set his oriental bowl down on the table, the greenish tea sloshing over the side, and stood to pace the room.

—For the love of God, do you people have any idea how much money I have on the line with this picture? I'm borrowing money from half of New Jersey and Brooklyn . . .

Sabine cut her glower across the room as he paced, her mouth thinning with sarcasm.

—*You people*, ah, *c'est bon*, the same ones who invented modern photography and cinema? And this person . . .

She drew one elegant hand down her indigo, lace-trimmed day dress.

— . . . is the human being that people pay to see in your reels. You might take money from investors who run glove factories and hog farms, but I am the big heart and bosom of this whole enterprise. Without me there is no film, no studio. Please don't ever forget it.

Hal Bender stopped pacing and silence gutted the room. He looked at Sabine, shook his head slowly, looked at Claude. The battle between the French and the Americans, between the Lumières and Edison, between art and commerce, between the French cuff and the derby hat, was suddenly intensely personal. Claude saw the betrayal on Hal Bender's face, the wounded reply he made with his eyes. He'd been enlisted to smooth things over between Claude and Sabine a hundred times, to expedite visas and build a stone cottage to satisfy an eccentric French actress's pedantic whims, and this was his thanks. He sat back down, folded his arms, but refused to look at Sabine.

Claude tried to ease the tension in the room.

—What are you hoping to learn with a visit to a sanitarium?

Pavel took up a large leather-bound volume from the couch beside him, opened it, and faced them, as if he were about to sing from a hymnal.

—Gentlemen, as you may know, I am conversant in the esoteric arts. For example, I have made a study of the homeopathic materia medica in my spare time . . .

—Jesus Christ and all the fucking saints, said Hal, looking out through the windows.

Pavel continued.

—Consider it a German treatise on human frailty. We now use it as part of our approach to a role. It allows for a more natural and truthful representation of the personality at hand. Allow me to highlight a few traits of Tuberculinum, the remedy and the tubercular personality type. Here—let's see—ah, yes . . .

He angled the homeopathic bible into the watery light of the windows.

—Tuberculars are hedonistic, stylish, and emotionally superficial . . . they crave freedom . . . they move through the world sensing they might suffocate, that the air is too heavy to breathe. A chill between the shoulder blades and an aversion to meat. They crave cold milk, want to use foul language, and are afraid of dogs.

Pavel looked up at them, grinning.

—Isn't it wonderful? A precise science of senses and moods!

Hal put his head into his hands and said, *I'd enjoy using some foul language right about now.*

Sabine had softened by the time she looked over at Claude.

—Your sister, when she was dying in the Paris hospital, did she have any of those traits?

Claude sensed a trap. She was asking him to choose between his allegiance to Hal and his devotion to her. He looked to Hal, who was still staring at the carpet, then back to Sabine. He'd invested every penny of his own savings in the feature's success. A trip upstate could jeopardize the rehearsal schedule. And if the weather turned bad in May they might lose shooting days, which would cause delays and increase costs.

—No, Odette didn't show any of those signs. She hated milk and she loved dogs.

Sabine tossed her head back, looked up at the ceiling, exasperated.

—You're lying, just to prove a point and embarrass me.

—You'll note, gentlemen, said Pavel, in Miss Montrose's contract, that she is entitled to photoplay approval before shooting. We feel this preparation will vastly improve her performance and the film.

Flushed in the face, Hal stood and buttoned his coat. He looked a few feet above the divan but wouldn't bring his eyes to settle on Sabine.

—I'm going to be plain. We begin filming on the first day of May. If Miss Montrose is not ready to shoot, for any reason barring her own death or incapacity, then we will sue her for breach of contract. She has already agreed to do the film. I'll be on set all day making sure construction is on schedule. The crew, at least, know the value of an honest day's work.

Sabine watched as Hal walked to the front door and went out into the daylight. He was a complete stranger to her. Where was the diplomat who'd brought her marzipan and wine after a fight with Claude?

Pavel brought the sprig of rosemary to his nose and closed his eyes.

—I would not call this an auspicious beginning.

—My tea tastes like acid, Sabine said. Pavel, will you leave Claude and me alone for a moment?

Pavel gave a nod and followed after Hal. She watched him go, then turned to Claude.

—A cat always lands on its feet . . . Do you remember that little film-strip you made years ago?

—Of course.

—A cat will also bite the hand that feeds her, if she's cornered. I have a good mind to get on the first boat back to the continent. The French respect me, at least . . . and they understand me.

She pulled some stray hair away from her face and tucked it behind one ear.

—We've bet everything we have on this film, said Claude.

—You sound like a businessman from Toledo.

—Is that so terrible?

—It's unimaginably disappointing. All this talk of money. I wouldn't even know how much I make in a year.

—That's a privilege of the rich.

Silence bloomed again. They both stared at Claude's shoes.

—She was scared of them, her whole life. At the end, in the hospital, she had terrifying dreams about dogs.

—Odette?

He nodded.

—And she made my father furious because she wouldn't eat meat when she was a child. *The Vegetarian of Alsace* was her nickname in primary school.

She looked at him.

—Does consumption find the person to infect or does the person find the disease?

—Ah, now that sounds more like Claude Ballard, the French cinematic visionary whom I have allowed into my bed precisely once.

—That was another lifetime.

—To me, it feels like yesterday.

He heard his own breath catch halfway up his throat.

—I remember your face in the mirror, she said. You looked like you'd seen a ghost. Or perhaps you saw yourself for the first time . . .

He was surprised she remembered that moment.

—You have always been like a ghost to me.

She put the tea bowls back onto the lacquered tray one by one. She carried them into the kitchen and he followed her.

—Let me smooth things over with Hal. But keep the Russian away from him.

She stared into the kitchen sink.

—I want to plunge into this woman's suffering. To soak in her life and ruin . . . it will make all the difference.

—Give me the details for the sanitarium and I'll see if we can arrange a visit.

—Thank you, Claude.

She walked across the floor to kiss his cheek, but found herself staring into his unflinching eyes. He had traveled a long way from that night in the hotel, with his Rhiny accent and his shabby top hat and the reel of his dying sister. She kissed him gently on the mouth, not out of love or lust, but as a kind of remembrance, almost as a farewell to the boy who'd resembled a provincial undertaker and who they'd both killed off in the lens of the mirror. She went back into the living room before she could regret the kiss or see that lovelorn mania washing over his face. Claude watched her walk away, the kiss peeling back the old, formidable ache.

A moment later, Pavel came to the front door, pointing down toward the cliffs.

—Lester Summers has just anchored his yacht down in the river at Edgewater. I thought you might like to go down to meet him.

Sabine stood in the doorway, hands on hips.

—I think I'll wait until he makes it up here with the rest of us. I've never met a yachtsman I didn't like better on dry land.

11

The Widow

Dorothy Harlow was living out the remainder of her days in a tuberculosis sanitarium near Saranac Lake. When Claude telephoned the sanitarium superintendent with whom Sabine had corresponded, a Dr. Ira Callow, he discovered that Sabine had never made it clear that she was researching a film role. Fumbling for a reasonable explanation, he said they were making a medical teaching film and wanted to interview Dorothy Harlow about her disease. The doctor said that normally a patient at her stage of the illness wasn't allowed company outside of immediate family, so Claude hinted at the possibility of a rather large donation to the sanitarium, an amount he hoped would get Sabine's attention, since the upstate expedition would certainly come out of her fee for the film. The doctor said that an exception could be made.

—The truth is, the doctor said, Dot will be lucky to see June. You must promise, though, that you won't make her laugh. That is one of the worst things for a pair of consumptive lungs.

Claude assured the doctor that there would be very little risk of laughter.

On the train ride north, Sabine slept much of the way, leaving Pavel to hum and reminisce while staring out at the passing hamlets and townships.

Claude, who'd come along to ensure they'd be back in time for rehearsals, brought along the photoplay with Pavel's scrawl in the margins, doing his best to make reasonable—and readable—notes for Nash Sully. He would be tasked with integrating the separate columns of handwriting into a type-written master shooting script.

Somewhere outside Saratoga Springs, Pavel floated a monologue about Chekhov's death from consumption, his deathbed vigil in the Black Forest, where he took a shot of camphor and a glass of champagne before turning in for the night one last time.

—You were there? Claude asked, looking up irritably from the photo-play.

Pavel didn't answer but turned from the whirring landscape to Claude.

—They sent his body back to Moscow in a refrigerated railway carriage designed for transporting oysters.

He looked back at the scrolling scenery.

—Anton deserved something a little more elevated than a shellfish locomotive . . .

Claude looked at Pavel's avian profile as he stared out at the rushing fo-liage, the hawkish, downturned nose and the hooded, imperious eyes. Sabine slept with her head slumped against his cashmere shoulder. Her Bal-tic big brother and philosophizing protector, Claude thought, even though he's a decade younger. Had Sabine ever associated with anyone her own age?

—After my sister died in a Paris hospital room, they wheeled her to the morgue on something resembling a wooden luggage cart. I collected her ashes the next morning in a shoebox. Famous or not, no one deserves the end they get . . .

Sabine woke for a beat, smiled blearily at Claude from the outskirts of a dream, then closed her eyes again.

The sanitarium motorcar waited for them at the station in Westport—not an ambulance, exactly, but somber, official, and vaguely funereal, with *Ad-irondack Cottage Sanitarium* painted austerely on the side. The driver was a tall, pale man in a wool cap—a recovered consumptive, he proudly announced—who loaded their bags and drove them quietly into the dis-trict of conifers and lakes.

•

An hour later, they motored down a long winding road that followed the bank of a river. They passed through the front iron gates right before dusk, when the sky was turning a smoky gold and the undergrowth among the beeches and aspens was beginning to choke with violet shadow. In the falling light, they came upon a small settlement of wooden cottages with glassed-in porches and an illuminated cobblestone church at the head of a macadam roadway.

This place reminded Claude of the remote Alsatian villages his father took him to explore when he was a young boy—a single row of pristine houses at the end of a daylong trek, rooms burnished by alpenglow under wide-gabled roofs, an atmosphere of eerie mountain quietude. They would spend the night in the hushed dormered rooms of an inn, barely talking over a dinner of knackwurst and braised red cabbage, then hike back down to the valley floor the next morning. His father picked and pressed wildflowers along the way and always emerged fortified by these hikes into the mountains, by the polite but distant service of the innkeeper and his wife, by the ribbons of cold alpine sunlight that streamed between summits. *These people live up here where no one bothers them*, his father would say. But Claude remembered the villages as aloof and secretive, and he sensed the same condition here. An old woman's face appeared beside a curtain, a world of pale lamplight behind her head.

The driver parked the motorcar outside the infirmary and directed them to the superintendent's cottage, where they would spend the night. He told them to keep their voices down, since most of the residents were retiring for the night or taking their supper in the refectory. They carried their suitcases along a paved walkway lined with trees and ornamental shrubs, up toward the church.

Because it was almost May the cooling night air carried an edge of pine-sap and moss. That smell always made Claude nostalgic for short winter nights of wood smoke and storytelling, for that brief window of his childhood when he could remember his mother's buoyant domestic presence in the house. She lit lamps, kindled fires, left out plates of strudel, told stories of her querulous Austrian grandparents. She rarely spoke

German, except when a place name or recipe or folk-song lyric demanded the correct pronunciation.

They headed toward a building that resembled a chalet, its windows low and streaked with twilight under the eaves. It was Sabine who first noticed the few dozen patients sitting in the refectory at long tables with their meals. They were all dressed for an avant-garde theater director's idea of alpine convalescence—the men shuffling along in leather leggings and sheepskin moccasins and cable-knit cardigans, one elderly gentleman in a chamois vest and kidskin gloves, a handful of women in knitted shawls and jodhpurs. Sabine stepped into a flowerbed to take a closer look, hooding her view through the window.

 —Oh, look, aren't these people fabulous in their felt footwear? It appears they are eating plates of sliced cold meat and drinking enormous glasses of milk. Can we go in?

 —We mustn't intrude. The superintendent is expecting us, said Claude.

Sabine straggled behind as they continued up the pathway to the superintendent's cottage. When Claude knocked, a sallow-faced woman in a dirndl appeared and introduced herself as Miriam Callow, the doctor's wife. The superintendent was doing his evening rounds and wouldn't return for some time. Miriam said she would prepare them some sandwiches and tea in the kitchen. She looked at Sabine, whose hair was unruly from the day's travel, then at the Russian in his moccasins and cashmere shawl. It occurred to Claude that Pavel had been dressing for a sanitarium all these years.

Sabine was shown to a large room with a double bed upstairs while Pavel and Claude were directed to the basement, to a small room with twin beds. Claude unpacked a few things from his suitcase while Pavel, facing east, did some stretching and breathing exercises at the foot of his bed. Claude was careful not to show Pavel that he'd brought along a compact camera in his luggage in case the circumstances allowed for the filming of the widow.

About halfway through their second cup of tea in the kitchen, Dr. Callow came into the house with a small Pekingese dog following after him. Apart from his white coat, he seemed to be the only sanitarium resident wearing civilian clothes—a tartan tie and tweed jacket, a pair of oxfords instead of something fashioned from felt or fur. He kissed his wife on the cheek, shook hands with everyone else, and took a cup of tea to the head of the kitchen table.

It wasn't clear why they weren't being hosted in the parlor; perhaps film people were the sort you made sandwiches for in the kitchen. The doctor made several nervous visual sorties over to Sabine, whose midlife continental beauty and elegance were conspicuous, even after a day of travel and in the jaundiced affections of a single Edison bulb overhead. They chatted about the train journey and the invigorating lake air. Then the doctor gave them a brief synopsis of the sanitarium's mission, about his days spent conducting experiments inoculating guinea pigs and rabbits and studying infected sputum under a microscope.

—Robert Louis Stevenson visited, you know, very early on . . . we have his complete works, signed and dedicated, over in the library. Dewey decimal is the system of choice over there, for all two thousand volumes. You'll find we run things like clockwork at the sanitarium. Convalescence is nothing but ordered restraint . . .

A few minutes before nine-thirty, Dr. Callow asked them all to come out onto the glassed-in porch to watch the observance of lights-out. They stood behind the louvered glass walls of the porch while the lights of the sanitarium went out, one by one, until the northern stars were the brightest things they could see. Even the lights behind the stained-glass windows of the church were snuffed. *The cure lives by a schedule*, Dr. Callow said, heading back into the hallway.

They stood at the foot of the stairs, saying good night.

—We'll have to invite you back to show a film sometime. Medical and educational films would be of great interest to our residents, I believe. We have lawyers, teachers, housewives, every sort.

—You should know that some of our motion pictures might excite a patient's breathing, said Sabine.

Claude had told Sabine about their medical-film cover story and he hoped she remembered.

—Quite right, yes, Dr. Callow said, we would have to choose carefully. Nothing with breaching ships or vertiginous heights! Very well, good night, all. Dorothy Harlow is expecting you to visit at nine in the morning. Oh, Mr. Ballard, there is the one matter we discussed on the telephone . . .

As the doctor crouched down to rub the Pekingese's rump, Claude realized the superintendent was prospecting for his donation.

—Of course. I will leave it on the kitchen table for you in an envelope.

The doctor and his wife disappeared upstairs. The others returned to the kitchen and their cups of tea.

—As a matter of interest, how much is my donation?

Claude knew he would enjoy the sound of the number.

—Enough to sting.

—The amount, please.

—One thousand dollars.

Pavel slurped his tea as he wrote in a notebook. Sabine stood and pushed in her chair.

—That does sting. And for that kind of money, I can surely dictate the terms of the visit. I'd like to meet with the widow alone tomorrow morning.

—As you wish, Pavel said. This is for *your* art.

Claude thought about the camera in his suitcase, about the value of capturing the widow on film. But something stopped him from calling after Sabine as she walked for the stairs. It was the thought of Odette's death endlessly looping for fickle audiences in Paris, New York, Sydney, and Brooklyn, for bored office workers with a few coins in their pockets. She'd died a thousand times for these strangers.

Unlike the other consumptives confined to absolute rest, Dorothy Harlow had been given an entire Queen Anne cottage for the final phase of her illness. She had bequeathed a large sum of money to the sanitarium, and in return they named the cottage where she was staying Harlow House. While the rest of the dying lay in the infirmary, in sun-scrubbed rooms separated by Dutch doors, Dorothy spent her time out on her private sun porch in an Adirondack recliner, playing solitaire and reading novels by Sir Arthur Conan Doyle. Occasionally she listened to a piece of classical music on a gramophone recording.

Sabine gathered all this information on her way over to the cottage, with the doctor at her side and the fussy little dog trotting a few feet behind. She asked about the risk of infection, and Callow assured her that every precaution was taken, from daily wet mopping to constant airflow to patients coughing into disposable handkerchiefs. Sabine had brought along a notebook and pencil and she jotted down something about the widow's white linen handkerchief, how it should be monogrammed with her dead husband's initials and become symbolic over the course of the film.

—The bacillus loves close quarters and we do our best to blast it with sunlight and air.

They rounded a corner and he gestured to the front steps of the cottage.

—She's all the way at the top, out on the porch. Just follow the music. There's a nurse on duty, but she won't bother you.

Sabine climbed the porch stairs and went inside the Queen Anne cottage. The rooms were sparse and airy—polished wooden floors with Amish rugs and sturdy walnut furniture, all the windows open, the gauzy curtains billowing gently. It smelled of linseed oil. A uniformed nurse in a bonnet sat completing some paperwork behind a small desk at the foot of the stairs. They exchanged polite nods. *Mrs. Harlow is expecting you*, said the nurse. Sabine thanked her and started up the stairs, careful not to touch the handrail; no matter what the good doctor and the latest science said, she suspected bacilli grew like a fungus along every surface of the house. She was glad she'd brought along her deerskin gloves and intended to keep them on for the duration of the visit. Somewhere near the top of the stairs she heard classical music—brooding and Germanic—coming from the sun porch. It was not the sort of music she could imagine slipping from the world to.

Through a set of French doors, she glimpsed the widow in profile, reclined in her Adirondack, her feet up, wrapped in a horse blanket and reading with a pair of white cotton gloves on her hands. One moccasin wagged slowly and arrhythmically to the music, almost as an afterthought. Sabine gently opened the French doors and saw that the sun porch was up in the treetops, submerged in a bowl of aspens and elms. *I hope I'm not disturbing you*, she said, coming in. *My name is Sabine Montrose.* The widow couldn't easily turn her head to see Sabine enter, but she gestured to the wicker chair opposite.

Sabine studied the widow's face for a moment in the dappling light of the tree crowns. Her skin was oddly luminous and smooth, like a piece of sea glass. There was a fringe of thinning, gray hair, but she couldn't have been more than forty with two children under the age of eleven. Her china-bone complexion had somehow made her ageless in the days or weeks before dying. Dorothy looked at Sabine over the rim of her reading glasses.

—When the comet passes we're going to move into a cloud of cyanide gas. The whole planet, you understand, could suffocate. Are you a doomsdayer?

—I tend to see the tragedy in things. Cyanide gas, for instance, wouldn't surprise me in the least.

Dorothy's face brightened, as if she'd at last found a sparring partner for her fevered bouts. She folded up her eyeglasses and set them on a side table that was spread with a half-finished game of solitaire. Then she closed her novel and set it in her lap—*The Hound of the Baskervilles*. Her expression changed.

—I'll be gone by then. But Leo and Cora . . .

She broke off, looked down at her gloved hands.

—Do you enjoy reading mystery stories, Mrs. Harlow?

—I do, said Dorothy. They keep me amused. Sherlock Holmes can infer a lot from very little. I like that in a man. The slow and plodding ones can all burn in hell, if you really want my opinion.

Sabine flashed her a smile.

—I couldn't agree more.

—You should call me Dorothy. Or Dot. They always called me that.

Her life was already slipping into past tense.

—Okay, Dot, I will. And please call me Sabine.

—I would shake your hand but the doctor forbids it.

Sabine nodded, leaned back in her chair, and removed her gloves, wanting to offer something up to Dorothy. She could feel the heat radiating off her skin.

—You're French, the widow said.

—Guilty.

—I have an ear for accents.

—Did you ever travel to Europe?

—James kept our travels strictly domestic, always by train, since he owned a railway. He didn't like the sea. I adored it, on the other hand. I grew up in Maine, clamming in the wet sand at low tide . . .

—Sounds wonderful. I grew up in the countryside. I didn't see the ocean until the first time I traveled to England.

A violin solo seared the space above the gramophone. Dorothy rubbed a fingertip along the edge of her novel spine.

—I was expecting students. Callow brings them in here sometimes, these butter-faced Bostonians who study the disease. Do you know the sort of boy who likes to take apart watches, or remove fly wings, and has his hair parted perfectly down the middle? Yes, I see you nodding, that's them. Some of them become doctors and they want to open up your lungs like a grandfather clock.

She adjusted herself against the inverted V of pillows behind her back.

—I've been reading a lot of Conan Doyle lately and I'll try out some induction, with your permission. Are you ready?

Sabine nodded. The widow's eyes were glinting and febrile in the quaking aspen-light.

—From the shoes and the dress, and from the unmarried hand, I'm going to say that you're a baroness from Europe. There's privilege in your bearing, but also an affinity with ordinary people. You've seen poverty. Perhaps you've done charity work, visited almshouses and the like. You took your gloves off, for example, to set me at ease and suggest you're not afraid of catching the disease. Perhaps you lost someone very dear to consumption and you never had a chance to say a proper goodbye. Is any of this close? Was there a mother who died from the disease?

—You got the unmarried part correct. I was once married. But my mother did not have the disease. She took her own life when I was young.

Sabine said it to pave the way for Dorothy's own intimacies. But apparently Dorothy either didn't hear it or had no interest in staring into the well of Sabine's own losses. Because the widow, her cheeks like the luminous insides of an oyster shell, looked down at the book in her lap and changed the subject.

—Why do you suppose Sherlock Holmes calls it deduction when it's mostly induction? That bothers me in every single one of these novels.

Was she superficial and trite, skimming the pond of their conversation with erratic questions and segues but unwilling to talk about what lurked beneath? Had she glimpsed her own underground river?

—I haven't read them, Sabine said.

—They're a good way to pass the time. Death by induction.

They sat through a leafy silence.

—If not a baroness, then who?

—I'm an actress. In pictures and on the stage. We came here because I wanted to meet you.

—And why is that?

Sabine took a long moment before answering. It was possible the woman would send her away if she knew the truth about the film. Then again, Dorothy was full of surprises. Sabine had been expecting a woman ravaged by the disease and instead found a woman who looked like she was burning with translucent good health, who might sit for eighteen hours a day reading the world's detective novels, listening to its boisterously sad symphonies, and writing restrained letters of farewell to distant relatives and lapsed friends. Her preparations for death looked nothing like Sabine had imagined.

—We're making a motion picture about you. Not you, exactly, but about your circumstance. I'm going to play a consumptive widow who seduces her hotel guests. I wanted to meet you so I could understand it better.

Sabine picked at one deerskin glove on the seat beside her while she gauged Dorothy's reaction. The widow blinked, considered.

—When you say *it*?

—Your life, said Sabine.

—And my death, I presume? Or at least my dying . . .

—Yes.

—I see. So you can steal a few choice details. Maybe the way I hold a book or what I do with my hands?

—Perhaps.

Sabine didn't know where to look. She settled on Dorothy's hands.

The gramophone guttered out and Sabine welcomed the chance to get up and tend to it. She stood at the gramophone and lifted the needle. *Another recording?* The widow shook her head, leaned back in her Adirondack, mulled things over. She made a distant, wheezing sound, as if the whole room were pressing down on her chest. Her face suddenly turned bright red and her eyes narrowed, then closed. The coughing fit was eerily quiet—a silent reel of exasperation. When she recovered, she took a sip of brown liquid in a glass beside her and brought a hand to her chest.

—In the picture you're making, whom do I seduce?

—Practically every man, married or not, above the age of sixteen.

Dorothy nodded, agreeing with this plotline.

—As it happens, I only ever slept with James on this earthly planet, and he used to leave his false teeth in a glass by the bed. I'd have to face the other way or make sure there was total darkness. A monster of the deep, those teeth, living in an ocean the size of a water tumbler. Can you imagine such a thing?

Sabine laughed and felt certain that it was impossible to shock this brazen woman.

—Sadly, I *can* imagine it.

Sabine took out her notebook.

—Do you mind if I ask you some questions, Dot? Some of them might be rather intimate.

Dorothy took another sip of her brown drink.

—Proceed.

—Let's begin with fears. Can you tell me what you are afraid of?

—Right this instant?

—Ever. In general.

—Let's see . . . that my children will be unloved. Of dying and not knowing it. That nothing I did in my life mattered one iota. I'm afraid of cheese that's been left out. And boredom and running out of things to read. Also, snails. Snail and slug poison was one thing I never ran out of at the big house in Albany.

—What do you dream about?

—My children mostly. Sometimes I see myself on a train at night, through the window, and I'm traveling through the desert.

—Where are you going?

—Mexico, I think.

Sabine wrote it down.

—Cravings?

—Sauerkraut. Almonds. Tinned peaches.

—Do you ever want to use foul language?

Dorothy puckered her mouth and squinted.

—How foul?

—Utter filth.

Now she was nodding matter-of-factly.

—Oh yes, like a whore of Babylon. I want to yell terrible obscenities so loud that the virgin nurse downstairs runs outside crying into her bonnet. I called her a louse once and blamed it on the fevers. At that moment, though, I felt as cool as a cucumber. I'm conniving when I want to be . . .

Sabine wrote it all down, enjoying this woman's brio immensely. She looked up at Dorothy, who was flushed again in the face, and tried to feel into those twin chasms of the body and the mind. Where exactly was a person's *essence* located? In Paris, watching melancholic barmaids and shopkeepers ply their trades and burnish their personalities, she was able to probe a person's insides by letting her mind drift and settle over them. With her attention suspended just above their heads, she absorbed them, a gathering cloud drawing up moisture from the ocean of the self. André Antoine and Pavel insisted that every person had their own atmosphere, that they carried it around with them like a personal weather front—a pair of shoes badly worn at the heel, a flinching, self-deprecating smile, a smell of fried onions about the frayed collar—and that these details told the story of what was burning inside. The tumult, the need, the want.

Sabine watched as the widow scratched at her hands through her cotton gloves.

—Your palms itch?

—Constantly.

—Give them a scratch. I won't tell.

Dorothy let her book drop to the floor, removed her gloves quickly, and raked at her palms for a few seconds. Her eyes fluttered with satisfaction. She flexed her fingers, curled them back and forth. Unlike the rest of her body, her hands were blotchy, red, and excoriated.

—Do you wake up irritable?

She shook her head.

—I wake up with a burning thirst and a chill. I sleep propped up, my body like a fortress in the open air.

She crossed her legs under the horse blanket.

—Do you know what I think? You should make your character be avenging a curse.

—How do you mean?

—There's a family curse in *The Hound of the Baskervilles*. The old aristocrat imprisoned a girl on the estate and a spectral hound seeks justice. Rips the old man's throat out. What will you wear?

Sabine smiled; Dorothy's mind was full of turns.

—A lot of long black gowns, I think.

—The longer the better . . . You could wear anything and look radiant. I imagine you've been stared at your whole life. It must get tedious, all that ogling. Being plain is far better.

Dorothy glanced out the windows into the treetops. Sabine saw that there was something sorrowful and enormous pushing at the skein of her thoughts.

—Why didn't anyone take in your children back in Albany?

The widow came back to the breezy room with a resigned sigh.

—James employed hundreds of men on the railways. If they went out on strike for better wages or conditions, he made sure they were fired. He hired Germans and Bohemians and Irishmen to fill in any shortfalls. They hated him down there. He built a mansion outside of town with a stone wall all the way around it. I always felt like we were living behind a moat. After James died and I got sick, our children were untouchable. It was like they had the plague in medieval Europe, like they were living out the family curse. If they never go back to Albany it will be too soon.

—Where are they now?

Sabine saw an image of the two waifs wandering through the hotel in the photoplay. She felt suddenly and hopelessly bereft.

—They're out in Westport, with the superintendent's sister. They visit me once a week, poor little darlings. They'll be here tomorrow for a few hours. When I pass, they'll go to boarding school and the sister has agreed to keep them on breaks and in the summers. Leo is very good with mathematics and Cora is a natural scholar in the humanities. I always read to her when she was small. *Little Women* and Dickens.

—You have no relatives who can take them in?

—On both sides, they want the dead tycoon's money but not his children. I'd rather a kind stranger look after them, to be perfectly honest.

Sabine tried to name the emotion on Dorothy's face but it eluded her.

—Oh God, it's the saddest thing I've ever heard.

Dorothy blinked and folded her arms.

—Callow says I'm not allowed to cry. It's bad for my lungs.

—I won't tell. Go ahead. I won't be far behind you.

The widow was already sobbing quietly, her eyes closed, her mouth faintly trembling. Sabine let Dorothy's unnamable loss burrow inside her and coil in with her own burdens and regrets. There was the shame at what her husband had done to the town, the fear of abandoning her children to an unknown fate, but there was also a pure white rage. The word *avenging* kept coming to mind. Why had she suggested a family curse? They cried together—quietly so the nurse wouldn't ascend the stairs to scold them. Dorothy dabbed at her eyes with a clean handkerchief and Sabine wiped her tears away with the back of one hand. The room emptied out like an exhalation.

Sabine reached out and touched the back of Dorothy's hand—it was on fire. Dorothy looked up at her.

—And what are you afraid of, Sabine Montrose?

—Oh, just about everything. Mediocrity, stupidity, ugliness, of never loving anyone with my whole heart. Loneliness. Stagnation. Standing water. Stray dogs and being murdered in my sleep. Of being forgotten or hated or ignored. Of being loved too much and being suffocated. I have dreams where I can't breathe.

Sabine slowly put her gloves back on, cinching them one finger at a time. She let the silence regather.

—What is the secret you're hoping to die with, Dorothy? I have no right to ask, but will you tell me?

Eyes on the shimmering tree crowns, Dorothy Harlow said:

—That I never loved him and that this is my punishment for it. The children always sensed it, that they were growing up in a household without love. This was our family curse, so to speak, the hound that wanted to rip our throats out. So, here it comes with the comet, the wrath from above . . . all that cyanide gas is coming just for me . . .

She adjusted her head, rubbed the side of her neck, closed her eyes. Sabine could feel the heat coming off her from a few feet away.

—Will you stay and meet Leo and Cora tomorrow when they come? It would mean the world to me.

—Of course, Dot. I'd be honored.

When Claude confessed that he'd brought a compact motion picture camera, Sabine insisted that he accompany her the next morning. In the footage of the widow visiting with her children, Sabine could be seen watching from a wicker chair, a tender expression on her face. Claude kept the camera in the corner of the sun porch while Dorothy read Conan Doyle aloud. The girl, her long blond hair in bows, sat on the edge of the recliner, her hand on her mother's moccasin, one finger curled against the sheepskin lip. The boy was more standoffish in his loosened tie and scuffed leather shoes, a book of puzzles in his lap and a pencil in one hand. He listened and nodded, but his attention was clearly on a mathematical or linguistic clue. The wind shook the trees outside, rippling the walls with delicate shadows that resembled shifting tea leaves.

Sabine studied the children's faces, jotting observations in her notebook. While he filmed, Claude watched the movements of her fountain pen, the pensive loops and slow-to-form punctuation, and wondered what kindness or insight she had reserved for these strangers. Dorothy Harlow enunciated bravely through a dramatic passage of the novel, and her son's attention was finally drawn into the story. The boy put the tip of his pencil to his lips and waited for the hound or the curse to present itself. But Dorothy delivered a cliffhanger, snapping the book shut with relish, and both her children erupted into protest. The daughter pressed her hands together and the boy said something angrily. The mother smiled benevolently but held her ground.

Later, when they watched the footage back in New Jersey, Sabine suggested that perhaps this was her way of delaying her own storyline, of ignoring the gas plumes and comets outside her window. They watched the part where Sabine said something encouraging to the children and touched the back of Leo's head, who softened under her hand. Then there was a moment when Sabine lifted her chin and turned directly to the camera, stared into the hooded lens, and raised one hand to her throat, as if to stifle a cough. *Look*, she said, watching it unspool with Claude, *you filmed the exact moment I dropped into Dorothy's heart and mind.*

12

Filming Begins

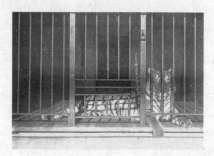

Every role is a seduction and this one was consummated with a homeo-pathic dose of Tuberculinum. For a week, Sabine had been studying the footage of Dorothy with her children and immersing herself in the photo-play, which had been revised to make the dead husband a begrudged rail-way tycoon. She paced through the cottage, reading aloud the dialogue title cards that moviegoers would never hear. She experimented with vocal gestures, vowels, and registers, with the sound of her voice trailing off into silence. Then, at Pavel's insistence, she took the remedy two days before production began—a small white pill that tasted of sugar.

In the cottage, she opened a bottle of burgundy, reclined on the divan with the photoplay, and began to experience what Pavel called *proving the remedy*. Her lungs felt heavy and constricted, her neck ached, and the sitting room had somehow become a furnace. She was convinced that she would burn up, so she rushed through the house, flinging open the curtains and windows and tearing off her clothes. In nothing but her gauzy underwear, she lay down on the cool tile of the kitchen floor, only to find that she was insatia-bly hungry. She raided the icebox, ate two cold chicken sandwiches over the sink, and repaired to the sitting room, feeling a little feverish. On the di-van, she fell asleep and passed quickly into unsettled dreams.

•

A night train roared through the desert, Leo and Cora pressed at a glimmering windowpane, and her own mother sat eating a meal of coq au vin in
the brassy, surgical light of the dining car. Sabine could somehow see into
all the train cars at once. Blue finches were swooping in and out of the open
windows as the train bawled along, and she saw a single white lily in a vase
on her mother's railcar dinner table. Meanwhile, her thirteen-year-old self
sat singing and crying in an adjacent compartment, in braids and a school
uniform, a suitcase neatly laid across her lap. When she woke, it was to a
feeling of immense sadness and bafflement. Where was the train headed?
And why was her mother eating coq au vin in the dining car?

Then a memory bloomed: Sabine coming home from school to find her
mother preparing a lavish dinner, as if it were her wedding anniversary. In
her best frock, Eliza Montrose sets the dining room table while the coq au
vin simmers, tells the story of killing the old barnyard rooster whose crow-
ing days were well behind him. A cup of his blood for thickening agent, the
feet and kidneys and coxcomb thrown in for good measure, she recounts her
grandmother's recipe like an incantation. It was, Sabine now realized, a tribute to the ancestors before joining them. Eliza persuades her husband to go
get some extra Beaujolais from the cellar, the vintage he's been squirreling
away for a future wedding or christening, and then they all sit and eat. Eliza
insists they each tell stories and share memories. She's recently been in the
hospital for a month, and now, she tells them, everything will be better. *But
what is the special occasion, maman?* Sabine asks. At this, Eliza looks at her
daughter calmly and blinks back the slightest suggestion of a tear. Quietly, quietly, she says, *How does it taste?*

For years, Sabine had tried to remember that look on her mother's face, but
it had evaded her. She saw plainly, at last, that it was exhaustion and relief,
the great burden of human days lifted. Sabine also understood that this
was the exact moment her childhood had ended, at the dinner table one
school night in October when she was twelve, when her mother patiently
ladled out the coq au vin as a woman who was already dead. The dinner
wasn't merely a farewell; it was a liturgy. Sabine had seen it in her eyes forty
years ago but hadn't been able to name it until just now, on the lapping
tide of a homeopathic remedy. She remembered wanting to catch her mother's

eyes again, to will her back to the living, but then one of the younger ones chimed in with, *I'm very cross with you, maman. You should have told us you were going to kill Samson. We didn't get to say goodbye.*

All this floated about her on the divan, the night her mother walked away from the house after dinner on the pretext of visiting a neighbor, only to drown herself in the river beyond the fields in her best dress. She'd been hiding in plain sight for so long. There was no note, but for months afterward they would find little talismans in their clothes hampers and bookshelves—chestnut leaves pressed into novels, her initials embroidered into a pair of the children's socks, her wedding ring tied to a ribbon, a breadcrumb trail of tiny goodbyes. Every role began with a wound and a spark, something to fuse the character to the actor's own shards of memory. What Sabine would carry from that October evening and apply to the widow was the look of teary calm on her mother's face. There was no guilt or remorse, just a meticulous plot. In her final hours, she wasn't punishing the living. She was savoring them.

Back in Paris, André Antoine had always insisted that authentic emotion for the actor began with stillness, with what he called *expressive motionless*. To put herself in the right frame of mind, Sabine spent the next morning paying close attention to everything around her: the lonesome dripping of a faucet, the particular tawdriness of a gray hair in the bathtub drain, the quickening pride of a bird preening on a windowsill. Nothing was too small to elicit her empathy. After a few hours of such attentiveness, she felt herself ready for the next step in her preparations.

As an exercise, she wrote a letter in character to a childhood friend back in France—a woman in Lyon who, over the years, had become accustomed to receiving acerbic, sad, or delusional missives from Phaedra and Ophelia. As the widow, Sabine wrote a short note, then added a postscript at the bottom: *I tell no one that it hurts to breathe.* When Sabine licked the envelope, the bitter gelatin taste of the gum-flap dropped her headlong into the widow's mouth and mind. Like Dorothy, the widow in the photoplay had hidden her loveless marriage from the world. Sabine realized the widow must have written countless letters over the years to keep people at bay, lest the loveless secret of her household be widely known. She feared pity more than anything else. Sabine rewrote the letter, this time in a brighter tone but with a subtext of inevitability. *The men have finished pruning the maze. The days are growing longer. Everything is as it should be.*

Next came the tiny auditions of action. It might be something as simple as washing her hands, or as complex as saying her prayers, but she attempted to trap the widow's atmosphere, the little weather front she carried around with her as she moved through the world. How does she wake (quickly), eat (voraciously), bathe (slowly, with very hot water), sing (high and trailing), spread jam on a piece of toast (thickly, with too much butter underneath)? The trick, if there was one, was to widen back so she could see all the carriages on the train at the same time.

Finally, she worked on her physical appearance, trying on the costumes and experimenting with makeup. Her nails were cut short, almost down to the cuticle, to prevent the widow from drawing blood when she scratched. She dressed in the black gown, applied some lavender powder to her neck and face, spread some kohl under her eyes, smeared some peppermint oil onto her hands to redden and irritate them, and slipped her gloves into place. Barefoot, her hair pulled up into a chignon, she looked into the mirror in her bedroom. The woman looking back was shockingly pale, hauntingly beautiful, and wholly unrecognizable.

The first night of filming, the production stage shone from the brow of the hill above the Palisades like an illuminated glasshouse. Inside the brightly lit space, Claude watched Sabine emerge from her dressing room through a piece of blue cellophane. He'd been experimenting with various filters for the camera and this one softened her otherworldly menace. He lowered the cellophane and examined her in the brunt of a medical carbon lamp—the contrast of black on powdered white, her hair up off her bare shoulders and the plunge of her neckline, a sapphire winking between her breasts like some Asiatic third eye, a gateway to enlightenment or ruin, depending on who was gazing into it, he thought, as she drifted closer in a cloud of peppermint oil. She walked by, eyes averted, summoning the role. He'd hoped that the rankling desire might dissipate as the film preparations began, as they edged closer to her cinematic death, but in fact it was unrelenting—a malaise that warped his thoughts and left him light-headed.

Meanwhile, Pavel was proving a nuisance on the set. In his self-appointed role as acting coach and mentor, he'd posted dozens of *Be Natural!* signs on the stage walls, out of frame, and in the actors' dressing rooms. And he had insisted on being part of blocking scenes. When Claude followed Sabine to block out the first scene with Lester Summers, Pavel fell in behind him in his embroidered waistcoat and twin fob watches, peeling an orange. He stood by listening, exploding citrus crescents inside his mouth, while Claude explained the logistics of the widow encountering the stranded traveler on her doorstep in the middle of the night.

Pavel walked over and offered both actors a piece of orange. As they chewed, he spoke to them in low, confiding tones.

—When Rosalind sees Harold Spruce arrive at the hotel for the first time, perhaps you are thinking, Sabine, it is merely a suggestion, about a time when you stole something as an enfant terrible in Burgundy. What could it be? No, no, don't tell me, just think on it. Gently, always from within. There is never an excuse for a big monkey face. Now, Mr. Summers, you want to consume her, eat her up like a piece of pound cake. Perhaps you are thinking of a great meal you have eaten, or of a woman you have devoured.

Lester Summers was short and thin and Sabine wondered whether he was capable of devouring a short stack of pancakes let alone a woman. Lester shrugged, his makeup clotting in the heat and glare.

—Lust is not a difficult thing to show on a man's face, Lester said. Now, if you don't mind, let's just run it.

Lester sighed and looked over at Chip Spalding, who was standing by with the animal trainer and the caged tiger. There was going to be a sequence with the animal and they'd been preparing for hours. After a week practicing stunt handoffs and maneuvers together, they had developed enough of a rapport that Chip felt comfortable offering up his studied impression of Pavel for Lester—shoulders up, chest and belly out, pacing, one hand stroking his chin while squinting into the middle distances. Lester and the lighting crew broke into laughter. Pavel still had his back turned but Sabine looked over just in time to see the final flourishes of the impression. Sabine blew Chip a stagey kiss and wagged her finger at him and then everyone was laughing at him, his eyes down, hands dropped to his sides, blushing in the medical lamplight.

Claude reasserted himself between the actors with his clipboard. Nash Sully leafed through the photoplay, dressed in a pair of breeches; his job was to call out underlined stage directions, read title cards on set, and make last-minute changes to the script before the camera rolled. The dialogue cards would be added during editing. Pavel moved to the periphery with his half-eaten orange, sensing but not fully understanding his ridicule.

—Remember, Claude said, the main camera swings down in a continuous shot from the level of the attic, after the tiger has trekked through the hotel. So, we will see Rosalind over Harold's shoulder. Let's try it with Sabine opening the door. Lighting crew, let's hot it up a notch. If we get it right, then we'll run the strip.

Sabine lifted the hem of her gown and took her mark behind the hotel's front door. She could see her reflection in the narrow glass panel set into the entranceway. She'd instructed the hair-and-makeup girl to make her face shockingly pale and luminous. *I want to look* fantomatique *and* ravissant, *understand, an oracle of the night,* she'd told the girl. And she'd argued with Claude and the costume designer about the cut of her dress. When they refused to take the neckline lower, she brought them a sketch of Agnès Sorel, mistress of Charles VII of France, standing in a courtly scene with her breasts exposed above a square neckline. *Regard,* Sabine had said, *that this saintly buxom depiction is from the fifteenth century. And Charles the First of England also sent his wife around with her* nichons *exposed and puckered. Both Charleses understood the power of a woman's* buste, *that it is part of her empire. Now, just a few more inches of hillside, if you please.* They conceded, and now, looking into the glass panel, she suspected she was too old for the unscrolled parchment of her upper breasts to appear flattering. *Merde,* she thought, I want to vanish.

The arc lights came up hot against her face, buzzing and sulfuric. She looked at Lester through the glass panel—dressed in a dinner jacket that looked as if it had been dragged through mud and brambles, his bow tie unraveled. The suggestion was that he'd clambered his way onto the estate, through the woods toward the hotel, after his motorcar had broken down on the highway. Sabine couldn't put her finger on why she disliked Lester Summers. He was too beautiful for a man, that was one thing, with delicate hands and a black pencil mustache the same thickness as his eyebrows. Then there was the matter of his height, a stature that brought to mind quips about Shetland ponies and stepladders. A clause of his contract was rumored to govern the distance of the camera so that he would never appear standing at full height beside another actor.

There was a long kiss coming up later that night—twenty seconds, right before the attic bedroom seduction scene (cutaway to moonlit, diaphanous curtains)—and she was already planning her strategy. She would accept his amorous intentions as an offering from the edge of her bed (she'd have to sit to avoid revealing his height), but mentally, she would think of the great kisses of her lifetime, of Louis Pasteur's nephew with his supple mouth and his impeccable breath, of her ex-husband, a methodical, lingual kisser, even of Claude Ballard, who tasted like a loaf of bread and kissed as if his life depended on it. At least 50 percent of a kiss was aromatic and she worried that Lester would smell like sour cherries and talcum powder.

—Quiet on the set, please! Claude yelled. Places, everybody! Actors, when you're ready.

Sabine closed her eyes and the word *ravenous* dropped into her mind.

—The doorbell rings . . . a hotel guest in the middle of the night! called Nash Sully.

Sabine opened the door and did her best not to squint into the carbonized moonlight. Even though the camera was going to look over Lester's shoulder at her, his face was alive with emotion. He let his eyes come up to her face slowly, taking her in by degrees, from the black hem of her dress to the hollow expression floating behind her eyes. Coming out of a mental fog, he said:

—I've broken down and somehow found my way here. Do you have a room for the night?

—The tiger appears in the doorway, from behind the widow's dress, Nash Sully called.

The tiger was, in fact, licking herself docilely in a cage over in the corner with Chip and the animal trainer. But Lester gave such a look of fright that Sabine was convinced for a moment that she could feel the animal bristling against her gown.

—We have a room. Would you like to come in?

She brought one hand up to her sapphire necklace to deliver her line, then she left her hand covering part of her chest, conscious, she now realized, of making contact with her own body. Rosalind may have been burning brightly but she was also blanching away, vanishing before everyone's eyes. The widow stood aside and the traveler came through the door.

—Perfect, actors, Claude said. Take a few minutes while we ready the camera.

Sabine and Lester had their hair and makeup checked and then they went outside to cool off. Lester lit a cigarette and blew smoke extravagantly up at the starlight.

—Was that all right? he asked, craning skyward.

Was it his studied self-doubt that annoyed her so?

—Yes, wonderful.

She could feel the night air against her exposed shoulders. Because Lester was due on another film later that summer, they were shooting all his courtship, conquest, and peril scenes first, and that was another source of irritation. Like the child actors—who weren't due for another six weeks—the film was dovetailing around his schedule. She held her hand out for his cigarette and he gladly handed it over. She took a long, deep pull and exhaled slowly. From the look on his face she could tell that he thought this was another stage of intimacy, the old dame of the continental theater sharing a smoke with the younger star, the breaking of bread, so to speak, but she was trying to taste the residue of his mouth against the cigarette paper, in anticipation of the upcoming kiss. Slightly fermented, she decided. Apple cider left too long on a sunny porch. They finished the cigarette in silence, handing it back and forth, the lights of Manhattan white and phosphorous across the river. *Shall we go in?* she said at last.

It came time to release the tiger and let it saunter through the cutaway hotel. The suspended camera would *swoon*—that was Nash Sully's word for it in the photoplay—from the widow in the attic, track the descending tiger, and finally arrive over Harold's shoulder on the doorstep, all in a single seamless, floating shot. In order to film it, the camera and director were positioned on a platform that could be raised or lowered by a series of pulleys and weights, two crewmembers giving it ballast at the other end of a fulcrum.

As Sabine climbed up to the attic to take her position, she found herself imagining Dorothy's house in Albany—the bed where she slept with her railway tycoon husband, his false teeth faintly effervescing in a nearby glass of water. The clocks ticking, the paintings gassing off their antique varnish, the dining room where they'd eaten so many cheerless meals and put on a brave front for the children. Stories of the railroad, perhaps, or seashore escapades in Maine, anything to keep the loveless hound from crossing the threshold and ripping out their throats. Many people lived a lie, Sabine thought, but not many people have died from it. Consumptives are the world's great liars, she decided, and it burns them alive.

After they'd rehearsed the descent a few times—Chip standing in for the tiger—Claude told everyone to be quiet on the set and the camera began to roll. Lester Summers stood below at his mark on the imitation stone steps while Sabine brushed her hair out in front of the full-length mirror in the attic. The animal trainer—in a flannel shirt, a revolver holstered at his side—unleashed and unmuzzled the Siberian tiger at the top of the stairs. Unseen by the camera, the trainer tried to coax the tiger down the stairs with a piece of sirloin attached to a long length of rope. Claude, craning into the viewfinder from the raised platform, told the two crewmembers holding the counterweight to lower him a few feet. From his vantage point, he saw the tiger's enormous head in profile, protruding from around the edge of a wall.

—Camera gliding right, called Claude. Now looking for the tiger on the stairs . . .

The trainer began to call out the tiger's name—*Bella, come, Bella*—but she wouldn't budge. Claude decided to keep the camera rolling while the animal deliberated.

—Actors, keep acting, camera still rolling. Do we need a bigger piece of meat? A carcass, perhaps?

The animal trainer was clearly embarrassed. He poked his head around the corner of the wall and shielded his eyes against the glare of the arc lamps.

—We've practiced it a dozen times. She'll come 'round. Sorry, Mr. Ballard.

He muttered a few things to himself and disappeared behind the wall again.

A moment later there came a torrential animal roar, followed by a man's full-throated scream. Sabine, still standing at the mirror, felt something electrical pass through her scalp and into the roots of her hair. She was unable to turn away from the scene captured in the full-length mirror—the animal trainer with the steak in his hand, only the limp hand was now attached to a wrist that happened to be secured inside the tiger's serrated mouth. A delicate strand of the animal's saliva threaded along its blackened gum line. Even she was surprised that she didn't scream or faint. She just kept looking into the mirror, where the tiger looked non-chalantly at a distant spot on the wall and the trainer's eyes met Sabine's apologetically.

—She did this once before . . .

The man panted, turned white, bit his bottom lip—did anyone on set even know his name?

— . . . but eventually she got bored and let it go. Right now, there's more pressure than actual puncturing. I startled you, that's all, isn't it, Bella?

Sabine could see the whites of his eyes in the mirror.

—You're going to be all right, she said. I promise.

She turned away to yell down the stairwell.

—Is anyone coming to take care of this? *Anyone?*

She watched as the tiger in the mirror shook its enormous head loose, side to side, as if slicking water off its jowls, and the man's drooping hand waved theatrically at the floor, as if beckoning down a mineshaft. When she saw a bright slash of blood against the pale, hairy wrist and against the black, shining gum line she gave herself permission to faint if she needed to. But she didn't faint, something she would regret later on account of her vivid, carnivorous dreams. She didn't want to startle the animal further, so she stood perfectly still at the mirror.

Then came the sound of Chip Spalding bounding up the stairs. He was saying *easy now, easy girl*, as he came closer. Bella lifted her head, reared up, this time causing a parabola of the trainer's blood to arc out into the room. Chip lowered himself slowly beside the trainer—Sabine saw it as a genuflection, a graceful sinner kneeling in church—reached for the man's holstered revolver, and fired two shots into the brindled fur of Bella's neck.

With the camera still clicking away, a cloud of blood burst open under the sodium arc lights, covering the animal trainer's face and Chip's arms and chest. It even spattered the train of Sabine's long gown. She turned at last from the mirror to see the tiger drop with such force that it took the trainer to the floor with it. Then Chip Spalding was prying open Bella's jaws, and Claude appeared, ripping off his shirt and tightening a tourniquet above the trainer's mangled wrist and hand. The lights suddenly went out, and in the darkness, with the carbon arcs ticking and cooling, they all heard the animal trainer calling for Bella like a lost lover. Somebody at last said his name. It was Rex Lander.

Production was halted while the custodial crew bleached the blood out of the attic and while Hal Bender sourced another tiger. Both Nash Sully and Claude suggested that the tiger could be cut from the photoplay, that the affected scenes could be easily rewritten, but Hal wouldn't hear of it. He thought of Edison's electrocution of a Coney Island elephant, of two trains colliding, of the need to keep up with the hunger for spectacle.

He had a lead from a circus in Florida, where a Bengal tiger was nearing retirement age, if only he could negotiate a fair price and delivery. In the meantime, Hal decided, it would be a thoughtful gesture to have Bella's body hauled off to a Fort Lee taxidermist. He could imagine the resurrected cat presiding over the lobby of the Bender Bijoux with its glaucous eyes and a plaque below, with the untold story of animal trainer bravery in moving pictures. But the taxidermist was unable to patch and fortify an animal of this size and damage, and eventually Hal settled for the mounted head. He took it with him to visit Rex Lander in the hospital.

•

The animal trainer lay back in his bed, his left arm amputated below the elbow and resting on a pillow, wrapped in bandages. He was an old amusement park bachelor, so the room contained only a handful of get-well cards and notes, mostly from the film crew. Sabine had sent a bonsai in a ceramic pot and it stood on the windowsill. Hal rested the tiger head on a side table, as if he'd brought in a basket of flowers or fruit, and looked over at the desolation sweeping across Rex Lander's face. Rex refused to look over at the head on the table but his eyes began to brim with tears. *Oh God*, he said, turning away, *please get it out of here.*

Slightly dumbfounded, Hal reached into his pocket and produced an envelope of cash. With his eyes down on the floor, he placed the money on the table. This feeling was familiar to him—the sudden humiliation of missing the mark. For years, out at the curbstone on Flatbush or Fulton, he'd read strangers as plainly as a book while he coaxed them into the novelty parlor, but he'd routinely misread his own flesh and blood, or friends who needed his kindness. He remembered bringing a girl at school an extravagant present after her father had died of pneumonia, as if the lacquered wooden box of ivory dominoes might offer distraction from her grief. Did he get this trait from Chester? He could remember him delivering tone-deaf gifts to Flossy after disappearing for three days at a time—snow globes, tulip bulbs, secondhand watches from the pawnshop. He picked up the head and walked back out into the corridor.

Within a week, a new tiger arrived at the studio from Florida and it cost Hal more than he cared to admit. Although he'd tried to negotiate a lease for Sumi—a four-hundred-pound male Bengal tiger—the circus sensed an opportunity to offload the twelve-year-old cat. To sweeten the deal, they threw in his trainer at a discounted daily rate. The cast and the crew came down to the loading dock to watch Sumi's arrival. It took eight men to lift his covered metal cage from the bed of the lorry.

Compared to the ageing Rex Lander, who dressed like a cowhand and was routinely unshaven, the new trainer appeared from the cabin of the lorry dressed as an international delegate for animal trainers, a professional brotherhood, he told them all, that was widely misunderstood. He wore a khaki safari suit, a waxed mustache, a holstered pearl-handled pistol. He carried a whip, a chair, and an embossed business card: *Cyril Beck—Wild Cat Specialist*.

As soon as Cyril removed the cover from the cage, Hal realized he'd paid a fortune for a tiger that nobody wanted—the big sleeping cat had a scarred, kinked tail and a patch of mange on its haunches. Sumi opened one eye, then the other, as Cyril entered the cage with the chair raised dramatically in front of him.

—Careful he doesn't drool on you, said Hal.

Cyril shot him a stare as he kneeled down to muzzle Sumi's enormous, drooping mouth. He attached a length of rope around the tiger's neck and led him out into the open.

Claude stood with Hal and Sabine.

—We'll shoot the old cat in profile, mostly at night. No one will know he looks half-dead, said Claude.

—Old or not, we're not taking any chances. The actors won't go any-where near this thing, said Hal.

He gestured to Chip Spalding, who'd been waiting off to one side and who came forward doubled as the widow—the long black gown, a dark wig, his neck and face powdered to whiten his freckles, even a smear of kohl under each eye. The crew whistled and groaned with pleasure while Chip sashayed along in his gown. Sabine folded her arms and took him in.

—He walks better in heels than I do.

—All those years of balancing on the high wire, said Claude.

Chip took the length of rope from Cyril and began to lead the tiger down the grassy slope, toward the cliffs, before turning and bringing Sumi back to the trainer.

—Can you paint stripes over the mange? We're back filming tomorrow.

—It's not mange, Mr. Bender, but a mild skin irritation. Feline eczema, in fact.

Hal shrugged and turned for the main house. A deflated Cyril took the rope from Chip and led Sumi back toward the cage.

—Wait please, Mr. Beck.

It was Sabine stepping forward. She stood between the tiger and Chip, her costumed doppelganger. She'd spent the morning horse riding at a nearby farm and was still wearing jodhpurs and a linen chemisette.

—May I?

The animal trainer bristled, still offended by the insult Hal had levied at his cat, then melted under her gaze.

—He likes his ears rubbed.

He took Sabine's hand and rested it on top of Sumi's muzzled head. She began to stroke the crown of his head, between the leather straps of his muzzle, working her fingers into the spaces behind each ear. They all watched as Sumi squinted up at Sabine.

—Do they purr? Sabine asked.

—No, the roaring cats don't purr, but look, he squints when he's happy. Amounts to the same thing.

Sabine looked at Cyril, seeking his permission. Then she took one hand and moved it down to the side of the animal's neck and left it there, to the place where Bella had been opened out to the world.

Sabine was different in the viewfinder. Claude had noticed it from the first night. Over the years she'd developed a number of trademark motifs and gestures—her reflective eyes coming up from the floor, her chin resting on her fingertips, a sigh that worked its way into her shoulders—but now everything had been pared back. Her arms barely left her sides and her face was expressionless until an emotion transfigured it. They used separate cameras for close-ups of the actors' faces, since the master shot couldn't vary its focal length to adequately take in the eyes and the mouth, and Claude was shocked to see the uncut celluloid from the close cameras. In the instant before a flash of anguish or lust or rage, Sabine's face was perfectly still. He pictured her floating on her back in a tranquil lake, staring up at the transit of clouds. The French word *détente* came to mind—a loosening and attentive quiet.

Even her voice had changed. It came from the pit of her stomach and the back of her throat instead of through her nose, not projected so much as unraveled. None of these sounds could be captured on film, and yet they vastly improved the scene and the performances of everyone around her.

Some lines surged and came back, broke off, and others were barely audible, uncoiling as strands of thin silver wire. Occasionally there came a rising, locomotive wail that hit him in the chest behind the main camera. It reminded him of the patients he'd filmed and documented at the hospital in Paris, the way a second, paradoxical self could be carried in the human chest and larynx, a hysteric's childlike voice or a neurotic's steady baritone.

The kissing scene in the makeshift attic bedroom with Lester, Sumi watching from a darkened corner of the room, unfolded less like a seduction and more like an act of animal magnetism. The mesmerized Lester came into the bedroom holding his shoes, perhaps to quiet his passage through the hotel, and the widow—who was drinking an absinthe cocktail—gestured offhandedly to the bed. He complied, sat on the edge of the mattress, gently placed his shoes on the floor beside his stocking feet.

They had all agreed that Sabine wouldn't stand over Lester, that she would sit beside him for the kiss, but once the camera started to roll she stayed standing, removed her earrings, and put them gently into his hands for safekeeping. Then she lifted his chin with one gloved hand, brought the absinthe cocktail to his lips, wiped his lips with her cottoned thumb after he'd taken a sip. Then she brought her face to his, still with the glass in hand. Lester, the diamond earrings winking in his open palms, kept his eyes open for most of the twenty-second kiss. Meanwhile, the widow's eyes were serenely closed, as if she were drawing a fortifying breath directly from Harold Spruce's mouth.

Asleep inside a kiss was the thought that came to Claude from behind the viewfinder. But he was surprised by the power of it. In real life, a kiss that long would have been accentuated by a sensual hand, by the tilt of a head, but this was oddly sedate and stylized. Lester's face, when it reappeared, was stricken. When the widow peeled back the covers on one side of the bed— this was close to the agreed-upon cut point—there was a look of total annihilation and defeat washing over him. He reclined very slowly and tenderly, an injured man lowering himself into a scalding bathtub. As soon as Lester's head touched the pillow, Claude yelled *cut!* and Lester sprang to his feet, dusting off the sleeves of his dinner jacket.

　　—That's not what we agreed on when we blocked this out.

He turned to Claude, then back to Sabine.

—Can we retake that one? At the very least, I'd like this poor sod to be standing on his own two feet before she puts her hooks into him.

Ignoring him, Sabine walked over to Pavel, who was standing in one corner of the attic with the photoplay. Claude heard them have a low-set exchange, then Pavel announced to the room:

—Sabine feels confident that the scene is appropriate for the circumstances.

—Let's keep improvisation to a minimum, said Claude. But the camera liked what it saw. Actors, take a short break.

Sabine wrapped herself in a silk robe and went outside to smoke a cigarette. Lester sat on the edge of the bed to put his shoes back on, still fuming. When Pavel edged past the camera, Claude reached out to touch his elbow.

—Can she still speak for herself?

Pavel offered up an oblique smile.

—She asked if I could relay her thinking. She's feeling fragile.

—Should I be worried?

—On the contrary, it works to your advantage. We're seeing her drift and detach.

Claude looked at him blankly and Pavel chuckled.

—They're all existentialists and nonconformists, these tubercular rascals . . .

Claude watched the baffling Russian head for the darkened stairwell.

The Comet

In the days leading up to the comet, Sabine didn't think the world was end-ing, but she suspected her spirit had been poisoned. She smelled it in the sulfurous aura of the arc lamps, sensed it in her dreams of the tiger prowl-ing along the cliff tops, saw it in the meals that Helena dutifully delivered on a tray to the cottage. Lapin à la cocotte—one of her childhood favorites—arrived in a clay pot like some Aztec sacrifice, bones separating from glis-tening flesh, smelling of scorched marrow and bitter thyme. She took the rabbit meat off the bone and fed it to a dog that belonged to the master carpenter, eating only the potatoes and carrots that remained in the pot.

She tried to pinpoint when this raking unease had first begun, but it was impossible to locate its source. It had been there long before Thérèse Raquin and Dorothy Harlow and the tiger, had perhaps always been there. She saw it now darkening the edges of all her memories—the early theater triumphs, her Greek island honeymoon, her barefoot days in the vineyards as a girl. She saw something new and unsettling in all these images, a shadow blot-ting out faces in an old photograph. Her discontent, her *toska*, had always been there.

The planet, or at least New York, would swim into the gassy tail of Halley's Comet on the night of May 18, 1910. If she had her way, she would have spent the evening in the bathtub with a glass of wine and her galley of Colette's *The Vagabond*, a gift from a Parisian publisher friend. Instead, Hal and Claude had given everyone the night off and Lester Summers was throwing a comet party on his yacht, still moored down in Edgewater. She suspected that Lester was trying to rekindle his reputation as a bon vivant, instead of the short, pouting figure they had all come to know.

The entire cast and crew were invited, the studio providing a driver and omnibus for transport. Dressed in a cochineal-red evening gown, she drove down with Pavel, Hal, Chip, and Claude in the studio's Oldsmobile, staring off at the river while the others exchanged production notes. Claude intended to film the comet's passage and held on to a wooden box camera. Down at the Palisades Amusement Park, they were offering dirigible rides over the city for comet enthusiasts who didn't believe tonight was the Apocalypse, or for those who wanted to embrace it.

The yacht was festooned with lights and red-white-and-blue bunting, decorated as if the comet's passing were more patriotic than cosmic. They walked up the gangplank, and Lester, dressed in a white dinner jacket, waited at the top to greet them. He shook hands with the men and kissed Sabine on both cheeks. *It's kind of you to come, cheri,* he said, smelling of pomade and gin. The deck was set up with recliners and wickerwork chairs, with tables of hors d'oeuvres and champagne. Lester was also apparently mixing cocktails, because soon he made a show of standing behind a rattan bar and hurling a metal shaker back and forth above his head. He offered his guests a choice of gin fizz, absinthe frappé, or sazerac. Sabine stood by the railing and sent Pavel to get her an absinthe frappé, giving Claude an opening to come stand by her.

—Do you know what Rimbaud said about drinking absinthe?
She didn't answer, but she turned from the railing to face Claude.
—He said the sensation is akin to the darkest forest melting into an open meadow.
—It tickles my nose and tongue, that's about all.
They'd barely spoken outside of the glasshouse since the incident with the tiger. While Claude filmed her on set, he often thought about the kiss in the cottage the day after her return, imagined that she'd been caught off guard by her own tenderness toward him.

—*Tout va bien?* he asked.

—What an odd question.

—Is it?

—Nothing is all right.

He leaned against the railing, looked at the runnels of hazy light above the city.

—When I see you in the viewfinder, you're a different person now.

—How so?

—You've become so still. It's like you're evaporating before our eyes.

—Like absinthe on a tongue?

He laughed.

—Is it contrived?

—No, it's very good for the role, but I barely recognize you.

Pavel arrived with Sabine's cocktail and handed it to her. Chip Spalding came over with a drink for Claude.

—Here's to the comet, said Chip, raising his glass of ginger ale.

Chip never drank, on account of his father's whiskeyed ruin. They all raised their glasses. Sabine took a sip of her absinthe cocktail and turned back to Claude.

—I think Rimbaud was wrong. It's more like drinking a tiny cloud.

At that moment a bright flash came from the other side of the deck, and for an instant Sabine thought it was the comet. But Hal Bender had organized a photographer to take some early publicity shots—the cast relaxing on a yacht moored in the Hudson—that he would circulate for the picture's release. Hal and Sabine, standoffish with each other since their confrontation in the stone cottage, looked at each other across the deck. Claude had persuaded Hal to stay on the sidelines, to let him handle the tinderbox of Sabine's emotions, but now Hal raised a glass to Sabine and it was unclear how she would respond. Flanked by Lester Summers and Nash Sully, Hal kept his glass in the air for an unnaturally long time. The longer he kept it there, the more attention it attracted. Even Lester's steward, deckhand, and captain shifted nervously in their white uniforms as they waited for the continental slight. Eventually, Sabine raised her absinthe frappé, though it was clear she was pointing it more toward the heavens than at Hal Bender. Claude heard somebody sigh with relief and realized it was his own nervous exhalation. He went to fetch his box camera and set it up on the foredeck.

•

At about ten-thirty the earth moved into the comet's icy tail, about thirteen million miles from its fiery head. This was the widely reported figure in the newspapers and everyone seemed to remember it, from newsboys to clergymen, because it emphasized the sheer and particular distance from calamity. Despite the intermittent clouds, New Yorkers came out of doors to see the auroral lights in the northeastern sky. People thronged onto hotel rooftops, along Broadway and Riverside Drive, packed into ferryboats and lined along the river bridges. *The New York Times* reported that "a million or so sky-gazers here were taking a lively interest in the heavens," and they all wanted to glimpse the edge of something cosmic. What would the comet do to the magnetic pole, to telegraph wires and atmospheric pressure, to the family pet?

On the Lower East Side, Italian children, clad in white, walked out of St. Patrick's Old Cathedral holding candles and chanting the Litany of the Blessed Virgin. People gawked and prayed in Central Park, marooned on blankets with bottles of wine and opera glasses. The hotels ran express elevators to their rooftops and upper floors, sponsored comet dinners and dances. On the rooftop of the Gotham, a night camp was set up, complete with wigwams and teepees and ticket-buying tourists. In the sun parlor of the Waldorf-Astoria, a telescope stood mounted in the center, under the electric torches, surrounded by six tables of women playing bridge, a consortium of the disinterested.

From Lester's yacht, they saw intermittent flashes over Manhattan, a spray of white light trailed by tiny arcs of fire. Claude caught much of it on film. The scintillations came in waves and lasted until two-thirty in the morning. They continued to drink and eat all through the eruptions of the night sky, occasionally pausing to applaud or comment on something particularly spectacular.

Standing silently on the foredeck with Pavel, Sabine felt unmoored from the proceedings. The planet spun, the comet pinwheeled, and Pavel had drunk too much champagne. He stood wobbling, grinning oafishly up at the cosmos. Under that fanning arc of light, she felt outside of herself, thought of Dorothy Harlow and her fixation that the comet was personal, that her

own falsehoods had somehow caused orbits and gravities to alter their natural courses. The human mind was capable of placing its own hurt and
muddle at the center of the universe. If you weren't properly tied to the living, then you were convinced that the planets were orbiting the sun of
your own discontent. She leaned into her glass and felt the absinthe dis-
solving under her nose. She took a sip and looked at a still-craning Pavel.
Something in her life needed to change.

    —I am sinking into oblivion, she said.

    He nodded, oblivious, humming up at the stars.

The festivities petered out just before dawn. Actors lay slumped in deck-
chairs, slurring stories of a profession in decline, tales of botched lines and
booing audiences, of the consummate thespian friend who'd become an em-
bittered hack. Chip, Hal, Claude, and Lester played poker in the cabin,
dinner jackets off, shirtsleeves rolled up. Sabine asked to be taken back to
the studio grounds and Pavel went with her in the motorcar. Mercifully he
was quiet and drifted off on the ride up the Palisades road, snoring himself
awake as the motorcar rattled over the cattle grate at the studio's main
entrance.

The driver dropped her at the stone cottage and took Pavel to the actors'
bunkhouse, where he was forced to sleep alongside the extras, with the
nameless hotel guests, the widow's gardener, the aeronaut, with people
the camera only ever saw in profile and at a distance. It was good to develop
humility, she told Pavel, to elevate those in your orbit, and so she packed
him off to the bunkhouse whenever she could. Inside the cottage, in the
dawning light, she went to the table in the kitchen and began to write
the letter she'd been thinking about for hours.

    May 19, 1910
    The Palisades, New Jersey
    Chère Madame,
        Tonight the comet lifted the train of her dress and left us in her fiery
    wake. Not an hour ago I was standing on a yacht owned by an over-
    billed actor and staring up through a diaphanous curtain of milky stars.
    It reminded me of everything transient and pulsing. I recall your idea that
    the comet was a harbinger of something terrible, perhaps your own death,

but I am writing to say it has awoken me from a rather long and dull sleep.

I see you sleeping toward The End in your recliner, propped up by all those pillows, swaddled in a horse blanket, and it makes me want to cry. I want to provide you with some tangible comfort, madame. For your consideration, I would like to extend the offer of adopting your son and daughter as my own. I realize this will come as a shock, especially from an unmarried, divorced actress in her fifties. It seems to me, however, that what your children need most is the loving attention of someone who can guide and protect them, who can not only tend to their material needs but also their spiritual necessities. Fame has given me many things, some of them unwelcome, but it has also provided a kind of shelter. A stone fortress. More and more, I want to spend my days immersed in the simpler pleasures de la vie.

You should know that I intend to marry, and this will expand my suitability for the task at hand. It will provide Leo and Cora with a loving father—a well mannered, caring, talented, and devoted man I have known for fifteen years. In the end, love chooses us, I think, and we have to embrace its imperfections and frailties. If we don't we end up alone on a desolate coastline. But because you confided in me, Dorothy, I will tell you that I don't know that I have ever loved anything or anyone with my whole heart. Your children, I swear to you, will be the formidable exception to this terrible average.

I know your prognosis is dwindling and in a few hours I will place a call to Dr. Callow, will dispatch this letter by private courier so that it arrives by nightfall. I will come to you with a fuller proposal before the week is out.

Votre amie dévouée,
Sabine Montrose

14

The Proposal

Sabine invited Claude to take a walk with her in the yew maze later that morning, after the comet party, as the city across the river slept off the hangover of its continued existence. The world had not ended, she thought, but her old life had vanished. She suspected that love was not a garden maze, but rather a series of ramparts, an avant-garde theater production that left its actors stranded on elevated, raked platforms. Nonetheless, she would propose marriage in the hedgerows to suggest they might find their way to the enigmatic heart of a great labyrinth together.

She stood at the leafy entrance and watched him walking toward her. He carried his notebook and hand lens, perhaps assuming they'd talk about that evening's shoot. He was forever jotting down production ideas, using arrows and boxes to block out or storyboard a scene, panning the space in front of him with his peephole glass. It occurred to Sabine that she mostly saw Claude with one eye closed and the other eye magnified. Didn't the one cancel out the other?

She'd chosen a practical outfit for the occasion—calf-length boots, a pale blue shirtwaist with a gored skirt—and she hoped her attire would send the right intrepid signal. This marriage would be an expedition into the unknown. She gestured for him to follow her into the maze.

•

The hedges were full of nesting thrushes, birds flitting in and out of the tightly packed under-branches. Sabine led them into several dead-end passageways, and each time she silently retraced her steps to choose another route. Claude flipped through his notebook.

—I have a map the head gardener made for me.

—That would be cheating.

Eventually they found the stone bench at the center. It was the peaceful, geometric hub of the labyrinth, the hedges planed to perfection, the morning sun raking in from an angle, the air rife with turf and juniper. Sabine told him to sit on the bench, but remained standing, her gloved hands clasped in front of her. Her hands—scorched with peppermint oil, concealed from view—connected her more than anything else to the widow. She felt Dorothy's hands scalding inside her own.

—I have made an offer to adopt Dorothy Harlow's children.

Claude removed his hat and looked down into its felt bowl, as if a reply were taped inside.

—I see.

He squinted up at the sun, looked back down into his hat, and finally over at her.

—I stopped trying to guess your inclinations a long time ago, Sabine. When did this come to you?

—Truthfully, from the moment I met her. It was like I'd been wandering through an empty house all these years, trying to find a room with a lamp on, something to give me purpose. When you filmed us together with the children, you saw it, I think. Or the camera did.

—I remember seeing something I hadn't seen on your face before.

—What was it?

—Devotion.

The birds flitted and wheeled in the hedged understories. A maze within a maze.

—The theater and the films aren't enough?

She shrugged.

—When I'm onstage, or in front of the camera, I feel invigorated, then I go back to my dressing room and look in the mirror. Or I see my reflection in the kitchen window of the cottage. There's a woman looking back at

me who is so terribly bored and lonely, who is vain and terrified of getting old.

—And what do you know about being a mother?

His voice took on a ragged edge.

—What's to know? You feed them and love them, no? You educate
them and read them stories, help them make their way into the world. Helena will always be with me, of course. That woman adores children. And
she is very devoted to me.

—So the children will be raised by two women . . .

It sounded resigned, almost philosophical.

—As it happens, I intend to add a husband to the equation. Not for
me, so much as for *lés enfants*. It will make everything simpler for the legal
arrangements.

Claude rubbed the back of his neck and put his hat back on. He'd built
himself a funeral pyre out of his longing and it had been burning for more
than a decade. Why had he so diligently been adding his own bones to the
fire like kindling all these years? He stood up from the stone bench, an unbroken line of dread and anger connecting him to the ground. He felt
light-headed and thirsty. His feet were numb. He didn't know where to
look.

—I need to make some preparations on the set. I assume you'll be
shooting your scenes tonight?

—I must leave for a day or two, but I will be back with the children.

Claude closed his eyes briefly, folded into the immense, jagged pressure in his chest.

—We're running out of money. Every delay is costing us a fortune.

—It cannot be helped. Dorothy is on her deathbed and the papers must
be signed.

Claude felt he might scream, or faint, so he turned to leave, but he was
suddenly faced with four competing hedgerow passages. He hesitated before beginning down one of them.

Sabine followed after him but his pace quickened. He veered into a side passage and fell into a loping trot. She chased after him, lifting her skirt,
calling him *imbécile* and *connard* as she ran. Claude had always been light on
his feet and she couldn't keep up, but then he took a wrong turn and she

followed him into a dead end. He refused to turn around. He just kept stamping his feet in front of the yew wall. She came closer, still out of breath.

—*Crétin* . . . please stop running . . . it's you I want to marry.

She pushed a big breath out to level her voice.

—If you would take an old lioness like me, knowing that she cannot be tamed.

It struck her how unceremonious and undignified all this was, running and panting through a maze of hedgerows. She thought of Chekhov's one-act farce, *The Marriage Proposal*, and how everything unravels from a single misunderstanding. Working up to his proposal, the smitten neighbor says to Natalie, . . . *my property, as you know, adjoins your own. If you will be so good as to remember, my meadows touch your birch woods.* It sounded like erotic poetry, like a euphemism for the melding of bodies and minds, but in fact Natalie hears only the beginning of a property dispute. She replies, *But are they yours?* Sabine reminded herself that the play does, in fact, end with a *yes*. Because Claude still hadn't turned around, she added, *Veux-tu m'épouser?* She watched his neck and shoulders loosen, his fingers uncurl at his sides. Later, she would tell him that she took the straightening fingers as her *yes*. When he turned around his face was pale, his mouth slightly open.

—You look like a thirsty cat wandering through a summer garden, she said.

—I don't understand anything you're saying.

—I'm asking if you would marry me and help raise Leo and Cora.

As a reprieve from the mangled feeling behind his rib cage he looked into the sight lines behind her head. The aperture of his mind had always been controlled by his eyes, so he let his gaze go out into the blued distances. He was thirty-three years old and nothing about his life made sense to him. A boy from an Alsatian village who'd moved to Paris to become a photographer's apprentice, a man who'd traveled halfway across the planet to make moving images and who now lived above the cliffs of New Jersey, who spent every waking moment thinking about his epic film, the strip that had begun in his mind as the cinematic death of the woman he'd loved hopelessly for fifteen years and who was now proposing marriage in front of him. He suddenly felt the resistance he'd been plying through, the dead weight of his languishing stupor. He saw the surface of his life as a great Arctic sea choked with pack ice.

—You look unwell. Do you need medicine?

He shook his head, came at the idea from a hazy depth.

—A proposal of marriage?

—I may faint from exasperation, she said.

He swallowed, gathered his thoughts in a straight line. There could be no deception or ambiguity.

—But you ask it as if we're sitting at different ends of the table and you need me to pass the butter. As if you just need a little butter on your bread . . .

—For God's sake, I just chased you through a labyrinth. Do you also need a violinist?

He was holding his hat again. The forlorn Alsatian undertaker, she thought, is still there. He had a bruised look in his eyes as they found his own feet.

—You've never loved me, Sabine, we both know that.

—Perhaps not the way you've gorged yourself on it. I've never loved anyone or anything like that. But you are dear to me and I admire you more than anyone else I can think of.

He looked at her, finally, paced a few steps.

—What you're offering is a marriage of convenience, two friends raising a widow's children together.

She noticed the way his fingertips worried the felt rim of his hat. His nails were bitten to the quick.

—It's unorthodox, I know. Then again, you're never going to marry that woman from Hoboken and we both know it. That ship has sailed. And now here comes a new ocean liner.

—Not exactly new.

She preened her gloves.

—They name ships after women and lots of them lie at the bottom of the ocean, he said.

—The ocean is a dangerous place. It's not for everybody.

—Who else is on the list? If I say no, who is next? Pavel?

—There is no one else, Claude. The truth is, I've lost all interest in men. I will do it alone if I have to and if the widow allows it.

•

He opened his notebook and flipped through some pages, as if he were about to block out a scene. Then he closed it and looked down at the ground, scanning the blades of grass for portents and omens—marauding ants severing the wings from a dragonfly, say, or a dead finch prostrate under the hedgerows—but all he saw was the perfectly sheared lawn. He thought of all the unreasonable demands he might make, thought of this as a film contract they might sign together, the clause that required her adoration, the manifesto that she place him at the center of everything, but it was like asking a waterfall to change its course, a knife to dull its blade. So instead of asking for her devotion, he settled for the one thing that would ensure a pleasurable descent.

—I would need a *wife* in all the connubial senses of the word.

She'd never understood why some men pretended sex was an indecipherable index at the back of some enormous tome. It was all they thought about, most of them, and yet each time it came near—a planet blotting out the sun—their minds turned to gelatin and their expressions went blank.

—If you're worried about amorous congress, then I'm happy to oblige.

He bit his lip, looked up from the book.

—You make it sound like a preference for having the bedroom window open at night.

—*Merde*, don't be such an infuriating cold fish. Speaking of the bedroom, you should know that I sleep always on the left side, that some nights I won't come to bed at all, that Helena brings me breakfast in bed on Sunday mornings, and that I snore in the wintertime when the blankets are piled on. Also, I will need you to bathe after dinner every night, or you will require your own room. Nothing upsets me more than strong odors after a meal.

Claude spoke to an invisible confidant to his left.

—This is not the way I thought it would happen.

—*I will have thee; but, by this light, I take thee for pity.*

He looked back at her.

—I don't want your disgusting pity.

—I'm quoting Shakespeare.

She cinched her gloves back to her elbows.

—But, to be truthful, I think you'd gladly take my pity. Because it's the closest thing you'll ever get to my undying heroic love. The whole thing couldn't be simpler. I need a husband, and you need to unload this misery you've been carrying half your life.

Now she was the one turning to leave.

—I leave for the sanitarium in a few hours. I hope you'll come with me to sign the papers as Leo and Cora's legal father.

Claude held his hat between his hands and wandered through the maze, head down, zigzagging his way back to the stone bench. As he sat, he couldn't quite place the emotions that swum through him. He removed his eyeglasses, untied his shoelaces, took off his shoes and socks, rubbed his bare feet across the cool, cropped lawn, tried to make sense of his own rippling thoughts without any clear-sighted distractions. Then something occurred to him and he was suddenly light-limbed and poised. Chip had once told him about the moment before a high burning dive, when the big fist finally unclamped from around his heart and he felt emptied out by the plummet itself, by the inevitability and simplicity of falling. The decision to fall was never made on the tightrope or cliff top, Chip said, but in the middle of the night, when you looked up at the ceiling and saw your own existence as a pinprick in eternity. Now, up on the wire, you were merely following the natural conclusion of whatever you'd fathomed above your head in the nighttime. Claude knew he would say yes, that it was a decision already made for him in a hotel room at the end of the last century, and so it wasn't indecision that kept him sitting on the stone bench, wrapped in the slack-edged embrace of his myopia, his bare toes caressing the sharp blades of grass. It was certainty. He wanted to linger awhile longer, delay his exit from the maze, imagine for a few more minutes that his life might still be his own.

They married two days later, in the sanitarium cure cottage where Dorothy lay dying. A Saturday morning in June, a justice of the peace presiding, the superintendent and his wife serving as witnesses. Dorothy observed the proceedings through a scrim of morphine and laudanum, propped up and faintly smiling from her bed, a scarf wrapped around her head. Sabine wore a white silk dress, Claude a seersucker suit with a paisley bow tie and gold

cufflinks. When the paperwork was complete, the superintendent took the
adoption papers over to Dorothy's bed for signature, but Claude and Sabine
weren't allowed to come any closer. There were no books by her bedside anymore, just the gramophone with its arm at rest. The doctor propped the
documents up at an angle so the widow could sign them without lifting
her head. When it was done, she held up one gloved hand to wish them well
and Sabine blew her a kiss just as Dorothy closed her eyes.

As they walked out into the northern sunshine, Sabine took Claude by
the arm and led him to the waiting motorcar. Dr. Callow had given them the
use of his lake cabin for their twenty-four-hour honeymoon. They needed to
be back in New Jersey and ready to shoot by Monday evening. They would
collect Leo and Cora from the superintendent's sister at lunchtime the next
day, before taking the train back to New Jersey.

But for now they had an afternoon and an evening to themselves, a cabin
with a lofted bedroom and a dock over the lake. The interior was full of
Callow's bacterial experiments and epidemiology texts, the kitchen crowded
with microscopes and porcelain dishes of unidentifiable ooze. It smelled of
iodine and vinegar. When they heard the motorcar drive away on the un-
paved road, Sabine climbed the ladder to the loft where a narrow pine bed
stood under a window. It was stuffy up here, so she opened the window.
Claude appeared at the top of the ladder.
    —This is obviously the place where the good doctor comes to get away
from his wife and to dream of tubercular sputum.
    He laughed at this and looked down at his feet.
    —Don't be nervous, she said. I will take care of everything, just like the
first time.

She closed the white gauzy curtains and casually began to undress. Compared to the last time Claude had seen her naked—more than fifteen years
ago—this occurred without flourish. If that first occasion was the unveiling of a bronzed monument in a park, this reminded him of someone removing a wrinkled frock from a clothes hanger. He looked at the creases in
her thighs and across her stomach from her undergarments, the tiny
dimples in her buttocks. He had agreed, in principle, to be pragmatic about
the arrangements of their new life. She needed a husband and he needed to

put this old burden to rest. You either throw the bottle of poison over the cliff top or you drink the whole thing down—he'd said something to that effect after the maze, when he'd gone to the cottage to tell her he was coming upstate. He'd never actually said *yes* until the *I do* of the ceremony. He'd said *I'll come with you*, that was all. Seeing her naked now at the foot of the knotted-pine bedframe, her gray-black hair down and unbrushed, her hands at her sides, palms out, allowed him to imagine for a fleeting second that he could still possess her body and mind.

He stood very still.

—Do you still like to have your wrists tied to the bedposts?

—Who can remember, it's been so long.

He removed his shoes and socks, folded his trousers neatly and laid them across a wicker chair. He took off his jacket and shirt and tie, folded them carefully. He straightened his eyeglasses on the bridge of his nose.

—Are you at the doctor's office or on your honeymoon?

He gave her a look. She blew him a kiss.

—Come sit on the edge of the bed.

He walked over naked, aware of the alpine breeze blowing against his privates as he passed the window. When he was sitting on the edge of the bed she took his hand and traced his fingers down her throat and breasts, down her stomach and between her legs. Then she had hold of his wrist, pressing the heel of his palm into her. Her eyes were open but blinking slowly the whole time. After a few moments she straddled him, sank down onto him with a small sigh, whispered *voici*, simple and satisfied, as if she'd just cleared a drain or cranked an automobile into submission, and began to rock back and forth.

He felt the air go out of him and for a minute or two he was oddly detached and thinking about the attic bedroom scenes on set, the widow's empty gaze as Sabine kissed him now for a small eternity, her head motionless, just the way she'd kissed Lester Summers under all those sodium lamps. Was she seducing him *in character*? But then she asked him to pull her hair before slipping her cool tongue between his lips. He heard himself groan into her open mouth as he took a handful up near the nape of her neck and then his mind went blank and clear.

•

A pantomime of love—this was the dispiriting thought that settled over him as she curled beside him after it was over. He reiterated that his condition for accepting her proposal was that they never live like brother and sister, that she perform all of the normal wifely duties. To which she answered:

—We will make love when I choose and I won't leave you languishing, but don't imagine I will ever cook or clean for you. And I have never darned a sock in my life. I also have a condition.

—What is that?

—That you don't smother me like some rescued spaniel. This might be an expedition into the unknown, but certain rules will still apply.

He resisted the impulse to stroke the back of her head as she lay beside him.

—Where will they go to school? he asked.

—I was thinking we would hire a tutor.

—There is a school in Fort Lee.

—We'll see. For now, it's summer and school is *en vacances*.

—Hal says that we will have an easy time at immigration with adopted American citizens.

—I don't want to become American.

—But our children *are* American.

—For now, she said, closing her eyes.

The superintendent's wife had sent along a wicker basket of supplies—wine, coffee, milk, hardboiled eggs, sandwiches, and a frosted cake. At dusk, they sat out on the wooden dock, their feet dangling in the lake, and ate their first meal together as a married couple. There were no wineglasses, so they drank from the tin mugs they found in the kitchen.

—This wine tastes like it might contain a cure for consumption, he said, drinking it down.

They toasted their marriage, the adopted children, the film. A loon swam into view, haunting the lake and marshes with its phantom call.

—It sounds like a wolf calling, he said.

—Or a dying baby.

She drank her wine, splashing her feet back and forth.

—How does it end?

He paused, considered the possibilities of what she meant, placed them in decreasing order of magnitude: the world, life, their marriage, the film.

—I still have not seen the final pages of the photoplay. Why are you keeping them from me?

—We're still working on the stunts and effects, to see if they are possible. We require a permit from the New Jersey fire warden, for one thing, and those are not easy to come by. Especially when Edison has every government official in the state in his back pocket.

—Surely something horrible happens to me, otherwise you wouldn't be so coy.

—An angry mob descends on the estate.

—Audiences will like that. What happens to her?

—There are two possible endings. In one the mob burns the estate to the ground and they pursue her out to the cliffs. She jumps rather than face what they will do to her.

—And the other version?

—She tries to escape in the airship but they set it on fire as it begins to float away. Lester Summers dangles from the ladder with a torch in his hands. She burns horribly and we see her fall in flames into the river far below. We see her sink down into the sludge, her face distorted and blackened . . . I've worked out a way to film from behind an aquarium tank, making it look as if it's all happening underwater.

They drank through a silence.

—I see. Either I leap to my death or I burn alive and drown.

—Chip will double you in either case. He'll wear your dress and a wig. You won't even need to be on set the day we shoot the final sequence.

—Why not have the widow and the children float away to safety in the airship, across the river?

—Audiences will want her punished.

—You mean you will.

The lake lapped, the loon called.

—And what happens to the children?

—The widow manages to hide her children in the maze before the mob arrives. There is a passageway for them to escape into the woods.

She took another sip from her tin mug.

—I've been thinking . . . I would like Leo and Cora to play the children. If they're willing, of course.

—How do you mean?

—In the film. We don't need to bring in child actors from Manhattan.

In Paris, André Antoine used real street urchins and vagrants for his tavern scenes and they were electrifying.

Claude looked over at her.

—They're about to lose their mother.

She stared into the lake as if her own childhood floated there.

—It's different for children. After my mother killed herself I began to memorize Baudelaire and recited poems because I wanted to be noticed for the first time. I missed her terribly, but I needed to be fully in the world. A child doesn't know what to do with grief. They carry it around like so much sand in their pockets . . . Besides, this way the poor darlings can stay right by our sides on the set.

She drained her mug and looked off at the darkening lake.

—You should choose the ending that burns me alive and sinks me to the bottom of the river. We should kill the beautiful monster off without mercy.

She handed him the empty mug, got to her feet, and walked back toward the cabin with her shoes in one hand.

The Mansion of Happiness

Claude did not expect happiness. But here it was, so compact and know-able it felt like a varnished birdhouse between his two big hands. The way they crammed into the stone cottage that summer, fell into a regimen of picnics and walks and parlor games. They summered like tourists at a lake-side resort. Sabine staged their mornings and afternoons, filled the rooms and hours with gramophone concerts, éclairs and lemonade, beach towels, puppets, tarot cards, Parcheesi. A board game was perennially laid out, mid-game, across one end of the kitchen table. Claude thought back to his own mother playing an old board game called the Mansion of Happiness, a spiral track of virtues and vices before the player ascended into heaven. Sabbath breakers, he remembered, were sent to the whipping post. Christian moral-ity had been important to his mother and he could feel her disapproval from the afterlife. What would she make of his film, his marriage?

The children shared a room with bunk beds and a window facing the woods, one side crammed with books and insects in jars, the other with paints and sketchpads. Cora was almost eleven, Leo nine. In the boy, Claude saw himself at that age—a fringe of brown hair that was forever in his eyes, a magnifying glass winking from a shirt pocket, shoelaces untied, a runner and a knee-scraper, a cataloguer of the natural world. Just like Leo, he'd also been a hoarder of stamps and bugs, a marauder of puzzles and riddles, and this had given his days two different pulses: long hours of quiet punctuated by bursts of scrambling energy. It was why his mother had nicknamed him *the housecat* by the time he was six. Cora, on the other hand, was a green-eyed painter and sketcher, a rescuer of nestlings and a singer with a high, clear voice. She was comfortable with adults, met their eyes steadily or spoke out against their imprecisions with an air of righteousness. Other children, sometimes her brother, were blots on her mental landscape and had to be ignored with unwavering devotion.

Both of them were serious-minded and inquisitive about household and worldly arrangements. They had, after all, been shuttled between a tycoon's mansion, a spinster's house near a railway station, and a film star's summer cottage, so they wanted to know when breakfast and dinner were served, how many people lived in the main house, whether Sabine and Claude had met in Paris, whether other children were expected—by birth or adoption—and if it was all right to open their bedroom window at night.

Other questions, over breakfast and lunch: *Do the French believe in God?* (Cora), *Is Helena a widow or an old maid?* (Leo). Sabine always answered them as directly as possible, but she also began posting a daily schedule in the kitchen each morning, like a call sheet, to give their new lives some ballast. A typical day read:

8:00 a.m. breakfast
9:00 a.m. walking along the cliffs
10:00 a.m. motorcar ride to the shore, swimming
12:00 noon picnic lunch
1:00 p.m. quiet time/dormir/reading
2:00 p.m. games or city excursion
5:00 p.m. dinner
6:00 p.m. report to set

After Helena served them all dinner in the cottage, Sabine read aloud in the parlor, Conan Doyle for Leo and *Little Women* for Cora, one before the other, with all the accents and dramatic gestures she could summon. Sometimes Claude hung a bedsheet on the mantel and projected an actuality for the children. From their spread blanket in the parlor, they stared up at their French counterparts at the seaside, a boy setting his toy boat before a wave and the salt-lipped girl running along the beach. Claude was careful not to show them his sister's death or other scenes that might frighten them. After a viewing, they interrogated him about the workings of the camera and projector, about how light could pierce the celluloid and the darkness.

He started taking them along on his trips into the city, where he visited a specialty camera and optical supply store. Once a week or so, they took the ferry over to Midtown and walked the dozen blocks to Appleton's to choose a new colored lens or a bottle of rubidine-red for tinting the film stock. Claude could have easily sent Nash Sully on these errands, but he loved to mill around in the store with its bromide smells and high, tiered shelving, the clerks adjusting cameras on swaths of velvet laid out on the countertops, hundreds of apertures staring out from behind glass-fronted display cases. They sold telescopes and trick cameras, rolls of film, photographic papers, refurbished projectors. Cora liked to study the novelty items—the Photoret pocket watch camera favored by private detectives, or the palm-sized, auto-spooling Minigraph, or the optical illusion sketches. Leo, meanwhile, headed straight for the telescopes and binoculars every time.

On their walks back to the ferry wharf, Leo stayed close, occasionally tugging Claude's sleeve when something caught his eye, while Cora strode out in front, carrying their purchases in a paper bag, singing in her high, pretty voice as if to clear the way. For the river crossing, Claude handed them strips of taffy and told them stories about his childhood, about collecting mushrooms with his father and the eerie alpine nights they slept up under the dormers of mountain inns. He also told them about a childhood spent watching—anthills below magnifying glasses, his garrulous Austrian grandfather behind a windowpane when he came to visit and smoked like a factory chimney outside, his older sister through a keyhole when she kidnapped the family Alsatian, Bernard, and kept him prisoner in her room. *You were a collector and a spy*, Cora said with her offhanded prescience. Leo added: *Our parents never let us stare because it's considered obnoxious.* Claude told them that the trick to ogling was to know when to look away.

After several of these trips, Claude couldn't resist buying them each a gift— Cora a book of optical illusions, Leo a pair of birding binoculars—and soon they were bringing their treasures along to the glassed-in production stage each night for wardrobe, hair, and makeup. Sabine told Claude not to spoil them, which was rich, he said, because she let them leave the table with food on their plates or braid her hair with dogwood flowers or climb on her back when they went swimming.

On set, between scenes, Leo and Cora were free to roam. Leo often sat perched on a stool beside Nash Sully, who had been promoted to assistant director and took care of mounting the cameras and warming the arc lamps and prepping the set before Claude's arrival. And Chip Spalding became an honorary uncle, entertaining them while Sabine and Claude worked into the night. He sometimes brought along the wallaby and let Leo and Cora feed it with grass while he told them stories about his daredevil days in Tamarama.

When Leo asked about Chip's scars—the cryptic puzzle of a daredevil's life—Chip talked about farm escapades, about droving and fencing and breaking horses, about the escape to the big city and setting himself on fire.
    —Your dad . . .
    He looked nervously at Cora, then modified it:
    — . . . the new one, he was the first to film the blazer stunt. Has he shown it to you yet? The one where I'm on fire and jumping into the ocean?
    They both looked at him.
    —Stop telling fibs, said Cora, wagging her finger.
    —I'll ask him to show you, said Chip.
    Leo was running a hand over the disc-shaped scar on Chip's left forearm. Whenever someone touched it, Chip swore he tasted lead and smelled smoke.

The children were never coached for their scenes. All they had to do was stare out the window, walk down the hallway, or play in their room. They never asked what the film was about, and neither Claude nor Sabine ever told them that their mother was the inspiration for the role of the widow. But Claude noticed the way that Sabine subtly prepared them for the camera. Right before they came onto the set the gramophone music in the cottage turned a little brooding and Germanic, just like the raking symphonies Dorothy had played from her sanitarium bedside. Or Sabine mentioned her own mother, in passing over dinner, as if to evoke the unnamable ache that all orphans reach for in the night.

•

They were not yet orphans, though. That didn't happen until July, when Claude received a telephone call in the main house from Dr. Callow.

—Dot slipped away on a wave of laudanum and morphine, the doctor said, with barely a murmur, a boat slipping quietly into a deep lake.

The doctor paused, coughed away from the telephone. Claude asked about funeral arrangements and Callow said that Dorothy's final will and testament, of which he was the executor, was very clear.

—She insisted that there be no ceremony of any kind. We have a plot for her in our own cemetery, out by the lake. Which brings me to this: your first payment, from the trust, will arrive next month. It must be deposited into an account with your name and your wife's name on it, per Dot's wishes. Oh, and will you let the children know of their mother's passing?

The doctor made telling the children about their mother's death sound like a formality, a matter of tucking a note under their pillows.

When Claude returned to the cottage, he told Sabine the news in the privacy of their bedroom. He'd envisioned she might have some wise and maternal way of handling such matters, but she began to weep unabashedly and—still with tears running down her cheeks—called the children into the bedroom from one end of the hallway. After explaining that their mother had been loosed from her body, she said, *She loved you both so very much and always will.* Staring down at his untied shoes, Leo said, *I don't like to cry.* Cora put her arm around his shoulder.

—Father didn't like it if we made a fuss of things. Is there a grave?

—Out by a lake, said Claude.

—She couldn't swim, said Leo, sniffling.

Sabine met these words with a fresh round of her own sobbing. She knelt on the floor and pulled the dumbfounded children into her embrace. From above, Claude watched their blinking, startled faces amid the net of Sabine's shining hair, then he patted the top of Sabine's head. *Alors, you're scaring them.* Sabine released them and Claude took them back to their bedroom. When he returned, he found her sprawled across the bed with her face in a pillow.

—Out of respect, there will be no filming tonight. It's only proper, she said.

Claude drew the curtains against the afternoon sun.

—You're grieving as if it was your mother who died all over again.

—Will you stroke my hair for just a minute? Then I will go and sleep in the children's room. They need my comfort.

—Or perhaps you need theirs.

There was nothing in the bedroom Claude shared with Sabine that suggested a man might dwell within. The draperies and eiderdown were laced and brocaded, the armoire smelled of jasmine and milled hand soap. His tailored clothes hung neatly, his English shoes polished and arranged on a shelf, but in truth he felt like a lodger. It didn't dissipate the relish he felt each night when he came to bed after midnight, the reels developed and drying in the lab, Sabine lying naked under the sheets.

True to her word, she fulfilled all of her wifely duties, though this was done between the hours of 6:00 and 7:00 a.m., twice a week before the children were up, on the days of her choosing. The exception was the week after Dorothy's death, when she made a habit of waking him five mornings in a row. He awoke to find her kissing his shoulder or stroking his leg, or sometimes she would dispense with the preliminaries and slide a hand down into his cotton drawers. The lovemaking was unhurried and experimental. Once she had lowered the drawbridge he was free to add some stage directions of his own. Sometimes, afterward, with a bite mark on his arm or a cramp in his leg, he would watch her fall back asleep and think: *I've married a terrifying Greek goddess. I should be terrified but I'm not.*

The film, meanwhile, continued to kill Sabine off one frame at a time. Although he no longer wanted to banish her to some cinematic afterlife, the celluloid seemed to have a mind of its own. Every angle, scene, and plot device pointed to an inevitable and tragic conclusion. To change the ending now—he briefly entertained her and the children floating across the Hudson in the dirigible—was to deny an audience its most basic impulse. Moviegoers favored endings that mimicked medieval morality plays, the restoration of balance. They wanted to see her burn alive.

·

With a month left to shoot, Claude began to think about an epic musical score to accompany his melodrama. The reels normally went out with a cue sheet from the studio, a listing of major scenes with suggested musical accompaniment, and this was a big improvement over the days of free-rein accompaniment, a house organist or violinist making it up as he went along. But because Claude wanted to control every aspect of the mood during the hour-long showing, he planned to commission a composer and a score. He convinced Hal that they needed an arrangement for a forty-piece orchestra and a sound effects man in the wings. The big symphonic sound would include pieces by Schubert, Dvořák, Schumann, Mozart, Grieg, Mahler, and Wagner. The smaller theaters, he knew, would bastardize the score, scale it down to a few musicians and an actor in the wings who could shatter glass or scream when the story called for it. The bigger movie houses—like the 1,100-seat Art Nouveau palace they were building on West Forty-second Street—would mount the film like an Italian opera.

Someone had built an exact replica of Sabine's life. There was a plaintive husband, two sensitive, intelligent children, a house full of games and puzzles and impromptu recitals. She immersed herself in the stage business of the household, the cutting of sandwiches and the bandaging of knees. It occurred to her that she had always been at her best onstage with a prop in her hand, with some small enterprise before her—the lighting of a match, say—and so it was in life. Years of listless contemplation had left her feeling untethered and now she felt firm and brimming, eager to wake each morning and put the kettle on. Bustling had never been so enjoyable.

They traipsed into the woods beside the studio property at dusk, inventing games and picking wildflowers. Leo and Cora never tired of hide-and-seek, of being pursued into the flowering dogwoods that spangled through the river light. While she counted, Sabine liked to lie under the canopy of fragrant trees and close her eyes, giving Claude and the children enough time to burrow into ditches or cover themselves with leaves in a shallow gulley. Sometimes, as she moved through the darkening trees, she called, *'Tis now the very witching time of night, when churchyards yawn, come out, come out, before I find you all.*

This often got a squeal of terrified delight from one of the children as they reassessed their fortresses and made for a deeper, darker place. She heard them scurry, whisper, plot. Leo, in particular, possessed a talent for camouflage and confinement. He insisted on hiding alone inside moss-barked, hollowed-out logs, flattened against stone ledges, or in the crook of two tree limbs, and each time Sabine found him, there was a moment of denial. He would stare out, disbelieving, while she peered into his violated sanctuary, then he would tear out of the spot and come bursting into her arms, knocking the wind out of her. Claude would admonish Leo for his roughness, but Sabine loved the raggedness of it, the last vestiges of untrammeled childhood as she lay back, leaves in her hair, and let him tickle her half to death.

It occurred to her sometime that summer that she was no longer afraid of the white days stretching at the end of her life. It wasn't happiness she'd found—she doubted she had the disposition or capacity for that abstraction—but joyous distraction, the wild good cheer of being alive and entertained by others. She had never felt so necessary, so amusing. Children were easy to make laugh—you imitated them, pouted when you didn't get your own way, sang at importune moments, played with accents, and belched when they least expected it. She gave herself completely to them, treated them as her confidants and co-conspirators.

She also felt herself swell and harden with a kind of fierce protectiveness. She had often wondered whether she was a moral coward, or too sensitive and easily intimidated, and now she knew in every muscle and nerve that she'd fight off Siberian wolves, jump in front of hurtling locomotives, or kill a man with her bare hands if the children were threatened. She carried this formidable knowledge everywhere she went, in the pit of her stomach, scanning a room or situation for reasons she might be tested. Bravery, she thought, was so much more interesting than beauty.

The Old Neighborhood

Money troubles are like women, Chester Bender used to say—they're fickle and want your undying attention. Hal could remember such loose talk in the kitchen after dinner, or once his father had settled in the living room with a teacup full of whiskey in his favorite chair. It all came back to him that summer, in early August, when he realized the studio was about to run out of money.

If the final eight-minute sequence hadn't called for a mob and a burning dirigible, or if the score wasn't a musical Taj Mahal, they might have been all right. As it stood, the budget had almost doubled, they were short close to $15,000, and the banks and creditors wouldn't budge. Without another infusion of cash he couldn't pay for extras or a composer, not to mention distribution and advertising. He persuaded a few individual investors to up their commitment, a few thousand here and there, but he found himself back in Brooklyn one Saturday afternoon in August, going to see Alroy Healy. He hated himself for it, tasted gunmetal at the thought of it, but in all the boroughs, it was Healy who could galvanize cash at short notice, who could have old John make an entry in the logbook and just like that you were on your way with a leather satchel in hand and a noose around your neck.

•

But no one seemed to know where Alroy was, so Hal moved from one taw-dry Brooklyn business to another, from the saloon to the mattress empo-rium to the poolroom. He finally found him at a pawnshop on Myrtle Avenue, a storefront with a large display window, a teeming showroom, and a cavernous warehouse set behind it. Arranged in the front window were the forfeited effects of other people's lives—a green bicycle, a collection of bone china, a divan, two violins, a guitar, a pair of polished oxfords, a set of Madras pajamas, a child's miniature train set.

Hal could remember coming here with his father twenty years earlier, al-ways using the side entrance for discretion, to pawn or redeem daguerreo-type equipment or a pair of cufflinks or the family's heirloom clock. Flossy either didn't know, or pretended not to know, and it always seemed to hap-pen on a Saturday afternoon, Chester's pockets empty and his mind shud-dering with the thought of having nothing to put in the collection plate the following morning. God, just like Alroy Healy, kept tabs on outstanding bets, and Chester had made it his habit to always make an offering in church to hedge against his own terrible luck.

Inside, the shopmen bustled behind the long wooden counter in their shirt-sleeves, a line three deep of workingmen and their wives, holding umbrel-las, bundles of clothes, billiard cues, fire irons. Hal asked one of the clerks where Alroy could be found and he was directed out through the ware-house to the manager's office. The space behind the storefront was filled with unredeemed stock, most of it on metal shelves, pawn tickets attached, and arranged by category: rows of ornaments, tools, clothing, furniture, paint-ings, sporting goods. Beside the loading dock was the windowed man-ager's office, where Alroy sat at a desk with a black Labrador at his side. Hal knocked on the door and was waved in after several seconds of scrutiny through the window.

Alroy puckered up a wolf whistle as Hal walked into the office. *Here we go, it's the fucking Prince of the Palisades. Fancy suit, Hal Bender, what is that, pop-lin?* In recent years, despite the studio's uneven balance sheet, Hal had taken to buying his shoes and suits from a Midtown clothier. In all his deal-ings with investors and distribution consortiums, he'd found it necessary to look the part of producer and impresario—imported brogues and tweeds and silk ties. Alroy gestured for him to sit, but continued to rub the dog's black muzzle and head.

Above the desk was a sign that read *Uncle Is In*. *Uncle* was an old Victorian moniker for pawnbroker, and people along the avenue, from the saloon to the pawnshop to the poolroom, all called him that, Uncle Alroy, because it was a sign of respect for the man who could bring cash between paydays or the angel of death upon your household. If there was anything avuncular about Alroy, Hal thought, it was in the worst possible way—the husband's brother who shows up to Christmas already drunk and proceeds to flirt with the host's wife and daughters.

Hal sat down in an overstuffed lounge chair and took in the office. Everything had the look of a lapsed pledge—a grandfather clock, a brooding old painting of a ship being tossed in a storm, a snuffbox with a masonic star set into the lid, a walking cane with somebody's initials engraved on the handle. The desk was piled high with ledgers and carbon-copy receipts.

—Looks like business is still good, Hal said.

—Not too bad, as a matter of fact. You know how folks are around here. They're tough and hardworking but prone to a spell here or there. A poor old bird out there, just a few minutes ago, tried to pawn her wedding ring and her undergarments. So I bring her back here for a private tutorial. They call this the confessional, the pawnbrokers, because it's where the worst cases come to unburden themselves. Which brings us to you, Hal Bender, because something tells me you're not here to play fetch with my dog.

—What's his name?

—Beauty, and she's a her.

—Pretty dog.

—Thus the name. Would you like a cigar?

—Why not.

Alroy pulled open a desk drawer, took out two cigars, and proceeded to trim and light both, before handing one to Hal. This seemed like some bizarre debtor's ritual, the man with the money leaving a trace of his own saliva on the proffered cigar. Hal took it and dried the end with two fingers below the edge of the desk so Alroy couldn't see. He brought it to his mouth and took a pull of smoke.

—Our big picture is about to release, starring Sabine Montrose and Lester Summers. The week of Halloween, if we can get the edits made.

—And what's this one about?

—A consumptive widow who runs an electrified hotel and preys on her male guests.

—Naturally.

Alroy chuckled into a stream of cigar smoke.

—The thing is . . .

—Oh boy, yes, there's always a thing. Without a *thing* I wouldn't be in business. Go on.

—We're cash-strapped and we need an injection of funds to finish out the film and pay for distribution.

Some nodding into a smoky pause.

—I see. And is there a particular number you had in mind for this painful injection?

Hal rolled his cigar between his fingertips and watched the dog go to the corner and lie on an afghan that somebody's Prussian grandmother had crocheted.

—We need fifteen thousand dollars, maybe twelve if there are no more hiccups.

Hal had never seen Alroy at a loss for words, but now there was an inscrutable expression on his face.

—Do you have any idea what that amount of money looks like?

Hal shrugged and waited to be told.

—You lay out the hundred dollar bills, one level deep, and they cover the top of this desk.

—I know it's a lot.

—Eight dollars a square foot.

—What's that?

—How much an apartment with a view costs on the Upper East Side.

—Right.

—So you're buying two of them with this amount of money. Two one-thousand-square-foot apartments. I assume the banks have all said you're out of your fucking braincase?

Hal nodded, crossed his legs.

—And whatever investors you've got over there in New Jersey, we can assume they also have no appetite for this scheme. Therefore, what we're left with is this: the son of a two-bit, shithouse gambler who wants to make it into the big leagues coming back to his old neighborhood for a visitation with Uncle in his walnut-colored church shoes. Your mother would not be pleased, Hal Bender.

—Flossy now lives in the Catskills in a cottage I paid cash for. Her opinion of this scheme has nothing to do with it. Is it possible? Can you secure that kind of money?

Alroy savored a whirl of cigar smoke against his tongue.

—Interesting ploy. Put the lender on the back foot, maybe inflame his pride and vanity like a case of hemorrhoids. Your old man would be tickled. He was a backer of such antics. One time I saw him fake a broken leg to get out of a debt payment.

Alroy looked across his desk at the mountain of receipts and documents.

—I can rustle together that amount and a lot more, but the question is what's my return on a risk of this largesse. If old John were sitting in that chair he would be farting into my upholstery and writing in the ledger right about now and saying the odds of getting back the funds are quite small. In his droopy-eyed, palsy-handed way, he'd say, *Alroy, I advise against it.*

—Where is old John?

—Buried in a plot out in the Flatlands.

—My condolences.

—He drank himself into a pine box. A prodigious accountant who couldn't keep tabs on what went into his own mouth. If I were willing to find that sort of money, you'd have to understand I'd need bona fide collateral and the interest would be widow-maker rates.

—I would only need the loan for a year, at the most. How much interest?

—Forty percent, calculated monthly, but paid in weekly installments. I would also need the title to whatever property you've got over there in the wilds of New Jersey.

—The bank's still got a note on the property.

—That's unfortunate.

—What about the title to the theater down the street?

—I doubt it's worth that much, but it's a start. How about you also put me in for a percentage of the new motion picture ticket sales?

—Three percent.

—Twenty.

—I can't do that. I have dozens of other investors I have to pay out.

—If the film doesn't see the light of day, then you've lost everything. Even Beauty can see that, can't you, girl?

—Twelve percent. That's all I can manage.

Alroy hummed, arranged a pile of carbon copies into a neat stack on his desk.

—Give me three days and then we'll meet back here for the final arrangements.

Hal rested his cigar on the ivory ashtray and got up to leave.

—Take it with you, Alroy said.

They shook hands and Alroy got up from behind the desk and opened the office door for Hal.

When Hal was halfway through the warehouse, Alroy came walking up behind him, the Labrador at his side.

—Actually, if you have a second, there's something I want to show you.

Hal followed him down into a row of shelved boxes, Alroy's head turned as he talked.

—The thing about pawnbrokers is they're superstitious and nostalgic. Sometimes, we keep things, like collectors, because we're drowning in other people's bad luck and we hope they'll come back for their goods. Technically, anything they don't claim is either mine outright or I can sell it at public auction. But sometimes I hold on to stock because I want things to take a turn for the better. Twenty to thirty percent of people don't ever reclaim their items.

He turned to face Hal.

—Do you know what that means?

—No idea, Hal said.

—That seventy to eighty percent of people find a way to solve their problems. That gives me comfort, it does.

He pulled down a dusty box from a shelf and handed it to Hal. On the lid, the word *Bender* had been written in ink. Hal didn't have time to brace himself before he was staring into the box, his mouth stiffening at the sight of Chester's church shoes, size twelve, a gold fob watch engraved with his initials, a box camera, a silver hip flask, assorted personal items, including a bone-handled hairbrush that had once belonged to Flossy.

—I want you to go ahead and take Chester's things. Not sure why I kept them all these years anyway, since I could have sold them off. Maybe send them to your ma up in the Catskills. But understand this, Hal Bender, if this arrangement goes sideways, if it falls in the trough, there's going to be a lot more than your old man's shoes in a box. I will take your life down to the studs to get this kind of money back. Do you comprehend my meaning?

Hal stared into the bloodshot, yellowed whites of Alroy's eyes. He nodded but said nothing, unsure whether he hated himself or Alroy Healy more in that particular moment. Then he was walking back through the warehouse and out into the bustling storefront, where Brooklyn on hard times stood fidgeting in line, a box of his father's unredeemed pledges in his hands.

Last Day of Shooting

The final sequence kept Chip Spalding awake at night. For weeks he'd been studying the last two pages of the photoplay, making notations, drawing schematics, but now that the final day of shooting was here, he felt sure he was going to die. Like other daredevils and high-wire performers, his thoughts turned ominous or religious on the eve of a harrowing stunt. His mind had always ticked over with the probabilities of life's hazards—December is the worst month for armed robbery, German shepherds are the dogs most likely to bite—but now he saw his death as clearly as his own callused fist.

Wearing a black velvet gown and a highly flammable wig, he would set himself on fire in the wire-frame gondola below the airship and jump into the Hudson, while the hydrogen-filled dirigible ignited above him as he fell. The fatal mistake that screened nightly in his dreams was a coil of rope wrapping around his left foot, so that when he jumped he never hit the river. Instead, he dangled by one leg from the exploding airship, upside down and on fire, while the fishermen and clammers of Manhattan and New Jersey looked on.

In his loft above the stables, he prepared himself for the stunt, but also for death. He took out the addressed letters he'd written years ago to his family and set them on his neatly made bed. Next, he picked up his mother's vellum-paged bible and flipped open to her favorite passages from Jeremiah, during the unrelenting drought. *They did not say, "Where is the LORD who brought us up from the land of Egypt, who led us in the wilderness, in a land of deserts and pits, in a land of drought and deep darkness, in a land that none passes through, where no man dwells?"* When he was growing up, his mother had viewed the Outback as a land of deserts and pits, and these words were her solace. Jeremiah became a story of a troubled man transformed into a prophet, a weak man becoming strong. Chip had seen himself in those passages, but also his father's failures, and the life his English mother might have had if she hadn't ended up stranded in the bush with a big brood of hungry kids and a drunkard for a husband.

He stood naked in front of the mirror, lathering himself in wool fat. The fire gel recipe hadn't changed much over the years, but now it contained more glycerol, making it gelatinous and harder to spread. From a distance of twenty feet, and with clothing covering all but the hands and head, the camera would never see it glistening amid all that fire. Once he was fully slicked, he put on a pair of wet cotton skivvies and then the velvet dress and the wig. The makeup girl would do his face, so he left it dry for now. The horses had been unsettled in the night, picking up on his mood, and he called down *easy now* while he stared at his ridiculous feminine double. He laughed nervously and took a bow into the mirror: *Nice knowing you, Mademoiselle Spalding.*

At least the final sequence was going to take place in daylight, on the rim of dawn, but that also meant they had a small window to get it right. Claude wanted to capture it in slanting light, Manhattan silvering up in the background. Besides, the dirigible could only be set alight once. Chip found himself holding his breath as he came out of the stables and walked across the field, as if the pocket of space in front of him were already scorched.

The set looked like a battleground, even before the sun was up. In an ingenious cost-cutting move, Hal and Claude had bussed in more than a hundred Bowery bums overnight to serve as extras for the mob scene. In exchange for fifty cents and two hot meals, the men were lured into an omnibus, twenty at a time, so they could spend the day shooting. Given the early hour, however, Chip could see that some of the men awaiting instructions up on the hill were still drunk, or half asleep. They were in their own tattered suits or overalls or shirtsleeves—that would be part of the effect, the suggestion of an entire town of spellbound, indolent men awaking from their stupors—while Helena moved among them with a cart, patiently handing out cups of coffee and donuts to sober or brace them awake. The burning torches wouldn't be handed out until the cameras were ready to roll.

Chip gave a wave as he walked down to the cliffs, and several of the bums whistled and cheered at the man in the black dress. There were three camera units that were going to film in parallel: Nash Sully and a crew up at the hotel stage with the Bowery men, Claude down at the cliffs with the dirigible, and a third cameraman lying down on the cantilevered cliff stage, six feet below the edge, aiming up as the airship floated out over the river. Once Chip was in makeup and doused in kerosene, he would head back up the hill and wait for Claude's signal through the bullhorn. The bums would light their torches, all the cameras would roll, and Chip would take off running as the mob pursued him down the hill.

An actor doubling as Lester Summers—who was already on another set in the mountains behind Los Angeles—would lead the charge. At the cliffs, Chip would launch the airship and begin to rise just as Lester's double took hold of the rope ladder. The double would jump back to earth after a few seconds, but not before setting the rope ladder on fire with his torch. Claude would film the advance, Nash Sully would film the retreat, and all three cameras would capture the incineration above the Hudson from the different vantage points. The burning hotel would be threaded in with the old footage of the razed mansion, a cutaway as the widow disappeared in flames into the river.

The final shots of Sabine and the children had been filmed the day before, in the garden maze and in the attic, so Chip was surprised to see Sabine, Pavel, and the bleary-eyed children sitting on a picnic blanket in the predawn light beside the cliffs. Sabine was braiding Cora's hair while Leo and Pavel were arranging a small flotilla of toy battleships across a tartan sea. When Chip caught his eye, Leo jumped up and came running over to him, an apple in one hand.

—Can I touch it? he said, chewing and pointing at Chip's gelatinous fingertips.

—Very gently. I need to keep every part of me slicked up.

Leo allowed his index finger to land on the gel for a brief moment, before rubbing some of the residue between his fingertips.

—Feels like the bottom of a slug, he said.

Sabine, Pavel, and Cora got off the blanket and came over.

—I'm surprised you're all on the set today, Chip said.

—I wouldn't miss my own terrifying death for anything, Sabine said.

—We wanted to see the consumptive go up in flames, to make sure it is realistic, Pavel said.

—Can I give you something for good luck? asked Sabine.

—I need all the luck I can get.

She produced a frayed blue ribbon from her dress pocket and tied it onto a button of the black velvet frock.

—This was part of the very first costume I ever wore onstage. I usually keep it in my pocket when I perform.

A talisman, Chip thought, because she also knows the whiff of death when she smells it.

—Are you sure you want the children to watch? It won't be too much for them?

—Nonsense. They deserve to see the blazing stunt that will make you famous.

She kissed his cheek.

—Tell the makeup girl not to be stingy with the lavender powder and the kohl. When she dies, I want her to be *ravissante*.

Chip turned for the staging area, where Jimmy Thorpe stood by the tethered dirigible. Since no one else could be in the dirigible with him when he set himself on fire, the airship would idle as soon as Chip moved away from the controls. Two dinghies with life preservers and a medic were floating on the Hudson, within a hundred yards of the designated impact spot, marked by a red buoy. The New Jersey Shellfish Protector, off duty and paid by the hour, was also floating below, keeping watch to ensure no fishermen or commercial boats came within the cordon.

Chip could feel his bowels feathering and his skin prickling under all that glycerin. His vision blurred and his windpipe tightened as the makeup girl applied the kohl and lavender powder. *Entering the chute* was how other daredevils described it, the narrowing of the mind's eye and the dimming away of sense in the final moments before you slipped beneath the surface. Jimmy Thorpe had once described how the airship was constructed—the big envelope fabricated from goldbeater's skin, from hundreds of cow or oxen intestines, all of it sealed to hold an entire atmosphere of hydrogen, chugged along by two seven-horsepower engines. He was being carried to his death, Chip thought, beneath the amalgamated stomachs of a herd of cattle. It was fitting, somehow, a return to the farm.

With his makeup applied, he asked for the tub of gel and smeared his face and neck while Claude inspected him. Once the gel was applied, across his lips and eyebrows and nostrils, he couldn't talk, so Claude didn't bother asking him how he felt about the sequence. Instead, they looked in silence one more time at the clipboard that listed the steps and the timing of each. Once he manned the airship, he had thirty seconds to drift before the burning fuse line neared the base of the muslin-wrapped gondola, then ten seconds to light himself on fire, stand, and jump from a height of one hundred feet. They had timed the ascent and calculated the pitch numerous times to ensure he could get over his watery target. But if a sudden gust of wind forced the airship back onto the cliffs, or if he couldn't clear the undercarriage, he would have a minute at most before the gas-filled envelope above his head burst into flame. He turned to Sabine and the children on the blanket and gave a salute, then he waved at a grave-looking Hal Bender, who was standing out of the shot in a camelhair coat with the collar up. Chip doused himself in kerosene and gave two thumbs up.

Chip walked back up the hill toward the hotel facade, the mob of men now with their torches lit. He was grateful to be in a pair of flesh-colored sandshoes, that Claude had allowed the widow to plunge to her death without heels. As he walked, he could taste wool fat in his mouth, could feel his heartbeat marauding his chest and ears. He got into position ten feet in front of Lester's double, Nash Sully peering into the mounted camera. One of the Bowery men let out a full-throated, baritone belch, a few others snickered, then Claude yelled *camera rolling* through the bullhorn, just as daylight seamed the sky behind Manhattan. Nash Sully yelled *Go!* and Chip took off running.

•

The velvet dress weighed a thousand pounds, thick and heavy as a stage curtain, and he could feel his emollient skin rubbing against it all the way down the slope, hear the slicking noise of fabric on glycerin. He tried to run like a woman, to approximate Sabine's high-arched gait, but in his adrenalized mind she existed only as a bounding panther, had perhaps always been that way, her shoulders and haunches loose and forever uncoiling. He sprinted for his life, under the weight of the dress, turned back to see his attackers, Lester's double out in front with a full grimace.

The Bowery men had fallen into staggered ranks, some of them roaring like Vikings and others wheezing, bent over, flailing. A few of them sat in the dewy grass or in slicks of mud, clutching a bung knee or inspecting a broken shoe. One man seemed to have had a close call with his woodcutter's beard and a lighted torch, because he was pawing at his own smoking face as he ran along. All the while Claude and Hal and Nash kept yelling for Chip to keep running, down the strait and into the gondola. *Come on, Chip!* they cheered, and for a second he heard his own father, drunk and yelling himself hoarse from the sidelines of a school carnival, the one domain where his father's pride was unabashed and Chip's shame was undiluted, the annual young Spalding rort of blue ribbons and athletic trophies. Another proof of imminent death, Chip half thought, his chest and feet pounding, your father yelling at you across the decades and hemispheres.

All he had to do was crawl into the metal frame, one hand over another, while Jimmy kept it in position and eddied the big floating cow stomach out over the edge. The crew and the spotters would handle the rope ladder, the burning fuse, and the actor who would briefly dangle from the lower rungs. He kept his head down, stayed low, felt the cold metal rails against his gelled-up hands as he climbed in, and then he was untethered and floating in air.

He saw the double drop a few feet from the rope ladder with his torch, thought the actor should have held on for a few more seconds, but now the river came into view between his feet. The Hudson had changed from a ribbon of black ink into a light box, a canyon of streaming silhouettes. He counted off the seconds, the little engines whirring then going silent when he cut them to shed some altitude.

They'd painted the cliff face with a black line to mark 100 feet. Years ago, a Dutchman had survived a bridge dive from almost 200 feet, Chip knew, but the truth was any time he tried his own luck above 120 he'd ended up with a broken wrist or rib and a concussion. He felt for the Ronson flint lighter in his dress pocket, the little pouch where he'd sewn it in for good measure. He watched the fuse burn up along the rope, counted down the last few seconds, and took a sight-line reading against the black mark on the rock face, then down at the target below. He was higher than he wanted to be, but he crouched down behind the muslin screen to light himself regardless, touching the yellow lighter flame to his feet and hands and torso. He kindled and ruffled with fire just as the fuse line made contact with the flammable muslin. He batted at the air in front of him—the camera always liked that—and straightened into a scrambling dive.

Two and a half seconds was never long enough to hold on to anything like thought. The shattering glass of the river, the bruising of his fingertips, the battering of his rib cage and lungs, each was so overwhelming that it extinguished whatever came in the seconds before. Time didn't dilate or stop during a high burning dive in Chip's experience; it continued on its arrow-like grudge, slicing away at eternity like a knife paring skin from an apple. He remembered vibrations, sounds, shards of color, bile burning like molten copper in his throat, but nothing like actual thought.

And then the first sign that he was still alive was a sensation of being swallowed by a great maw of pain and cold and the sound of his extinguishing skin. He was always surprised that his skin hadn't been peeled clean from his body. Then a constellation of underwater stars as his lungs ballooned him back to the surface. When his head broke up out of the water that August dawn in the summer of 1910, he heard an enormous inhalation. It was the epic surprise of air.

18

The Premiere

For a week, the widow's kohl-rimmed eyes floated above Manhattan from the side of an airship. Her pale, lavender-powdered face could be seen in subway cars and on lampposts and billboards. As part of a publicity campaign, Hal arranged to have special matchbooks made up and handed out in saloons so that each time a man struck a match Sabine Montrose stared back at him through a veil of sulfurous fumes. *The Widow Awaits*, said the caption, and from the other side of the matchbook a tiger glowered up at the smoker.

They rented out a cavernous Broadway theater with 1,016 seats and an orchestra pit that could accommodate a hundred musicians. The venue was typically used for operas and touring symphonies, but the Saturday night before Halloween in 1910 it would house Claude Ballard's grand cinematic experiment. Movie palaces and a steady stream of feature-length films were another five years away, and the average New Yorker had never seen a film spanning more than twenty minutes. America's cities and towns were still full of storefront theaters and nickelodeons and vaudeville houses that showed reels as a sideline. D. W. Griffith, whose three-hour epic *The Birth of a Nation* wouldn't come out until 1915, released more than half a dozen titles in 1910, including the first film to be made in Hollywood, a seventeen-minute reel called *In Old California*. *All this is to say*, Claude would remind interviewers in later years, *that we were ahead of our time.*

But there were no red carpets, limousines, or photographer flashbulbs on the night of the premiere, just a thousand people clogging the sidewalk on West Forty-second. Advance ticket sales had secured the entire house, allowing Bender & Ballard to extend the film's run on Broadway and into smaller theaters in all five boroughs and New Jersey. If Hal's projections were correct, the movie was going to turn a profit within a month.

When the moviemakers pulled up to the sea of people in a touring car, there were *Sold Out* placards in the ticket-booth windows and ten ushers standing abreast at the big glass doors in their epaulets and brass buttons. The crowd parted for Sabine Montrose in her red cochineal dress, Pavel at her side in his embroidered waistcoat and twin fob watches. Chip got out and squinted at the crowd, shaking his head, followed by Hal and Claude. As they stepped onto the pavement, neither of them spoke or looked at each other, for fear of piercing the fabric of what they'd conjured together.

As Claude moved toward the Beaux Arts facade he felt the buzz of the crowd in his fingertips. Chip, walking at his side, said, *Can you believe it?*, and Claude was surprised to discover he'd always imagined this night as a kind of inevitability. He'd been led here, he thought, by an unbroken chain of events, by a series of maladies and fixations from his own life, his childhood fever in the attic and his mother's death, his myopia, his sister's consumption, the move to Paris, the audition for the Lumières, the tour as a concession agent, the rooftop conservatory, his lovelorn obsession with Sabine, all of it somehow cascading and buffeting him to this cavernous theater and this blaze of lights. Even the carpeted staircase and the flocked wallpaper as they followed the usher up to their seats seemed part of some elaborate, auspicious plan, the embossed green parrots and pomegranates and tulips beckoning with Eastern promise.

The usher led them to a balcony box, where five name cards had been placed on the red velvet opera chairs: Claude and Sabine in front, Hal and Chip in the second row, Pavel in the rear. Helena was back at the cottage with the children. Claude had come earlier in the week to inspect the equipment, to make sure the long throw from the projector to the oversized screen still allowed for adequate illumination, but he hadn't seen the auditorium from this vantage point, the chasm of raked seating, the vaulted, domed ceiling that seemed to float without support from the marbled columns.

He watched the crowd bustling in, half of them in tuxedos and pearls and the other half straight from their day about town. He studied the deep recess of the orchestra pit, caught the glint of French horns and the slant of violin bows. They had commissioned a custom-made Excela Soundograph, an air cabinet that housed fifty sound effects, and an apprentice prop master had been employed to pull its levers and push its buttons during the screening. Hal and Claude had agreed that merely having a sound effects man with thunder sheets, wind whistles, and horse-hoof coconuts was unthinkable.

Claude noticed that Sabine was staring up at the blank screen, at the acre of white silk, an empty champagne flute in hand, ashen-faced with nerves. He reached for her hand but it lay limp and cold beneath his. Claude felt his mind slacken in the final seconds before the house lights went down. He knew every frame and angle of the film by heart and yet he couldn't imagine what was about to unfold. His champagne glass shook gently and he tried to calm his breathing. Sabine suddenly clenched his hand but did not look at him as the canyon below bloated with darkness. Music drifted from below the lip of the stage, a fog of oboes and cellos and violins.

The fade comes in above the Palisades and we're floating across the dark river, descending over a ravaged garden with a yew maze. A gothic hotel facade comes into view, a single light shining from a round attic window. We glimpse a menacing silhouette prowling across the front porch. In the pall—a large cat, a tiger, lying across the front entranceway like some guardian to an ancient crypt.

The prop boy at the Excela Soundograph launched a tiger's snarling roar into the auditorium and Claude watched it ripple through the crowd. It pinned heads to the back of seats, hurled gasps up at the stratospheric ceiling. He watched the exhilarated moviegoers settle into the blue-gray twilight, the ones who leaned toward the screen smiling and the ones who leaned back, the armrest white-knucklers and the nervous spouse whisperers. A woman's shaken voice asked the darkness *What on earth was that?* and received a gentle shushing from her neighbors. When the first title card appeared on-screen—*THE ELECTRIC HOTEL, starring MADAME SABINE MONTROSE*—scores of people shifted in their seats to point or wave up at the high-altitude box seats and Sabine gave them a brief flourish of her hand. It reminded Claude of a monarch's aloof wave, an austere gesture from a stateroom balcony as an ocean liner pulls out to sea.

We see the rooms in profile, stacked like boxes. The widow stands in her long black gown in front of the mirror, in her elbow-length white gloves, brushing her hair in her attic bedroom. A four-poster bed behind her. She shudders and coughs into a white monogrammed handkerchief and a close view reveals an island of blood.

Claude was dismayed to see that on a screen the size of an Olympic swimming pool the tiny island of blood was more like a continent and that the first third of the theater had their heads turned to the side. It was too much, even from the high seats, and he regretted the decision to insert the close shot from the second camera.

Then he watched them all being lured back to the celluloid with every subsequent shot of the opening—the glimpse of the children in their bedroom, the zigzagging descent through the house, the rooms cutaway like a diorama, the widow and the tiger walking out to the cliffs under the moonlight. And when the dirigible descended into view, looming above the darkened river with the slight churning of propeller blades and a lone clarinet rising from the orchestra pit, he saw their heads lift and their mouths open.

A rope ladder descends from above and the widow carefully climbs up toward the airship in her gown, one foot after another, rising out of the frame. Now we see the airship floating across the Hudson toward Manhattan's tessellations of window-light.

For the next hour, Claude shifted his attention between the screen and the thousand moviegoers immersed in his celluloid dream. Every cut and effect was seamless. The stranded motorist arriving in the middle of the night, disheveled and covered in mud, who watches his suitcases ascend the stairs as if by magnetism. The flickering light bulbs when the widow

walks through a room. The children's dollhouse animated with moving figures and furniture. The tiger lurking in the shadows, its mangy hide and
painted stripes invisible to the camera.

The illusion was to make it all feel alive and unfolding now, to feel as caus-
ally connected as the flowing branches of a river, when in fact it was sixteen lies per second, the slipstream of frames that caused the human eye to
imagine perpetual motion. In the early days, a forty-five-second reel of a
sailboat leaving a dock in Marseilles or a white-frocked baby tottering above
a goldfish bowl in Lyon, viewed in a hotel basement, was enough to rouse an
audience because no one had ever seen a projected image shimmer with life
in every corner and plane. Each view was a silver-skinned mystery, a tran-
scribed minute of existence.

Now they were all aficionados of the human drama, the grocery clerk and
the banker's wife and the businessman, laying everything out on a mental
wire of juxtaposition and suggestion. It was the viewer, Claude knew, who
provided his own narrative powers to complete the picture, who placed one
thing against another. A traveler staring up wantonly at a woman's silhouette
in an attic window and then the same man in a darkened stairwell, clutching a candle, moving toward a widow's lofted bedroom, were not inherently
connected. They were two strips of celluloid nitrate glued together, filmed
on separate days, in fact, the actors not standing within shouting distance
of one another, and yet they were unfolding, irrevocably, at this moment in
time. It was a fiction without seams.

During the bedroom seduction scene, when Sabine sipped her absinthe
cocktail and placed her diamond earrings into Lester Summers's open
palms, as she lifted his chin for a long, stupefying kiss, a consortium of the
morally offended looked up toward the balcony of moviemakers. Claude
watched Sabine as she glanced down into the valley of accusation, refusing
to linger, and returned her gaze to the screen. When he saw society women
in the expensive seats preening their gloves and giving little shakes of their
heads he realized he'd collapsed their world into the widow's. They judged
the widow, and therefore Sabine Montrose, no differently than if she were a
fallen acquaintance they saw flitting along the storefront windows on the other
side of the street. In the theater, every actor walked onstage at the end—

villains and heroes and torchbearers alike—to take a bow and relinquish their roles and therefore the audience in the full brunt of the floodlights. In film, for better or worse, there was no renunciation of the conceit.

Claude watched the audience relax into the final sequence, confident that the vengeance they'd been craving since the lingering attic kiss was now at hand. Chip Spalding, doubled as the widow, ran toward the Palisades in the dawning light, a brooding Grieg composition playing at his heels. The horde of Bowery men, some of them holding torches, others wielding flintlocks and pitchforks, came running and silently roaring down the hill, an army of the deranged and the besotted in pursuit of the widow. The Soundograph played a battle cry, a tribe of clansmen descending on their enemies.

She makes it to the cliff's edge and scrambles into the gondola of the airship, one of her pursuers dangling briefly from a rope below. A sputtering flame kindles and wicks up the rope as the dirigible eddies out over the river. We see the widow float away from the cliffs, the city glinting in the morning light behind her. She crouches, stands, bursts into flame . . .

Sabine's prerecorded phonographic scream shattered the hemisphere of plaster and gloomy air above their heads. It shot out of the Soundograph as the widow batted at the space in front of her and dropped into a scrambling high fall. The airship erupted into flames while she fell, raking at the river as it rushed to meet her, and she hit the Hudson with an epic splash and a flume of smoke. The sound of a boulder hitting a body of water came an instant too late, Claude knew, but then the whole auditorium was underwater and no one seemed to care. For good measure, the auditorium surged with the sound of river rapids and gushing water.

Filmed from behind a narrow glass aquarium tank, the frames tinted green-blue and slow-motioned, the widow descended toward the bottom of the river, her arms languishing above her head, her singed gown billowing around her like the luminous skirts of a jellyfish. In fact, Claude remembered three men lowering Chip Spalding from a winch in a harness while a fan blew up his skirts. An eel—elegant as a sine curve—swam by in the glass tank that acted as a second lens wrapped in front of the camera. The murky bottom of the river was three feet on the other side of the glass tank, nothing more

than a mountain of heaped silt and improvised wreckage and flotsam in a
darkened corner of the production stage. The widow lay in the mud, her eyes
open and fixed on the fathomless world above.

*A slick of daylight on the surface of the river. Then we are rising again, this time
above the Palisades and back toward New Jersey, above a burning mansion surrounded by a mob with torches. We watch the conflagration for a moment but the
camera still floats, passing over the gardens. The last thing we see, as we float by, is
the yew maze and the two children standing at the center of its geometric heart, craning up and looking back at us as we pull away.*

The orchestra let the final images unfold without accompaniment, their
bows and horns at rest, and when the houselights came up the silence continued for a very long time. People continued to stare up at the blank
screen, unsure of what they'd witnessed. Eventually, men tightened cufflinks and watchbands, women adjusted shawls, and then a few people stood
up from the close-in seats. Everyone then followed their lead, as if emerging from a long and stupefying eulogy, drifting into the aisle in a daze, their
eyes down on the carpet. Claude watched them shuffle for the exits and out
toward Broadway, listened for their reactions down in the auditorium, but it
was eerily quiet.

When the filmmakers descended the stairs into the lobby, no one was waiting for autographs or milling around to catch a glimpse of the widow in
the flesh. But there happened to be a few people still collecting their coats
from the cloakroom attendant, two affluent couples waiting for their furs
and camelhair coats. They turned around just in time to see Sabine stepping tenderly down the stairs in her red cochineal dress, her eyes dark and
shining and tender with what she'd just endured. *You didn't just kill off the
beautiful monster,* she would tell Claude in bed that night, *you burned her at the
stake.* One woman over at the cloakroom window, a socialite ablaze in diamond earrings, a mink stole around her shoulders, lifted her eyes to Sabine
and tapped her husband on the sleeve. And then the four of them stood for
a moment, transfixed by the vision of a wrecked Sabine descending the stairs.
One of the husbands guided his wife toward the glass doors along Broadway and in a low, grave voice he said, *Well, look at that, it's the vampiric
whore back from the dead.*

Edison's Attack

In the two weeks before the letter arrived from Edison and his lawyers, more than one hundred thousand people saw *The Electric Hotel* in New York and New Jersey. In hotel bars and lounges all over the city, there was an uptick in women ordering absinthe frappés and the department stores couldn't stock enough black evening gowns and lavender powder and kohl. Despite the film's moral hazards, it received enthusiastic notices and reviews in the dailies and film journals. A critic writing in *The Moving Picture World* called it *a harrowing work of genius, a moving picture coup of macabre storytelling.* The *Ciné-Journal* described it as *a moral plague that will nonetheless leave audiences rapt and gasping.*

Within a few days of the premiere, bags of mail began to show up at the studio, some of them addressed to *The Moviemakers*, but most of them addressed to *Sabine Montrose,* or *That Woman, The Widow, The Consumptive, The Vamp, The Harlot, The Whore Montrose.* Pavel oversaw the handling of the letters, the careful sorting and parceling out to Sabine. She had always made a habit of reading and occasionally responding to her fan mail, but this onslaught was different. The mailbags piled up in Hal's office, most of the letters unread.

The Edison demand letter arrived on a Friday afternoon, hand delivered by a law clerk who'd traveled from Edison's complex in West Orange, New

Jersey, some twenty-five miles west. Hal and Claude were in the film lab, overseeing the packing of celluloid prints for national distribution. The lab crew worked in shifts to hand tint, dry, and pack the reels for shipping. Every theater would get a wooden crate with the labeled canisters, the musical score, and a set of publicity stills, including a signed photograph of the actors on Lester Summers's yacht.

They took the letter to Hal's office but neither of them could bring themselves to open it. Eventually, Hal sat at his desk, reached for a letter opener, and sliced the envelope open with a tiny sword. Between the tiger head on the wall behind his desk, with its glassy eyes and formaldehyde vapors, and the rheumatic image of a younger Edison on the back of his door, the portrait from the Brooklyn parlor, he read the letter several times before handing it to Claude. For years he'd burnished his contempt for Edison, rubbed it like bronze and kept the portrait as proof of how far they'd come. The Wizard of Menlo Park had tried to patent or otherwise copyright various forms of motion and light, would patent human breath itself if he could find the legal precedent, and here he was firing a litigious canon directly at the Palisades.

The letter itemized the violation of a filmstrip patent (US772647) held by the Motion Picture Patents Company, several camera mechanism infringements, and a customs law violation that had occurred by illegally importing foreign celluloid without paying stamp duty. It also mentioned the New Jersey fire codes that were routinely ignored in the manufacture and storage of flammable celluloid, *with said filmstrips further used for hazardous fire stunts that jeopardize the New Jersey public safety and contradict the state civil code for navigation of waterways.*

The final paragraph read: *Unless the film is pulled from distribution immediately, the General Film Company and its agents will be forced to remove all theaters currently exhibiting* The Electric Hotel *from its distribution agreements, effective at midnight tonight. Carbon copies of this letter have been sent to affected theaters, the New Jersey Fire Warden, and the state waterways commissioner.*

After Claude read the letter he slumped into an easy chair, unable to speak, and then something on Hal's desk came alive and the world was split in two by a ringing telephone. Hal knew it would be a theater calling to say they would have to cease exhibiting the film to stay in business, but for a brief moment he was convinced it was his father calling from the afterlife with a dispatch. He could see Chester Bender roused from a nap in the apartment living room, fresh from a three-day stupor of booze and poker losses, scratching at his paunch and brimming with saloon philosophy: *A dog that chases carriage wheels will eventually come to harm* . . .

To the theater owner on the other end of the line, Hal said he understood, that he would arrange for the pickup of the reels, and then he quietly replaced the Bakelite receiver onto its cradle. A few minutes later, the phone rang again and Hal unplugged the transmission cord from the wall. He reached into a desk drawer to retrieve a bottle of whiskey and poured them both a few fingers of single malt into two tumblers. They sat quietly, the afternoon light scaling up off the river, sipping whiskey, each man lost to his personalized version of ruin.

Hal looked at the box of his father's unredeemed pawnshop pledges sitting on a metal filing cabinet. He didn't have the heart to send the shoes, hairbrush, and personal effects to Flossy in the Catskills, and studying the box now, with Alroy Healy's block-case *BENDER* on the side, he realized that the end in his mind had always been a small caliber bullet from the muzzle of a gun. He saw himself sitting there in his office with its telephone and wall safe and tiger head, sitting in his bespoke suit and Italian loafers, an ashcan tycoon from Flatbush Avenue and Myrtle and Fulton who couldn't outrun his own fate. He was a gambler's son, a curbstone hustler, had always been a dog chasing after a churning carriage wheel.

For Claude, the picture of ruin was a room without windows. It was a scene unframed by a viewfinder. For two decades he'd lived an extraordinary life, traveled the globe assembling footage, a diplomat of the moving image, cheered on in taverns and theatrical palaces. He'd slept with and married a famous actress. The idea of his celluloid masterpiece languishing in a metal cabinet while Edison dragged them through the courts was unthinkable. He had created something new in cinema, he was sure of it, five thousand feet of spectacle and revelation, consumptive visions in china blue and rubidine red, a story of our darkest selves. He imagined himself living out his

days as a traveling projectionist, forever turning a crank between vaudeville acts or auditorium travel lectures. He saw himself on a Paris street
corner in a sackcloth suit, mistaken for a mortician.

As if summoned by their desolate moods, Chip Spalding appeared in the
office, one arm in a sling, his eyebrows growing back in tiny clumps, a slight
limp when he walked. During the high burning fall he'd torn some carti-
lage in his left knee, broken his wrist, and singed off his eyebrows and what
little remained of his body hair. The long black wig had protected his head
of wiry, cedar-colored hair.

—Who died? he said, limping in.

Hal handed him the letter and he stood by the window to read it.

—Even with the ticket sales so far, Hal said, we're way behind on the
debt. If the film gets pulled now, we'll end up owing about forty thousand.

Hal's face was unreadable, his eyes on the wall.

—Do you know any lawyers? Claude asked Hal.

Hal sipped his whiskey, shook his head.

—The Benders have never been big on jurisprudence.

The room fell silent. Chip looked up at the mounted head of the tiger and
thought about the moment he'd put two bullets into the side of the animal's
neck. There was a split second when the bullet was roaring through an artery,
when the tiger's eyes were walled back but still blinking, when somehow the
animal knew it was both still alive and already dead. *Death throbs in the veins
of the living*, he thought. Maybe he should return to Australia, take up an honest day's work, and live in a caravan back behind some far-flung beach. You
could do worse than wake every morning to the unfurled cobalt of the Pacific.

The thing was, he'd never liked bullies, had always stood up for the short or
gimp or poofy kids at school, the convent boys who came over to the public side of education when their family farms turned to cinders and dust in
the great drought. He'd always been a scrapper, a playground pugilist, and
he wasn't about to let his fire stunt go unobserved because of some lording
inventor and magnate.

—Why don't we go talk to Edison directly? Chip asked.

Hal brought his attention back from the wall.

—What, we just motor over there and show up unannounced? Go have
a chat with Mr. Edison?

Chip set the letter back on the desktop, facedown.

—The one thing my father taught me was that when your opponent has a height and weight advantage, you ambush the bastard.

Claude sat nodding with his hands clenched in his lap.

When they arrived at the gates to the laboratory complex in West Orange, a security guard checked them in and a telephone call was made to Mr. Edison's office. Deliberations ensued and they were told that Mr. Meadowcroft, Edison's secretary, would come down to meet them. Meadowcroft arrived in a charcoal suit and bow tie, a British accent clipping his vowels and throwing up the intonation at the end of his sentences. He shook hands with each of them, introduced himself as new to the post of secretary, but said he was a former partner in a law firm that had worked with Mr. Edison since the beginning.

He led them on an impromptu tour, took them past the various buildings, machine shops and laboratories, the employee restaurant and the department of decorative and miniature lamps. There was no mention of film or motion pictures; those had long been decamped to the Manhattan and Bronx operations. Claude wondered where they were hiding the Black Maria, Edison's first studio—a black box the size of a house that featured hinged roof panels that opened up to the sunlight.

Meadowcroft made a point of stopping by the punch clock in the entrance to the main building to show them that Edison himself punched in every morning before eight, that he was just another workingman. Then they were led into a big open room with tall windows and hanging light shades. The silver-haired inventor sat at a rolltop desk, leaning back in a wooden swivel chair, surrounded by a cortege of assistants in dark suits and bow ties, each of them taking turns to lean into his good ear to give an update from the realms of commerce and invention.

Hal saw that his nemesis was a man in his sixties in a crumpled white linen suit, despite the fact that it was November, a man, perhaps, who had no use for seasonal attire or social customs, who found such things a baffling bit of noise. There was a straw boater on the desk, a half-eaten cheese sandwich, a pile of engineering books, and a scatter of phonograph records in their paper sleeves. He had a kind, avuncular face, and each time he cupped his right ear to listen to the bent-over messenger the attendant got so close that he almost kissed the side of Edison's poised head.

Meadowcroft told them to take a seat at a long table that was spread with blueprints and he went over to deliver his own dispatch, to kiss the halo of white hair beside Edison's right ear. The inventor looked over and delivered a raffish grin, as if Meadowcroft had just told his employer that a dozen naked girls were on their way in to dance for him. Hal clasped his hands on the tabletop and wondered what had just been whispered. *The hustlers from the Palisades have come to hand you their testicles like a pair of iron Baoding balls.* He pictured Edison rotating the Chinese meditation balls in one hand as he peered into a microscope or stood behind a lectern. Edison took a bite of his cheese sandwich, waved his assistants off with a loose, distracted hand, then rolled himself over to the table, his backside never leaving the wooden swivel chair.

Meadowcroft sat at one end of the table, beside Edison's good ear, and proceeded to take minutes.

—Let it be known that I am recording the minutes of this meeting, at four-fifteen p.m. on this Friday, November eleventh, 1910, held between Mr. Thomas Edison and Misters Bender, Ballard, and Spalding. Gentlemen, you may proceed with your business.

Hal didn't know how to begin, so he just passed the letter across the table. Edison picked it up, put on a pair of wire-frame spectacles, read it while chewing with concentration.

—Apart from some capitalization misfires, I'd say this is a handsomely worded letter. The intention is very clear and robust.

It dawned on Hal that Edison had perhaps signed but never read the letter, that its summarized contents had been whispered into his right ear along with something about a delayed shipment of tungsten wires. Then, judging by the pleased look on Meadowcroft's face, he wondered whether the secretary had written the letter himself. There *was* something smugly Anglo-Saxon in its construction.

—Which one is the lawyer? Edison asked Meadowcroft loudly.

Claude noticed that there was a miniature rubble field of cheese crumbs on Edison's lapels. He thought back to his first meeting with the Lumière brothers, the way they'd dressed like aldermen. They had seemed like men on the verge of history; Edison seemed on the verge of a nap. Meadowcroft leaned in and told Edison that there was no lawyer currently representing the visitors.

—Sir, said Hal, we'd like to come to some agreement about the distribution of our new film. Theaters all over New York and New Jersey are pulling it as we speak because of this letter.

Meadowcroft relayed the message.

—Yes, Edison said. I expect they are.

—But we've never knowingly violated any of your patents or copyrights.

This was a lie and they all knew it. Meadowcroft spoke mockingly:

—He says they didn't *knowingly* violate any of your patents.

Edison looked out over the table, above their heads.

—Have you gentlemen heard of Hertzian waves?

—What now? asked Hal.

—In this very room, there might be fifty wireless messages being transmitted and we would never know. Completely invisible to us. And yet this hub of space is alive with meaning. The unknown, gentlemen, is something for which I am always preparing. Now, I am going to ask you a question . . .

Hal, Claude, and Chip all looked at one another. Was he a madman or a New Jersey Confucius?

—What are you here for? Edison asked.

—As I just mentioned, we want to discuss the alleged patent infringements and the distribution of our new film, said Hal.

—No, no, said Edison, annoyed, wetting his lips, not here in this room, here on earth. What are you each here for?

It seemed like a trap, so Hal said nothing.

—I was put here to make pictures, said Claude.

—To cheat death, said Chip.

Meadowcroft relayed the messages to a smiling Edison.

The inventor sat quietly for a moment, warming to some private theme. Later, Hal would recognize this as its own kind of incandescence, the way his face flushed like a filament.

—I was put here, good sirs, to tinker and illuminate. Nothing more or less. Sometimes I improve on the work of others, and sometimes I make a thing from scratch. In the matter of projected images, I believe we're still rumbling along . . .

He ran a palm across his hair, combing it into place with two fingers.

—The human imagination, you see, is such a finite container. We must kill off the weaker ideas and pursue the stronger ones. It's the same in nature, no?

Hal leaned forward to implore him.

—If we can't get our film into the theaters, then we'll go bankrupt. Have you seen it? Perhaps if you watch it then you'll understand what's at stake. It's the most innovative and expensive film ever made.

To Meadowcroft's relay, Edison said:

—I'm not much interested in watching pictures. I'm sure it's quite accomplished, the legal tethers notwithstanding.

There was a long pause. Edison looked out through the tall windows, leaned forward in his chair.

—Here's a story: I used to fish at a particular stream not far from here. I'd take off sometimes at lunch and grab a rod and see what I could pull out of the stream. However, soon everyone knew where I would go to clear my head and they'd follow me there with business. You know what happened?

None of them answered.

—The fish stopped coming, so I started to fish at night, when no one else was around . . . night fishing is a wonderful time for imagining the future, I've found. Now, gentlemen, I have correspondence to get to. Also, we're holding a concert in the music room at five if you'd like to stay.

Just as Edison began to swivel his chair toward his rolltop desk and his waiting cheese sandwich, it was Chip Spalding who stood up, arm in a sling, mostly without eyebrows.

—Just one moment, he said, clearing his throat.

Meadowcroft put a hand on Edison's shoulder and the old man turned around. Chip limped over so that he was close enough to Edison's right ear that he could make his speech without translation. He put one hand on the back of the chair, grazing Edison's shoulder as he leaned over.

—You pretend to be a regular fellow, punching in like a working chap, but the truth is, Mr. Edison, with all due respect, you're a ruthless mogul, no different from Carnegie or Rockefeller or Vanderbilt. You surround yourself with fancy solicitors, potter around in your laboratory, while you sue the bejesus out of any man who comes up against you. It's cowardly, it is, and you ought to be ashamed of yourself. We're just trying to make a living. This filmstrip of ours, it's got everything we have in it. It might as well be made from our own intestines. Let us run with it wherever we can. We're begging you . . .

Edison had been staring into the distance during Chip's speech. When it was over, he offered up a cryptic smile.

—A lot of us are fishing nowadays in the same waters. Nonetheless, all the best spots are already taken.

They all watched as he turned slowly in his chair and wheeled himself back to his rolltop desk. He picked up his cheese sandwich and took a bite. Meadowcroft, now in the manner of a saloon doorman, placed one hand on Chip's elbow, the one without the sling, and said, *I will see you gentlemen out.*

They came upon the studio in the early hours of evening, a few windows lit up in the main house and the porch light on over at the cottage. In the cool night air, the yew maze breathed out an intoxicating juniper breath. Now that production was complete, the hotel facade had been dismantled and the production stage stripped bare. There had been little talk of the next production, so most of the crew had gone in search of other work. Hal parked the motorcar on the gravel drive and told them they'd assemble in the morning to discuss their options. He said good night and walked silently into the house, his shoulders slumped.

Chip headed out to the stables, to the equine comfort of his sleeping loft, while Claude walked toward the stone cottage. More than anything, he wanted to eat a bowl of soup, play a board game with Leo, and watch Sabine brush out Cora's hair. He wanted to make love to Sabine to wash away some of the dread in his chest. This film had begun as a ploy to rescue his mind from the ravages of unrequited love, and instead it had turned into the death sequence of the entire studio. Without a wider release, they'd be lucky to see out the rest of the year.

•

When he opened the door to the cottage he noticed how dark and cold it was, how the fireplace was barren, the lanterns unlit. He walked back toward the children's bedroom, expecting to find Sabine dozing with Leo and Cora against her shoulders, a Conan Doyle novel splayed across her chest. But the room was empty. He moved down the hallway, toward his own brocaded and pillowed bedroom, calling out as he went. The chest of drawers was emptied, the armoire door ajar, a few scarves and camisoles tossed over the bed.

He walked into the darkened kitchen and lit the kerosene lamp. There was a mailbag propped onto a chair, dozens of letters ripped from their envelopes and strewn across the floor. On the countertop, a notecard had been placed against a vase of flowers and his hands were trembling as he picked it up:

> *My dearest friend and husband, I can no longer endure it. We will be safe, but far away. Je regrette. —SM.*

He was out the door and running toward the actors' bunkhouses, then sprinting up the porch stairs and through the main house, calling out to Pavel and Helena. Hal came out of his office clutching a whiskey bottle and they looked at each other through the darkened interior, two strangers in the hallways of hell.

—The security guard at the gate says they took the old horse and carriage an hour after we went to see Edison. She must have been waiting for her chance.

Claude looked down at the notecard in his hands, flipped it over and over, as if he'd missed an addendum or a postscript.

—What about the Russian and the maid?

—Gone as well.

—She must have grabbed one of the mailbags from your office.

Claude took the bottle of whiskey from Hal, brought it halfway to his lips, stopped. He handed the bottle back to Hal and walked down the darkened hallway and out into the cool night. Back in the cottage, as he stood by the light of the kerosene lantern to read some of the opened letters, it fell through him that she was never coming back.

Vamp,

    What has the world done to deserve your European contempt and mockery? How we let you into this country is beyond a thinking man's sense. You should go back to your homeland where they eat babies and drown in sexual vice.

    Harry T. Simmons

Madame,

    You have changed me. When I seen your face and hair, I knew I was a goner. You floated up above the city like a dream. Please consider this a proposal of marriage and know that I will send for you soon, my love. Whatever impediments lay on the broken road, I will sweep them aside in this ardent pursuit. My name is John Gordon Hyatt and I am a man of some means. Until soon, amour. JGH

Sabine Montrose,

    You represent perhaps the greatest threat to civil society. In regards to your recent film "The Electric Hotel" I am writing to tell you that Christian married women everywhere will mull your name alongside the devil's, for it is in his company that you belong. An archangel seductress and a Vampyre ripped from Poe.

    Miss Sybil Plum of New Jersey

Permit me, dear madame, an admirer and scribbler at times, to address you in a friendly manner, for I feel that I am an intimate and long acquaintance of yours. My addressing you is to satisfy a long pent-up desire that has been filling my heart for years. I only wish I had you in a room quietly by myself and free of interruption for half an hour. I would strap you on a table, your feet on the floor, making a fine half crescent at a certain part of your body, convex-side upper-most, I would bare you to the skin, and then proceed to ply a stout leather strap with knotted tails to your buttocks. Heavens! I enjoy the very idea of it. There would be no delay between sentence and execution. I would consider my deed righteous. But in the tempest, torrent, and whirlwind of my passion, I would beget a calmness of scientific applications. I would study the torture with exceeding joy as I saw the blisters and welts accumulating under my scientific handling. Then I would untie you, madame, and lead you to the sofa, and then love you back into heartedness and joy before snuffing it all at once. You would call me master in the voice you once reserved for Phaedra.

Yours till we meet across the Jordan

—JM

P.S. Perhaps when I kill you and your waifs I will become the most important person in your life.

20

The Monogrammed Suitcase

Toward the end of 1963, Claude sometimes called Martin in the middle of the night. These phone calls never began with *hello* or *hope you weren't sleeping*, they just launched into the middle of his tumbling thoughts. One night, he said his whole life had been a misunderstanding. Another time, he told Martin that D. W. Griffith, before having a stroke and dying under the chandelier in the Knickerbocker lobby, had been drunk and singing and walking down the hallway of the eleventh floor in his boxer shorts.

—Do you know, Martin, what his last words on this planet were?

—I couldn't guess.

—He said *I've been gone so long I don't remember what they call me.*

Claude couldn't sleep for the month after the Kennedy assassination. He'd watched 1963 unfold between the pages of the newspapers in the lobby—the introduction of zip codes, the closing of Alcatraz, the anti-segregation sit-ins, an airliner crashing into the Florida Everglades—and it all made sense to him as a series of headlines, as dispatches from the second half of the twentieth century. But November 22 and its aftermath didn't fit the pattern; it seemed to come from outside history.

Since he didn't own a television, he'd come down to the lobby after someone knocked on his door to tell him that the president had been shot. In the

Spanish mortuary pall of the lobby, he saw a group of residents huddled around a television set, the doorman, Sid, quietly weeping with his gold-braided cap in his hands, and Susan Berg, wrapped in her bathrobe, pacing in circles and saying, *We are all tainted by this, every last one of us.* Claude could remember looking out the windows of the lobby, where he usually saw secretaries and underwriters bustling to and from the Guaranty Office Building, but now the streets were empty, cars pulled off at the curb, a small crowd consoling one another, huddled in front of an appliance store with televisions in the window.

In the days that followed, Claude made his foraging and photography circuits through vacant lots and along hillsides and streets, only to find the city's mood had changed. Among the college dropouts on the strip or waitresses staring out the windows of a diner, there was a dazed, bewildered expression. Car horns were eerily silent, as if a honk might offend the somber motorist in front, and the love songs of the previous summer petered out on the radio in favor of Johnny Cash's "Ring of Fire." Strangers held doors and elevators a little longer for one another, nodded hello out on the curbstone a little more often. One Monday morning, Claude photographed three men in gabardine suits changing a flat tire for an elderly woman who was stranded at the corner of Hollywood and Vine.

After so many sleepless nights, he returned from these expeditions to collapse into his armchair by the window in his apartment. He removed his eyeglasses, leaned his head back to stare into the vagueness above, and quickly fell into fitful sleep and troubled dreams. He saw images of a funereal presidential limousine and the shining blacktop tarmac in Dallas, but they were spliced together with impressions of the tiger's head in Hal Bender's office, its eyes fixed on the window where the Palisades and the river and Manhattan floated through a summery haze, or the widow falling from the burning zeppelin, and then a sequence of Irene Lentz's jump from the eleventh floor of the hotel from the previous November, her feet idling back and forth from the bathroom window ledge as if she were testing the waters of a deep pool. In the dream, she nudged herself off into space and fell toward the concrete awning in total silence while Claude craned up helplessly from the sidewalk. She moved through the chlorinated Los Angeles sunshine in slow motion, languidly, as if the air had become water.

•

Claude never made it his habit to impose his dreams on a conversation, so he didn't tell Martin about his nightmares when he telephoned in the small hours. Martin, who said he was ashamed to be from the same state that killed Kennedy, let Claude talk about whatever was on his mind. He talked about the five thousand canisters of undeveloped film he kept in a lightproof storage closet in his living room, three decades of shutter clicks.

—You've never exposed the negatives? Martin asked.

—When I worked as a wedding photographer all those years ago, I always sent the negatives to a lab, but the ones I took for myself I never developed. Until that second they hit the chemical bath, every image is perfect in my mind. I have one of Betty Grable slumped at the bar with a bouquet of flowers on the empty stool beside her. And I have one of Marilyn Monroe up on the sundeck in her bikini. She liked to sunbathe up there and listen to baseball games on a transistor radio. I took one on the day of the assassination that shows a heartbroken Susan Berg kissing the manager's English setter on the top of his head.

Claude could hear Martin drawing on a cigarette.

—They sound incredible . . . Maybe we could organize an exhibition after we show the feature.

Martin was working on a restoration of *The Electric Hotel* and planned to exhibit a remastered version in the spring, as part of his dissertation in film history.

—No, no, you mustn't touch the photographic negatives until I'm gone.

There was a long pause, then a crackling lick of static that curled around the silence.

—It appears we're down to the last batch of celluloid. Can we meet on Tuesday?

Claude looked over at the ravaged suitcase he'd dragged out from under his bed. It was the leather valise he'd used to carry equipment and supplies during the early days of the war in Belgium.

—It *is* Tuesday, Martin said.

—Then I will see you in a few hours.

By nine that morning they were sitting in Claude's living room, staring at the suitcase on the floor. Claude knew that history could show up in a ravaged suitcase or a battered metal trunk but he also knew this valise contained his own ashes, the cinders after the Mansion of Happiness had been burned to the ground. It hadn't been opened since 1929, since the year Claude moved into the hotel. The brass latches were stippled with verdigris, the dark leather striated with mold, and there was a flaking gold monogram—*S.M.M.*

—Are those Sabine's initials?

Claude nodded and Martin got on his knees to open the latches, releasing a damp cloud of bromide and leather. Inside was a bundle of rusting film canisters, lashed together with twine, along with a first aid kit, a military field canteen, some letters and notebooks, and several compact box cameras.

—She left the suitcase behind in New Jersey after she vanished. I don't know why I kept it. In Europe, during the war, it held everything I had.

Two weeks later, they watched some of the restored suitcase footage in a small screening room at the university, the projector throwing out its submarine light. Starbursts of damaged emulsion dissolved against the screen, then a landscape juddered into view. A silent field of mud, tree stumps, and trenches smoking against the twilight. The swaying camera—looking out over a hillside from a grove of pinewoods—didn't appear to be mounted on a tripod. A German soldier in a spiked helmet and jackboots emerged from outside the frame and walked onto the field to survey the scene. A few other soldiers were behind him, unwinding a long hose.

Seeing it all these years later, it took Claude a moment to realize that it was a flamethrower on the first soldier's back. At first it looked innocuous enough, like a couple of oxygen tanks and a garden hose, but then a white flame came spewing from the nozzle, unfurling like a ribbon of magnesium.

They watched as the French soldiers were lit on fire, scrambling out of their trenches, flailing against coils of barbed wire. They raked silently at the air in front of them. A few of them took off running onto the muddy field until they fell to the ground, batting at their own flaming heads.

The projector thrummed through its gears and the footage grained to black for ten seconds, as if entering a tunnel, before coming back. Another man entered the viewfinder, walking down the hillside. The camera appeared to be sitting on the ground now, just staring out vacantly. The man was bone-shouldered, stooped, and uncertain on his feet, wearing a motley uniform with a forage cap instead of a helmet. He stepped across the smoking lunar landscape, oblivious to the burning turmoil all around him, and provided silent instructions to the German soldier. The stage direction was so un-hurried that it could have been a rehearsal for a boarding school tragedy. Then the gaunt man trudged back up the hill toward the camera, and for a second his gaze cut into the lens.

Claude asked Martin to pause the projector as he moved just a few feet from the screen. The image fell out of focus, abstracted into a field of flinty specks and mercury-colored pinpoints, but there was no mistaking his own face transposed across the decades. *Yes*, he said, *continue*.

The German soldier, now clear on his stage business out on the field, dragged a lifeless French soldier and propped him against a barbed-wire entanglement, his woolen infantry jacket braiding with smoke. Then the camera, manned once more, came in for a jostling close-up: the Frenchman's charred head thrown back, his face stricken, O-mouthed and incredulous. And then there was a wall of white static, a thousand soundless detona-tions as the film guttered into black.

The First Escape

Sabine on the night train. Not the woman but the girl at thirteen, running away a year after her mother's suicide. The dream on the divan, on the wave of Tuberculinum, had conjured a girl in tears, singing to herself in a compartment while her dead mother ate coq au vin in the dining car. But the truth of that spring night was she'd sat in her school uniform, drumming her fingertips on her calfskin valise, not scouring with shame at leaving her younger brother and sister and grief-addled father, but filling with exhilaration.

She'd told the conductor she was visiting a sick aunt in Paris, a missionary who'd contracted typhoid in the tropics. He punched her ticket and brought her hot chocolate in a tin mug to console her, told her to watch out for pickpockets in the Paris station and streets. To reassure the conductor, she told him her uncle was sending his carriage from the château because she had never seen Paris and this seemed like the most exuberant form of wealth she could imagine. She drank her hot chocolate, flushing with the audacity and meticulousness of her escape—the squirreling away of money, the suitcase she'd left packed in a granary on the way to school, the hunk of cheese and bread she'd wrapped as provisions in waxed paper.

•

She arrived in the city on the rim of a new workday, in the midst of Hauss-mann's final opus. After years of construction, the medieval town was still being plundered and reborn, the kinked alleyways widened into streets, the streets into boulevards, a work crew on every corner. Parisians ignored it all on their way to work—the little Arcadian woodlands shimmering from va-cant lots, the dredging of cesspools and graveling of sinkholes, the zincing of roofs and whitewashing of shutters. The chalk-colored stone facades and blue awnings and wrought-iron balconies. The public pissoirs where rings of frock-coated men stood urinating into metal wedges. The imported shade of a thousand chestnut and linden trees hauled in from the countryside.

The pedestrians looked unfazed by all this beauty and rubble, Sabine thought, accepted it as plainly as street names and seasons. An emperor was bludgeoning the present to build them an airy future, blasting daylight into the brickwork ravines. Her valise banged against her knees as she walked along, neck craned, the tide of the city and its people pulling her along.

For a week she went by the name Wilhelmina, worked in a tannery during the day and mimed or sang for strangers on street corners in the evenings. She lived in a narrow room above a tobacconist, in a Montmartre cul-de-sac that had not yet been quarried for the Grand Project. Her clothes and hair smelled of pipe smoke, her hands of tallow. Her head throbbed from exhaustion when she performed each night, pushing her pretty voice up from her stomach and into her nose, unthreading it the way her mother had taught her.

When she mimed, she liked to mimic posh female pedestrians bustling along to the opera or vaudeville houses, tickets in hand, cinching their gloves self-importantly. A Burgundy girl up on her arches, promenading and preen-ing like a countess—this always got a laugh from those ringed around her. A scattering of centimes into her open valise, where she also kept her makeup and props. Each night she introduced something new into her act: an argu-ment between two hand puppets, a fright wig, an impression, a tambourine.

She noticed the way the boys and men looked at her in Paris. It was not like the sidling glances of her classmates or the offhanded affections from men old enough to be her father back in Burgundy. It was unabashed and cunning, a narrowing through a gun sight. She felt it wherever she went, along the planking of the serpentine alleyways in Montmartre, from behind the smoky windows of a chandler or a cooper, but also along the broad promenades, through the aqueous lens of a monocle.

Something new and unnamable hovered about her, an aura in a gas lamp, and she saw it in their lustful calculating eyes and heard it in their cajoling voices. A few of the men started small talk when they dropped money into her suitcase, guessing that she was much older than thirteen. They all liked the sound of her name, Wilhelmina, the Germanic force of that initial V sound, of their front teeth grazing their lower lips.

A vision of a Paris life seemed within her grasp. She'd heard of girls, not much older than her, living in the dormitories above Le Bon Marché on rue de Sèvres. She could imagine herself into a future where she was a shopgirl during the day, selling bolts of ribbon and silk and crinoline, and a performer at night, an actress dressed in primrose and claret, offering up electrifying speeches to sobbing theatergoers. The affectionate public would give her playful nicknames—*la cloche* (the bell), *le moineau* (the sparrow)—and fill her dressing room with flowers. There was never a husband in her imaginings, just a circle of admirers and benefactors, and the sisterhood above the department store, the girls from the provinces who had the wrong accents and were all running away from something. It was Sabine, in this vision, who negotiated with store management and asked for an increase in wages. Even here, she would admit years later, she'd cast herself as the heroine and rescuer.

In the span of a week, she'd become expert at navigating the city. She knew where to buy bread and soup, where to wash her clothes, but she didn't know how to decline a man's unwanted invitations. Her mother had taught her to simply look away, to smile politely and look for a nearby distraction, but she'd never told her what to do when an older gentleman offers to buy you dinner and you're starving, repeats his invitation and stands over you while you pack up a valise of silk scarves and puppets.

—I have daughters not much younger than you, mademoiselle, back in Lyon. Let me buy you a brasserie plate. This is the third time I've watched you this week. Wonderful, splendid. You are destined for great things, *ma petite poupée.*

•

And so she followed this pot-bellied father into the soupy fug of a brasserie, the light braiding through the pipe smoke, the smell of mutton and onions already in her hair. She accepted a plate of sausages, ate enough cheese and bread and wine to make up for the days of hunger, for the time she'd briefly fainted at the tannery, when she'd found her arms waxed up to the elbows in tallow. The gentleman from Lyon prattled and sang little ditties that came to mind, helped her on with her shawl when it was time to retire, insisted on walking her back to her accommodations.

And it was here that her earliest vision of Paris was snatched from her grasp, the Bon Marché and the dormitory above it, the street theater and patriotic songs she belted for strangers, when he grabbed her from behind as she crept up the iron stairs behind the tobacconist. She'd been warned not to make a racket by her landlord, a man who seemed to rise for work in the middle of the night, and somehow this stayed with her, an admonition against noise after dark, as the Lyonnaise put his arms all around her, squeezing her rib cage and whispering *ma petite poupée* into her neck and ears.

A molten river flooded down her spine. She told him to stop, tried to break free and elbow him in the stomach, but his grip only tightened as it encircled her breasts. Her legs, especially her calves, were sinewy and strong from so many years of mashing Gamay grapes, so when she brought her ankle up behind her, piston-like, it gave a sharp jolt and she heard a long coil of air run out of him as he fell back onto the iron stairs.

She turned to see him reaching for a handhold in the air as he fell, his twill frockcoat flapping out like the wings of a bat. Lights and commotion came from the apartments up above as she hurried down the stairs and crouched to see whether he was still breathing. Blood crowned slowly around his head, but his eyes were still open. He blinked up at her wordlessly as the tobacconist landlord appeared at the top of the stairs, peering down and calling out with a lantern in one hand.

Then she was running into the snaking alleyways, wending her way toward the train station, her valise bashing at her knees, the city swallowed by night. During her arrival, the construction had been a sign of new beginnings, the broadening streets a new horizon, but now she tripped on a mason's pail of mortar, on a quarryman's sledgehammer, almost fell headfirst into a roped-off mound of gypsum.

She was battered and bruised by the time she made it to the station and bought a ticket back to Burgundy. Hands shaking, out of breath, she waited the three hours until departure time at the far end of the platform, sitting on her valise, her scarf around her head and shoulders. Something ragged coursed through her, and at first she thought it was the lingering terror of the man's arms squeezing her breath out, his voice sparking down her spine. She'd run aground, retreated from her own great future. In the train compartment she would sing to cheer herself up, blinking back tears, her reflection ghosting in the night of the windowpanes, the valise on her lap. All those years later, the shame came back to her on the shores of a homeopathic remedy, not for running away but for returning home.

22

War Correspondents

As a borough, Brooklyn was now a graveyard in Hal's mind. His brothers had fled to Boston, where they both worked as projectionists, and there was bound to be at least one Myrtle Avenue poolroom or tavern bounty on his head. Before Alroy Healy took over the Bender Bijoux to reclaim some of his debts, Hal had managed to remove some posters and fixtures from the lobby and a single opera chair—1A—from the auditorium. He hauled them over to the small apartment they all shared in Queens, put the red plush chair in the cramped sitting room, facing the window above the street. At night, when they came home from a day shooting advertisements for cruise ship companies or the opening of a new skyscraper, they all stared at 1A by the window, but none of them would sit in it.

For Hal, it was a piece of salvage, a reminder that no one would see their epic production. If he'd toed the line with Edison's copyrights, if Claude hadn't created a vampiric widow who seduced audiences but also drew their wrath, if Sabine Montrose hadn't opened the mailbags . . . It made him heartsick every time he looked at the chair, running the gearwheels of their ruin afresh. For Claude, 1A was occupied by a nameless moviegoer. Depending on his mood, he felt the invisible presence of a terrified woman who sits in the dark with her fingers laced across her eyes, or the clerk who hums too loudly with the music, or the country uncle who clucks and shakes his head, murmuring *idiots* up at the projection booth. It had always been impossible, Claude thought, to appease the fearful and the oblivious and the scornful with the same passage of music and celluloid.

It was Chip who finally sat in the chair and broke the spell. He plunked down one evening, a plate of spaghetti in his lap, looking out over the busy street with his mouth full. When he felt them both staring at him in disbelief, he shrugged, said, *I don't believe in curses*, twirled his fork into his noodles. *Besides, I can see into the piano showroom across the way when I sit here. It's the night polishers I like to watch, the way they buff all that lacquered wood with a cloth in each hand. Look at the frenzied bastards . . . Best seat in the house!*

For four years, they lived above a greengrocer, made filmstrips of wax museum openings and civic ribbon cuttings. Hal prospected for the work, Claude manned the camera, and the closest Chip came to a stunt was sliding down a banister in a tuxedo to promote a new luxury ocean liner. Mostly, he hauled the equipment and made props. With whatever money they could save, they each plotted their own escapes and comebacks. Chip and Hal saved to move out to Hollywood, and Claude kept a firm of private investigators on retainer to locate Sabine and the children. Early on, the firm had checked steamer passenger logs, wired Sabine's acquaintances in Paris, and spoken with the superintendent of the upstate tuberculosis sanitarium, but there was no trace of them. They sent letters to acquaintances of Pavel and Helena, but nobody responded. As her legal husband, Claude was able to check for withdrawals from the bank account he shared with Sabine, where the monthly deposits were made from the widow's estate. He imagined there would be a paper trail, a dotted line of withdrawal locations, but not a penny had been touched.

On the basis of his adopted, albeit missing, children, Claude was granted American citizenship after taking night classes in civics and English grammar. Although he had to technically renounce his allegiance to all foreign governments, they let him keep his French passport even after he acquired an American one. He was free to leave the United States and return, to search the ends of the earth for Sabine and the children, but he couldn't think where to begin.

•

He pictured Leo, now thirteen, and Cora, fifteen, living in a thatched-roof house up on stilts in French Polynesia, or in equatorial Africa, living in some kind of expatriate compound and sleeping under mosquito netting. Whatever deprivations he conjured for them, it was impossible to extend the same to Sabine. She hated insects and the heat too much to have taken up a new life in the tropics. There were two tiny islands, French protectorates off the coast of Newfoundland, St. Pierre and Miquelon, and he tried to imagine them there until he read about their blustery winters and the fishermen who spoke a coarsened and obscure dialect of French. They might have had gendarmes and francs, but Sabine could never live on some rocky outpost like that. His mind kept gravitating to distant francophone countries and territories, to places far enough away and small enough that no one would trouble her. Wherever she was, he saw her in disguise, changing her name, growing old and anonymous. He imagined her exile with such detail that it became his own, setting him adrift in the middle of a crowded room or street.

He'd carried want for so long that he wasn't prepared for loss. It ate at his insides, coiled around his dreams, swung through the ticking orbits of his fob watch. At night, he surrendered to the melancholy that had been ebbing through him all day and lay in bed to contemplate the losses of his life. Everything seemed to flow back to the attic bedroom and the fever, to the swooning boy on the brink. The past and the present were connected the way his father said mushrooms were, fungi and spores conspiring with messages below the dirt, so in his mind, he tried to pluck himself from the fever, get up onto his feet, and stagger out through the bedroom door to go sit by his mother, who was dying of smallpox in the next room. But the boy lying in the closed attic bedroom wouldn't budge. He tried to remember murmurs through the wall, imagined that perhaps her last words were German, since they were also her first, or that she had called out his name. Somehow, if he could hear her voice, he was certain it held a message for him. Then he pictured the moment the painting at the foot of his bed—a girl sleeping in a forest—stippled out of focus, the instant the fever warped the luminous corneal oceans that lapped over his eyeballs. He wanted to believe that she had died in the same moment he'd lost his perfect vision.

All his losses seemed to roost and burrow together at night. In the smears of street light from his window, his narrow bed in Queens sagged into his childhood bed in Alsace. It was the same person sighing through the same lungs. He thought the boy's thoughts, swam through his feelings, and the boy, in turn, was somehow prescient of his own future burdens. Sometimes Claude thought of himself as the abandoned husband and father as he floated his *whys* and *wheres* into the hazy cosmos above his head. Other times, when the melancholy softened, he traced Sabine's flight back to his own decision to make her a beautiful monster. In doing so, he'd turned the world against her, and therefore against himself. He wondered whether, in that closed room up in the attic, half a lifetime ago, he'd been the one to close the door to keep his mother's unraveling voice at bay. Sorrow, he thought now, had always been waiting for him on the other side of that door.

In August 1914, Hal Bender saw their chance at redemption. Like his other big ideas—a moviemaking glassworks above the Palisades, the Bender Bijoux with its Model B cinématographe and cake emporium—it came to him all at once and fully formed, an epiphany that felt religious in its power.

He didn't tell Claude or Chip that he'd made an appointment with the Belgian consul after hearing him interviewed on the radio, that he'd taken his only remaining tailored suit out of its garment bag, polished his Italian brogues, and gone into Manhattan like the old days of wooing bankers and magnates to finance a film. There was no flip chart or projector this time, because the proposition was so simple that it didn't need to be conjured on butcher paper or celluloid: Bender & Ballard would donate 80 percent of ticket sales to the Belgian Red Cross in return for unfettered access to film the German invasion anywhere inside the country.

The consul was a beleaguered career diplomat in a moth-colored suit. He thanked Hal for his proposal, but kept looking at his watch.

—I will make some telephone calls and be in touch. However, we expect this will all be over very soon. Belgium, after all, has a ring of fortresses around every city . . . We've been defending our turf for centuries . . .

Hal knew the look of an investor with cold feet, knew when a Brooklynite was shambling down Fulton Street, worrying the coins in his trouser pocket but not quite ready to part with them. So he stood, buttoned his coat, and shook hands with the diplomat. Casually, almost as an afterthought, he added:

—If nothing else, we should document this big German embarrassment. I'll let you consider and return in the morning.

When he came back the next day, he carried a copy of *The New York Times* with the headline "ANTWERP PREPARES FOR A SIEGE," ready for another round of lobbying. There was no need: three letters were waiting, signed and sealed, including a letter of introduction to a government official in Antwerp, plus a document the diplomat referred to as the *laissez-passer*.

—Your films, Mr. Bender, must persuade the world to come to us in our time of need.

Hal put the letters into his coat pocket, shook the consul's hand, and went out into the street.

On the train ride back to Queens he rehearsed what he would say to Claude and Chip: *We've been living like misers and monks, worrying that Alroy Healy will show up one night with his henchmen, too afraid to bring a woman or prospective spouse through that door, into the black pit of our lives, and Claude already broken and loveless, a waste of a great cinematic mind, if you ask me, and me afraid to step foot back in Brooklyn, the streets I know like my own two hands, the place where I was born and where my father died in debt, which is the Bender family curse, as far as I can tell. The city's dead to us and we're dead to it. We're of no use here . . .*

His speech sounded convincing, even patriotic, in his mind. It had the zeal of the curbstone evangelist. When he delivered it, though, he didn't get more than a third of the way in before Chip waved his hand from 1A, told him to give it a rest, that of course they'd bloody well go to Belgium because what else was there for them.

—Besides, I'm too short to join up with the Australian army. They won't take any man under five feet six inches and I'm one inch in the red. So this is probably the next best thing for a shrimp like me.

It was Claude who took his time, picking up the official letters in their envelopes, weighing them in his hands. For years Hal had watched him slip away into sorrow and distraction, his eyes floating across the empty space in a room. Claude looked down at his scuffed oxfords.

—We will need the right shoes for Belgium. I hear the mud can be murder.

A five-day steamer passage to Liverpool, an overnight ferry to the Netherlands, a barge up the river Scheldt. Within a week they found themselves in Antwerp, joining an army of photographers, journalists, and war tourists from all over the world. Whereas the French and British had forbidden foreign correspondents from traveling with the military, the Belgians were lax. But every horse, lorry, and motorcar had been commandeered for the war effort, so most newspapermen couldn't get out of the city and into the hinterland of besieged towns. They filed their stories *from the back of the front*, dispatched from the upper rooms of the Hotel St. Antoine.

As part of Hal's deal with the Red Cross and the Belgium government, they were provided with a ninety-horsepower Berline, now painted elephant-gray, that had once belonged to a florist from Ghent. With Chip at the wheel, they made daily trips into the shelled-out moonscapes of Flanders, stopping every few miles at a German or Belgian checkpoint. In addition to the government letters and the *laissez-passer*, they also carried cartons of Chesterfield cigarettes and racy postcards. It was usually a combination of credentials, passwords, and pornography that got them waved through a checkpoint.

When they were out filming a skirmish, they carried more weight than artillerymen—Graflexes, hand-held Aeroscopes, a cinématographe, the Pathé movie camera, film canisters, tripods, log books. They carried rolls of muslin and built crude filming shelters, like deer blinds, so that the hand-cranking from the tripod didn't look like the grinding of a machine gun.

Claude carried the Italian cowhide suitcase that Sabine had left behind when she'd vanished. Monogrammed with her initials, he'd filled it with spare cameras, extra rolls of film, rations, cigarettes, a sheath of her letters, a field diary, a first aid kit, and reels for showing the troops. The Belgian soldiers made fun of him for his *petite valise*, chided him in three languages, accused him of looking like a tourist on the Riviera. But he had no use for rucksacks, preferred the hard shell and compartments of the suitcase, the way it doubled as a seat or lap desk. He wiped it down at night with mink oil, this elegant piece of wreckage from his former life.

They spent a week filming skirmishes along the roadway or out in the smoking fields. To personalize the desolation, to give it human scale, Claude captured the residue of the fighting, the fine silt that covered the hedgerows across Flanders, the flecks of Belgian blue cloth in the treetops. His intercuts included a pair of false teeth resting on the windowsill of a burned-out farmhouse, and a single row house left standing in a ransacked village, its door marked in white chalk—*Nicht phindern*, Do not pillage.

There were hours of artillery fire and mortar attacks, then entire afternoons of calm, the Berline scouting for new locations, coasting between checkpoints with its little American flags flapping neutrally from the side mirrors, camera out the window. Claude filmed the German observation balloons—the big gray Boches—rising through the blued distances like great primordial brains.

The Belgian uniforms were endlessly filmable, too. Cavalrymen trimmed in scarlet piping and oilskin hats, artillerymen in navy blue wool coats with brass buttons. They made the plundering of the human body all the more disturbing—a severed arm out in a field of mud with epaulets still pinned to the shoulder. Claude found himself, after a week, acutely aware of joinery and sockets, not just in the human body but in the hinges of a cupboard or armoire that had been dragged out into a ransacked village square by a German brigade.

The Germans carried arson field kits, little tins filled with lozenges of sulfur and matches for setting a town ablaze. Sometimes they turned a motorcar into a flamethrower, fitting its petrol tank with a pump, a hose, and a spray nozzle and then driving slowly through the streets, one soldier at the wheel, another two pumping and spewing flames up at the houses. Before they razed a town or village they painted warnings on church walls—*Good people of this town, do not plunder*—and hung the Kaiser's flag from the bell tower.

Claude filmed it all, sometimes concealed in a tree, or behind a low wall, and he felt his mind swinging out like a gate. Everything in the world waited to be burned, dismantled, unhinged, blown apart. It was all he could think about when he went to bed each night, peering up at the veracity of his own bare knuckles.

Some nights they showed reels in abandoned farmhouses and barns, projecting images of Paris and Tamarama and New Jersey onto makeshift screens of burlap as a reprieve for the Belgian officers and conscripts. For the first time in years, Claude manned the projector, unspooling Sabine bathing in a rooftop conservatory, a Parisian couple kissing in a doorway, the teenage daredevil in flames above the ocean.

He had a powerful sense of cranking through the entrails of his old life. The soldiers stared up at the filmstrips, mesmerized or heckling or groaning with pleasure. When Sabine blew a cloud of soapsuds into the air above the rooftops of Manhattan he could hear the whole barn of soldiers shifting on their wooden benches at the same time. When she waved at the camera he undercranked the projector to slow her movements on-screen, as if he might delay his own ruin.

But these men in their beautiful uniforms had their own ruin in mind, sitting in a darkened barn on the outskirts of Antwerp one evening in late August. Brussels had fallen and now the field army had retreated behind Antwerp's ring of fortifications. All but a few buildings had been leveled to clear the sight lines before a German siege. As he cranked a scene of Paris onto the burlap, he wondered about these cavalrymen's lives, about their regrets and longings.

A cavalry officer accompanied the reels with a violin, quietly at first, as window-shoppers pointed into the storefronts along the Boulevard des Capucines, as a woman sold bread from a bicycle. Here was Paris, a sister to fallen Brussels, flaunting her springtime bloom. Couples picnicked in a municipal park and the omnibus came glinting through noontime. The violinist changed tempo during Sabine's rooftop bathing, worked into an upbeat waltz that had the men cheering and tapping their boot heels. By the time Chip's high fall fluttered against the burlap, the officer had become a virtuoso and they all watched as the daredevil plunged burning into a sea of violin sharps.

That August night, after the reels, Claude went outside for a cigarette and to stand among the tethered cavalry horses. He rubbed the white diamond on a mare's forehead and blew smoke up into the cooling night. There was a mineral smell in the air that reminded him of iron balcony railings after a downpour, of drowsy afternoons in his little Paris garret before he'd gone to work for the Lumière brothers almost twenty years ago. Tucked inside the mansard roofline of a crumbling old building, his whole world had been a single room with a tiny portal window on one wall, a camera, he understood now—a darkened box behind the glass aperture of the oval windowpane, a recess where he'd been exposed and developed into someone new. He caressed the horse's jawline, stared into the brown knowing of one eye. He could see himself looking back in the half light of his burning cigarette. The world was a baffling mystery to him.

The mare blinked, twitched one ear, nickered. Her eyes walled back. Claude looked up into the night sky, craning, but saw only a gauzy vault of stars. A second later, an immense pressure pounded through his chest and the air keened.

On the other side of the roadway, the impact sent a cascade of dirt and tree limbs into the air. Sulfur rippling through the treetops, filaments of blue-yellow flame and white smoke rising above the dark woods. Claude could feel the wrenching of timbers in the back of his teeth and wondered if they'd failed to blacken the barn windows enough, if the gaslit projector had drawn the artillery.

There was yelling, suddenly, in Dutch and French, then a burst of Flemish cursing, as the cavalrymen came running from the barn. Claude crouched beside the mare, his palms cupped over his ears, before he had the wherewithal to fetch the Aeroscope camera and a lantern from the trunk of the Berline. Leaning against the hood, he filmed the men mounting their terrified horses. The violinist, it turned out, rode the mare with the white forehead, his instrument now strung over one shoulder like a rifle.

They drove south, away from Antwerp, into a territory of ruined beet and asparagus fields. Somewhere north of Brussels, they encountered a pocket of fighting. A band of Flemish peasants had taken up position in a roadside ditch, behind sandbags and barbed-wire entanglements, while the Germans were firing down from a wooded hillside.

In the rain, the filmmakers hauled their equipment down into the ditch, but it was too narrow to set up the tripods. Because the Aeroscope was compact and required no hand-cranking—a chamber of compressed air kept it spooling—Claude could run it in the narrowest of spaces, even when he was on the move. He leaned against a sandbag, crouched low to the ground, and panned the fields on the other side of the road. There were bodies lying in the wet grass and he could tell they'd been there for days. At the Salpêtrière in Paris, Claude had photographed disease progressions and autopsies, so he knew something about the gas-filled ministrations of a corpse, the way a body bloated with nitrogen and phosphorus. Turning blue-white and rigid in the rain and heat, these dead men assumed various poses, some of them sitting bolt upright, others reclining with their hands clasped in front of them, poised to make a speech from the afterlife.

Claude turned the camera from the dead back to the living. When they'd first arrived, the village holdouts had been young men in vivid uniforms; now they were boys and grizzled old men in shirtsleeves. A Belgian mastiff—one of the dogs the army used for hauling the machine-gun battery like a sled—lay curled and sleeping in the ditch.

Claude wanted to go out to the bend in the road, out toward the wooded perimeter of the hillside behind them, to see if he could get some images of the skirmish from above. Almost all of his shots so far were low and lacked perspective; he wanted an angle that would capture the field strewn with bodies and the smoking, leafless trees along the roadway. He wanted audiences, from Brooklyn to San Francisco, to understand this desolation.

He told Chip and Hal his plan and moved along the ditch with his suitcase in one hand, the rolling Aeroscope in the other, the Graflex attached to the tripod on his back. Before he got to the bend in the road, a reservist who introduced himself as a tram conductor insisted on having his moving image taken. He was a gunner now, in charge of a lone mortar, his hands blackened from cordite. *My mother and sisters can watch this when I'm gone.* He said it in Flemish, and one of the French-speaking boys nearby translated it for Claude. He turned the camera and filmed a few seconds of the barrel-chested man grinning under his waxed mustache.

The gap between the ditch and the edge of the wood was no more than twenty feet. But in order to get across it, Claude asked the former tram conductor to provide some cover. The gunner sent artillery fire into the German thicket up above, briefly quelling the volleys of the machine gunners, while Claude edged out into the gap on his stomach, dragging the suitcase along the ground beside him, the weight of the Graflex and tripod pressing against his back. When he reached the start of the wood, he crawled then got to his feet, hurried for a stand of oaks and pinewoods. He crouched behind a big tree and waited for the German machine gunners to start up again, but an eerie silence fell over the road and opposite hillside.

From up on the rise he could see that the field of bodies stretched a few hundred feet, that there were dozens of dead men and horses out there, that the Germans had artillery dugouts deep in the opposing woods. In the relative quiet, the sound traveled along the spine of the hills, so he could hear smatterings of German and French and Dutch.

The battery dog in the Belgian ditch barked a single time, apparently startled by the quiet. In this unofficial pause he removed the tripod and Graflex from his back, pumped air into the Aeroscope, and loaded it with fresh film. He aimed the aperture through a clearing and waited for the fighting to begin again. Five minutes of quiet passed, then fifteen. It began to rain again and then it poured down. From this vantage point, the muddy water in the field and ditches became runnels of tarnished silver.

When the greenish flaming arcs finally shot out of the German thicket, Claude began to roll film. Rockets pin-wheeled into high parabolas over the roadway, some of them exploding in midair, erupting into brief clouds of light, before streaming into capillaries of smoke. To make a moviegoer understand war, he thought, all he had to do was keep the film rolling and capture the explosion of light in a downpour. But then the rockets began veering toward the wood and the ridgeline, splintering the treetops and setting the upper branches aflame. A rocket shot into the trees, less than twenty feet away, and there was an enormous flash all around him.

He found himself on his back, deafened, staring up through the oak crowns. He blinked, unable to move, watching the leaves delicately thread with smoke. His eyeglasses were still on his face but one lens was cracked. The first few shards of sound came back but they were distant and underwater. Then there was another observer, standing behind his thoughts and the hairline fissure in his spectacles, someone unhurried and speculative, who studied the purling smoke overhead and thought about the violinist's horse and Sabine's slender hands, about the sprigs of lavender she used to wrap inside her traveling trunks of clothes and bedsheets.

He watched the oak leaves vibrate in the rain while this mental river floated by. He saw his own reflection in the diamond-headed horse's eye and knew it was a kind of preparation, a moment of staring into his own fate. He waited for it to happen, felt at peace with it, but then his ribs were trembling and he realized he was covered in blood.

Coming back to his own body, he sat up and clutched his stomach. The wood was on fire from below, a line of burning trees moving uphill. He got to his knees, mouth open, squinting through the smoke, and began to search on all fours for his cameras and tripod and suitcase. Eventually he found them buried under mounds of dirt and leaves and shattered tree limbs. He got to his feet, staggered away from the flames, up the ridgeline with his suitcase and cameras, using the tripod as a makeshift crutch, deeper into the wood. Behind him, still from under the waves of artillery, he heard the muffled, distorted sound of the Belgians yelling and the machine-gunner dog barking. Then he heard the faint ticking of the Aeroscope, felt it whirring in his hand. For a brief moment, he had the sensation of holding his own beating heart inside a balled fist.

23

The Belgian Woods

When the moon set it was so black he could barely see his own trembling hands. He'd once been nimble in the darkroom, had learned to plumb hidden spaces under Albert Londe's direction at the hospital, so he settled at the base of a tree and dragged the suitcase across his lap, opened its latches, and let his fingertips probe the compartments. In the first aid kit, he found two fresh bandages, some gauze, a bottle of rubbing alcohol; in the mess kit there were four tins of preserved meat, some crackers, half a canteen of water.

He lifted his bloodied shirt and began to unpeel the soaked bandage. As the air made contact with his wounds, he heard his own howling voice and closed his eyes. For an instant he saw his dead mother and sister, Ada and Odette, sitting at the kitchen table in his childhood home. They stared up at him as he took a seat.

All day he'd thought he was going to collapse and die, but instead he'd merely fainted half a dozen times, no more than a blink, the flick of a light switch. When he pressed the rubbing alcohol back into his wounds, into the dozen welts studded across his chest and stomach, he knew he'd fainted again because he came to with his hands limp in the dirt. He breathed through his mouth, looked into the darkness, unrolled a fresh bandage over the squares of gauze. For added pressure, he tore strips of muslin from the wrappings of the film canisters and tied them around his ribs.

He leaned back against the tree and felt inside the suitcase again. The Belgian Red Cross had given each of them a vial of morphine, a token of wartime thanks for their efforts, and it gave him some measure of comfort, rubbing the edges of the wooden case with his fingertips, imagining the moment when he would allow himself to swim into an ocean of morphine. He'd resolved not to use any of it for the pain so that he could escape it all at once if the time came.

Above the treetops, somewhere far-off, searchlights panned the night sky and he could hear distant ordinance. It was the sound of surf detonating on a reef. Inside his fever, there were moments when he felt himself receding, where he became nothing but the erratic pulse of his own thoughts. This was faintly familiar to him, a distant memory of his convalescence in the attic. In the woods, as he staggered along with the suitcase, he'd found himself unpacking his mind as if to spread his life out on a table, assembling his childhood, his mother's death, his years in Paris, Odette's hospitalization, the Lumières, his obsession with Sabine, the rise and fall of the film company, one event after the next, arranged in a row, because the chronology seemed important but also tenuous. On the night of *The Electric Hotel*'s premiere he'd imagined that the cascading events of his life had led him to a cinematic cathedral, to a thousand people waiting to be immersed in his visions, but those same events had, in fact, also conspired to place him in these woods with his insides seeping against cotton bandages.

During the night, he slept in short fevered bursts, waking to stare into the darkened wood, sometimes wondering where and who he was. He could feel his heart beating in the serrated edges of his shrapnel wounds. The same impartial stranger who'd stared up into the quaking leaves right after the explosion on the hillside was still there, puzzling it all out, the way that pain slowed time, the countless inventory of hours and seconds. *Our bodies are made of time*, the stranger said to Claude.

❧

In the dawning light, there was smoke rising through the trees, no more than a mile away. Claude tried to eat a handful of mushrooms he'd foraged the day before, but he couldn't get past their fungal reek. He smoked a Chesterfield to calm his shaking hands and surveyed his torso. His wounds were beginning to turn. He knew it from the malty, acrid smell and the blooms of verdigris and yellow in the gauze bandages. He packed up the suitcase, fastened the latches and straps, slung the Graflex and tripod on his back, got to his feet by first rolling into a crawl and then forcing himself into a kneel. It was clear to him by now that he was unwilling to die in the woods without his equipment, that not a single camera or canister could be left behind to lighten his load. With both hands against a tree trunk, he supported his weight and pushed himself gradually upright.

When he was standing, he leaned his head against the tree to throw up several times. His eyes felt bruised and tender and they kept flooding with tears. But either he was going to get back down on the forest floor and empty the vial of morphine into his arm, or he was going to find the source of the smoke. A burning village, fleeing refugees, a German outpost, or a Belgian sortie, it didn't much matter. Staying in the woods meant the certainty of death. He crouched slowly, keeping his torso stiff, and reached for the suitcase handle. He walked toward the smoke, picked a line through the trees.

In a quarter mile he came onto an exposed meadow down below the ridgeline. A few sheep grazed in the drowsy, early light. He skirted the edge of the clearing and looked out from a stone ledge. He could see a macadam road and a blackened church steeple jutting above the tree crowns. The exact source of the smoke was unclear. It drifted up in broad sheets and ribbons, thinned out into an acre of sun-streaked fog. Suitcase in hand, he hobbled downhill along a narrow footpath. He limped out of the trees, shambling into the broadening daylight.

From the roadside ditch he saw roofless stone houses and the hulk of the church. Fragments of stained glass—blue and vermillion—clung to gothic portals in triangles of lead. A German tricolor had been draped over a fountain in the square, and furniture lay in piles on the cobblestone, battlements of armoires and kitchen tables. A pyramid of chairs and clothing burned nearby but there were no villagers to be seen. A gray-green field car stood parked at the head of the square.

Then he noticed there was a soldier in a spiked helmet crouched against the hood, his Mauser raised and aimed at this bookish traveling gypsy, some Belgian peasant or refugee wandering in from the woods with a suitcase of stale bread and family heirlooms. But there might also be dynamite in the suitcase, or a stolen civic guard revolver, and the getup on his back could have been a rifle attached to a tripod. In his delirium, Claude felt connected to the wire of the soldier's thoughts, felt it uncoiling from the barrel of his gun.

The soldier yelled indecipherably. Claude set the suitcase on the ground and raised his arms into the air. Two other soldiers appeared. They came toward him, three of them, weapons raised, including a rifle with its bayonet attached. He had imagined this moment of contact many times, pictured the way he would approach a German checkpoint with a sense of friendly caution. Now that it was here, the probability of being shot seemed overwhelming. Claude reached very slowly into his pocket for the handkerchief-sized silk American flag. He didn't have the strength to wave it, so he just held it in front of his chest and said *Hoch der Kaiser!* half-heartedly. He tried to remember the storyline of working for a German consortium of newspapers back in the United States. He had been separated from his journalist colleagues during the bombardment beyond the woods.

The first word he understood from the Germans was *spion*. Before her death, his Austrian mother had rarely spoken German around the house, and her native tongue was often a source of embarrassment to her. But it always crept into her French pronunciation, a bony hand inside a satin glove. They were calling him a spy, gesturing for him to open his suitcase. In the gap between his Franco-American English and their Prussian or Bavarian or Austrian style of German there was bound to be confusion. It was a linguistic canyon where he might be shot for a botched vowel or unnatural pause.

Then one of them, a fresh-faced enlistee, said in perfect English:
   —We would like you to open the suitcase or we'll have to shoot.

Claude put the American flag back in his pocket, removed the Graflex and tripod from his back, kneeled beside the briefcase, laid it flat, unlatched the lid. When he spoke, his voice was hoarse and thin.

—American, journalist camera operator. I am covering the war for some German newspapers in America.

—Which papers?

Two names came to him.

—*Der Deutsche Correpondent . . . Scranton Wochenblatt.*

—Open the suitcase.

Claude breathed and steadied his hands. He lifted the lid to reveal the film canisters and equipment, the rations and first aid kit. There was a flurry of indignant German among the men.

—What are you filming with the cameras?

—My colleagues and I were on the other side of the hills. I was separated from them during the battle.

—Bring the suitcase and stand up.

Claude latched the suitcase lid and got to his feet, one hand clutching his stomach where blood was again seeping through his shirt. The soldiers pointed with their rifles, this time toward the village square. He walked along the road, the three of them a few feet behind.

As if to explain his flawless accent, the English speaker said:

—I am Lance Corporal Marcus Kaufer. I lived in the Bronx before the war. Almost American, I was. Played baseball in a church league championship . . . keep walking toward the fountain. My sister still lives in Schenectady. Do you know it?

—Yes. I live in New York most of the year.

—But your accent is different. You were not born there.

—No, he said, staggering along. I've lived in many places.

They led him into the square, where facades were missing from houses and inns, exposing a cross-section of rooms and copper plumbing. A bathtub in a decimated attic still had a white towel laid across its rim. A black lacquered piano had been dropped into a cobblestone courtyard, its innards sprawled in all directions.

Around a bend: two German officers, pistols holstered, sitting at an ornate mahogany dining room table out in the street. The table was spread with empty wineglasses, bread and jam, a jewelry box, a field telephone, battle-field maps. Kaufer gave a brief summary of what had transpired out on the road. The officers looked at Claude the whole time. He was holding the tiny American flag again, clutching it over his bleeding middle. One of the officers stood up from the table and approached, Marcus Kaufer retained as translator.

—The commandant would like to review your documents and posses-sions. Please put all your things on the table. Empty your pockets out as well.

Claude struggled to lift the suitcase but he managed to set it on the table. He opened the lid and went through the compartments. He laid out his American passport, the letter from the Belgian Red Cross, and the *laissez-passer*. The commanding officer had a distracted, theoretical air, and he studied the documents closely, holding one letter up into the pale smoky sunshine. He murmured something to himself, spoke a few words of German to his underling, before turning his attention to the suitcase.

He methodically removed each item and placed it on the table, forming several neat rows. To handle the bloodied gauze, he first put on his leather field gloves. When everything was removed, he studied each item—craning up into the viewfinder of the Aeroscope, or examining the backs of the lewd postcards, perhaps for signs of cryptic marks or handwriting. When he came to the notebook, the pages scribbled with annotations about shooting reels and locations and times of day, Claude realized everything was written in French. The kid from the Bronx was already onto his accent anyway. But the officer seemed unfazed as he turned the pages of the notebook. Then Claude remembered that he'd sealed his French passport behind the silk lin-ing in the suitcase, in an envelope just below the cowhide exterior. That could be the linchpin for his undoing.

The officer said a few words in German and the private relayed them to Claude.

—We will take you to see a medic. And the commander will retain your possessions in the meantime. For safekeeping. He would also like to make a detailed inventory.

Claude breathed through a flare-up of pain.

—As an American, I'm a neutral party. You've got no right to detain me.

—Everything will be all right.

Claude watched as two soldiers began to make an inventory of his possessions, one of them writing down the items in a field book as the other called out the German name for the object. As the soldier led him toward the gray Mercedes he heard the words from behind him—*pornographie*, *kamera*, *zigarette*, *film* . . . Then he recognized the word *Morphium* and it struck him with its beauty and power. It sounded like the name of a battleship, H.M.S. *Morphium*, empress of the opioid oceans, guardian of sleep. He realized his ears had been ringing ever since the explosion in the woods, the world shunting and soughing, but now everything slackened and fell loose about him. As he collapsed into the dirt, this beautiful German word kept breaking over him like a wave . . . *Mor-ph-ium, Moor-ph-iuuuum. Moor-ph-iuuuuuuuum.*

24

The Château

Claude woke propped with feather pillows, the sound of piano music rippling along a stone passageway outside his door. For a moment, without his glasses, he sensed that he'd died in the Belgian woods and this was the afterworld—a stony concerto in the fog of eternity. He blinked and swallowed, turned his head slowly. He reached out a hand next to the bed, an old habit, made a sortie for his spectacles along the wood-grained nightstand, brought the wire frames to his face. The fissure in the right lens brought everything back, the woods, his capture. Through the doorway he could see the top of a broad stairwell, a wall of sconces and baroque tapestries. And there was a man sitting in a chair at his bedside. It was the English speaker from the roadside, the kid from the Bronx.

The German looked at him over the rim of a field manual, nodding to the gravitas of the music. Pulling the bedsheet back, Claude saw that there were fresh bandages wrapped around his stomach, sections of taped gauze on his chest. When he lifted the edge of a bandage he could see a miniature railway of sutures, the skin pinched and blue-gray along the seams.

 —They sewed you up at the *Feldlazarett*.
Claude looked up at the raftered ceiling.

—I am Lance Corporal Marcus Kaufer. We met in the village. Do you remember?

Claude nodded, winced. His head had been replaced with an anvil.

—Where are my things?

—Downstairs. The Oberstleutnant is eager to meet you. Can you hear him at the piano? He's quite well known for his Brahms. As a youngster, he performed in Berlin concert halls. I will fetch you something to put on.

Kaufer dug through an armoire and produced a gingham nightshirt. He came over to the bed, lifted Claude's arms one by one, and slipped his head through the collar.

—There is food and company downstairs. You must be famished.

Kaufer extended his elbow and Claude grimaced as he turned his upper body for the first time.

The lance corporal led him out into the stone passageway and down the stairwell, one careful step at a time. Hanging from the walls were gold-threaded tapestries—visitations and saints—and a series of brooding portraits, Flemish ancestors with their mastiffs and blowzy wives. The oriental strip of rug felt warm against Claude's bare feet all the way down the stairs, but there was a chilling smell of moss and wet slate to the air.

On the bottom landing, Kaufer led him gingerly into a sun parlor, where a group of officers were standing around a white grand piano in their full regalia—gray-green tunics, polished boots, spurs, dress swords, walnut-colored leather holsters. Claude suddenly became conscious of his bare knees and the flimsy gingham nightshirt.

The white piano and the Oberstleutnant were directly beneath a skylight. The officer looked up, nodded, and finished playing his passage. He had a brash, Hindenburg-style mustache but feminine, patrician features—small blue eyes and a nose that was narrow and delicate. One hand perched on his scabbard, he came forward and held his other hand out for Claude to shake.

—You will forgive my English in advance, yes? I am Oberstleutnant Graf Bessler, head of the new photographic and information unit in Belgium. We're all very pleased you're arriving here.

He said something to Kaufer while gesturing back out into the hall-way. There was a clicking of heels and the clinking of spurs on the stone floor as the officers followed Bessler out of the sun parlor.

—The Oberstleutnant would like to offer you some refreshments in the dining room, said Kaufer.

They came into a long room with an enormous fireplace and a wall of lead-framed windows that overlooked a garden in high, white bloom. The table could seat twenty in ladder-backed chairs, but Bessler gestured to one end, where a half-eaten smorgasbord was laid out.

—I hope you don't mind, but we had a little nibble before you came down.

—Your English is just fine, said Claude, sitting down.

—And yours! said Bessler, to a hearty round of laughter. For an American.

—There is the matter of my things. My suitcase, my equipment . . .

Bessler spoke in German to Kaufer, who took a seat beside Claude.

—Everything has been carefully safeguarded and put into a room for you to inspect after we eat.

The table was laid out with hunks of rye bread, wedges of cheese, sliced apple, three bottles of schnapps. A Flemish woman appeared in the door-way, eyes down, carrying a pot of stew to the table. She ladled it into ce-ramic bowls and silently handed them around to the officers, Bessler first. Claude was the last to be served. Kaufer translated Bessler's remarks:

—Gentlemen, this may be the last time we eat oxtail stew that is not from a can. The war will have its deprivations, but Paris is not far off. Let us raise a glass to the motherland and the Kaiser!

They all raised a glass except for Claude, who continued to eat. The stew tasted strongly of onions but he couldn't remember the last time he'd eaten a meal. How long had he been lying upstairs? The Germans ate up, dip-ping hunks of rye bread into their bowls and shooting back tiny glasses of schnapps. Kaufer translated between mouthfuls.

—The army unit that swept through here on their way to Louvain was a little overzealous. They removed all the copper pipes and kettles, for ex-ample, from the nearby brewery. They almost stripped out the château's pipes, its plumbing, before I put a stop to things. They mean well, because the metal is taken back to a German foundry for weapons, but I think we've gotten off on the wrong foot . . .

At first, Kaufer translated it as *the wrong shoe*, but then he corrected himself. Claude took a sip of schnapps and it burned his throat.

—War is a series of misunderstandings, if you ask me, Mr. Ballard.

—So far, America agrees with you.

They ate for a few moments without talking. Then Bessler puckered between mouthfuls, chewed around the edges of a question.

—Tell me, how did you come to work for the German newspapers?

—I'm an American, but my mother was Austrian. I got the job through family connections. They were looking for someone to make photographs and reels, to take a neutral position.

—And you grew up in America?

—We traveled a lot for my father's business. But New Jersey has been home for some time.

Bessler nodded.

—Years ago I was in charge of the German Federation of Tourism Agencies, in Berlin, and I entertained journalists from all over the world. We hosted Africans and Slovaks and Australians. I like to think I have an ear for accents, but yours has me stumped. It is a soupy mess, if you don't mind my saying so. A big vat of goulash!

The officers laughed at Kaufer's alternate translations—*messy broth, jumbled stew, soupy mess, vat of goulash.*

—Accents are funny things, said Claude.

He tried to be conscious of his francophone vowels, the way Hal had instructed him to rectify them in the front of his mouth. What had become of Chip and Hal in the aftermath of the hillside fighting? Bessler perched a hunk of cheese onto a stub of rye bread.

—You don't speak German, even though your mother was Austrian?

He inspected the bread from multiple angles before settling on a corner to bite.

—Barely a word. *Nacht* and *bitte* are about the extent of it.

Bessler chewed into a faint smile.

When the meal was over, Kaufer and Bessler led Claude down the hallway while the other officers went outside to smoke cigars. In what looked like a medieval armory—a stone floor with wall sconces, hanging chain mail, and a long wooden table—his suitcase and its contents had been laid out and sorted: the Aeroscope, the cinématographe, the Graflex, the Pathé, the reels, the first aid kit, the opened notebook, all of its pages written in French. The silk lining of the suitcase lid, where he'd carefully sewn in his French passport, had been sliced open. Both his passports—French and American—were neatly arranged beside the suitcase.

Bessler folded his arms and circled the table, picking up an item then carefully placing it back on the table.

—Perhaps your father was French? Ballard is quite Gallic, if you ask me. And you appear to write in French fluently.

—We spent time in France for his business. I went to school a few years there.

—I see. Where in France?

—Alsace-Lorraine.

—Ah, then, practically a part of Germany anyway. Nationality is a complicated matter, don't you agree?

—I should probably check in with the American consulate in Brussels. So they know I am safe.

—Yes, especially since the French consulate has been closed.

Bessler let his spurs scrape on the stone floor—a knife blade on whetstone—before giving Kaufer a chuffed, satisfied smile. He looked like a man who has just finished dressing a Christmas tree.

—As it happens, we have already contacted the authorities to make certain enquiries. Just to verify your status. We cannot be too careful with spies roaming around the countryside. Are your cameras in working order?

Claude picked up the dented Aeroscope and looked through the viewfinder.

—This one looks to be damaged, but I'll have to check the others.

Bessler took out a cigarette from a tin case he carried in his breast pocket. He offered one to Claude and lit it for him. As long as the reels are in metal canisters, Claude thought, the nitrates will be safe. Kaufer took a step back, translating but out of their field of vision.

—I am a great admirer of American films . . . We are slowly coming around to this kind of art in Germany, but for now my friends in the General

Staff of the army are hesitant. They want to make propaganda films that are nothing but iron eagles and unfurling flags. If we want to win over the American mind and heart, I believe we must appeal to their love of entertainment.

He circled the table, one hand along the edge.

—To this end, we are setting up a film company in New York, which will handle distribution. There is even talk of buying a small chain of theaters. I wonder if you might consider being our cameraman on the frontlines, to see this war from a German vantage point. Some films will be for the American market and some for Germany, for the men who stoke the fires. Would you consider our invitation? After all, you have had quite the American film career already. You understand the moviegoer from Manhattan to Maine.

Bessler grinned, delighted with his phrasing. Claude looked out the window where the German officers were standing on the flagstone patio, sending up filaments of cigar smoke under a canopy of trees.

—You know my work?

—You are far too modest to introduce yourself as a German newspaperman. We've been lucky enough to see some of the Bender & Ballard films back in Berlin. And even though my colleagues would criticize such a stance, I am still a fan of Sabine Montrose. They all think she is a symbol of French hedonism.

Bessler let out a smoky breath.

—But, if you ask me, Claude Ballard, art is art, wherever it blooms.

Claude looked again at the open suitcase, his life emptied and arranged.

—In the short term, we will need to send your photographs and footage to Berlin for developing, but soon enough we will set you up with your own laboratory. I wonder if you might inspect all of your equipment to make sure it's in working order. And don't worry about extra film. Rest assured, we have brought plenty of that with us. Tomorrow, we will go into Louvain for our first shooting expedition.

Bessler picked up the two passports and tapped them on the edge of the table.

—And I will hold on to these for safekeeping. Very well, we will leave you to it. Kaufer will be just outside in the hallway should you need anything.

Bessler turned, took a step, then came back.

—Oh, and if you know your prescription, we will arrange to have new spectacles made for you. We can't have you be the eyes of the German people unless you can see without impairment.

Claude was surprised by how calm he felt in the armory, alone with his cameras. Something had dropped away in the Belgian woods, the rotating shutter of death so close at hand, so that the idea of being held captive, of being shuttled through the German hinterland of war, seemed almost impersonal, an event wired in from afar. He realized he no longer cared what happened to him. The ache and anger over Sabine also seemed distant, abstract, as if he'd closed the pages of a wearying novel. He asked Kaufer to fetch him some dusting cloths and a work lamp and hunched over the long table.

It comforted him to disassemble and clean the cameras one mechanism at a time. The inside of a camera or projector had always been a sanctuary of mechanical logic, the gears and sprockets and chambers like the workings of a clock. Time could be parsed by a second hand or by light exposure, the present calibrating into the past, and he liked to think he had some control over its passage with a pair of needle-nose pliers in hand, straightening a set of metal teeth or loosening the tension in a wheel. If the tension wasn't right, if something wobbled, then it was written into the frame. If a speck of dust or grit or a thumbprint attached itself to the meniscus of the lens then everything was lost.

The Pathé, Graflex, and cinématographe were sturdy designs and had come through relatively unscathed, but the Aeroscope had been dropped in the woods. Its lens mounting had detached, allowing light to seep into the main chamber. When he opened the side gate he already knew the footage of the hillside bombardment had been exposed and ruined. There was, perhaps, a way to solder the lens in place and seal the inside with tape, but he found himself extracting the film and using the brass air pump to refill the autowind feature. He listened to the quiet pneumatic hissing, watched the sprockets and spools turn. Then something occurred to him from deep within this mechanical reverie.

He remembered the trick cameras in the Manhattan camera supply store, Appleton's, the way Cora had been fascinated with the Photoret, the pocket watch camera for private detectives, with its tiny discs of celluloid, and the Minigraph, which rolled film automatically, powered by compressed air, and fit into the palm of your hand. It was, essentially, an Aeroscope built at one tenth the scale.

Claude didn't have a way to scale down the workings of the Aeroscope, but it occurred to him that he had a way to hide them inside the chamber of the big wooden Graflex. He opened the larger camera and began to take measurements. If he drilled a small hole in the bottom corner of the front faceplate, he could position the Aeroscope lens and gears behind it, snug beneath the nonmoving parts. He could coil the small tube where the compressed air fed from the hand pump inside, visible only if the camera was fully open. A small lever on the bottom could release the air so that the mechanisms could move within, without any hand-cranking. A Trojan horse camera, an eye within an eye. It would allow him to film things the Germans didn't want him to capture.

When Kaufer came to check on his progress several hours later, Claude told him the Aeroscope was ruined, but he could use it for spare parts.

—The others still need some work. A few more hours.

The lance corporal went to resume his hallway post. From outside the door, he said:

—Do not stay up all night. The Oberstleutnant wants you well rested for our big day of shooting tomorrow.

25

The Sack of Louvain

For a week they made filming expeditions into Louvain. Bessler provided Claude with new glasses and a uniform, something to set him apart and underscore his ambiguous nationality—an American army shirt, a pair of British riding breeches, French puttees, and a blue Highlander's forage cap. The suitcase stayed back at the château, but he carried a tripod, spare film, and two cameras—the Pathé in hand and the modified Graflex strapped to his side, big as a parlor phonograph.

As they drove the Opel staff car into Louvain each day, Claude saw that the roadways were full of fleeing villagers. He couldn't film them without being noticed but he made a point of remembering certain images. Men trundling wheelbarrows with infants aboard, old women hobbling along with bread and potatoes in pillowcases. A young barefoot girl in her nightgown carrying a canary in a wire cage.

In the city, the gothic university smoldered, its library transformed into catacombs of plaster and rubble. Thousands of volumes had been plundered and lit on fire, so that the streets blew with the papery embers of medieval texts and nineteenth-century novels, with ashen leaves of cryptic prose.

•

Claude took his direction about what to film from Bessler, who moved about the smoking ruins and shuttered storefronts like Cecil B. DeMille on the set of an epic, a tin whistle around his neck on a silver chain. He would ask a group of clean-shaven infantrymen to pose in front of a decimated church or beside a goulash cannon, briefly frame the scene between his hands, then instruct Claude to begin filming, first with the motion picture camera, then with the still. *Perhaps you can angle up to get the Kaiser's flag flapping from the bell tower as well, Mr. Ballard, so we get a sense of the scaling.* His stage directions came through Lance Corporal Kaufer, complete with the interpreter's own errors, omissions, and misunderstandings. *How does it look like in the* fotoapparat? *Is the light vexing?*

While Bessler and Kaufer scouted out the next location and scene, Claude kept his finger on the small lever he'd fashioned at the bottom of the Graf-lex, spooling the second camera within. He could keep the box camera by his side, at waist-height, looking in the other direction, while the Aero-scope sprockets laced through the perforations in the celluloid. It wasn't soundless, but there was enough atmospheric noise—distant ordinance, the singing of soldiers, the revving of touring cars—that it went unno-ticed. In this way, he captured corpses of women and children mutilated by bayonets, a dozen Jesuit priests made to line up naked against a yellow sandstone wall, a ditch filled with dead horses, a mountain of smoldering books.

Since he barely looked at these images while he was filming them, it was only back at the château that they scoured through him. He'd been al-lowed to convert a small pantry adjacent to the armory into a darkroom with a red safelight. After he sealed the film stock bound for the official lab in Berlin, he removed the Aeroscope reel and placed it into a canister. Since Bessler and Kaufer wouldn't risk exposing propaganda footage by opening the darkroom door, Claude knew he had time to secure a good hiding place. He moved the mat that stood at the entrance to the pantry, pried up three floorboards, and placed the canister below. As long as he was careful and Bessler didn't count the linear feet of celluloid, he could perhaps keep aside ten percent of the film he was given for the Trojan camera.

•

He sat cross-legged on the pantry floor, bathed in the phosphorous atmosphere of the safelight, the day's plunder falling through him. Across one dead woman's chest an infantryman had carved his initials. And there was a field of human limbs and Belgian blue cloth back behind the cathedral. When he closed his eyes, he felt the stranger breathing inside, the silent witness and cataloguer from the woods.

Bessler insisted that Claude eat dinner with the officers in the main dining room every night, his motley uniform a source of tableside amusement. They ate beef from a nearby farm and whatever vegetables the Belgian cook could pull from the garden. After dinner, they asked Claude to show some reels with his cinématographe, and he was surprised to find that it was the falling cat that delighted the Germans the most, the veracity of a cat landing on its feet from a height.

One night, after a piano concert and a screening, Bessler invited the men to gather around the field telephone in the parlor. He took the receiver from a young private and waited, one eye closed. *My orderly has just made the connection with Berlin . . . ah, quiet please, here we are!* Claude stood off to one side, expecting a speech to come through from a general or high commander, but instead came the sound of a man's baritone voice reciting Goethe. He couldn't understand more than a few lines, porting them from German to French, but then Kaufer dutifully laid them out in English: *The dust rises, in the middle of the night . . . no, in lower, in deep night . . . when on the narrow bridge . . . The traveler shivers . . . or trembles. I hear you, when with a dull roar, the wave is rising. In the quiet grove I often go to listen when all is silent . . .*

The connection dropped before the recital could finish, which brought a pained expression to Bessler's face. The orderly offered to try again, but the Oberstleutnant waved him off and kept repeating *tiefer Nacht*, deep night, as he surveyed the gently drunk men before him. *Gentlemen, Antwerp awaits. Very soon, it will be time to cross that narrow bridge.* He said good night to them all, put one hand on the scabbard of his dress sword, and retired for the evening. He'd claimed the ornate guest bedroom in the stone tower of the château, the bedroom where, according to the housemaid, Franz Liszt had once slept and written a symphonic poem.

26

Antwerp

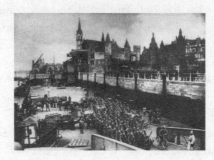

Chip couldn't shake the feeling that Claude Ballard had stolen his fate. He thought about the way he'd cheated a fiery death a thousand times and then here was the Frenchman, haplessly wandering into the blaze with a suitcase full of silver nitrate film stock, an incendiary device that would have blown him asunder. They'd scrambled up the hillside while the Germans continued to bombard the wood, calling his name, but there was no sign of him, and then the mortar fire threatened to close off the road below. The Belgians retreated and they fled to the Berline, driving north through a hailstorm of shrapnel.

In Antwerp, a month later, as the Germans encircled the city with heavy artillery, Chip found himself imagining Claude's bones, undiscovered for years, bleaching on a Belgian hillside. Or they would silver and scale with all those nitrates. His mind had always flowed this way, toward the morbid resting point of a scenario. In preparation for the attack, the Belgians had cleared the sight lines around the city, leveling chestnut trees and châteaux walls, sowing the potato and beet fields with electrified entanglements. At night, when the army tested the electrifications, the wires sometimes picked up radio signals and crosstalk—flurries of advertisements for laundry soap and Bavarian folk music drifting in from the hinterland. Chip listened to it when he couldn't sleep, and he was sure it was death's faint crackling anthem.

He imagined his old life in Tamarama, clambering up tree ropes and falling from the wire, forever slicked with fire gel. Claude Ballard had appeared like some Gallic philosopher, screening his titillations in the musk and brine of the sideshow tent for gypsy acrobats and the foremen alike, then shambling up to Chip's lean-to that dusk, big-knuckled hands butterflying behind his back. Say he'd never wandered up that day. Would Chip have lost an arm by now to a tiger shark, or would he have skulked home to his mother and her vellum-paged bible? Would he be breaking horses on some droughty fringe of land out west? He was submerged at night, pressed under the surf of his own thoughts.

He had an inkling to go volunteer with the Munro Ambulance Corps after he and Hal were done filming the German advance on Antwerp. Since he was too short to enlist with the Australian Imperial Force, he could make himself useful hauling the wounded from the trenches to the field hospitals. He would be calm and calculating in a crisis, giving well-annunciated orders to those around him. Hadn't he always been the one with the clear head and eyes when everyone around him went squiffy with fright? He'd seen graziers and actors and showmen faint at the sight of blood, or wobble when a situation turned flinty. In fact, when everyone stood like wax figurines during the tiger attack on the set of *The Electric Hotel*, he'd been the one to bound up the stairs, seize Rex Lander's revolver, and fire two bullets into the side of the big jungle cat's brindled neck.

They'd been able to buy equipment and film stock from a Pathé agent fleeing Antwerp. When the reels were finished, Hal was going to take them to England and tour for the Red Cross, donating the profits to their cause. While they waited for the siege, they lived in a three-story redbrick row house full of expats, journalists, and photographers in the southeastern quarter of the city. They lived on the top floor, *Collier's Weekly* and the *Chicago Tribune* were on the second floor, and the Dutch vice-consul had the first floor all to himself. Rents were cheap, the neighborhoods thinning out by the hour and the day. The war tourists had all fled the city after a zeppelin night raid dropped a dozen bombs on the Place Verte in late August.

•

Because nobody seemed to know when or how the advance would happen, Chip traded cigarettes and brandy for information from the garrisoned soldiers. The Germans were hauling Big Berthas and Škodas from Essen by train, then using teams of circus horses to move them into a wide perimeter around the city. Each thousand-pound shell had a range of nearly eight miles, so it was clear the attack was never going to come by road or field, that the city had felled its trees and hedgerows for nothing. *A game of shuttlecock* was the unofficial phrase in the garrisons, an eight-mile lob over the net of fortifications and electrified entanglements.

In late September, Hal and Chip stood on a hillside filming the first bombardment. A balloonist sent radio signals back to the Germans to improve their aim against the fortifications while the artillery fire riffled against the sheer blue sky. A Bertha shell began as a distant, throaty recoil, then it became a thrashing copper wire in the air. It continued to thrash and keen for a second after impact, a sonic afterimage as it gouged a house-sized divot into the beehives of concrete and men. Chip felt the shock waves a quarter mile away, felt it chatter into his teeth and testicles.

By early October, the Belgian king had fled to the coast and the British evacuated the city with London double-decker buses. Along the Scheldt, thousands of refugees crammed into skiffs, barges, and ferryboats bound for Holland. The mayor of Antwerp surrendered on October 10 and the first German soldiers entered the city—a battalion of cyclists, rifles slung over their shoulders, singing "Die Wacht am Rhein" in two-part harmony.

Hal and Chip filmed the advance from the balcony of the American consulate: thousands of soldiers on a torrent of kettledrums, uhlan lancers on feathered horses, the infantry in knee-high boots with green sprigs in their lapels and thin cigars clenched between their teeth. When the field artillery rumbled across the cobblestone, the city's few remaining windowpanes rattled, the cannoneers sitting inscrutable and Buddha-like atop their caissons.

The city had been without municipal water or services for a week, so it reeked of garbage, unflushed drains, and sewers. The sanitation and signal corps detached and fanned out singing into the empty, putrid streets and boulevards, already at work to make the city habitable again. A column of cyclists unrolled telephone wires and began to attach them to street lamps and electric posts. Fire hoses were uncoiled and opened out against the grime.

Hal aimed the Pathé at an open lorry bed that was carrying dozens of violins in their slender, curved black cases. *An entire division of serenaders*, he said to Chip. Then came a fleet of Opel staff cars, their gray hoods raked and winking in the sunshine, the officers holding stiff salutes against their hat brims for an imaginary audience.

In one touring car, Hal could see a cameraman hand-cranking footage, perched across the luggage mount from the backseat. He seemed to be filming the sanitation and signal corps as they wended through the streets. Through the viewfinder, Hal could see only a sliver of the man's face behind the camera, darkened by the shadow of his peaked forage cap, but he noticed he was overcranking the film, which would slow and dull the march when it was eventually projected.

A month later, when Hal developed the reels for the Red Cross tour, he would see Claude Ballard's face flicker into view above the luggage mount of the Opel staff car. He would make telephone calls and write letters to the American Legation, send a telegram to Chip declaring Claude Ballard officially resurrected. But for now he was oblivious, side-mouthing a comment to Chip about the amateurishness of German propaganda. He panned elsewhere, got caught up in the Škodas arriving like hundreds of telescopes craned up at the stars.

The road to the coast was so clogged with refugees that Hal and Chip eventually decided to leave the Berline and travel on foot. They loaded their equipment into a wheelbarrow and fell in with Flemish peasants and factory workers. The potato fields were trampled and trimmed in barbed wire, the roadsides dotted with wooden crosses. Farmers let their livestock wander across the landscape, sheep and cattle and pigs, set their houses and barns on fire as a departing gift for the Germans.

•

After two days of walking and then riding on a London double-decker bus, they arrived in Ostend, where Taube airplanes whinnied overhead. The pilots dropped hand-bombs from their open-air cockpits, fired their pistols at refugees as they loaded onto steamers. Hal and Chip waited for the steamer to Dover among the hordes of people at the docks. To avoid inspection on the other side of the English Channel, Hal would leave the cameras with Chip and travel with the celluloid sewn into the lining of his heavy overcoat. From Dover, he would travel to the Red Cross headquarters in London.

They stood saying goodbye as the steamer filled with panicked crowds. British soldiers were forcing families to leave behind their household effects to make more room on the ship, so the docks were littered with china, farm implements, chairs, wheelbarrows, carpets. Donkey carts laden with mattresses and bundles of clothes wandered along the sand dunes, unattended.

A cold breeze came off the North Sea. Chip blew into his hands, craned up at a droning Taube.

—When will you go back to America?

—Once the reels have toured England. I'd like to show them in New York and Chicago and San Francisco next.

They stared over at the gangplank, where a crate of chickens was being passed overhead, back down to the docks.

—I'll make enquiries about Claude's family, make sure they're notified, said Hal.

A silence settled in below the wind off the dunes. Chip saw the image of Claude's unclaimed bones silvering and bleaching on a hillside again.

—When Claude and I traveled out into the bush, and he was trying to get me to come to America . . . you know what he said about you?

—What?

—That he'd received a letter of interest from a gifted moving picture salesman, a Brooklyn kid who sounded like he could sell lace undergarments to a nun. He called you a salesman extraordinaire.

Hal laughed at this.

—Hasn't done me much good up to this point. But who knows, this could be a fresh start. Maybe I'll see you in Hollywood when all this is over. A burning man is always in high demand.

Chip grinned, shook his head.

—That last burn just about killed me.

They both surveyed the smoking line of warships against the darkening horizon.

—Well, do me a favor and don't get yourself killed hauling stretchers for the ambulance corps.

—At this point, I consider the grim reaper a little hanky I carry around in my back pocket. Pressed and folded like a church lady's tear blotter . . .

They shook hands, then Chip bundled Hal into a two-armed embrace. He could smell the celluloid and feel the heaviness of Hal's gabardine trench coat.

Chip watched Hal merge into the welter of moving people and baggage. He remembered the stories of Hal hustling along Flatbush Avenue as a teenager, drawing in the noonday crowd with his banter and sandwich board signs, and he could see him clearly, this streetwise kid rocking on his heels and looking into the depths of a moviegoer's want. Somehow he'd known the medium's real power before Edison or the Lumières, understood that it was a silver mirror more than a big blue window. People wanted escape, sure, but first they wanted the shock of recognition.

Turning from the docks, Chip conjured a future for Hal in California. He settled on a new life with Hal as impresario and studio boss, camelhair collar up, double-breasted suit lapels shining under a chandelier. He saw the big sloping maw of an American automobile, the beachside house with the view, the wife from the art department or typing pool, because Hal never did have the stomach for actresses. He'd choose a girl who seemed like she could have grown up on Flatbush Avenue. When Chip imagined himself in California all he could see was the tin and cobalt of the Pacific, a return to the ocean, a meeting with Tamarama's distant, northern cousin.

In the town of Furnes, twenty miles south, Chip volunteered as a driver for the Munro Ambulance Corps. He lived with a group of British nurses and doctors, but also aristocrats and novelists and painters who'd volunteered for the cause. They slept in the dormitories of a Catholic college where the classrooms were converted into wards, the cellars into operating theaters. The college professors worked as orderlies, Keats scholars and chemists cleaning grates and sweeping floors and writing letters for the wounded.

Chip drove into Dunkirk for the mail and to buy provisions each day before joining the twenty ambulances that left for the front at night. They gathered the wounded along the Yser River, from dressing-stations near the trenches, and brought them to the waiting ambulance trains. At midnight, the trains shunted back into Furnes with the evacuated soldiers. Red Cross orderlies unloaded the men—studded with shrapnel, gaping with wounds—and took them to the college. By the light of guttering candles, the nurses triaged head wounds, tended the shell-shocked and the frostbitten, while down in the wine cellar the surgeons removed limbs and sutured the dying.

When he was off duty, Chip wandered the wards to read aloud or write letters for the convalescing soldiers. The French had called up the entire empire, so that the beds were full of Senegalese and Algerian fighters, Zouaves in mud-covered red trousers and cutaway jackets. They slept on mattresses filled with straw and wood shavings, groaned from the cold in the jaundiced light of tallow candles. Chip also found his way to an orphanage where the children were cared for by nuns and a few volunteers. There was an American woman named Alice Cartwright, a teacher from Santa Barbara. After he finished playing soccer and cards with the boys, she made him cups of tea and offered him milk biscuits she'd kept aside. He brought her nosegays and cowslips, whatever still grew along the roadside ditches, bought her white cotton handkerchiefs at the bazaar.

He sometimes filmed images along the trenches at dawn, after he'd driven the last of the wounded from the dressing stations to the ambulance trains. He'd never had an eye for composition, but he remembered the kinds of things Claude had captured and arranged inside the viewfinder. So he filmed the Christmas Day truce, the impromptu soccer matches out in no-man's-land, the pyramid of spiked German helmets the Belgians kept as war trophies, the fox terrier guarding the stoop of a burned-out house in a ransacked village. He adopted the dog and brought it along, to the delight of Alice and the children at the orphanage.

Death had always been lurking in the folds of Chip's life—in the bearing of a stunt, in the undertow of a blunder or bad luck—but now it was something that fouled up the air. Gangrenous damp wool and cinders and trench foot. The pestilence was so potent that he often found himself smelling the hem of a laundered hand towel, or the leaves of a redwood, as a reprieve from the carnage. He would never see the human body the same way again, the heart like a big fleshy plum sitting inside a man's chest, the ribs flimsy as a wire birdcage. Mid-morning, when he woke from his few hours of sleep after hauling the wounded all night, his first thought was of his own death. Best-case scenario, at thirty-four, he suspected he was halfway there.

By April 1915, the field hospital had been moved to Hooge, and Chip was all out of film. So there was no way to capture Madame Curie and her daughter walking through the X-ray department, or the miasma of the first German chlorine gas attacks, the green-white brume above the trenches. He carried a respirator soaked in hyposulphate, heard his own breathing chug when his ears and throat bloated with fear. When he proposed to Alice Cartwright at the orphanage one spring afternoon he could still taste sulfur in the back of his throat. He was swallowing and blinking back tears when Alice's eyes came up quick and blue and hopeful from the fox terrier in her lap. War seemed to heighten and flatten romance at precisely the same time.

They were married the next day in a Catholic chapel in Hoogestadt, a dozen people in attendance, nurses, doctors, novelists and painters and ambulance drivers. Alice Cartwright, daughter of an elementary school principal, was married in a lilac day dress borrowed from Madame Curie. This would become the glimmering detail they would offer up in the many years of their marriage, the inventor of radium standing that wartime morning in the cloister.

27

Exile

Sabine often thought that she had been preparing for exile her whole life. For years she'd imagined the endless white days in a stone cottage along the Brittany coast, saw herself as an old woman eating solitary meals, moving from room to room in her robe, a dog-eared novel by the bathtub. Her eventual banishment, whenever she'd conjured it, was listless, sun-bleached, and aloof. But after five years of living under an assumed name, she also understood that exile was a kind of devotion. The Catalan herder she employed to tend her sheep and orchards, in his bright sash and floppy red barrettino, lived in a cave and burned votive candles on his ancestral shrine to the Virgin Mary. In her mind, the vigils of exile—the discretion, the banking arrangements, the winter house in Barcelona—were no less devout. In order to maintain the faith, she had to uphold a body of esoteric rules and observances.

Claude Ballard appeared nightly in her dreams and regrets. Often, he was standing at the edge of a mountain lake, pants rolled up, his pale silvery feet immersed in the frigid water, a few trout moping through the stony green shallows nearby. Or he was standing behind his tripod on the suspended stage below the Palisades, hand-cranking his camera while a burning man dangled below a zeppelin. Her visions were animated with tigers and trains, with envelopes addressed to her in menacing cursive.

•

There was also the daily weight of Claude dimming away in Leo's and Cora's memories. At first, she spoke of him as a blood relation who, for complicated reasons, could no longer visit. By the end of the first year, their questions were less frequent, but also more direct. Green-eyed Cora, always ferreting out untruths, asked why he wasn't coming if they were married, to which Sabine replied, *We were never meant to be together. We married not for love, but so we could adopt you both.*

Sabine often held the summer they'd all spent together in her mind, their little tourist camp above the Hudson, as one of the happiest times of her life. But it was also a falsehood, a house of paper and glass. She liked to imagine that she had unburdened him, once and for all, that he might have gone on to other more fortifying loves, perhaps a marriage with children of his own. Each night, though, she felt the truth of the matter uncoil in the pit of her stomach: it was *she* who had been unburdened. Ever since she'd run away on the train to Paris at thirteen, the audacity of leaving had always been her greatest exhilaration. The shedding of a skin. The lighting of new lamps. It was staying in one place—or returning home—that terrified her.

She went by the name Désirée Mouret, after a Zola character, and lived quietly with Leo, Cora, Helena, and a Catalan housemaid. Pavel stayed for months at a time but frequently traveled to give lectures or take up a residency with a theater somewhere. From April through the end of November each year, they lived in the mountainside town of Ordino, in a rambling stone house that had belonged to an Andorran baron. The wife had been murdered—or so the town legend went—and the baron fled with his children to France, leaving his furniture and belongings behind, right down to the sheet music and the chessboard inlaid with lapis butterfly wings.

They usually wintered in Barcelona, or sometimes in Greece or Corsica, where Pavel brought a well-paying international delegation of thespians and directors, followers who'd embraced his framework. Sabine never performed, but she sometimes joined them for their dramatic exercises and workshops, or offered up stories about the triumph of naturalism. *You cannot make progress,* she told them, *until you embrace the indefinable ache.* She signed autographs and they signed nondisclosure agreements. She told them she lived most of the year in the house of a murdered Andorran baroness, a detail they would never forget.

Andorra was a natural hideaway, a hermitage clamped onto a Pyrenean valley, wedged between Spain and France. In its own way, it was a nation of exiles, of people who had turned their backs on the world. A country smaller than Chicago, a principality governed jointly and absently by the president of France and His Serene Highness, the Archbishop of Urgell. A country with two postal systems, one French, one Spanish, and a flock of carrier pigeons that still flew mail out into the deep valleys blocked with snow during the long Pyrenean winters.

Andorrans had a reputation for being taciturn and secretive, a condition, Sabine thought, that came with their mountain hermitage. Their houses were made from dark native limestone, with roofs of blue slate. Many houses were windowless and they sealed the weather and the world out with big wooden shutters. Their secrecy also served a practical function, since they were also great smugglers of tobacco. Every family had an uncle or a cousin who, when he wasn't tending the orchards or sheepfolds, led a mule or two along the Gran Valira river to a clandestine meeting place where he would sell untaxed tobacco or cigarettes to Spaniards and Frenchmen.

The six hundred people who lived in the capital, Andorra la Vella, and the hundred or so who lived around Ordino, all suspected she was in exile, the handsome *vieja* with her teenage children, but from what they couldn't be sure. There was a Hungarian aristocrat and his wife who lived anonymously in the capital, as well as a washed-up British writer, so fleeing a former life was not unheard-of. It wasn't until a merchant began to show novelty films above his store that she noticed the Andorrans staring at her through shop windows or along the stone footpaths. She braced herself for a Catholic backlash, for Catalan women in their mantillas turning her business away at the bakeries and greengrocers, but instead they offered her discounts and knowing looks. Secrets were a kind of currency among the five Andorran parishes, and now she was in their debt.

For Cora's sixteenth birthday, in June 1915, Sabine decided to throw a party and invite the townspeople of Andorra la Vella and Ordino as a way of thanking them for their years of hospitality and discretion. Although Cora didn't attend the local school—she and Leo were tutored by a polyglot Spanish nun and a retired French mathematics professor—word had passed down the valley that the pretty summering American girl was now of marriageable age. So the locals mistook the birthday girl for a debutante, and two hundred townspeople picked their way up the steep rocky path to the limestone house that overlooked the valley. They brought with them all manner of gifts and marital enticements—deeds of trust, sheep, chickens, bushels of barley and wheat, handmade figurines, Catalan embroidery.

The Hungarian aristocrats and the British writer also came, though they kept their distance from each other. Technically, their nations were at war, though the bloody battles named after rivers and woods seemed like abstractions up in the mountains. Andorra, despite not having an army, had also declared war on Germany as a show of allegiance with its parent nations. Sabine sometimes forgot the war was raging to the north, but now she remembered as she saw the Hungarians avoiding the Englishman out on the veranda. They stood at opposite ends of the ironwork railing, looking off into the valley as a cool afternoon breeze blew through the surrounding larches and cypress trees. Cora, looking mortified in a silk frock a local seamstress had made for her, stood over by the cake and punch table, politely accepting sacks of grain and sheaths of tobacco. A sheepherder's boy presented her with a baby chick cupped between two hands and she blushed as the crowd cooed.

Leo, a fourteen-year-old who liked to find the logical flaws in adult arguments, who spent his days with stamps, insects, detective novels, and crosswords and his nights with a telescope, stood talking to the British writer, a man named Reginald Bellows. Sabine watched them from across the room, noticed something solicitous in the way Bellows tilted his head and leaned in whenever Leo was talking. She remembered that the writer only ever introduced himself as Bellows, as if to suggest a chummy boarding school upbringing.

When the candles were blown out, and the birthday songs were sung in three languages, Sabine took two pieces of cake over to the Hungarians and chatted with them for a few minutes. They were polite, a little stiff, the husband mustached and wolfish in his charcoal woolen suit and the wife all in white, dressed as if for a wedding. Then she took two pieces of cake over to Leo and Reginald Bellows, interrupting whatever interrogation was unfolding. The writer took the piece of cake and cut into it with a fork. He spoke between bites.

—I'm surprised you invited the Hungarians.

Sabine licked a flake of icing from her thumb.

—Mr. Bellows, I was rather hoping the war wouldn't make its way above three thousand feet.

They all looked over at the Hungarian couple standing off to one side, silently eating their cake.

—What were you boys talking about?

Leo, his mouth full of cake, said:

—The Huns and our life back in America.

—Don't call them that.

Bellows shifted onto the balls of his feet, clearing his throat.

—I'm surprised you have any affection for the Germans, Madame Mouret, given the predicament in France.

—I like to think of myself as a humanist, not a nationalist.

—Tell that to the Belgians.

—Leo, would you mind helping your sister gather up her gifts? She looks exhausted, poor thing. We'll make some toasts in just a minute.

They both watched Leo cross the veranda with his cake plate in hand. Sabine saw the way the girls looked at him and decided, in that moment, that he needed a haircut and that they would spend the summer in Corsica.

After a silence, Reginald Bellows said:

—Zola, isn't it?

—What's that?

—Désirée Mouret is an obscure character in *The Fortune of the Rougons*, that insufferable twenty-volume novel project he slaved away on.

—It's not a crime to be named after a character from literature.

—Of course not. But I would have thought, now that your films have surfaced here in town, that you'd go back to your birth name.

She felt her breath quicken, then she looked into his face—gin-blossomed and wary, his brashness a kind of compensation. She saw the peevish, fretful boy of his youth, perhaps not bullied in the Anglican boarding school where he learned to masturbate and read Byron, but certainly shunned as an outsider, the boy who quoted Latin proverbs at precisely the wrong moment. She felt into his atmosphere, the little weather front swirling about him.

—Is it true that you once wrote novels?

—Guilty as charged. Emphasis on *once*.

He morselled another bite of cake into his small mouth. She watched him chew, rabbit-like, marveling at the thinness of his lips. She had never trusted a man with a stingy mouth.

—But I have also written essays and journalism over the years. I still write the odd piece that I send to an editor in London.

—It must get lonely, being so far from the literary scene.

—Oh, I prefer it. Far from the hoi polloi . . .

There was a long silence between them.

—Do you get lonely up here, Miss Montrose?

She felt her reply strike the air like a sulfur match.

—If that is flirtation, Mr. Bellows, you might direct it at me instead of at your cake plate.

She watched him redden, saw a glimmer of anger water his eyes.

—It was merely a question, he said, swallowing.

—Well, all the same, I'd appreciate it if you didn't interrogate Leo, or egg him on with nonsense about the pillaging Huns. We came here for privacy, just like you. I hope you enjoy your cake. Please take some home with you. Life can be hard when one lives alone.

As Sabine walked away, she heard the clinking of glassware and realized that Reginald Bellows was now tapping a spoon on a champagne flute. It took her another long moment to realize that he intended on proposing a toast before all two hundred of her guests. Incredulous, she watched him stand on a chair so that he could be better seen.

He moistened his thin mouth, stared into the eye of his champagne flute, then brought his regard obliquely out into the audience.

—Compadres, *mis amigos*, I thought I'd raise a glass to our birthday girl, the fetching Cora, who will no doubt be kept in grain and livestock forever after.

A quiet chuckle. A few low-set translations for the older Catalans.

—But birthdays are also an occasion to remember history and the forces that have brought us here. Had it not been for your distant peasant ancestors from the County of Urgell, who fled the rampaging Moors as they devoured Iberia, we wouldn't be standing in this beguiling spot. From the very beginning, Andorra has been a place to hide.

He looked at Sabine, then over at the Hungarian couple.

—But the world is shrinking, and it's getting harder and harder to outrun history, whether it's personal history or history with a capital *H*. So as we raise a glass to Cora, let us also raise a glass to her mother, the very talented and famous actress, Sabine Montrose, and to our Hungarian aristocrats, the Count Bethlen and his wife, who, if I'm not mistaken, had ancestors fighting off the Bavarians at the same time your Catalans were fighting the Muslims. How times have changed! Now the Bavarians and Hungarians are fighting on a united German front . . . but that is another matter. Here's to Cora, and to history, and to the mountain valley that allows us all to hide!

Sabine refused to raise her glass but she watched the townspeople dutifully acknowledge the toast. She took in the room and noticed that the Hungarians had already fled. She saw the tops of their graying heads as they picked their way delicately down the steep path that led from the house.

EXILE IN EUROPE'S HIGHEST CAPITAL
By Reginald Bellows, Special Correspondent

By now many of us know the story of Sabine Montrose and her rise to fame. A Burgundy farm girl who made a name for herself in the Paris theater scene and beyond, Montrose also went on to star in cinematic roles, including her scandalizing bathtub nude scene. Then, in 1910, under the direction of Claude Ballard, she starred in the doomed film *The Electric Hotel*. Not seen in this country, the film was pulled from distribution following a series of electrifying lawsuits and entreaties from the inventor and tycoon Thomas Edison. While we are left to wonder about what moral hazards sauntered across the screen in said film, we can now rest in the certainty of what happened to the actress herself.

For more than five years, Sabine Montrose has lived a secluded life with her two adopted children in Europe, spending her summers in the remote and tiny country of Andorra, a principality shared by Spain and France. Going by the name of Désirée Mouret, an obscure character from an ill-fated Zola novel series, Sabine Montrose lives an eccentric, decadent lifestyle. In the evenings, she can be seen drinking cocktails in a cochineal dress on the blue slate veranda of her Ordino house overlooking the valley, a manor that once belonged to an Andorran baron. She imports luxury goods brought in by mule train, everything from silk to caviar to champagne. She is rumored to have a bathtub made from pure copper, manufactured by the same French firm who installed the torch for the Statue of Liberty. Her adoptive charges, American by birth, are tutored by professors and overeducated nuns and taken to various portside villas during the long Pyrenean winter, lest they fall in with the local peasants. While Montrose is still technically married to Claude Ballard, all evidence suggests they are now estranged.

Further down the valley, in the capital of Andorra la Vella, a Hungarian aristocrat and his wife hide from history. Count Bethlen was driven out of Budapest after his political alliances shifted with the monarchy. Among his business interests back in his homeland is a munitions factory that sold its wares to both German and French parties. Now confiscated by the Austro-Hungarian war machine, the factory is producing thousands of shells a day that pummel British and French trenches along the Belgian and Normandy coastlines.

Such are the vagaries of the rich and exiled in a nation that was founded as a hiding spot from invading Muslims . . .

28

The Blackout

A storm swept through Los Angeles a month before Martin's exhibition of *The Electric Hotel*. The clouds darkened and flashed over the Hollywood Hills, causing blackouts across the city. They sat together in Claude's kitchenette drinking tea, the table lamp flickering. Claude was telling Martin about the ravages of Belgium as he watched the capillaries of lightning travel along the base of the clouds. He remembered the Boche balloons in the skies above Flanders from half a century ago, the way they resembled enormous gray brains.

Sometimes, out in the street, when he was on his route to photograph the rug sellers in Little Armenia, or the goateed man who sat with a typewriter writing poems for strangers on Vine Street, he looked skyward and saw a commercial blimp. His throat went dry as he craned up, and for a moment he didn't see the *Goodyear* or *Budweiser* lettering and he was convinced that this floating specter had been dogging him for decades, his life somehow tethered to it. The lights flickered again in his kitchenette.

—Maybe memory is just electricity passing through us. Old voltage in the joints, he said.

Martin had brought over some photocopies of old newspaper articles he'd uncovered at the university library. Claude pressed the one about Sabine's

exile in Andorra to the window, staring into the crosshatching of micro-
fiche lines.

—Are you surprised this is where she ended up?

—Nobody vanishes into thin air forever.

—You already knew about Andorra?

Claude looked at their doubles in the darkening windowpane.

—I often wonder about what happened to Leo and Cora . . .

—Did they keep their own last names? I can do some research.

—I think so, yes, Harlow.

Martin moved the other articles across the table. One was Hal Bender's obit-
uary from the early 1950s. After running a studio for decades, he retired,
left his studio to his son, spent his twilight years restoring a sailboat, and
published a memoir entitled *The Brooklyn Lumières*. Martin pulled a copy of
the book from his rucksack and placed it on the table.

—There's quite a lot in there about you.

Claude ran his fingertips over the cover image of the Bender Bijoux at
the corner of Flatbush Avenue and Fulton Street in Brooklyn. It showed a
crowd of people—men in derby hats, women in day frocks—standing in
line at the ticket booth. He couldn't bring himself to open it.

—That's your copy. I found it in a used bookstore in Santa Monica.

—Thank you.

The lights went out for a few seconds. When they came back on, Martin slid
another photocopy across the table, this one with a picture and caption of
Chip Spalding in front of his stunt gym in Venice Beach. Taken in the
1940s, it showed a squinting Chip in khakis and a windbreaker—still wiry
and athletic in his sixties—flanked by would-be stuntmen.

—Somehow he's still alive, Martin said.

—The Australian?

—He married an American and they settled down in Venice Beach
after the first war. He had regular work as a stuntman with the studios and
then he ran his own stunt gym for thirty years.

Claude read the article to himself, his lips trembling as he mouthed
along.

—Where is Chip now?

—His wife passed away and he's living in a nursing home. I called the stunt gym, which is now a judo dojo, and the owner told me where he ended up after he sold the building.

—We all ended up in Hollywood, one way or another, but I never once saw them again after the war. Venice Beach might as well have been Venezuela.

They listened to the rain and wind for a moment. Then a thunderclap rattled the windowpane and Claude's suite went dark. The refrigerator hummed into silence and they heard a commotion out in the hallway. Doors were being opened and residents were talking to one another as they came out of their rooms. Claude cocked his head to one side, listening to the voices.

—We need to go check on Susan. She's terrified of storms. On top of the refrigerator, you will find a flashlight.

They descended the stairs to the ninth floor and passed Susan Berg out in the corridor. She was wearing slippers and a tattered negligee, her hair tied back with a threadbare scarf.

—Is he still here? she said to Claude.

—Who?

—I heard he was dancing just now out on the Lido patio. Valentino. Everyone is hurrying down to see him.

Rudolph Valentino had died years before the hotel opened.

—It's just a storm, Claude said. We've lost power.

He touched her arm very gently, coaxing her back to 1964. She took hold of his elbow and they turned back toward her apartment.

—Well, I insist that you boys stay for dinner.

It was after midnight.

—I can't be alone in an electrical storm, she said definitively. It's a widely known fact.

—We would be delighted to join you, wouldn't we, Martin?

—Of course.

And then they were stepping into Susan Berg's sulfurous living room, their hostess already busying herself in the cluttered kitchen. The smell of the soup warming on the gas burner came all at once—a weather front of fermented cabbage and curdled milk. With the flashlight, Claude picked out the archeology of the living room for Martin's benefit: the snake plants that somehow thrived in the subterranean fug, the dusty bookshelves filled with volumes on Egyptian numerology, art history, zoology, and Hitler, the film industry plaques and tarnished trophies, the peeling production shots of Susan in her twenties, in a bikini or a nightgown, ablaze in diamonds and coy beauty. The bathroom was visible with its damp laundry, a dozen gauzy undergarments hanging like pennants.

—Under no circumstances do you eat the soup, Claude said quietly.

Claude watched Martin's panicked face as Susan singsonged them to the table. In the area next to the kitchenette there were two steaming bowls of soup placed at one end of a wooden table. At the other end, there was an enormous jigsaw puzzle laid out, half completed, depicting a Dutch Golden Age winter scene, peasants frolicking and skating on a frozen river. They both sat very quietly, lowering themselves into the hemisphere of soup steam.

—Be careful not to get soup on my Avercamp.

—You will not be dining with us, Susan? Claude asked.

—Oh no, I never eat past twilight. It's how I keep my figure.

Claude nodded, spooned through the soup, creating little swirls and eddies. Martin followed suit.

—Delicious, Claude said.

His spoon hadn't once left his bowl.

—Wonderful, Martin said. How did you make it?

—My mother grew up in Idaho pulling potatoes out of the ground. Consider us people of the broth.

They both made a show of clattering their spoons on the ceramic bowls, and Susan didn't seem to notice that they weren't eating. She bent over the Dutch Golden Age at the other end of the table. Claude unscrewed the cap from the flashlight and the tiny bulb cupped the table in its pale embrace. The storm was now headed out into the valley, growing fainter by the minute.

At some point, Martin asked Susan if she remembered any of Sabine Montrose's film roles. She considered this while she placed a piece of jigsawed ice into the frozen river.

—Oh yes, she moved like a swan in front of the camera. That long white neck, all that floating grace. When you watched her, though, you wondered how something so pure and fierce could just swim by like that . . . Personally, I always wanted to grab her by that long pale neck and pluck her goddamned feathers. I wanted to make a pillow out of those white feathers and sleep on it every night. That's how we all felt about her . . .

Claude laughed, not mockingly, but with an appreciation for Susan's phrasing.

—No, no, Susan, you are mistaken. Swans mate for life, I believe. She was more like a praying mantis . . . The females, you see, eat the heads of their mates during sexual congress.

Susan looked up, delighted, and gave a chortle that involved her shoulders. But then she collected herself and continued in her own vein.

—In England, the Queen owns all of the swans. Did you boys know that? .

They both shook their heads.

—Oh yes. A royal pedigree that dates back centuries. I have a book on swans if you'd like to borrow it. Somewhere on the shelf over there with the Hitler biographies. The boys are called cobs, the girls pens. And they sometimes call a flock of swans a lamentation . . . Isn't it marvelous?

When the power came back on, they'd been listening to Susan's monologue on swans for several minutes. Her rooms didn't blanch with light, since she lived in permanent low-wattage. Instead, a few lamps came on and the radio began to murmur. Claude said, *Susan, I am afraid we cannot finish our second helpings of soup. Will you forgive us?* She looked down at the winter scene in the new lamplight.

—Just this once I will allow it. But you must come back. There is always something simmering on the stovetop.

Claude switched the flashlight off and put it into his pocket. Susan opened the door for them and kissed Claude tenderly on the cheek before they set off into the fluorescent hallway. As they walked toward the stairwell, Claude said:

—When I first came to the hotel, I used to take women out on dates. Susan Berg and I had a series of unfortunate suppers and an ill-fated weekend on Catalina Island.

—What happened?

—I was going to ask her to marry me. I went for a walk along the beach, trying to pluck up the courage, and didn't come back for hours. I left her waiting in the hotel lobby half the night. She didn't speak to me again for years, until she finally went a bit mad in 1957. Then I started to bring her soup bones and check in on her. She didn't forgive me for what I did to her . . . she just forgot. Sometimes I see it in her eyes . . . the vague certainty that she's been deeply wronged by me.

They stood in the cement stairwell, someone whistling jauntily above.

—Why didn't you marry her?

Claude stopped and looked down at his hands.

—Something in me wouldn't budge. I had every intention of starting over. It was like an errand I meant to run for fifty years.

29

The Messenger

In the journals Claude kept in the floorboards of the château, he paid careful attention to time. Meals and weather were time-stamped in his looped cursive, right next to filming locations and the names of plundered villages. The descriptions were flat, almost mechanical, as if verbs and nouns were the only things that hadn't been looted. He wrote of paraffin and sugar, chicory and salt. The verb *ravager* appeared frequently. A town where all the inhabitants buried their silver, china, and clocks in the ground was said to be *ticking under our feet*. A roadside incineration of bodies was noted as a *mound of more than twenty deceased persons*.

At 4:15 p.m. on August 20, 1915, the word *Flammenwerfer* appeared in the journal. Bessler had filled dinnertime conversation with reports of the specialist regiment that had been formed to dispense *Greek fire*. The description of seeing the flamethrower in action was matter-of-fact. It included no mention of filming his fellow Frenchmen in flames, or directing Lance Corporal Kaufer to prop a burned soldier against a barbed-wire entanglement. Instead, he wrote: *A range of no more than twenty yards, the Flammenwerfer runs out of fuel in two minutes. The trenches must be very close together. Six men to operate. Easy targets for enemy fire without the protection of a parapet.*

•

That summer Claude weighed little more than 120 pounds. He had to cinch his British riding trousers with a length of rope to keep them from falling off his waist. His hands shook when he loaded a camera, and a persistent cough rattled through his chest. His nails were bitten to the quick and he frequently blacked out—tiny flickers of a neural switch. Some of his footage swerved into a corona of daylight in the middle of a harrowing scene, as if the viewer were being forced to stare into the sun.

Most nights, he ate alone in his basement bedroom. Kaufer brought him a tray of leftovers and sometimes snuck a piece of chocolate or some sugar cubes under a saucer. Every once in a while, Bessler summoned him to the dinner table, especially if a visiting dignitary or an officer of the high command was visiting from Berlin. Claude was ordered to shave and put on a fresh shirt, to tell stories of the Palisades, of Thomas Edison, American tycoon and hero, sending them all bankrupt. Bessler told his guests that Claude Ballard, a pioneer in the film world, was working on a masterpiece of propaganda that they would soon unveil in Brussels. By now Claude had a full laboratory at his disposal—developing chemicals, a Williamson motor-driven printer, a supply of German positive and negative film stock.

Hal Bender was able to send a letter to Claude that summer through the American Legation in Brussels, along with the newspaper clipping about Sabine's exile. It was forwarded from Brussels to Berlin to Louvain to the château. Between Herbert Hoover's Commission for Relief in Belgium and American diplomatic pressure, the sway of a neutral power was mounting. Claude knew that everything was riding on Bessler's cinematic debut, a war film he was calling *The Victor's Crown*.

Each Sunday afternoon, Claude showed Bessler the week's footage and they talked about how it should be edited together. The only official frames to be included from the *Flammenwerfer* reel were the hillside pans of scorched bodies, the aftermath softened by dusk. After the premiere, Bessler hoped to put the film into wider distribution. Movie ticket sales in Brussels had tripled since occupation, he told Claude, and the sidewalk cafés were crowded with German soldiers on leave from the trenches, their pockets full of banknotes.

•

Claude didn't write about the newspaper article in his journals, but he wrote the word *Andorra* at the top of an otherwise blank page. He taped the article on the wall of his basement room. As he stared up at it, the room seemed to dim away. The tiny country with its blue slate verandas was unfathomable, the detail of the copper bathtub impossible. He pictured Leo and Cora with their rarefied lessons. He remembered his mother teaching him how to read, his father bringing him to see the wildflowers pressed inside the family bible, a world within a world. When he became aware of the room again everything was inscrutable: his knuckles, his breath, the gauzy membrane of his own thoughts. In a jar beside the bed, he saw that he'd kept months of nail clippings and strands of his own hair and he couldn't think why.

The unexploded bomb appeared in the château garden amid the celery and radishes. The gardener, a peasant from a nearby village, went out to weed and water one morning when he found the twenty-pound aerial shell, its nose dug a few inches into the soil. He informed Bessler and his officers, who were eating buckwheat pancakes on the flagstone terrace, and they hurried out to inspect. Claude followed them and they all stood there deliberating in the early, slanting light. There were colored bands of red and white wrapping the explosive but nobody knew what they meant. They were many miles from the real fighting, and no British planes had flown over this territory. Claude pictured a villager delivering this messenger in the basket of a bicycle under the cover of night, saw a man on his knees, planting the shell in the Belgian soil with a trowel.

Bessler rushed inside to telephone the ordnance corps and prepared to evacuate. He told his men that he had no idea whether the bomb was powerful enough to gouge a six-foot crater or break all the windows in the château. *We will take no chances,* he said. *I used to run a tourist bureau and now I'm expected to be an expert in artillery and munitions.* The officers, Berliners with literature and engineering degrees, rushed between rooms and began loading the Opel staff cars. Claude descended the stairs to the basement. He packed his camera equipment into his suitcase and went to retrieve the footage from under the pantry darkroom floorboards.

•

Something new took hold of him. He understood that he could move through the house invisibly, detached from his body, because there had always been tiny gaps in time, hidden passages and crawl spaces where he'd moved undetected. While the château erupted into commotion he finished packing his suitcase and methodically took down the newspaper clipping and folded it into his pocket. He understood the shell was a signal for action, its tailfins a perfect X on a map. He left his belongings on his cot and walked up the stairs and out into the garden. The bomb was still there, lying half-submerged amid the bolting celery stalks.

By the time Claude lifted the shell out of the dirt and carried it into the château, cradling it gently in his arms, the Germans were assembled in the drawing room and ready to evacuate. He stood with it by the white grand piano and the telephone, the space under the skylight where the officers gathered in the evenings to listen to Brahms or a crackling recital from Berlin. He was amazed at how steady he felt with the cool metal against his forearms, the color draining from his captors' faces. He thought of Chip Spalding on the tightrope, an emperor of burning air.

Bessler worried the top of his cognac-colored holster with his fingertips.

—I want the lance corporal to drive me to Brussels, Claude said.

Bessler touched his fingertips together, puckered.

—I want to be delivered to the American Legation. You will retrieve my passports and place them on top of the piano. The lance corporal will fetch my suitcase and tripod while the rest of you wait outside.

Claude saw himself riding in the front seat of the Opel staff car, Kaufer's hands on the steering wheel at precisely ten and two o'clock.

—You will never get through the checkpoints, said Bessler.

—You'll call ahead and make sure I do.

Bessler pushed out his lower lip and switched to German:

—Even if I did, there's always a hypothetical soldier who takes matters into his own hands. A Mauser fires as you speed away. The staff car blows up on the roadside. Worst-case scenario is a dead lance corporal and a suspected spy who's carrying at least one enemy passport.

•

Before Kaufer could translate, Claude realized he'd caught every word of it, that he'd always understood more German than he'd admitted. His mother spoke it to him when he was very young and, later, when she was very sick, the language of fairy tales and convalescence and death. He also realized, looking at Bessler's pale, aristocratic face, that he'd mistaken the Oberst-leutnant for a war bureaucrat, for an aesthete with no stomach for death. In fact, standing there, Bessler would unscrew the nose cone on the bomb just to prove a point.

Bessler told the officers to go wait outside on the terrace. Kaufer remained by Bessler's side, ready to translate.

—I intend to carry this the entire way to Brussels, said Claude.

—What then? Nothing is getting in or out of Belgium, not even a tele-gram, without German approval. You think we'd let you just walk out with your suitcase and cameras?

Claude felt the shell tight against his rib cage.

—I promise you, after we show our film in Brussels, you will be free to leave. You have my word.

—You've kept me here as a prisoner for almost a year.

—Nonsense. You've been our guest.

The room filled with northern sunshine. Bessler closed his eyes for a mo-ment in concentration before removing the pistol from his holster and rais-ing it in the air. From a distance of eight feet, he began to walk closer, the muzzle aimed directly at Claude's head.

—At university, I used to play a lot of poker and dice. Games of chance. So I was always thinking about the odds of this or that occurring. Num-bers exist like layers of a mystery, like the delicate passages of a Goethe poem . . .

Kaufer felt compelled to whisper a translation as Bessler came closer.

—The odds that the bomb is still alive, the chances that you will drop it to find out, the probability that you expect to be killed. I'd rather not shoot you, but by now we have enough good footage and you're not the only person in Belgium who can glue strips of celluloid together. I'd also rather not explode into a million tiny pieces . . .

The muzzle of the gun was now a few inches from Claude's right temple.

—*Wenn auf dem schmalen Stege, Der Wandrer bebt . . .*

Kaufer murmured:

—*When on the narrow bridge, the traveler trembles . . .*

Only Claude was not trembling. His hands were steady. He was aware of the weight of the shell, of the sunlight on the back of his neck.

—Please set the shell down very gently. We will all drive away and wait for the ordnance corps to arrive and nothing will be mentioned in my report to Berlin. Don't think America will risk the Kaiser's wrath over an Alsatian with two passports. If the sack of Louvain didn't force them into the war, then what will?

Claude felt the château floor drop away. He was ten years old, standing beside his father with the open bible, leafing between pressed wildflowers.

—*Wildblume*, he said, *fleur sauvage.*

—He's gone quite mad, Bessler said to Kaufer.

The muzzle of Bessler's pistol was now touching Claude's temple, and for an instant, when he saw the expression on Kaufer's face, he thought that he'd been shot, or that he'd entered the cramped dark foyer of a tiny blackout. But Bessler had said something low and menacing and the lance corporal took a step closer to lift the shell out of Claude's cradled arms. The first sign that Claude had acquiesced was the uncanny sight of the banded metal shell resting on the sun-glossed lid of the white grand piano.

Everything was different now. Claude was confined to the basement and to the pantry darkroom, Kaufer and two officers taking shifts to guard him, even when he showed his progress on *The Victor's Crown* for Bessler. Kaufer no longer brought him sweets concealed on the meal tray. Instead, he looked at his boots, ignoring the fact of Claude's existence.

One afternoon, Claude said to him:

—When we were in the field with the flamethrower, I saw you through the Pathé, after you'd moved the French soldier into position. You were weeping, very softly. You walked away from us, from where Bessler and I were standing on the hill, to make sure nobody would see. I saw you wipe your eyes with the back of your sleeve, filmed it in fact.

Kaufer refused to look over at him, and Claude turned back to editing the footage. The room was drowning in acetone. Finally, Kaufer said:

—After the film shows in Brussels, they intend to send you to a work camp in Königsberg.

By October, *The Victor's Crown* was ready to screen. In the Brussels district of Sint-Gillis, Bessler commandeered a movie theater, the Diamont Palace, and invited an audience of occupation officials, German high command, a handful of foreign journalists from neutral powers, the American Legation, and the Commission for Relief in Belgium. He told his men that he wanted to show the world that Germany had conducted an orderly, humane annexation of Belgium, that across the three administrative zones trains were running, bridges were being repaired, and paraffin lamps were burning.

In his filming and editing instructions to Claude, he'd been careful to exclude anything that would suggest troop movements or strategic positions. And the fighting scenes tended to show the afterglow of victory rather than the terror of battle. Bessler had even deliberated about whether or not to include a shot of poisoned Belgian carrier pigeons lying limp in their wire cages. In the end, he asked Claude to take the frames out.

The Brussels cinema was a Moorish auditorium walled in by ornate stalls and balconies, the proscenium flanked by an enormous trompe l'oeil. Kaufer showed Claude to the projection booth—a narrow white room perched at the back of the auditorium—and promptly bolted the door behind him. Claude set down his leather suitcase and metal box of reels.

They had arrived several hours early so that he could become familiar with the projection equipment and they could rehearse the thirty-minute film with a live military band. A dozen Austrians—the Alpenkorps—were going to play Blankenburg marches while the action unfolded. No improvisation would be permitted, so the military band needed to time their sheet music against the action on-screen. They had also arrived early, Claude suspected, to ensure that he didn't interact with any of the American delegates or journalists who might attend the screening.

Behind two glass viewports, the projection booth walls were yellowed from years of carbon arc lamps burning through a nitrate fog. There was a bank of heavy metal filing cabinets, each one full of canisters and spare projector parts, and a small exhaust vent positioned above two hulking German projectors. Claude opened the projectors to take stock of their moving parts. Each one had a Maltese cross mechanism that spooled and shuttered the frames.

He unpacked two reels from the metal case and two from the suitcase. Each was a thousand feet long, roughly fifteen minutes, labeled A, B, C, and D. The A and B reels were Bessler's official footage, carefully edited according to his mandates. These would be loaded, one in each projector, for the rehearsal with the military band. When a cue dot appeared at the end of reel A, Claude would start the second projector and unspool reel B. When it was time for the live performance, he would swap B for C, which contained three minutes of alternate footage right at the very end. Reel D was a copy of reel C, and Claude decided to stash it in the space behind the exhaust grate above the two projectors. He couldn't imagine who would find it, or how, and now he wished he'd buried the copy in the ground at the château. Before the incident with the bomb, he might have sent the backup copy into Louvain with the Flemish gardener.

He sat on the projectionist's wooden stool and waited for the band to arrive. Lately, there were entire minutes where he felt loosed from his body and mind. He studied an offcut of celluloid curled on the floor and suddenly saw himself emulsified into the filmstrip. There were four closed doors in a hallway and he stood knocking on one of them. When there was no answer, he opened the door to see Sabine Montrose reclined in a copper bathtub, her eyes smeared with kohl, the head of a Bengal tiger mounted and hovering in the darkness behind her.

He closed the door and continued to the next room, where a neatly made cot stood under an open window. The sun was setting outside and the raking light projected up behind an orchard, spangling the branches and leaves onto the walls and ceiling. He stepped inside the room, closed the door, and lay down on the bed to stare up at the tree crowns floating and tessellating above his head. In the daydream, he watched himself fall asleep.

When he heard the band arrive he stood up and slid open one of the glass viewports. In their pike-gray uniforms and calfskin boots, the Prussians held their instruments delicately between white-gloved hands, flugel-horns and trumpets and highland snare drums. It was hard to imagine the Alpenkorps engaged in anything but musical combat. Bessler consulted with the feather-hatted, brass-medallioned conductor, a man dressed for a coronation.

Music stands assembled, sheet music splayed, the band tuned their instruments with brassy innuendoes and syncopated riffs. Bessler stood to the side to give them some room as they assembled below the lip of the stage, the silk movie screen a floating field of white above their heads. The Oberst-leutnant gave in to a jaunty smile when the first Blankenburg march started up. Soon he received a demure nod from the conductor and Bessler waved up at the projection booth. Claude turned on the first projector, heard the prickle of the arc lamp as it blanched the first frame.

The rehearsal went perfectly. They opened with "Unter Kaisers Fahnen" (Under the Emperor's Banner) and closed with "Adlerflug" (Flying Eagle). For a year, Bessler had heard this upbeat, martial arrangement in his head as they filmed and edited. The march through the streets of Antwerp, the waves of kettledrummers and cavalrymen, it all seemed choreographed to the music. Thirty minutes before showtime, the band went outside for a cigarette and Claude swapped out the reel in the second projector.

Bessler unbolted the projection booth door and came inside with two cham-pagne flutes just as Claude was closing the projector hatch. Claude couldn't remember the last time they'd stood together without Kaufer's speculative translations between them.

—What did you think of this arrangement? Bessler asked.

—Suitable.

—I agree so, too. Would you like some champagne? I have some for you.

—No, thank you.

Bessler shrugged and set down the second champagne flute on top of a filing cabinet.

—I consider this a night of celebration. All our hard work leading us here. I feel myself happy and content.

Without Kaufer to even out his phrasing, Bessler sounded sentimental and dithering. Then Claude remembered the Oberstleutnant's eyes when he'd touched Claude's temple with the cold muzzle of his pistol—they were like two chips of ice at the bottom of a scotch glass. Later, when the commotion had passed, even with the guards stationed outside the pantry darkroom, Bessler acted as if nothing had happened. The ordnance corps discovered the bomb was dead and carted it off and it was never mentioned again. But standing in the projection booth, Bessler's breath smelling of gherkins and champagne, Claude realized there was no way to undo the chill kiss of gunmetal against his pulsing forehead.

—The projectors are sent from the factory in Leipzig. How do you like him?

—So far so good.

—*C'est bon?*

Claude said nothing.

—You must miss *Französisch*. I cannot imagine cutting out my mother tongue like you.

Bessler paced the booth a little, contemplating something as he sipped his champagne.

—I will let you in to a little secret. We receive a word that Herbert Hoover is in town from London and will be attending tonight's performance. Der Kaiser is not happy with the coal baron at all. He lets the relief commission distribute their food every month to the locals, but he thinks it's sending the wrong message. As you know, the Belgians are perfectly, ah, *fähig*, for feeding themselves if they could organize and tend the fields in orderly fashion. We have seen it with our own eyes!

—The camera sees the truth.

—Precisely. Did you know they have their own flag?

—Who?

—The Commission for Relief in Belgium.

—I didn't know.

—And their own fleet of ships as well.

From out in the lobby, the sound of boot heels on marble. Bessler threw
back his champagne flute and drained his glass.

—Our guests are beginning to arrive. I must scuttle. *Viel Glück!*

He closed the door, sliding the bolt into place, and Claude moved two of
the filing cabinets in front of the entranceway.

The audience was mostly military men in full regalia. The few women—
wives of high-ranking bureaucrats—looked underdressed beside so many
feathered brigade hats and ribboned medals. From the projection booth,
Claude tried to discern the foreign journalists and American delegates. He
saw a group of men in workaday suits, some with cameras and notepads,
doffing their homburgs and fedoras as they shook hands with the Germans.
Through the open viewport, he heard snippets of Dutch and Swedish and
English. When everyone was seated with a glass of champagne, Bessler
and Kaufer took to the stage.

Kaufer translated Bessler's welcome speech for the English speakers in the
audience, a concession to American neutrality. One hand on his scabbard,
the other between the brass buttons of his tunic, the Oberstleutnant told the
audience that Germany had been a reluctant occupier, that it had acted in
self-preservation.

—In cities like Liège and Louvain, we discovered that the so-called neutrality was a mask for Flemish hostility toward Germany. Tonight, as we
will demonstrate in the language of cinema, the German army is a benevolent and necessary occupier. In the words of the Kaiser, *We must pray for the
triumph of our weapons and prove this oath to the last drop of blood.* This film is
our prayer and our proof. We hope you enjoy!

Bessler gave a nod up to the projection booth, Claude uncapped the light
from the first projector, and the Alpenkorps leaned into a Blankenburg
march. They sounded like a municipal brass band on a Sunday afternoon as
German infantrymen lined up at a goulash cannon, tin plates held plain-

tively in the dawning light. Then a Bavarian engineering corps labored on a train trestle, plying pneumatic drills and welding torches, while a procession of pigtailed young Belgian girls delivered cans of coffee and plates of *butterbrot*.

There were scenes of Prussian cavalrymen helping a farmer recapture his herd of dairy cattle, and soldiers filling bags of sand. Images of Belgian soldiers were noticeably absent until a sequence opened on a work camp, where a group of bearded prisoners performed calisthenics against a backdrop of northern woods in high summer.

The march through Antwerp, even at reduced speed, was a display of choreographed military might. The army gendarmes and the uhlan lancers on horseback, martial and glowering, the singing infantrymen with their cheap cigars, the field artillery and the cannoneers serene as Tibetan lamas. The signal corps on bicycles, uncoiling telephone wires through the empty streets.

A general and his officers standing in the cavernous dining room of an abandoned abbey. Their bowls and dinner plates pushed to one side as they confer around the edges of a map with wax pencils. Bessler wanted it to show their methodical planning, a moment of topographical reverie, but on closer inspection the map was upside down from where the general stood. And at the edge of the frame there was a plate of Strassbourg goose livers, anchovies, and rum chocolate, bright packets of tinfoil and cardboard on display. Other signs of decadence followed, a bottle of Eiswein at the edge of a gingham tablecloth. Claude watched the back of Bessler's head in the front row, nodding slowly, a fraction behind the marching beat.

After the cue dot, the second projector hummed and spooled. From behind the glass viewport, Claude watched the serried trenches, the impromptu visit of a chaplain inside a muslin-covered triage unit gouged into the mud, the German wounded on stretchers, the flamethrower unit coming over the parapet, the dead Frenchman, reclined and tendriled in smoke, his scorched face bathed in twilight.

The swapped-out footage was three minutes of desolation and cruelty. It began with Lance Corporal Kaufer wiping tears from his eyes on the

Flammenwerfer battlefield before cutting to a barn in Louvain. A priest, naked except for his clerical collar, was being hoisted by his wrists up to the rafters. Below him, German soldiers assembled and lit a bonfire. The theme of incineration continued with a mound of burning books and an abbey being plundered by Prussian lancers hurling sulfur lozenges. To maximize the impact, Claude had glued together a series of cuts that showed a woman's bayonetted body, a young girl being dragged by her hair by a German officer, the men of a village being hauled away at gunpoint. A stretch of barren no-man's-land widened back to reveal a field of human limbs in ribbons and tatters of blue fabric.

From behind the closed viewport, Claude saw the reaction of the Germans as a pantomime of outrage. Bessler was up onstage, trying to pull the trompe l'oeil over the screen, and Kaufer was running toward the back of the auditorium with his hands in the air. A German officer removed his revolver and took aim at one of the projection booth viewports. Claude remained standing at the glass and waited to either be shot or see the improvised intertitle he'd filmed with his notebook:

> *A message from the projectionist:*
> *My name is Claude Ballard.*
> *I am an American citizen being held against my will.*

Claude stared down into the blue-lit ocean of the auditorium and waited for the bullet. The Alpenkorps was somehow still playing through the uproar, a silent underwater symphony through the glass viewport. Bessler had removed his dress sword and used it to slash at the projection screen while the filmstrip continued. Some of the foreign journalists flashbulbed the pandemonium with their cameras, strobing the German bureaucrats as they rushed for the exits with their wives.

When Claude heard them ramming at the metal door of the projection booth, he thought the filing cabinets would slow them down or deflect the first few bullets. He turned off the second projector and sat on the floor, the machine ticking and cooling against his back. He closed his eyes, brought his knees in to his chest. The flurry of voices at the door began to separate into layers and strands—a wide swath of incensed High German, some Dutch glottal concern, then a narrow strip of reasonable American English, insistent and low and modulated.

One baritone voice cut in below all the others:

—Mr. Ballard, are you there? Can you hear me?

The voice came from the end of a long corridor and somehow Claude could not answer or open his eyes. He was on the fringe of a blackout, felt himself being wicked away.

—Sir, are you all right? We intend to get you out, just hold tight.

In later years, Claude would insist that this voice belonged to Herbert Hoover, the future president of the United States, and that he was calling to him as if he'd fallen down a mineshaft. When the Great Depression hit, Claude would lean in to the wireless in his hotel suite to parse the president's speeches about the wintertime privations of the poor and the rallying of the American spirit, comparing the voice to what he'd burrowed into the back of his mind, when Herbert Hoover called his name and lifted him out of the darkening well.

30

Faux Paris

Claude often thought of the three-minute strip of war celluloid as his real masterpiece. The British and French used the footage as proof of German atrocities, not only in propaganda films but also as fodder in subsequent war-crimes trials. The Commission for Relief in Belgium used it to fuel fund-raising efforts and many Americans saw it as a sign that they should consider entering the war.

Hal Bender, still touring with his reels, saw the harrowing strip in London and wrote another letter to Claude, care of the Relief Commission, but this one never got through the mail censors. In Germany and occupied Belgium, *The Victor's Crown* was never seen again. Oberstleutnant Graf Bessler was recalled to Berlin and spent the remainder of the war as a petty bureaucrat in charge of sourcing rubber for military bicycle tires.

Under the protection of the American Legation and the Red Cross, Claude was smuggled out of Brussels, slipping into France behind Ypres. After con-valescing for a month in a hospital in Calais, he was given a choice of either returning to the United States via London or relocating to Paris. He chose the latter, not because he had any great affection for the city of his youth, but because he wanted to ensure there were no traces of the dreamer who'd set off almost twenty years earlier as an agent for the Lumière brothers. New Jersey and Hollywood were also impossible to imagine after a year filming the entrails of war.

Claude barely recognized Paris. Fearing a prolonged siege, the military had brought in livestock from the countryside, and the sound of lowing cattle filled the boulevards and streets. The bronze statues and stone monuments were heaped in sandbags, the Eiffel Tower trimmed with machine guns. The Louvre was closed, the paintings dispatched to Toulouse, and the train stations were glass-domed cities of gamboling dogs and head-scarfed refugees. Government palaces and grand hotels had been turned into military hospitals.

Women's skirts, meanwhile, grew shorter, their footwear sturdier, and socialite magazines ran articles about what to wear when taking refuge from a zeppelin attack. New words were invented: a female postal worker was a *factrice*; a *munitionnette* was a woman working in a munitions factory. Bohemian Paris was also in retreat. Jean Cocteau was said to now work as a Red Cross ambulance driver.

Claude rented a room in Montparnasse, above a violinmaker, and took a job as a taxi driver. Celluloid film stock was almost impossible to obtain, so he stored his cameras and equipment under his narrow bed and forgot about picture making. Although Paris taxi drivers were notoriously impatient and irascible, they had become national heroes after hundreds of red Renault AG1s drove reservists up to the First Battle of the Marne. Dutifully following city regulations, the taxi drivers had kept their meters running and later sent the government the bill. Four thousand soldiers were taxied to the front in two days.

Claude took solace in the routine of driving the Renault twelve hours a day, in the winding chaos of the streets and in the glimpsed lives of his passengers. The motorcar was high, sleek, and narrow, designed for the serpentine passageways of the city, and he could comfortably seat three people in the sealed compartment behind the driver's bench. Because he never heard their conversations, he had to surmise their pasts and futures from the initial directions and the payment of the fare. An accent, a weary look, a tattered scarf or ermine shawl. As he had with the looping mechanisms inside a projector and camera, he became intimate with the Renault's engine, the way it stuttered in the cold and chortled after a long idle.

Despite his prewar film career and his footage of the Germans, no one seemed to know who Claude was in Paris, and he relished the anonymity. He walked past the installations of his former life as if they belonged to a museum of the past. The old aperture window of his garret roofline apartment. The Salpêtrière hospital, now full of wounded soldiers, where his old mentor, Londe, mapped the walking cadences of hysterics, the consumption institute where his sister died in a room filling with winter light. He was a wartime flâneur, taking walks of atonement through his old stomping grounds.

He sometimes thought about driving out to Lyon to make amends with the Lumière brothers, who were now investing in color autochrome photographs, but he couldn't imagine what he would tell them, or why they would care. He ate one meal a day and drove until his whole body hummed. On Sunday afternoons, he bathed in the silty Seine as a kind of penance. At night, when he couldn't sleep, he walked out into the streets to look up at the river of stars. With so many lights snuffed after curfew, the sky was a tumult of blackness and starlight above his head. In every way possible, his life was becoming smaller and simpler. He wanted to reduce daily existence to its struts and filaments, to some underlying structure that could not fill with deceit.

But his loneliness hung all about him, like a smell from the tanneries. At night, before the curfew, behind the wheel of the Renault, he saw the headlamps pick through the darkened streets and felt weightless of time and body, a floating witness to everything around him. His daytime visions and blackouts subsided but his dreams were run through with trench horrors and severed limbs. He never charged a fare for soldiers on leave. Sometimes, as he stared into a young Frenchman's face, he tried to discern whether he would come back from the front. There were entire days where he felt clairvoyant and omniscient: *That boy will die in flames. That woman has never loved anyone but herself.*

By early 1918, everything had changed in the war. The Americans were now fighting in Europe, the Germans were bombing Paris and London with their Gotha heavy bombers, and the Paris-Geschütz—a ten-story siege gun with a range of eighty miles—had landed shells inside city churches and metro stations. Claude continued to drive his red Renault through the streets, the stained-glass windows removed from Notre Dame, the brothels overflowing with British and American enlistees.

Despite its hold on the city, the war now felt like an abstraction to Claude, a series of parabolas and probabilities. Without the daily footage of atrocities, it became newspaper ink and omnibus stories. He pictured the Paris Gun launching its ten-foot shells, saw them scraping the gas-blue flame of the stratosphere. On Good Friday 1918, a shell came through the roof of a church in Saint-Gervais, killing eighty-eight people. In his mind, there was nothing personal about this kind of carnage. It was both random and mathematical.

Then one morning the war took a ride in his taxi. A French officer and a military engineer directed him fifteen miles north of the city, to the quiet district of Maisons-Laffitte, where a secret and enormous faux Paris was being built on a different stretch of the Seine. The fake city was being designed to fool the Gotha bombers at night—complete with replicas of the Arc de Triomphe and Gare du Nord, fully functioning train tracks that carried empty carriages, mock buildings constructed like movie sets, their skylights painted with translucent paint to suggest the grimy lights of factories and warehouses.

They asked if Claude would be willing to supervise the optical effects, to ensure that the illusion was convincing from above. The project already employed dozens of theater set designers, electrical and mechanical engineers, carpenters, painters, and a hundred workmen. But they needed a film director's eye and someone who also knew the German mind-set.

Since Claude wasn't allowed to tell anyone of his new work, the military asked him to continue driving taxis during the day and to work on faux

Paris at night. Each night, after dinner, he drove up to Maisons-Laffitte
and toured the day's progress. The rooftops were set facades, a skin of
fabric, wood, and mastic, and he liked to view them from an observation
booth that doubled as a train signal tower. But he needed more height if he
was going to capture a Gotha pilot's view. So he asked his military con-
tacts to source a working Aeroscope camera, some celluloid, and a weather
balloon.

Once a week, he attached a small basket to the balloon, positioned the rolling camera, and sent the apparatus up on the end of a thousand feet of
rope. Just as the Germans radioed artillery calibrations from observation
balloons at the front, Claude was able to adjust the mounting movie set by
viewing it from above. Paris was a scroll of parchment, a glimpse of riverine light and hazy industrial skylights and steeples and gargoyles and trains.
Germans had an eye for the symbolic, and for the aesthetically pleasing, so
he made sure there were tiny painted wooden boats on the Seine with faint
red pilot lights and mannequins dutifully night fishing.

The war ended before faux Paris could ever be fully tested. In a train compartment out in the French countryside, the rival powers signed a peace
treaty and the Armistice swung through Europe at 11:00 a.m. on November 11, another mathematical portent. The treaty was signed at 5:00 a.m.
but the fighting continued for six hours, a fact that would haunt Claude in
later years, the idea that a few thousand men could be both alive and dead
for a morning. When the church bells started pealing across Paris, when the
students erupted into the streets, carrying soldiers aloft, Claude found himself heading south of the city in the Renault.

He drove for two days along chalky, tree-lined roads, through hamlets and
villages and towns that were just now hearing of the Armistice, their cafés
and taverns hung with flags. Burgundy vintners waved at him from their
browning fields, dairy farmers from haylofts, the madness of a Paris taxi
joyriding south. The world was full of fellow feeling, despite the bracing
weather of November. They let him pay for petrol but nobody would let
him pay for a meal or a glass of wine or a bed for the night. He shrugged

when they asked him where he was headed, thanked them for their hospitality, and honked his horn patriotically as he headed farther south.

In redbrick Toulouse, the weather sharpened and he bought supplies and made enquiries about getting up into the Pyrenees. From the town of Axles-Thermes, with its casino and sulfur baths, the locals said, there was a mule road up into Andorra, but no passage for a motorcar. But he could motor into Spain and follow the white macadam road that led from La Seu d'Urgell up into the mountains. They warned him of Pyrenean storms, of lawless mountain clans, of the sawtooth massif where Catalan herders and smugglers had been hiding for a thousand years. When a grocer asked him what business took him to L'Andorre, he thought about all the ways he might answer. Finally, he said, *Everything.*

31

Andorra

A Paris taxi motoring into the main square of Andorra la Vella, the streets empty on a rainy November afternoon. A few dozen locals, up and down the valley, stricken with *la gripe*, dying in shuttered rooms under slate roofs, their doors marked with tiny yellow flags. After ravaging Europe for a year, the Spanish influenza had arrived in the Pyrenees just the month before. So it was a Catalan doctor in a wool cap who came out to meet the parked Renault, a surgical mask secured to his face under an umbrella. Around the square, a few onlookers appeared behind rain-streaked windowpanes.

The doctor asked whether Claude would submit to a physical examination on account of *la gripe*. Claude stepped under the umbrella and removed his jacket. The doctor listened to his lungs, took his temperature, looked down his throat, and asked him what brought him to town. He told the man that he was looking for the household of Sabine Montrose. The doctor fell quiet, recoiled into the ancient, empty room of Andorran discretion and secrecy. Claude said, *I am her estranged husband,* and this elicited a casual nod as the doctor pointed with his stethoscope to a church-spired town cleaved into the northern wall of the valley. *Siempre arriba, en Ordino, cerca de la iglesia.* He handed Claude a white cloth face mask.

•

As Claude cranked the engine of the Renault, the doctor asked in Catalan, then in French:

—Is it true?

—That I am her husband?

—That the war is over.

Claude nodded and settled behind the wheel to slowly release the clutch. It occurred to him for the first time that he had technically stolen the motorcar from his employer and driven it more than six hundred miles. He'd had the presence of mind to pack up all of his possessions, to slip into the crowded streets without his violinmaker landlord noticing his suitcase and equipment, but it was only now that he admitted that he had no plans to return to Paris.

He drove farther north into the valley in the pelting rain, wound up a rutted mule path, eventually parked the Renault alongside the ancient stone church in Ordino. A big house presided over the street, mortared in clay, roofed with blue slate, its tall windows shining behind a long wrought-iron balcony. Claude found his way to an archway that gave onto a courtyard garden with a fountain and a set of zigzagging steps that led to the house's main entrance.

He was out of breath by the time he reached the top landing, hands on hips, staring at the small yellow flag nailed to the weathered old door. He stamped the mud off his boots, knocked, waited, clutched the face mask between his hands, felt light-headed from the smell of rain and wet limestone.

Helena, still brisk in her seventies, opened the door and dried her hands down a white apron, clearly bothered by this mid-afternoon intrusion. It took her a few squinting seconds to recognize the pale wire of a man standing before her in the rain, to complete the mental calculation that ported Claude Ballard from the Palisades to the Pyrenees. She shook her head, rubbed her bare arms, her eyes blotting with tears.

I have come to see Sabine and the children, he said unnecessarily, but Helena was still staring through her own memories and Claude saw himself as she might, the way he'd shown up with his Alsatian undertaker's hat on

Sabine's fortieth birthday, waiting out in the hotel hallway with his light box in tow, shimmering Parisian boulevards and plummeting cats onto a bedsheet that doubled as a screen, and now he stood there all over again, shifting his weight from foot to foot, a ravaged ghost in the alpine rain. Had he been standing out in the rain for twenty-two years? Gesturing to the yellow flag on the door, he said, *Qui?*

She said nothing, but opened the door wider and took his drenched overcoat. She led him silently toward the great room that overlooked the valley, his boots dripping as he walked. The room was a perched jewel box, dark wooden rafters hung with ironwork candelabras, fencing masks and French impressionists on the walls, gold-and-blue Persian rugs brightening the big-timbered floors. He had the sensation of walking into the back of a theater during a play, of actors blocked and arranged and facing downstage. Two women stood at the window, watching a cataract of sunlight widening above the other end of the valley. He'd expected a different scene and play, perhaps a salon farce, a few pompous expat literary types and serious-minded actors, maybe Pavel standing on a chair pontificating about the subtle machinery of the mind. Standing inside this jewel box, he understood that time was a pebble, something he could slip into his pocket or rest under his tongue. Helena sighed and it broke the spell at the window.

Cora was the first to turn around, now a pretty green-eyed woman at the cusp of twenty. Almost in fright, she touched the back of Sabine's hand, and the actress turned slowly around. Claude remained motionless, studying her face amid the glassed-in clouds and vales and summit balds behind her head. She came into focus as a straight-backed woman in her early sixties, wearing a gray velvet day dress. Her hair was neatly pinned up, off her long pale neck, and her face was the color of candlewax. In all the years he'd stared at Sabine through the viewfinder, he had never seen this particular face. Wordless, unmade, inscrutable.

He felt emptied out by her wan expression, bird-boned with relief. For years he'd imagined this moment as a reckoning, feared that the old ache would thicken in his throat, mangle through his stomach, but now he felt light and steady and desireless on his feet. He'd plucked a bomb out of a celery garden, exhibited German atrocities while Berliners sat in feathered hats, driven a taxicab from Paris to the Pyrenees, filmed hysterics, his dying sister, a dark melodrama that had changed everything. Now it all seemed to have happened to someone else. But this particular emptiness was happening to him alone. He had traveled years and continents and hundreds of miles to feel this strain of nothingness. There was no way—or reason—to speak any of this, so he just looked at her blankly.

Then he noticed the white face masks around their necks and it occurred to him that Leo was the one dying of the Spanish flu in a room at the back of the house or above the salon. The disease, he remembered, favored the young. He would be almost eighteen by now, a boy running into the smoke-mirrored hallways of manhood. Claude thought of the shifting wood-light above the Hudson, of the astonished look on Leo's face when he was discovered in the crook of a tree during a game of hide-and-seek.

Sabine eventually moved from the window and came toward him. She said to Cora, *Do you remember Claude Ballard, from our days in America?* Cora could only nod. The rainstorm had swept in a Catalan vision, a hallucination from an ancestral shrine. Sabine raised one hand in the air and he thought of a conductor's hesitation before a difficult symphony, the way the music hovered just in front, unplayed and therefore still perfect, like an undeveloped photograph. She was unsure how to begin. He smelled of damp wool, of something unspeakable. To touch his face or shoulder was unimaginable.

—Is it you?
—More or less.

Cora said she would fetch some tea and she joined Helena, who had been watching from the doorway. Sabine's hand had been in the air for a very long time. Finally, she used it to point to a divan.
—I'm drenched to the bone.
—No matter.

He settled on the divan and she sat opposite, on the edge of a wingback chair. He took out a handkerchief and wiped his face. He knew he would have to ask directly, that she was too preoccupied with her own onslaught to address the obvious specter in the room.

—Where is Leo?

She shook her head.

—Oh dear, of course. No, no, he's safe and sound. Studying at Oxford. His first term, such as it is, with half his classmates off in the trenches.

—The yellow flag. *Qui?*

Claude pointed to the back of the house and for a moment he imagined a husband dying of fevers.

—Poor old Pavel. The doctor says he may not live through the night.

—I'm very sorry to hear that.

—We were told to send him to the quarantine station in Barcelona, but we couldn't do it. Instead we wear masks and gloves whenever we go in. Helena has been the most industrious nurse. For years they quarreled, now she's his cherished confidante, writes letters to his family in St. Petersburg for him . . .

—That's very kind of her.

The silence, when it gathered, was interrupted by the arrival of Cora with a tray. She poured them all tea and sat on the divan next to Claude. Cora's look of worry had vanished and now there was some of Helena's briskness, a pre-occupation with china and a sugar bowl and spoons. Sabine looked off at the window, at the marbling underbelly of clouds. When she came back to the room, her voice unraveled.

—Oh dear God, what did I do to you, Claude?

—Don't flatter yourself, madame. This is mostly my own doing.

Sabine dabbed at her eyes with a handkerchief, offered up a careworn smile.

—Hal Bender wrote me about you. Told me what happened during the war. It's unimaginable . . . I never wrote back to him, I'm ashamed to say.

When Cora picked up the thread of a cheerier topic, Claude realized it was with an orphan's instinct for pragmatism and self-preservation. She was not about to sit through a maudlin recounting of betrayal and misplaced de-sire. The girl had lost both her parents and her homeland before the age of twelve.

—I remember you playing board games and showing us films above the mantel. You taught us how to swim in the Hudson River. Leo used to call you Clowd because he couldn't pronounce your name the way you said it.

They all smiled at this.

—How has life been for you up in the mountains, Cora?

—Dull, mostly. I prefer Barcelona, but Sabine thinks I'll end up with a Spanish grocer for a husband if we spend too much time there.

Of course she called her Sabine instead of Mother. Claude looked at Cora's face, tried to discern traces of Dorothy Harlow, but he remembered nothing from the sanitarium except the vials of sputum lined up in the doctor's cabin. Their one-night honeymoon at the lake. That atmosphere of bacteria and inoculation should have been a portent of the coming ruin.

—What will you do? he asked Cora.

—I'm going to study law at the Sorbonne next year.

Claude blinked, smiled weakly, sipped his tea. He was happy for their bright, promising lives, but it all seemed unfathomable. Oxford, the Sorbonne. One day there would be a wedding, he thought, to a diplomat or a statesman. There had never been a place for him in their lives. Even back in New Jersey he'd been standing outside the firelight, staring through the window at the hearth. The Mansion of Happiness was an unwinnable board game that eventually had to be packed up and put away. He'd always known that, even then.

They talked of their shared summer in the Palisades, of the Andorran litany of religious festivals, of the visitors who occasionally came through the town. Nobody mentioned the war. Claude offered up nothing of his recent years except to say that lately he drove a taxi and lived above a Paris violinmaker's workshop and it often sounded like cats being tortured below. This got a generous laugh from Cora.

After an hour, Sabine asked if Claude would like to spend the night and take a hot bath. When he accepted, Helena boiled the water in the kitchen and then Sabine prepared the bathroom like a sanctuary, laying out a lavender-scented towel, lighting candles in glass jars, filling the tub with fragrant, steaming water. She placed some hot coals in the brasero to warm the room, placed some clean clothes that belonged to the Basque gardener on a stool.

It was the enormous copper bathtub sitting below the dormer window that unnerved Claude. In the basement of the château, he'd read about the copper tub and it seemed like a shining emissary from a vanished world, an image of oblivious wealth and privilege and safety. He removed his damp clothes, stood naked at the edge of the tub, his feet cold on the white marble floor.

When he lowered himself into the hot water, he was surprised by the sound of a very old man's rheumatic moan. It was an exhalation that swallowed the room. His life used to feel unyielding to him but now it felt warmly contained inside the tub. His hands and his fingernails, the knuckles and kneecaps, the uncoiling thread of his own breath and thoughts, these were all entirely knowable. Apart from his dreams, there was nothing he could think of that frightened him and the feeling was like being wrapped in a goldbeater's skin, a zeppelin's membrane filling with helium. He was a forty-two-year-old man reclined in a copper bathtub, perched above three thousand feet. He was about to begin all over again, perhaps make another film, start out small, careful, unafraid. He took his time in the tub, scrubbed himself clean, submerged his head so that he could hear the steady tempo of his own heartbeat.

After dinner, Helena announced that Pavel had asked to see Claude. He walked toward the back of the house and up a narrow wooden staircase, his face mask in place, a pair of cotton gloves on his hands. The children's bedrooms and a guest room were up here, the latter converted into a sickroom for Pavel. Claude thought of Bedouins and desert encampments as he entered, a paraffin lamp burning, the walls whitewashed and hung with Turkish prayer rugs, the canopy above the bed an enormous sash of red arabesque. Beneath it, Pavel lay propped with pillows, his cropped head diamond-pricked with sweat, his eyes yellowed and bloodshot. A sheet was pulled up to his bare, bristled chest. In one blotched hand he held a sprig of rosemary. Claude sat on the stool beside the bed. Pavel was the first to speak.

—I don't know who is looking worse, you or me.
—Definitely you.
Pavel blinked into an abstract smile.
—You look like someone starving that they pull from a coal mine. A survivor of calamity.

—The war changes people.

He lifted the rosemary sprig to his nose.

—I can only imagine what you've seen. And here I am the one dying, a ridiculous bourgeois malcontent . . .

His mouth opened and closed a few times.

—I am the oldest and fattest man in the village *avec la grippe*.

—You're not very old.

Another faint, dry-lipped smile. His eyes were once imperious and quick, Claude remembered, always seemed to be peering down at you from a height, or he was staring into the middle distances where a new theory or idea coalesced. Now his gaze was sidelong and slow and yellowed with fever.

—I was never sick in my life. Healthy as oxen. There was a Russian flu epidemic . . . when I was young, and it didn't lay a single finger on me. Not a pinkie. I've always pictured my lungs like two hot-air balloons . . . waiting to float me away.

It occurred to Claude that respiratory complaints had shaped the course of his entire life. Odette, the widow, the feature film with a tubercular seductress, and now this pair of wheezing Slavic lungs drawing him in from under the canopy. *The world is too much for some people to breathe.* Pavel turned his head to one side.

—We might not have had Romantic poetry without ailments of the lungs, Claude said. You're in good company.

—Chekhov blazed the trail for me, among others.

—I remember you telling me the story of his death one time on a train.

— . . . the glass of champagne, the hotel room in Germany, the oyster train car they used to haul his body back to Russia . . .

Pavel's breathing turned hooked and phlegmatic.

—One time . . . this was some years ago, I met the bellhop who worked at the hotel where he died. He was the messenger sent for the doctor. Do you know what he told me?

Claude shook his head.

—That Chekhov's dying breath sounded like a bull being lanced through its side. That his wife, Olga, grabbed the doctor by the lapels and screamed into his face. She was hysterical, you understand . . . and they both sat out with her on the iron balcony until dawn . . . and then they smuggled the body out of the hotel in a laundry basket . . . so as not to upset the other guests.

He looked down at the sprig of rosemary, wincing and panting with pain.

—When Olga told that story in later years . . . she never mentioned any of that. She said he took the glass of champagne and went off peacefully . . . a canoe slipping into a lake.

Pavel closed his eyes, seemed to doze off for a full minute, before coming back as if no time had elapsed.

—Will you tell me about the war?

—What do you want to know?

—Everything. We have been so cloistered up here. They say millions have died, and I barely know the names of three battles. We've been drunk on peace up here in the mountains, dithering our days away. I am sorry for that . . . Leo wanted to enlist, but Sabine wouldn't let him. Will you tell me what you saw?

Claude stared into the shadows in the bowl of paraffin lamplight.

—Why don't I show you?

⚓

Since there was no electricity, Claude had to improvise a limelight lantern in the lamphouse of the projector. It took him several trips to carry his equipment up from the Renault, and by the time he set the projector up at the foot of Pavel's bed, it was well after midnight. Cora and Helena had gone to bed, but Sabine insisted on staying up. Pavel's illness had turned her into Helena's assistant, taking the night shift as the bearer of compresses and broths and lemon-scented spring water. Pavel sat propped in bed, marooned in pillows, blinking drowsily up at the whitewashed wall. Claude threaded the war footage and warmed the projector. Sabine sat on the other side of the bed, holding Pavel's hand in a white cotton glove.

The wall granulated and seamed with light. Prussians on horseback in the ancient city of Louvain, moving among the ruins. Mustached, hale, staring solemnly at the camera from under their spiked and feathered helmets. Belgian prisoners of war performing star jumps and lunges in the northern woods. Then the march through Antwerp, the city an abandoned fortress of church spires and stone facades, the infantrymen with their cheap cigars and boyish grins, the bicycling signal corps with a thousand feet of uncoiling wire. Claude could see in Sabine's face, and hear in Pavel's lulled breathing, a slight sense of relief. They briefly mistook the cavalcading and marching for the actual stuff of war.

A dinner plate with goose livers. A chilled and salted oyster on a pewter plate. The wax pencil beside the waterproof invasion map. The close-ups were as staged as baroque still lifes. Only when the smoking trenches appeared in the twilight, when the flamethrower came over the parapet, did the footage seem improvised and lifelike. The unfurling ribbon of magnesium, the pandemonium of men on fire, batting at their own heads and arms, the cameo of Claude walking onto the smoking field, the lance corporal propping up a charred, dead Frenchman . . .

Sabine sat quietly weeping beside Pavel's bed, dabbing at her eyes with a handkerchief above her face mask. Pavel was staring up at the wall, unblinking, swallowing, mumbling to himself in Russian and French and English. When the naked priest was hoisted by his wrists to the barn rafters, a bonfire lit from below, it was the first time that Claude had ever seen Sabine avert her eyes from a filmstrip. Pavel continued to stare but his breathing quickened. He began talking to the sky of red fabric above him, quoting from Chekhov's letters and plays.

—My father was a peasant who pulled onions from the earth . . . but here I am in a white waistcoat and yellow shoes . . . a pearl out of an oyster.

The projector chattered through its gears. A mound of burning books incinerated against the whitewashed wall. Through the slightly ajar window above the paraffin lamp, a black moth fluttered into the room.

—Just think about it and examine me . . . and you'll find I'm still a peasant down to the marrow of my bones . . . all my theories just scraps of paper in my pocket . . . so many beautiful shreds . . .

The moth avoided the fiery gulf of the paraffin lamp, but wafted drowsily through the air toward the spooling projector. A lunarscape of bare, smoking trees, some of them trimmed with tatters of Belgian uniform fabric.

—I don't know why one can't chase two rabbits at the same time . . . if you have the hounds, go ahead and pursue . . .

The moth fluttered and warped in front of the projector's eye, into the frame, its griffinlike silhouette darkening the wall of European twilight.

Claude waited for it to find a way inside the projector, to burn up against the lamphouse, but it fluttered into the upper draughts of the room, circled above their heads. Pavel took his last breath somewhere during this flight, a sprig of rosemary across his chest, his eyes closed, his mouth open. His face and hands were birdlike, his mouth a gothic archway. Claude had seen so much death but this one was small and personal. It carried a name and a weight.

Claude snuffed the projector and sat on the other side of the bed. They both watched the black moth circle in the cone of light above the paraffin lamp.

—He wanted to understand how it really happened, Sabine said, how it might have felt. A student of naturalism to his dying breath.

—There is no understanding what happened.

Claude listened to the ticking of the cooling projector gears.

—Where will you bury him?

—Up in the mountains. He liked it here, the peasants and their funny hats. Where will you go?

—Back to America, I think. Europe is a burial ground for me now.

—It makes me so sad to look at you. I see it plain as day—the war finished what I started.

—Your vanity has always been shocking. I was always going to be doomed in love. If not you, then someone or something else.

—In case it matters, I'm sorry for everything.

Claude watched the moth flutter toward the open window, watched it recoil in the lamplight.

—I'm sure it matters . . . but right now I can't think how.

—Since that first escape to Paris, when I was thirteen, I was never going to give myself to anyone. Not even myself. Cora and Leo, that's the closest I've ever come.

—If only you'd warned me.

—I was nothing but warnings, Claude. One ringing alarm bell after another.

—I was deaf back then. Blind, too.

Claude crossed to the projector, opened the side gate, and began to unload the reel. He turned to the window and opened it wide, giving the battering moth a clear shot at the alpine night. Sabine said she would like to sit with Pavel's body for a while longer.

—In the morning, Helena will make us breakfast. Please stay as long as you like. Cora will likely cross-examine you over crêpes suzette. Leo's bedroom is made up for you, at the other end of the house.

Claude said good night and carried his equipment out into the hallway. In Leo's bedroom, he lit a lamp and studied the bookshelves and the framed coin collections, the telescope jutting from one corner. He was careful not to disturb anything. The room smelled of India rubber and ink and stamp glue. He removed his shoes and lay on the bed without removing his jacket or peeling back the covers. He blew out the lamp and stared into the darkness for a while, tried to sleep but stirred into the small blue hours, transfixed by the idea of the first day of a new life, of making his own escape beyond the sunless valley floor.

He carried his shoes and equipment through the darkened house, made two trips, sat out on the slate stoop to tie up his laces, walked down the steep stairs to the courtyard and up the cobblestone street to the Renault. He could not look back at the house for fear he'd woken them, that they'd all be standing in the picture window in their nightgowns with candles. He packed his equipment in the trunk, poured the spare gasoline into the tank, cranked the engine until it sputtered to life. And then he was driving into the floor of the dark valley, down through the Pyrenees in his Paris taxi, the meter running and the *occupied* light on just for a lark, the oceanic night awash in flint-and-white stars and smelling of slate and juniper and lichen. He drove all the way to the Barcelona docks during daylight, slept in his taxi, bought a ticket on the next steamer to America. For half a century, he would think about the Renault AG1 parked down at the Spanish dockyards, imagining that it had remained untouched all these years, stolen and with its meter still running.

32

Return to the River

Chip Spalding lived at the Tahitian Sunrise Villas, a palm-treed pocket of assisted living wedged between Playa del Rey and LAX. As Martin drove south to pick him up on the day of the screening, Claude stared out the window, cameras strapped across his chest, waiting for the Pacific to glimmer into view. Apart from an occasional taxicab for grocery shopping or a wedding photography gig, Claude had managed to avoid automobiles since before Woodrow Wilson was in office. His mental map of L.A. was a five-mile walking radius that began in the hotel lobby and ended a few blocks east of the 101. As they wended south of Venice, it took him a moment to realize that the snub-nosed leviathans bellying down over the ocean were jetliners, wheels down, metal flanks like burning chrome in the sunshine. He had traveled the world by the time he was twenty, but the idea of packing a suitcase and getting airborne was unthinkable. The jet age, like cinematic sound, was something he could do without.

In his big-heeled boots, Martin was riding the clutch of his Buick. Claude thought of his wartime Renault, of its difficult little gearbox and the way it whinnied up a hillside. Sometimes it stalled out on a Montmartre side street and he'd have to hold the clutch in for a long, winding coast until the engine sputtered over. He asked Martin about the horsepower of the Buick

LeSabre and was shocked to hear 250. The buggy he'd driven along the streets of Paris and up into the mountains of Andorra more than forty years ago had had a nine-horsepower engine. They pulled into a parking lot surrounded by tropical motifs—banana trees and buildings with island names and lanais and big-shuttered windows. They signed in at the front desk of the main building and a young nurse named Angela went to find Chip Spalding. Claude watched her pass through two glass doors in her floral-print uniform, down a long corridor that was painted avocado green. She stopped in a sitting area, where the frail and befuddled sat under plaid blankets in front of a television set. Claude could imagine dying alone in his hotel suite, surrounded by vinegared celluloid and jaundiced newsprint, but that flickering nonexistence at the end of the hallway had always terrified him. As he watched Angela begin to push a short wiry man down the corridor in a wheelchair, he felt his breath catch in the back of his throat.

—Did we know he was a cripple?

Martin flushed, shook his head.

—When I called, they said he had to have a nurse with him all day. I figured it was something like that. By the way, they don't call them cripples anymore. Not since the Depression.

They both looked down the corridor and saw that Angela's face was exuberant with laughter as she pushed Chip along. He was wearing a monogrammed, bright orange windbreaker, khaki trousers, a pair of white tennis shoes, his thinning hair raked back into a comb-over.

—He looks like he's dressed to be lost at sea. What do they say now? Paraplegic?

—They just don't say anything.

Claude took the pressed handkerchief from the breast pocket of his glen plaid suit and cleaned his bifocals. Chip was still side-mouthing the tail-end of a story as Angela wheeled him into the foyer, something about the Tahitian Villas sock thief and how he didn't take proper account of a generation of monogrammers.

— . . . so the shift nurse lifts Arthur's polyester pant leg and there's the incrimination, right on his bloody ankle. Didn't take Scotland Yard to solve that one.

Angela laughed and parked Chip in front of his visitors. He squinted up at them, his mouth slightly open, a breath mint on his tongue. Claude bent down to shake Chip's hand but Chip brought the Frenchman and his cameras into a craning hug.

—Surprised you're still in the picture business, Monsieur Ballard. You must be at least a hundred by now.

—You're no spring rooster, either. May I film you for a few seconds?

—Only if you make me look like Errol Flynn.

Claude straightened, held up the Bell & Howell, spooled a few seconds of Chip with one arm extended for a swordfight.

—Last time I saw you it was on a hillside full of machinegun fire in Belgium. I sent you some letters after the war and they never got a response. Hal and I assumed you were dead. Resurrected only to die in a flophouse in West Hollywood . . .

—What happened to your legs?

—*Claude*, admonished Martin.

—Nerve damage. One too many falls. Not much feeling below the waist. In fact, it's pretty much dead down there in the nether regions. The nurses try, but it's like deep space in that particular department.

Angela gave Chip's shoulder a playful slap. Claude blinked, unsure of where to look, and introduced Martin.

—He is the one who has restored the old reels. Despite his cowboy boots, he's a film historian with a Ph.D.

—Almost, said Martin. I still have to defend my dissertation.

—Is it true we're getting tuxedos for the premiere? asked Chip.

—The premiere was in 1910, Claude corrected. This is a second release.

—It's true, said Martin, thanks to Hal Bender's son. He's also donated one of their downtown theaters and paid for a limo.

Chip nodded, zipped and unzipped some pockets in his windbreaker, removed a roll of antacids, a pair of bent aviator sunglasses, some electrical tape, a pocketknife, before settling on a tin of breath mints. He offered them around and they all took one, trying to find the right words in the minty silence.

—I haven't been in a limousine since Alice's funeral five years ago, said Chip. Maybe this will be a happier occasion. Now I'll need Angela at my tuxedo fitting to help snug me into the pant legs. She's certified in that area.

Chip put his sunglasses on.

—She's with us all day and night, said Martin. I was thinking we could get lunch in Venice Beach first. Does that suit everyone?

Angela said she knew just the place.

•

After Martin and Angela lifted Chip into the backseat of the Buick they drove down to the beach and found Angela's favorite restaurant along the boardwalk. It looked to Claude like a shanty made of driftwood and strung with empty wine bottles and fishing nets, though she assured them all that the fish tacos and cheeseburgers were excellent. Claude sat next to Chip at one end of a picnic table on the patio, the boardwalk in its noonday splendor. They watched buskers singing and playing guitars, bodybuilders with buzz cuts pussyfooting through the sand in their Speedos. A group of surfers came bounding up the beach in their half-peeled wetsuits, laughing and slicking saltwater from their hair, dopey with bronzed youth.

—You never went back to Australia? Claude asked.

—A few times. Funerals mostly. After university, one of my sons took a job with IBM in Sydney, if you can believe it. I should go back one day. If all else fails, my ashes will be scattered off the Tamarama cliffs. Strict instructions.

—Of course you will be cremated. You said one of your sons. How many are there?

—Alice and me had five kids all up. Three boys, two girls. You never married again?

—No, no, never.

—Sabine Montrose was enough to turn a man off women for life, I reckon. It's like if you eat bad liver, even one time, then offal is murder all of a sudden. Whatever happened to her?

—By all accounts, she died an old woman under a blue slate roof in Andorra. Ask Martin. He's the expert on all of our lives these days.

Claude looked down at the other end of the table. It was possible Martin was flirting with Angela in his slouching Texan way. She was laughing and rolling her eyes between bites of her fish taco.

—What's so funny down there, you two? Chip asked.

—Claude, I was telling Angela about our candlelight dinner with Susan Berg during the blackout.

—Ah, Claude said, poor Susan. You might say she is the Genghis Khan of broth.

Angela was an easy laugh, so this got another generous titter.

•

Claude and Hal watched a bodybuilder limbering on the sand with hand weights. After a moment, Claude turned his attention to Chip's scarred hands and wrists, to the half-moon calluses on his knuckles.

—You and Hal stayed in touch?

Claude watched the boardwalk float by in Chip's sunglasses.

—God yeah, Chip said, pointing with his chin. We used to play hand-ball just over there and sometimes in Santa Monica, every Sunday morning instead of going to church. Hal playing handball as an old man was something to behold, a singlet tucked into nylon shorts like a wrestler, socks pulled up, never yelling or cursing but slapping the tennis ball like some Viking avenging his ancestors. I took bets, like I was his personal bookie, and the newbies never believed he was once a studio head. He looked like a retired mechanic from Thousand Oaks.

The image made Claude smile, Hal Bender as a hustling old Brooklynite.

—He got me steady stunt work with the studios over the years, said Chip. Burning falls, helicopter jumps, general combat. One time I rode a saloon piano down a flight of stairs for one of his westerns. He was good to me, Hal was. You remember Alroy Healy, the debt monger from the old neighborhood?

Claude considered the name, let it hover in the tin-white sky above the boardwalk.

—The one who took over the theater?

—Bingo. Also the alleged murderer of Hal's old man. Well, apparently he was still owed from back in the day, so he shows up on Hal's back lot one day looking for his arrears. This is twenty years after the fact, mind you, and he looks like an Irish wolfhound from the pound, with a couple of missing teeth and a hobo's whiskey bottle in a paper bag.

—What did Hal do?

Chip took a sip of his iced tea, lifted the bun of his cheeseburger, removed the onions to the side of his plate.

—You're thinking revenge, I can see it in your eyes. How do you like the bifocals, by the way? I always feel like I have a concussion when I put mine on.

—I have grown accustomed to them. What did Hal do?

The lid back on the bun, Chip took a bite, chewed, washed it down with a swig of iced tea.

—So he gives Alroy the royal treatment, takes him on a tour of the set we're filming on, introduces him as a family friend from back east to the director and some stars, makes him feel like perhaps bygones have come into play, but then here's the surprise move. The haymaker, if you will.

Another bite of hamburger, some careful navigation around a missing rear molar.

—He asks Alroy if he'd like to be an extra in that day's shoot, that he can arrange it with the director. Can't remember the name of the film now, but I had to do a jump from a balcony into a hotel swimming pool. Hal tells Alroy that he's going to be in the sequence and all he has to do is smoke a cigar while lounging on a pool float. I have to do a practice run anyway, so Hal asks me and the director if I can do it with the Irishman in the pool, whether I can jump as close to the bastard as possible, without actually killing him. So I jump from the balcony, fifty feet up, and land within a foot of Alroy Healy blowing smoke into the air. He goes under like a torpedoed battleship, gasping for air, thrashing and yelling all the way back to Red Hook. Eventually I drag him sputtering to the side of the pool and tell him that he's a murdering son of a whore that's not owed a fucking cent, that if he ever sets his pockmarked arse back on the premises then security will break his goddamn legs, and failing that I would be happy to oblige. He leaves the lot soaked and holding his shoes. I'll never forget it.

Martin and Angela had stopped talking and were looking down at the other end of the table. Claude realized he was still holding a fish taco two inches from his mouth.

—Sorry all, got a bit carried away, Chip said.

—Did Alroy ever come back? Claude asked.

—Never. And the best part was that we captured it all on film, just for the dailies. Hal kept that little outtake in his own collection, like it was a snuff film to prove the past had finally been put to rest.

No, no, Claude thought, the past never stops banging at the doors of the present. We pack it into tattered suitcases, lock it into rusting metal trunks beneath our beds, press it between yellowed pages of newsprint, but it hangs over us at night like a poisonous cloud, seeps into our shirt collars and bedclothes. They ate for a few moments, listening to Angela tell stories of Chip's antics at the nursing home, the way he commandeered the television remote if a movie came on that featured one of his stunts. Sometimes he yelled admonishments or cheered at the TV during an action sequence.

Martin looked at his watch and asked if everyone was ready for their formalwear fitting. Chip pointed at Angela's daisy-print uniform.

—Do the scrubs come in black?

—Don't worry, Mr. Spalding, I packed along a dress and heels for your special occasion.

At the downtown formalwear store, Claude and Chip chose white dinner jackets and black cummerbunds, with a white carnation in the lapel. Martin wore a bolo tie with silver tips and a Navajo turquoise slide, and Angela changed into a sapphire evening gown, something she confessed she hadn't worn since her sister's wedding. When the limousine picked them up at the designated spot, they took a leisurely route toward the theater, moving through downtown and past Elysian Park and the new Dodger Stadium.

As they drew closer to the venue, Claude saw immediately that the Fulton Théatre on Broadway was Hal Bender's love letter to the Bender Bijoux. It had a bull-nosed nickel ticket booth stenciled in gold and a stucco facade full of carved gods and griffins. Martin had warned them on the car ride not to expect red carpet and a crowd, but there were twenty or so people gathered in the foyer, spilling out onto the curbstone in their eveningwear. As the chauffeur and Angela navigated Chip back into his wheelchair, a round of applause started up and Chip grinned as they wheeled him inside. Claude captured their entrance into the cheering foyer with his Bell & Howell.

Claude took a flute of champagne from a waiter with a tray and began to walk around the lobby, camera in hand. This seemed to delay the deluge of introductions that awaited, mostly to Martin's university colleagues. Here was Hal Bender's ode to Flossy's Brooklyn cake emporium—a glass cabinet stocked with cigars and cigarettes and matchbooks—and here were the red velvet drapes with the gold ropes. Then, in one corner, Hal had erected a shrine—the single plush opera chair from the Queens apartment, 1A, a gramophone on a table, then a Model B cinématographe on a tripod beside it. The crowning touch was the ossified head of Bella, the Siberian tiger, hanging on the wall, her mouth slightly open, her eyes yellow and glazed. The Bell & Howell was still filming in Claude's hand, but he loosened his grip and let it fall to his waist. Chip's voice came from somewhere down there.

—Did you know he kept the head under his bed in that fleabag apartment we all shared?

—I never knew. I remember the chair, that's it.

—For years he kept the tiger head in his studio office out here, said it came in handy during contract negotiations, then he moved it when they took over the theater and renovated it. It was a good-luck charm for him, if you can believe it, a talisman to ward off the evils of the past.

Claude pictured the Queens apartment above a greengrocer. He'd been so distracted by Sabine's flight and the studio's ruin that he wouldn't have noticed a tiger's head on the dinner table.

Martin appeared smiling in his tuxedo.

—Are you two going to stand over here by yourselves all night? Some people want to talk to you before the film starts.

—Show us the way, Chip said, maneuvering himself into a turn.

Martin led them over to three people standing with cocktails in hand. The older man and woman were in their sixties and scholarly in their attentions, perhaps film historians from the university, both of them nodding seriously at the fast talker with the cigarette, a producer of some kind with studio war stories and tales of celebrity excess.

—Our guests of honor, Martin said, gesturing back to Chip and Claude.

They all turned to greet them. Claude watched as the younger man greeted Chip and it was clear that they knew each other. It was Simon Bender, Hal's son, the current owner of the family studio and chain of theaters. He was tan and broad-shouldered, loose with his hands and charismatic smile. He shook Claude's hand slowly, saying *what a pleasure*, one hand over the top. The older gentleman was smiling at him over his champagne flute and then the woman was suddenly blinking back a tear.

—And I believe you know Cora and Leo Harlow, said Martin.

Claude felt the Bell & Howell humming in his right hand, understood that it was still running beside his pant leg, pointing shakily at the parquet floor. Somewhere there was the thought of raising it up to eye level, of capturing their earnest, brimming faces, but his hand wouldn't budge. He remembered filming them in the room up in the tree crowns at the sanitarium, their mother's face like sea glass, delicate and somehow ageless. He remembered Cora's earnest interrogations and clear-voiced singing, Leo's scabbed knees and his magnifying glasses, the summer they all lived together in the embrace of a beautiful lie up on the Palisades. He didn't want anyone to speak and somehow it was Cora who knew it and moved to silently embrace him. Then Leo came over and put one arm around Claude's shoulders and he was sealed between the siblings. To get a teary laugh from his sister, Leo said, *Monsieur Clowd, it has been a very, very long time.*

They moved to Chip next, kneeling down on either side of his wheelchair and folding him into a hug. When they stood there was some wiping away of tears, an exhalation, a sense of nowhere to begin. To break the silence, Claude asked them about their lives. Leo was a tenured professor of astronomy in Hawaii with a wife and grandchildren, and Cora was an appellate judge in New Orleans, married to a lawyer, both of them about to retire.

—No children? asked Claude.

—My own childhood seemed like a cruelty that I didn't want to inflict on someone else, said Cora. I felt like we'd been kidnapped from everything we knew.

—You'll remember that my sister always speaks her mind.

—I do remember that, said Claude. She never suffered fools or untruths.

—Well, said Leo, I like to think my two daughters were happy prisoners. They grew up on the beach, learned how to fish and bodysurf by the time they were ten.

—There's no place like the ocean, said Chip.

—And you did not remarry? asked Cora, looking at Claude.

—I lost my appetite.

A bell rang at the other end of the lobby and an usher began to call people inside the auditorium. Claude walked between Leo and Cora, Chip wheeling just in front with Angela at his side.

—What happened to Sabine, in the end? Claude asked.

—Honestly, said Leo, she was at her happiest as an old woman. She and Helena hiked up in the Pyrenees, gambled at the casino in Barcelona, started a charity for war orphans. When they buried her, there was an Andorran twenty-one-gun salute and she insisted that her headstone read *Désirée Mouret*, after the obscure Zola character. She said it was to throw future biographers off her misguided trail. She was buried right next to Pavel. The only thing on his headstone were the words *Be Natural!*

—They remained themselves, even in death, said Claude, incredulous.

They walked in silence for a moment. The ruins of the past had presided over his life for fifty years, had sat on a mantel like ashes in a brass urn. He might have made other films, loved other women, not gone looking for his own demise in the Belgian woods. For half a century, he'd been reckless in his caution, drunk on it.

—I am sorry I didn't stay in touch after my visit at the end of the war, said Claude. It was too painful, I think. Cora, weren't you about to go study at the Sorbonne?

—I left Andorra not long after you came. I spent a year at the Sorbonne, then I petitioned Yale Law School and they let me in as one of the first women. Sabine never forgave me for it.

—What was there to forgive? asked Claude.

—She always felt America had turned against her, that she'd had a kind of spiritual death here. Me coming back here was a betrayal. In my early twenties, we went years without seeing each other. Then Stephen and I started to visit Spain in the summers and we saw her then. She would only speak to us in French, even though Stephen didn't speak any. I loved her, but she was difficult.

—Yes, said Claude, I think I remember that.

They all laughed at this.

Inside the auditorium, Martin and Simon Bender directed them down to the reserved seats in the front row. Claude sat between Leo and Cora, Chip on the aisle with Angela beside him. They watched as Martin took the stage to make some remarks before the screening. He spoke about growing up in the back of a Hill Country movie house with his ailing grandparents. *I was born in the wrong century Claude told me one day at the diner, and possibly on the wrong continent.* He made gentle fun of Claude for his Dijon-colored suits and existential shrugging, remembered the first time he walked into the cloud of vinegar that passed for his hotel suite. Claude listened as if from afar, waiting for the lights to go down so that he could be alone with the flood of the past.

Right before the feature played and the pianist started up, there was a minute or two of original promotional footage that Martin had restored. The projectionist floated aerial shots of the film studio in Fort Lee, taken from a Palisades Amusement Park airship. The enormous glasshouse of the production stage up on the brow of the hill, glinting in the Atlantic sunshine, and the geometric heart of the yew maze as the camera angled down to the Palisades, where six people stood waving from the cliff tops: Claude and Sabine, Leo and Cora, Hal and Chip. Claude's free arm linked through Sabine's, the children in front of them. This was the summer before everything came undone, a glimpsed room in the Mansion of Happiness. Claude stared at his younger self and expected to feel pity or loss, some inexpressible weariness for all that was to come, but he felt nothing but awe for these figments standing at the edge of New Jersey, waving to the camera as it spooled the present into the past, beckoning to the audience through the evanescent light above the river.

FIN

Acknowledgments

As with any work of historical fiction, I am indebted to many books and primary sources. Some of the letters from moviegoers to Sabine Montrose are modeled on letters from readers that were sent to Mark Twain and collected in *Dear Mark Twain: Letters from His Readers*, edited by R. Kent Rasmussen. They have been adapted and used with the editor's permission. The idea of characters having an "atmosphere" in the book is derived from Virginia Woolf's 1924 lecture "Mr. Bennett and Mrs. Brown." While many books were useful for researching the silent era, I am especially indebted to Kevin Brownlow's *The Parade's Gone By*, Richard Koszarski's *Fort Lee: The Film Town*, Eileen Bowser's *The Transformation of Cinema, 1907–1915* (History of the American Cinema), and *American Cinematographers in the Great War, 1914–1918*, by James W. Castellan, Ron van Dopperen, and Cooper C. Graham. Special thanks to Ron van Dopperen for helping me locate an image at the U.S. Army Signal Corps collection at the National Archives.

My editors, Sarah Crichton and Jane Palfreyman, and my agents, Emily Forland and Gaby Naher, each contributed something important to this novel as it progressed—insight, encouragement, and sometimes challenging questions. It is a better book because of their efforts and I'm deeply thankful for that. A special thanks to Jeremy Pollet, for always being up for an obscure research excursion, and to Michael Parker, for his careful early reading of the manuscript.

Finally, my deepest love and gratitude to my wife, Emily, and my two daughters, Mikaila and Gemma. Their encouragement, patience, and support mean the world to me.

ILLUSTRATION CREDITS

Chapter 1: Tichnor Brothers, Publisher. "Hollywood Knickerbocker Hotel, Hollywood, California." Postcard, ca. 1930–1945. Boston Public Library, Tichnor Brothers Collection #63646. Public domain image of postcard retrieved from Wikimedia Commons, https://commons.wikimedia.org/wiki/File:Hollywood_Knickerbocker_Hotel,_Hollywood,_California_(63646).jpg (accessed August 3, 2018).

Chapter 2: Marcellin Auzolle. Film poster for Cinématographe Lumière, 1896. Shared under a Creative Commons Attribution-Share Alike 3.0 Unported license and retrieved from Wikimedia Commons, https://commons.wikimedia.org/wiki/File:Poster_Cinematographe_Lumiere.jpg (accessed August 3, 2018).

Chapter 3: Lafayette Photo, London. Portrait of Sarah Bernhardt as Hamlet. Photograph, June 1899. Public domain image from the Library of Congress Prints and Photographs Online Catalog (digital ID cph.3g06529), retrieved from Wikimedia Commons, https://en.wikipedia.org/wiki/File:Bernhardt_Hamlet2.jpg (accessed August 3, 2018).

Chapter 4: Henry King. Bondi Aquarium, Tamarama, Sydney, Australia. Photograph, 1890. Public domain image from the Tyrrell Collection, Powerhouse Museum, Sydney, retrieved from Wikimedia Commons, https://commons.wikimedia.org/wiki/File:Tamarama_Bondi_Aquarium.jpg#file (accessed August 3, 2018).

Chapter 5: William James. Auditorium Theatre at 382 Queen Street West, Toronto. Photograph, circa 1910. Public domain image from the City of Toronto Archives, listed under archival citation Fonds 1244, Item 320C, retrieved from Wikimedia Commons, https://commons.wikimedia.org/wiki/File:Auditorium_Theatre_in_Toronto.jpg (accessed August 3, 2018).

Chapter 6: D. Sharon Pruitt of Pink Sherbert Photography (www.pinksherbert.com). *Grungy Dirty Dark Vintage Viewfinder Film Camera Lens Glass Texture*. Photograph, 2012. Shared under a Creative Commons Attribution 2.0 Generic license, retrieved from Wikimedia Commons, https://commons.wikimedia.org/wiki/File:Grungy_Dirty_Dark

_Vintage_Viewfinder_Film_Camera_Lens_Glass_Texture_(8225064806).jpg (accessed August 3, 2018).

Chapter 7: Pathé Exchange. Still from the production of the American film serial *The House of Hate* with Pearl White and Antonio Moreno, with director George B. Seitz and cinematographer Arthur Charles Miller. Photograph, 1922 (book publishing date). Public domain image from page 151 of William Lord Wright, *Photoplay Writing*, New York City: Falk Publishing Co., 1922, retrieved from Wikimedia Commons, https:// commons.wikimedia.org/wiki/File:The_House_of_Hate_(1918)_-_1.jpg (accessed August 3, 2018).

Chapter 8: Adam Jones, Ph.D. *Facade of Abandoned Mansion Along the Paseo, Merida, Mexico.* Photograph, 2012. Shared under the Creative Commons Attribution-Share Alike 3.0 Unported license, retrieved from Wikimedia Commons, https://commons.wikimedia.org /wiki/File:Facade_of_Abandoned_Mansion_along_the_Paseo_-_Merida_-_Mexico .jpg (accessed August 3, 2018).

Chapter 10: Ellery Sedwick and Frank Leslie, *Frank Leslie's Popular Monthly*, v. 41, 1896. Sketch. Public domain image taken from page 627 of above-mentioned title, retrieved from the Hathi Trust (www.hathitrust.org) Digital Library, https://babel.hathitrust.org/cgi/pt?id =inu.32000000494437;view=1up;seq=647 (accessed August 3, 2018).

Chapter 11: Unknown photographer. Rainbow Lake Sanatorium. Date unknown. Courtesy of Adirondack Experience.

Chapter 12: C. C. Pierce. Caged tiger at the Los Angeles Zoo. Digital reproduction of glass plate negatives, circa 1920. A public domain image from the Title Insurance and Trust, and C. C. Pierce Photography Collection within the California Historical Society Collection at the University of Southern California. Retrieved from Wikimedia Commons, https:// commons.wikimedia.org/wiki/File:Caged_tiger_at_the_Los_Angeles_Zoo,_ca.1920 _(CHS-9748).jpg (accessed August 3, 2018).

Chapter 13: Unknown author. Halley's Comet, as seen on May 25, 1910, at its greatest light. Unknown format, May 25, 1910. Public domain image from the Digital Library of Slovenia, retrieved from Wikimedia Commons, https://commons.wikimedia.org/wiki /File:Halleyev_komet_1910.jpg (accessed August 3, 2018).

Chapter 14: Internet Archive Book images, *American Homes and Gardens.* The maze at Hampton Court, England. Photograph, 1910. Public domain image taken from page 425 of above-mentioned title, retrieved from Wikimedia Commons, https://commons.wikimedia .org/wiki/File:American_homes_and_gardens_(1910)_(18157514225).jpg (accessed August 3, 2018).

Chapter 15: William and Stephen B. Ives. Mansion of Happiness. Photograph of a game board from 1843. Public domain image retrieved from Wikimedia Commons, https://commons .wikimedia.org/wiki/File:FirstAmericanPrintrunOfThe_MansionOfHappiness.jpg (accessed August 6, 2018).

Chapter 16: Edward Read. *Saturday Night at a Pawnbroker's.* Drawing, 1901. Public domain image taken from page 38 of *Living London* (1902), edited by George R. Sims and published by Cassell and Company, Limited, retrieved from https://books.google.com/books?id =-NY-AAAYAAJ&dq=From+Living+London,+published+c.1901&source=gbs _navlinks_s (accessed August 6, 2018).

Chapter 17: Bain News Service, publisher. Baldwin balloon in flight over spectators. Reproduction of a glass negative, undated. Public domain image from the George Grantham Bain Collection at the Library of Congress's Prints and Photographs division under the

digital ID ggbain.03980, retrieved from Wikimedia Commons, https://commons.wikimedia
.org/wiki/File:Baldwin_balloon_(dirigible),_in_flight_over_spectators_LCCN2014683974
.jpg (accessed August 6, 2018).

Chapter 18: Unknown photographer. Horizontal view from stage looking south—Granada
Theatre, 6425–6441 North Sheridan Road, Chicago, Cook County, IL. Photograph,
after 1933. Public domain image from the Historic American Buildings Survey of the
National Park Service, retrieved from Wikimedia Commons, https://commons
.wikimedia.org/wiki/File:HORIZONTAL_VIEW_FROM_STAGE_LOOKING
SOUTH.-_Granada_Theatre,_6425-6441_North_Sheridan_Road,_Chicago,_Cook
_County,_IL_HABS_ILL,16-CHIG,109-19.tif (accessed August 6, 2018).

Chapter 19: A. Radclyffe Dugmore. Portrait of Thomas Alva Edison. Photograph, no later
than 1905. Public domain image retrieved from Wikimedia Commons, https://commons
.wikimedia.org/wiki/File:Portrait_of_Thomas_A._Edison.jpg (accessed August 8,
2018).

Chapter 20: Auckland Museum. Combined desk and document case, made of wood and covered with leather, which belonged to Sir Frederick Whitaker (1812–1891), premier of New
Zealand. Photograph of nineteenth-century object. Image is shared under a Creative
Commons Attribution 4.0 International license, from the Collection of Auckland Museum Tamaki Paenga Hira, 1965.78.823, col.0083, ocm2361, 1995x2.175, and retrieved
from Wikimedia Commons, https://commons.wikimedia.org/wiki/File:Desk,_portable
_(AM_1965.78.823-6).jpg (accessed August 8, 2018).

Chapter 21: Photographer unknown but probably Charles Marville. Boulevard Haussmann,
Paris, France. Photograph print mounted on cardboard: albumen silver, circa 1853–1870.
Public domain image from the State Library of Victoria under the Accession Number
H88.19/90a, retrieved from Wikimedia Commons, https://commons.wikimedia.org/wiki
/File:Charles_Marville,_Boulevard_Haussmann,_de_la_rue_du_Havre,_ca
._1853%E2%80%9370.jpg (accessed August 8, 2018).

Chapter 22: Photographer identified as S.C. Mr. E. B. Hatrick, Sergeant A. Duff (center) representing the Committee on Public Information at the front near Sommedieue, France.
Photograph, 1918. Public domain image from the U.S. Signal Corps Collection at the
National Archives and Records Administration digital catalog, record number 111-SC
-11382, https://catalog.archives.gov/id/55183049.

Chapter 23: Jaroslav A. Polák. *Praktica BC1—Wood*. Photograph, 2016. Public domain image retrieved from Flickr, https://flic.kr/p/GS5aGZ (accessed August 8, 2018).

Chapter 24: Bert Kaufmann. Front of the Château Miranda (Château de Noisy), Celles, Belgium.
Photograph, 2012. Image provided under the Creative Commons Attribution-Share Alike
2.0 Generic license, retrieved from Wikimedia Commons, https://commons.wikimedia.org
/wiki/File:Castle_Miranda,_front_entrance_(BW).jpg (accessed August 8, 2018).

Chapter 25: Bain News Service, publisher. Louvain Library in Belgium. Photograph from a glass
negative, 1914. Public domain image from the Library of Congress's Prints and Photographs division under the digital ID ggbain.17303, retrieved from Wikimedia Commons, https://commons.wikimedia.org/wiki/File:Library_-_Louvain_LCCN2014697569
.tif (accessed August 8, 2018).

Chapter 26: *German Troops Arrive at Antwerp*. October 8, 1914. Photo by Mondadori Portfolio via
Getty Images.

Chapter 27: Boigandorra. Andorra la Vella. Photograph, 1920. Image provided under the
Creative Commons Attribution-Share Alike 4.0 International license, retrieved from

Wikimedia Commons, https://commons.wikimedia.org/wiki/File:Andorra_la_Vella_al _1920.jpg (accessed August 8, 2018).

Chapter 28: Boss Tweed. *Manhattan Blackout.* Photograph, 2012. Image provided under the Creative Commons Attribution 2.0 Generic license, retrieved from Flickr, https://flic.kr/p /dp3eNb (accessed August 8, 2018).

Chapter 29: State Library of New South Wales collection. The pictorial panorama of the Great War: embracing Egypt, Gallipoli, Palestine, France, Belgium, Germany and the Navy, from an exhibition of war photographs in natural color, produced by Colart's Studio, Melbourne. Hand-colored photograph, 1917. Public domain image retrieved from Wikimedia Commons, https://commons.wikimedia.org/wiki/File:Liquid_fire,_or_Flammenwerfer _(13940668626).jpg (accessed August 9, 2018).

Chapter 30: Cartographer Louis Bretez, engraver Claude Lucas. Plan de Paris: commencé l'année 1734. Image of map from 1734. Public domain image from the Norman B. Leventhal Map Center at the Boston Public Library, retrieved from Wikimedia Commons, https://commons.wikimedia.org/wiki/File:Turgot_map_of_Paris,_sheet_6_-_Norman _B._Leventhal_Map_Center.jpg (accessed August 9, 2018).

Chapter 31: Jean-August Brutails. Andorre-la-Vieille; vue Générale. Photograph, date unknown. Public domain image from the Bordeaux Montaigne University (Bordeaux, France), retrieved from Wikimedia Commons, https://commons.wikimedia.org/wiki/File:Andorre -la-Vieille_-_J-A_Brutails_-_Universit%C3%A9_Bordeaux_Montaigne_-_1707.jpg (accessed August 9, 2018).

Chapter 32: Keystone View Company, publisher. Picturesque Palisades of the Hudson River, looking north, New Jersey. Photograph, circa 1920. A public domain image from the New York Public Library's Digital Library under the digital ID G90F453_052F, retrieved from Wikimedia Commons, https://commons.wikimedia.org/wiki/File:Picturesque_Palisades _of_the_Hudson_River,_looking_north,_New_Jersey,_by_Keystone_View_Company .png (accessed August 9, 2018)